PRAISE FOR
WHERE THE HEART IS

Winner of the Walker Percy Award

"This crisp, tight, beautifully written work never goes a word too far. . . . Prizewinning writers Clyde Edgerton, E. Annie Proulx, and Barbara Kingsolver may have to move over to make room for Billie Letts."
—*Dallas Morning News*

"Read the book. You won't regret it." **—*Milwaukee Journal-Sentinel***

"An engaging novel written with a light spirit and an almost always deft touch."
—*The Times* (London)

"You can't go wrong with characters like these. . . . WHERE THE HEART IS . . . is quick and funny, and you absolutely *see* these people."
—*Miami Herald*

"It isn't only that Billie Letts has a talent for humor and an ear for Wal-Mart vernaculars, but that she has a genuine affection for her characters. Novalee and Sister and Forney are marvelously real, and they make reading WHERE THE HEART IS pure pleasure."
—Robley Wilson, editor of *The North American Review*

"A feel-good read." **—*San Antonio Express-News***

"At times wistful and at others hilarious, WHERE THE HEART IS will leave you uplifted and renewed." **—*Burlington Free Press***

"Enormously fresh and captivating . . . as readable as a serial in the *Saturday Evening Post*."
—*Tulsa World*

"A heartfelt and gratifying read. . . . Letts's wacky characters are depicted with humor and hope. . . . A lively, affecting first novel."
—*Publishers Weekly* (starred review)

"A feel-good story, centered in America's heartland, where dreams can still come true and people still care enough about each other to give a leg up when it is needed. . . . A wonderful inspirational book that causes chuckles and tears." ***—Midwest Book Review***

"What a debut novel: Letts herself is a whirlwind through life, collecting and remembering, knowing exactly 'WHERE THE HEART IS.' . . . In hearts as warm as July, life is wonderful: Letts knows that, and tells it well." ***—Indianapolis News***

"An endearing, quirky tale." ***—Women's Wear Daily***

"Entertaining . . . a nice message to hear." ***—Hartford Courant***

"Giving names and faces to America's trailer parks and their residents, WHERE THE HEART IS pulls you into their fictional lives with realism, accuracy, and emotion. . . . You'll cheer for Novalee." ***—Evansville Press*** **(Illinois)**

"[A] modern, must-read, all-American morality tale." ***—She*** **magazine**

"A delightfully good yarn. . . . A fine first novel . . . [that] takes the reader on a journey that's not soon forgotten." ***—The State*** **(SC)**

• • •

Other books by Billie Letts

The Honk and Holler Opening Soon

Shoot the Moon

Made in the U.S.A.

Publisher's note: This novel is a work of fiction. Names, characters, places, and incidents either are the product of the author's imagination or are used fictitiously, and any resemblance to actual persons, living or dead, events, or locales is entirely coincidental.

Grateful acknowledgments are given to the following:

Benson Music Group, Inc. for portions of lyrics from "Farther Along," by J.R. Baxter, Jr., and W.B. Stevens. Copyright 1937 by Stamps Baxter Music / BMI. All rights reserved. Used by permission of Benson Music Group, Inc.

Doubleday and Company to reprint an excerpt from "In a Dark Time," by Theodore Roethke.

The Poetry of Robert Frost, Copyright 1936 by Robert Frost. Copyright © 1964 by Leslie Frost Ballantine. Copyright © 1969 by Henry Holt & Co., Inc. Reprinted by permission of Henry Holt & Co., Inc. Grateful acknowledgment is also made to Jonathan Cape and the Estate of Robert Frost for permission to quote from *The Poetry of Robert Frost*, edited by Edward Connery Lathem.

Selections from *The Negro Speaks of Rivers* by Langston Hughes reprinted by permission of Harold Ober Associates, Inc. Copyright © 1951 by Knopf.

Shawn Letts for portions of lyrics from "Beat of a Heart," music and lyrics by Shawn Letts. Copyright © 1992. All rights reserved. Used by permission.

Grand Central Publishing
Hachette Book Group
1290 Avenue of the Americas
New York, NY 10104
www.HachetteBookGroup.com

Printed in the United States of America
Originally published in hardcover by Hachette Book Group.
First Trade Edition: June 1998
Reissued: April 2000
Value-priced reissue: June 2015
10 9 8 7 6 5 4 3 2 1

Grand Central Publishing is a division of Hachette Book Group, Inc.
The Grand Central Publishing name and logo is a trademark of Hachette Book Group, Inc.

The publisher is not responsible for websites (or their content) that are not owned by the publisher.

Library of Congress Cataloging-in-Publication Data
Letts, Billie.
Where the heart is / Billie Letts
p. cm.
ISBN 978-0-446-67221-4
I. Title.
PS3562.E856W48 1995
813'54—dc20 94-43079
CIP

Book design by Giorgetta Bell McRee

ISBN 978-1-4555-3511-8 (value-priced pbk. reissue)

where the heart is

Billie Letts

GRAND CENTRAL PUBLISHING

NEW YORK BOSTON

For Dennis

who trusts the truth of miracle and magic

Grateful appreciation goes to:

my writers' group: Marion and Elbert Hill, Glenda Zumwalt, Betty and Bob Swearengin—a tough bunch of readers who wouldn't let me quit;

my good friends: Howard Starks, Katy Morris, Doris Andrews and Brad Cushman, who laughed and cried in all the right places; and Vicky Ellis, whose computer virtuosity was available day and night;

my family: Tracy, Shawn and Shariffah, Dana and Deborah, because they think my book is as good as my chicken fried steak and gravy; and others "who seem like family": Holly Wantuch and Amy and John McLean;

my editor: Jamie Raab, who guided me gently and with humor;

my agent: Elaine Markson, who took me to dinner in New Orleans and made me feel like a writer;

my students, who said, "Tell us what happens next," so I did;

and to everyone in Oklahoma and Tennessee who took my calls, gave me their time and tried to answer my questions.

Part One

Chapter One

NOVALEE NATION, seventeen, seven months pregnant, thirty-seven pounds overweight—and superstitious about sevens—shifted uncomfortably in the seat of the old Plymouth and ran her hands down the curve of her belly.

For most people, sevens were lucky. But not for her. She'd had a bad history with them, starting with her seventh birthday, the day Momma Nell ran away with a baseball umpire named Fred. Then, when Novalee was in the seventh grade, her only friend, Rhonda Talley, stole an ice cream truck for her boyfriend and got sent to the Tennessee State School for Girls in Tullahoma.

By then, Novalee knew there was something screwy about sevens, so she tried to stay clear of them. *But sometimes,* she thought, *you just can't see a thing coming at you.*

And that's how she got stabbed. She just didn't see it coming.

It happened right after she dropped out of school and started waiting tables at Red's, a job that didn't have anything to do with sevens. A regular named Gladys went crazy one night—threw her beer bottle through the front window and started yelling crazy things about seeing Jesus, all the time calling Red the Holy Ghost. Novalee tried to calm her down, but Gladys was just too confused. She jumped at Novalee with a steak knife, slashed her from wrist to elbow, and the emergency room doctor took seventy-seven stitches to close her up. No, Novalee didn't trust sevens.

But she didn't have sevens on her mind as she twisted and squirmed, trying to compromise with a hateful pain pressing against her pelvis. She needed to stop again, but it was too soon to ask. They had stopped once since Fort Smith, but already Novalee's bladder felt like a water balloon.

They were somewhere in eastern Oklahoma on a farm-to-market road that didn't even show up on her Amoco map, but a faded billboard promoting a Fourth of July fireworks show promised that Muldrow was twelve miles ahead.

The road was a narrow, buckled blacktop, little used and long neglected. Old surface patches, cracked and split like torn black scabs, had coughed up jimsonweed and bedrock. But the big Plymouth rode it hard at a steady seventy-five and Willy Jack Pickens handled it like he had a thousand pounds of wild stallion between his legs.

Willy Jack was a year older, twenty-five pounds lighter and four inches shorter than Novalee. He wore cowboy boots with newspaper stuffed inside to make himself look taller. Novalee thought he looked like John Cougar Mellencamp, but he believed he looked more like Bruce Springsteen, who Willy Jack said was only five foot two.

Willy Jack was crazy about short musicians, especially those who were shorter than he was. No matter how drunk he got, he could remember that Prince was five one and a quarter and Mick Jagger was five two and a half. Willy Jack had a great memory.

Roadside signs warned of tight curves ahead, but Willy Jack kept the needle at seventy-five. Novalee wanted to ask him to slow down; instead, she prayed silently that they would not meet any oncoming traffic.

They could have been driving on a turnpike if they had gone farther north, a toll road that would have taken them through Tulsa and Oklahoma City, but Willy Jack said he wouldn't pay a penny to drive on a road paid for with taxpayers' money. Though he had never been a taxpayer himself, he had strong feelings about such things. Besides, he had said, there were lots of roads heading to California, roads that didn't cost a penny.

He misjudged the first curve, dropping the right front tire onto the shoulder and sending a shimmy through the car that made Novalee's bladder quiver. She unsnapped her seat belt and scooted her hips forward on the seat, trying to shift her weight in a way that would ease the pressure, but it didn't help. She had to go.

"Hon, I'm gonna have to stop again."

"Goddamn, Novalee." Willy Jack slapped the steering wheel with both hands. "You just went."

"Yeah, but . . ."

"Not more'n fifty miles back."

"Well, I can wait awhile."

"You know how long it's gonna take us to get there if you have to pee ever fifty miles?"

"I don't mean right this minute. I can wait."

Willy Jack was in a bad mood because of the camera. Novalee had bought a Polaroid before they left because she wanted him to take a picture of her at every state line they crossed, with her posed beside signs like, WELCOME TO

ARKANSAS, and OKLAHOMA, THE SOONER STATE. She wanted to frame those pictures so someday she could show their baby how they had traveled west like the covered wagons did on their way to California.

Willy Jack told her it was a stupid idea, but he had taken her picture when they crossed into Arkansas because he had seen a bar called the Razorback just across the highway and he wanted a beer. They were twenty miles down the road when Novalee missed the camera and discovered Willy Jack had left it in the bar. She begged him to go back for it and he did, but only because he wanted another beer. But when they drove into Oklahoma, Willy Jack had refused to stop and take her picture so they'd had a fight.

Novalee felt warm and sticky. She rolled down her window and let the hot outside air blast her in the face. The air conditioner in the Plymouth had stopped working long before Willy Jack bought it with her fifty dollars. In fact, almost everything in the car had stopped working so it had ended up in a junkyard just outside Knoxville where Willy Jack had found it. He had replaced a universal joint, the carburetor, the distributor, a brake drum and the muffler, but he had not replaced the floorboard where a piece the size of a platter had rusted out. He'd covered the hole with a TV tray, but Novalee was afraid the tray would slide and her feet would slip through the hole and be ripped off on the highway. When she would lean forward to check the tray, she could see at its edges the pavement whirling by, just inches below her feet, an experience that only increased her need to relieve herself.

She tried to get her mind off her bladder, first by counting fence posts, then by trying to remember the lyrics to "Love Me Tender," but that didn't work. Finally, she pulled her book of pictures out of the plastic beach bag on the seat beside her.

She had been collecting pictures from magazines since she was little . . . pictures of bedrooms with old quilts and four-poster beds, kitchens with copper pots and blue china, living rooms with sleeping Lassies curled on bright rugs, and walls covered with family pictures in gold frames. Before, these rooms had existed only in the pages of magazines she bought at garage sales in Tellico Plains, Tennessee. But now, she was on her way to California—on her way to live in such rooms.

"Look, hon." She held a picture out to Willy Jack. "Here's that Mickey Mouse lamp I told you about. That's what I want to put in the baby's room."

Willy Jack turned on the radio and started twisting the knob, but all he got was static.

"I hope we can get a two-story house with a balcony that overlooks the ocean."

"Hell, Novalee. You can't see the ocean from Bakersfield."

"Well, maybe a pond then. I want to get one of those patio tables with an umbrella over it where we can sit with the baby and drink chocolate milk and watch the sun go down."

Novalee dreamed of all kinds of houses—two-story houses, log cabins, condominiums, ranch houses—anything fixed to the ground. She had never lived in a place that didn't have wheels under it. She had lived in seven house trailers—one a double-wide, a camping trailer, two mobile homes, a fifth-wheel, a burned Winnebago and a railroad car—part of a motel called the Chattanooga Choo Choo.

She held up another picture. "Look at these ducks here on this wall. Aren't they cute?"

Willy Jack turned the wheel sharply, trying to run over a turtle at the edge of the road.

"I just hate it when you do that," Novalee said. "Why do you want to kill turtles? They don't bother anything."

Willy Jack turned the radio dial and picked up "Graceland," by Paul Simon, who Willy Jack said was three and a half inches shorter than he was.

When they passed the Muldrow water tower, Novalee put her picture book away. The thought of so much water was almost more than she could bear.

"I bet they'll have a bathroom in this town."

"Oh, I wouldn't be surprised," Willy Jack said. "Almost every town has one. You think they'll have a little hot water, too? Maybe you'd like to soak in a hot tub. Huh? That sound good to you?"

"Dammit, Willy Jack, I have to go to the bathroom."

Willy Jack turned the volume up on the radio and beat out the song's rhythm on the dash. As they roared through Muldrow, Novalee tightened the muscles between her legs and tried not to think about swimming pools or iced tea.

She dug the map out again and figured the next chance she would have to stop, short of a head-on collision, was another twenty miles down the road in a town called Sequoyah. She peeked at the gas gauge and was discouraged to see they still had a half tank.

For a while, she played a silent game of running through the alphabet searching for a name for the baby. For A she thought of Angel and Abbie; for B she liked Bordon and Babbette, but she was just too miserable to concentrate, so she quit before she got to C.

She had aches and pains from her top to her bottom. Her head had been hurting all morning, but she didn't have any aspirin with her. Her feet were killing her, too. They were so swollen that the straps of her red sandals bit into her ankles and pinched her toes until they were throbbing. She couldn't reach the buckles, but by rubbing one sandal against the other, she was finally able to wiggle out of them, and for that, she was grateful.

"Wish I had some gum," she said.

Her mouth was dry and her throat felt scratchy. She had a half bottle of warm Coke in the back seat, but she knew if she drank it, it would only make her bladder fuller.

"Red's wife says she had trouble with her bladder when she was pregnant. She thinks that's why she had to have a C section."

"What the hell's a C section?"

"A caesarean. That's when they cut your belly open to get the baby out."

"Now don't you go planning on that, Novalee. That'll cost a damned fortune."

"It's not something you plan, Willy Jack. Not like you *plan* a birthday party. It's just something that happens. And I don't know how much it costs. Besides, you're going to be making good money."

"Yeah, and I don't want it spent before it's in my pocket, either."

Willy Jack was going to California to go to work for the railroad. He had a cousin there named J. Paul who had made it big working for the Union Pacific. And when Willy Jack had heard from J. Paul, just two weeks ago, he got excited and wanted to leave right away.

Novalee thought it was strange for Willy Jack to be excited about work, but she said she was not about to look a gift horse in the mouth, so as soon as she picked up her check at Red's, they left Tellico Plains and she didn't look back.

It was the chance she had dreamed about, the chance to live in a real home. She and Willy Jack had been staying in a camping trailer parked beside Red's, but the plumbing didn't work so they had to use the bathroom inside the cafe. She knew a job with the railroad would guarantee she would not have to live on top of wheels ever again. She knew that for sure.

But what she didn't know was that Willy Jack was going to Bakersfield to chop off one of his fingers. He hadn't told her the whole story.

He hadn't told her that a month after J. Paul started to work, he got his thumb cut off in a coupling clamp, an injury for which he received a cash settlement of sixty-five thousand dollars and an additional eight hundred dollars a month for the rest of his life. J. Paul used the money to buy a quick-lube shop and moved into a townhouse at the edge of a miniature golf course.

Hearing that had created in Willy Jack an intense interest in his own fingers. He noticed them, *really* noticed them for the first time in his life. He began to study each one. He figured out that thumbs and index fingers did most of the work, middle fingers were for communication, ring fingers were for rings, and little fingers were pretty much unnecessary. For Willy Jack, a southpaw, the little finger of his right hand was absolutely useless. And it was the one he would sacrifice, the one he intended to trade for greyhounds and race horses. It was the one that would take him to Santa Anita and Hollywood Park where he'd drink sloe gin fizzes and wear silk shirts and send his bets to the windows on silver trays.

But Novalee didn't know all that. She only knew he was going to Bakersfield to go to work for the railroad. He figured that was all she needed to know. And if Willy Jack was an expert on anything, it was what Novalee needed to know.

"Want to feel the baby?" she asked him.

He acted as if he hadn't heard her.

"Here." She held her hand out for his, but he left it dangling over the top of the steering wheel.

"Give me your hand." She lifted his hand from the wheel and guided it to her belly, then laid it flat against her, against the mound of her navel.

"Feel that?"

"No."

"Can't you feel that tiny little bomp . . . bomp . . . bomp?"

"I don't feel nothin'."

Willy Jack tried to pull his hand back, but she held it and moved it lower, pressing his fingers into the curve just above her pelvis.

"Feel right there." Her voice was soft, no more than a whisper. "That's where the heart is." She held his hand there a moment, then he jerked it away.

"Couldn't prove it by me," he said as he reached for a cigarette.

Novalee felt like she might cry then, but she didn't exactly know why. It was the way she felt sometimes at night when she heard a train whistle in the distance . . . a feeling she couldn't explain, not even to herself.

She leaned her head back against the seat and closed her eyes, trying to find a way to make time pass faster. She mentally began to decorate the nursery. She put the oak crib beneath the window and a rocker in the corner beside the changing table. She folded the small quilt with cows jumping over the moon and put it beside the stuffed animals . . .

As she drifted into sleep, she saw herself thin again, wearing her skinny denim dress and holding a baby, her baby, its face covered with a soft white blanket. Filled with joy and expectation, she gently peeled the blanket back, but discovered another blanket beneath it. She folded that back only to find another . . . and another.

Then, she heard a train whistle, faint, but growing louder. She looked up to see a locomotive speeding toward her and the baby. She stood frozen between the rails as the train bore down on them.

She tried to jump clear, to run, but her body was heavy, weighted, and the ground beneath, spongy and sticky, sucked at her feet. She fell then, and from her knees and with all her energy, she lifted the baby over the rail and pushed it away from the tracks, away from danger.

Then, the blast of the whistle split the air. She tried to drag herself across the rail, but she moved like a giant slug, inching her way across the hot curve of metal. A hiss of steam and rush of scalding air brushed her legs when, in one desperate lunge, she was across. She was free.

She tried to stand, but her legs were twisted sinew and shards of bone. The train had severed her feet.

The scream started deep in her belly, then roared through her lungs.

"What the hell's the matter with you, Novalee?" Willy Jack yelled.

Yanking herself from sleep, Novalee was terrified to feel the rush of hot air coming through the floorboard. She knew without looking that the TV tray was gone.

She turned to look out the back window, dreading what she would see—her feet, mangled like road kill, torn and bloody in the middle of the highway.

But what she saw were her red sandals, empty of feet, skidding and bouncing down the road.

"What are you smiling about?" Willy Jack asked.

"Just a dream I had."

She didn't want to tell him about the shoes. It was the only pair she had and she knew he'd gripe about the money another pair would cost. Besides, they were on a real highway coming into a real town and Novalee didn't want to get him mad again or she'd never get to a bathroom.

"Oh, look. There's a Wal-Mart. Let's stop there."

"Thought you had to pee."

"They have bathrooms in Wal-Mart, you know."

Willy Jack swerved across two lanes and onto the access road while Novalee tried to figure her way around a problem. She didn't have more than a dollar in her beach bag. Willy Jack had all the cash.

"Hon, I'm gonna need some money."

"They gonna charge you to pee?"

He drove across the parking lot like he was making a pit stop and whipped the big Plymouth into the handicapped parking space nearest the entrance.

"Five dollars will be enough."

"What for?"

"I'm gonna buy some houseshoes."

"Houseshoes? Why? We're in a car."

"My feet are swollen. I can't get my sandals back on."

"Jesus Christ, Novalee. We're going clear across the country and you're gonna be wearing houseshoes?"

"Who's gonna see?"

"You mean ever time we stop, you're gonna be traipsing around in houseshoes?"

"Well, we don't stop very much, do we?"

"Okay. Get some houseshoes. Get some polky dot houseshoes. Some green polky dot houseshoes so everyone will be sure to notice you."

"I don't want polka dot houseshoes."

"Get you some with elephants on them then. Yeah! An elephant in elephant houseshoes."

"That's mean, Willy Jack. That's real mean."

"Goddamn, Novalee."

"I have to buy *some* kind of shoes."

She hoped that would be enough of an explanation, but she knew it wouldn't. And though he didn't actually say "Why," his face said it.

"My sandals fell through the floor."

She smiled at him then, a tentative smile, an invitation to see the humor in what had happened, but he declined the offer. He stared at her long enough to melt her smile, then he turned, spit out the window and shook his head in disgust. Finally, digging in the pocket of his jeans, he pulled out a handful of crumpled bills. His movements, exaggerated and quick, were designed to show her he was right on the edge. He pitched a ten at her, then crammed the rest back in his pocket.

"I won't be long," she told him as she climbed out of the car.

"Yeah."

"Don't you want to come in. Stretch your legs?"

"No. I don't."

"Want me to bring you some popcorn?"

"Just go on, Novalee."

She could feel his eyes on her as she walked away. She tried to move her body as she had when they first met, when he was unable to keep his hands away from her, when her breasts and belly and thighs were tight and smooth. But she knew what he was seeing now. She knew how she looked.

The single stall in the bathroom was taken. Novalee pressed her legs together and tried to hold her breath.

When she heard the toilet flush, she was sure she was going to make it, but when the door didn't open, she was sure she wasn't.

"I'm sorry," she said as she tapped on the door, "but I've got to get in there now."

A little girl, still struggling with buttons, opened the door, then jumped out of the way as Novalee rushed by.

Once inside, Novalee didn't take time to lock the door or cover the seat with paper. She didn't even check to make sure there was paper on the roll. She just peed and peed, then laughed out loud, her eyes flooded with tears at the joy of release. Novalee took pleasure in small victories.

As she washed at the sink, she studied herself in the mirror, then wished she hadn't. Her skin, though unblemished and smooth, looked sallow, and her eyes, a light shade of green, were ringed with dark circles. Her hickory-colored hair, long and thick, had pulled loose from the clip at her neck and was frizzed into thin tight ringlets.

She splashed cold water on her face, smoothed her hair with wet hands, then dug in her beach bag for lipstick, but couldn't find any. Finally, she pinched her cheeks for color and decided not to look in any more mirrors until she could expect a better picture.

She went directly to the shoe department, knowing she had already taken too much time. The cheapest houseshoes she could find had little polka dots, so she settled quickly for a pair of rubber thongs.

At the checkout stand, she fidgeted impatiently while the man in front of her wrote out a check. By the time the checker dragged the thongs across the scanner, Novalee was caught up in the headlines of the *National Examiner*. She handed the checker the ten-dollar-bill while she puzzled over the picture of a newborn who was two thousand years old.

"Ma'am. Here's your change."

"Oh, sorry." Novalee held out her hand.

"Seven dollars and seventy-seven cents."

Novalee tried to jerk her hand back, but before she could, the coins dropped onto her palm.

"No," she shouted as she flung the money across the floor. "No." Dizzy, she staggered as she turned and started running.

She knew he was gone, knew before she reached the door. She could see it all, see it as if she were watching a movie. She could see herself running, calling his name—the parking space empty, the Plymouth gone.

He was going to California and he had left her behind . . . left her with her magazine dreams of old quilts and blue china and family pictures in gold frames.

Chapter Two

SHE WOULDN'T REMEMBER it all, even later. She wouldn't remember the man who found her camera in the handicapped parking space. She wouldn't remember the clerk pressing the money into her hand or the manager leading her to the bench just inside the door.

But she did remember someone wanting to call an ambulance and she did remember saying she was all right, telling them her boyfriend had gone to get the car fixed and would pick her up later.

And little by little, as they went to lunch . . . sneaked a smoke . . . stocked more shelves, as clerks and stock boys and managers drifted by, they forgot the pregnant girl on the bench by the door, sitting under a red, white and blue banner that said MADE IN AMERICA.

By two o'clock she was hungry. She ate popcorn and drank Cokes from tall plastic cups. She had two Paydays and went to the bathroom twice. She tried to think of what she should do, but thinking about it made her tired and caused her head to throb, so she ate another Payday and went to the bathroom again.

Just before three, a bony little woman with blue hair and no eyebrows rushed up and smiled into Novalee's face.

"Ruth Ann? Ruth Ann Mott! Well, I declare. Little Ruth Ann. Why honey, I haven't seen you since your momma passed. What's that been? Twelve, fourteen years?"

"No, ma'am, I'm not Ruth Ann."

"Don't you remember me, honey? I'm Sister Husband. You remember me. Thelma Husband. Course, that's not what you called me back then. You called me 'Telma' because you couldn't say 'Thelma.' But everyone calls me Sister Husband now."

"But my name isn't—"

"Last time I saw you, you wasn't more'n a baby. And here you are about to *have* a baby. Don't that beat all? Where do you live now, Ruth Ann?"

"Well, I've been living in Tennessee, but—"

"Tennessee. I had a cousin lived in Tennessee. School teacher. But when she was in her midlife, she had an operation."

Sister Husband lowered her voice and leaned closer to Novalee.

"Hysterectomy, it was. And you know after that, she couldn't spell anymore. Couldn't spell 'cat,' so they said. She had to give up her school teaching, of course. But that was a shame, wasn't it?"

"Yes, ma'am. It was."

"Tennessee. So, you just moving back, honey? Coming back home now?"

"Well, not exactly. But it looks like I might be here awhile."

"Oh, that's good, Ruthie. I think that's good. 'Cause

home gives you something no other place can. You know what that is?"

"No, ma'am."

"Your history, Ruthie. Home is where your history begins."

"Yes, ma'am."

"The late Brother Husband said, 'Home is the place that'll catch you when you fall. And we *all* fall.' That's what the late Brother Husband used to say."

"Was he your husband?"

"No. He was my brother. A real man of God. You go to church, Ruthie? You go regular to church?"

"Not regular."

"Well, that's good. I think that's good. Sunday School . . . Bible study . . . prayer meetings. Now that's just too much church. Ain't nobody so full a sin they need that much church."

"Yes, ma'am."

"No reason to work so hard at it. Me? I just have one job to do now. Just one job. You know what that is?"

"I guess it's to save souls."

"Oh, no, Ruth Ann. The Lord saves souls. I save wheat pennies. No, my one job is to give away Bibles. That's what the Lord wants me to do. Do you read the Bible, Ruth Ann?"

"Well, not much."

"That's good. I think that's good. Folks read too much of it, they get confused. Read a little and you're just a little confused. Read a lot and you're a lot confused. And that's why I just give out a chapter at a time. That way, folks can deal with their confusion as it comes. You understand what I'm saying, Ruth Ann?"

"Yes, ma'am. I think I do." Novalee touched the scar on her arm in remembrance of Gladys.

"Wish I had a Bible chapter to give you, honey, but I went by the bus station and gave away my last Deuteronomy and two Lamentations. Met a woman going to New Orleans. Any woman on her way to New Orleans can't have too many Lamentations. But I don't have a chapter left. I feel real bad about that."

"Oh, that's okay."

"I'll get some more run off tomorrow. I'll print you out an Obadiah. Obadiah won't confuse you much. But I'm not going to leave you empty-handed now, honey. Come with me."

Sister Husband wheeled and started for the door, then turned and motioned to Novalee.

"Come on, Ruth Ann."

Novalee wasn't quite sure why she followed the blue-haired woman out the door and across the parking lot, but she figured it couldn't bring her much more trouble than she already had. Sister Husband marched her way to a banged-up blue Toyota pickup rigged to resemble a Conestoga wagon with a canvas cover over the bed. But the canvas was torn and the wire arches supporting it were bent, leaving the top drooping in the middle. On the side of the truck was a sign in white lettering: THE WELCOME WAGON.

Sister Husband opened the door and pulled out a straw basket with a red bow tied to the handle. She held the basket in front of her and pulled herself up tall and straight, like a soldier at attention.

"Let me be among the first to welcome you home," she said with the cadence and inflection of a bad public speaker. "And on behalf of the city, I would like to present you with this basket of gifts from the merchants and bankers to make this, your homecoming, as pleasant as possible."

"Thank you." Novalee took the basket.

"Look here, Ruth Ann. It's got matches, a phone book, emery boards. Here's some discount coupons and a map of the city. There's just one thing though. See this appointment book?"

Novalee nodded.

"I ran out of these last week. This was the only one I could find for myself, so I wrote two or three of my own appointments in there. My AA meetings. But if you aren't an alcoholic, then you'll know those dates aren't for you."

"No ma'am, I'm not."

"Good. I think that's good. But remember, we all fall. That's what the late Brother Husband used to say."

"Sister Husband. Can I take your picture?"

If the question surprised her, Sister Husband didn't show it. "Why, Ruth Ann. How sweet," she said. She took off her glasses and sucked in her stomach until Novalee snapped the camera. They watched together as the picture developed.

"Oh, looks like my eyes are crossed. I always take such awful pictures."

"No, it's good."

"You really think so?"

"Yes, I do."

"You're sweet, Ruth Ann. Real sweet."

Sister Husband gave Novalee a quick hug, then she climbed in the Toyota and started it up.

"I live on Evergreen, Ruthie. You'll find it on your map. Last house on the left. You come out there anytime you can. And bring that baby! You two will always be welcome."

"Thank you, Sister Husband. And I'm gonna put this picture in a frame to keep for my baby."

Sister Husband drove away, but Novalee stood in the parking lot and waved at the little covered wagon heading west until it was out of sight.

Back inside the store, Novalee stopped at a wooden porch swing displayed near the door. She ran her hand across the dark wood and thought of cool yellow porches and morning glories thick on white trellises.

"Old man out on Sticker Creek makes porch swings out of hickory."

She turned toward the voice and the big black man sitting on her bench.

"Those won't last," he said. "Threads'll strip in that soft wood. You want a swing that'll last, go out on Sticker Creek."

"Where's that?" she asked.

"You new in town?"

"Yes. No. Well, I haven't been here very long."

"A newcomer then."

He smiled and scooted over on the bench, an invitation for her to join him.

He was the blackest man Novalee had ever seen, so black his skin reflected light. She thought if she leaned close enough, she could see herself in his face. He was dressed in a suit and had a briefcase on the floor beside him. Novalee had never seen a black man with a briefcase before.

She put her plastic beach bag and the welcome basket between them, giving herself little room at the other end of the bench.

"My name's Whitecotton. Moses Whitecotton."

"Oh." She started to tell him hers, but changed her mind.

"Some of my family shortened their name to White. But that's not their name. Name's Whitecotton."

"Why'd they change it?"

"They found some shame in it. Said it was a slave name. But it's theirs. And it's mine."

Moses Whitecotton was still for a moment, staring off at something Novalee couldn't see.

"Name's important," he said. "Keeps track of who you are."

"I guess so."

"That's right. Name's an important thing. You picked a name for your baby yet?"

"No, but I got some I'm thinking about."

"Well, take your time. Can't rush a thing like that. Name's too important to hurry."

Novalee reached into her beach bag and pulled out a package of Life Savers, then she put the bag on the floor, under the bench. The top Life Saver was green, her favorite, but she offered it to Moses Whitecotton.

"Thanks, but I'm a diabetic. Can't take sugar."

"You know," she said as she popped the Life Saver into her mouth. "I've been thinking about Wendi, with an i, or maybe Candy, if it's a girl."

"Get your baby a name that means something. A sturdy name. Strong name. Name that's gonna withstand a lot of bad times. A lot of hurt."

"I never thought of that."

"I used to be an engraver . . . trophies, plaques. Cut gravestones, too. You do a thing like that, you think about names."

"Yeah, I guess you would."

"See, the name you pick out is gonna be with your baby

when nothing else is. When nobody is. 'Cause you ain't always gonna be there."

"Oh, I'm never gonna leave her. The way some people just leave, go right out of your life. I'm never gonna do that."

"But you're not gonna live forever. You're gonna die. We're all gonna die. Me. Her. You."

Novalee swallowed her Life Saver.

"You're dying right now. Right this minute." He looked at his watch, said, "Right this second," then tapped it with his finger. "See there? That second passed. It's gone. Not gonna come again. And while I'm talking to you, every second I'm talking, a second is passing. Gone. Count them up. Count them down. They're gone. Each one bringing you closer to your dying time."

"I don't like to think about that."

"You ever think about this? Every year you live, you pass the anniversary of your death. Now, you don't know what day it is, of course. You follow what I'm saying?"

Novalee nodded, but just barely, as if too much movement might break her concentration.

"Look here. Say you're gonna die on December eighth. Course, you don't *know* the date because you're still alive. But every year you live, you pass December eighth without knowing it's the anniversary of your death. You see what I mean?"

"Yeah." Novalee was wide-eyed, stunned by this startling new idea. "I'd never thought of that."

"No, not a lot of folks do. But listen. You're gonna die. But your name's not. No. It's gonna be written in somebody's Bible, printed in some newspaper. Cut into your gravestone. See, that name has a history."

"And home is the place where your history begins," she said softly.

"And that history is gonna be there when you're not."

He turned his palms up, hands open . . . empty. He had given her all he could and she had taken it.

"Here," he said. He picked up his briefcase and while he adjusted it on his lap, Novalee moved the Welcome Wagon basket to the other side of her and scooted over next to Moses Whitecotton. The briefcase was full of pictures.

"Why do you have all of those?"

"I'm a photographer now. Go around to stores and take pictures of babies."

"Can I see some?"

He shuffled through a dozen pictures. Babies smiling, frowning, crying. Brown babies, black babies, white babies. Curly haired, blue-eyed, red-haired and bald.

"You bring your baby in here a few months from now, I'll take her picture for free."

"You will?"

"Sure. Here's what I'm looking for."

Moses Whitecotton handed Novalee a satin baby book. "We give these away with a hundred-dollar order." He opened the first page. "That's where you write in your baby's name. Be sure it's the right one."

"I will."

He reassembled the pictures in his briefcase and snapped it shut.

"Mr. Whitecotton, could I take your picture?"

"Mine?"

She nodded.

"Sure."

Novalee took the camera out of the beach bag, stood in front of him and snapped the picture.

Just then, a young man, blond and polished, stepped between them.

"Hi, I'm Reggie Lewis. My girl said you were waiting to see me? Is it Mose?"

"No. It's Moses Whitecotton."

"Oh. Okay. You want to come back to my office?" Reggie walked off, leading the way.

Moses Whitecotton offered his hand to Novalee. "Good luck."

His hand was sturdy, strong and Novalee liked the way it felt to have her hand in his.

"Thank you for the baby book."

"My pleasure," he said, then he walked away.

Novalee watched him go, then looked at the picture in her hand, the picture of Moses Whitecotton, and for a moment, just for a moment, she thought she saw herself in his face.

At just after seven, Novalee had a chili dog and a root beer float. Then she bought a copy of the *American Baby Magazine*, hoping to find a list of names to choose from, but it didn't have one. Instead, she read an article entitled "Staying Fit During Pregnancy," which prompted her to have a package of beef jerky for extra protein and then to take a brisk walk. She circled the parking lot three times, breathing deeply from her diaphragm as the article had suggested, but the Oklahoma heat tired her quickly and she plodded through the last lap.

She looked up when a pickup pulled in and parked nearby. The back was filled with small trees, their roots wrapped in burlap. A hand-lettered sign on the side of the truck read, BEN GOODLUCK NURSERY. EARTH CARE GROWERS.

The driver, a tall, thin Indian man, got out and went

into the store. His passenger, a young boy, waited in the truck.

Novalee walked over, studied the sign for a few seconds, then traced the word "Goodluck" with her finger. The boy, a ten-year-old copy of the man, leaned out his window and watched her.

"Is your name Goodluck?" she asked.

The boy nodded.

"Wish that was my name."

"Why?"

"Because that's a strong name. A name that's gonna withstand a lot of bad times."

"I guess so," he said. "What happened to your arm?" He touched the scar very lightly.

"I had some bad luck." Novalee pointed to the bed of the truck. "What kind of trees are those?"

"Buckeyes."

"I never heard of those."

The boy jumped out, fished in his pocket and pulled out a hard, brown nut . . . polished, shining.

"Here." He held it out to her.

"What is it?"

"A buckeye."

Novalee took it and rolled it around in the palm of her hand.

"It's lucky," he said.

"How do you know?"

"My grandpa told me. This was his grandpa's, then his. And now it's mine."

"Did they have good luck?"

He nodded. "They were good hunters. So am I."

"Does it only bring good luck in hunting?"

"No. It's good for lots of stuff. Lets you find things you

need. Helps you find your way home if you get lost. Lots of stuff."

Novalee held the buckeye out to him.

"Make a wish first," he said.

"A wish?"

"Yeah. Hold it in your hand and make a wish."

"But it's not my good luck charm. It's yours."

"Yeah, but it'll work. Try it."

"Okay." Novalee clamped her fingers around the buckeye and closed her eyes tight, like a child waiting to be surprised. When she finished, she gave it back to the boy.

"What did you wish for?" he asked.

"If I tell you, it won't come true."

"Nah. That's just when you wish on a star."

"Can I take your picture?"

"I guess so."

"Stand right there by the door of your truck so I can get your name, too. There. Just a little to the left. Good."

Novalee snapped the picture just as the boy's father returned to the truck.

"You ready to go, Benny?"

"Okay." He opened the door and got in, then smiled at Novalee. "Well, bye."

"Bye, Benny Goodluck."

The boy waved as the truck pulled away. Novalee crossed the parking lot, headed back to the store.

"Ma'am. Ma'am."

She turned and shielded her eyes from the sun.

"Wait up," Benny Goodluck called. He was running toward her, carrying one of the little buckeye trees. "Here. It's for you."

"For me? Why?"

"For good luck." He put the tree down in the handicapped parking space.

"Oh, Benny. You knew what I wished for."

"Yes, ma'am. I did."

Then he turned and ran back to his father.

Novalee was looking at baby clothes when the intercom clicked on. The voice sounded tinny and distant, like a bad connection.

"Attention Wal-Mart shoppers. The time is now nine o'clock and your Wal-Mart Discount City is closing.

Novalee's breath caught and she felt lightheaded.

"Please bring your final selections to . . .

Something surged in her chest, something hot and painful.

"We would like to remind you of our store hours . . .

Her heart raced, the beat irregular, heavy.

"We are open from nine . . .

Her mouth felt slick and tasted of cold chili.

"And, as always, thank you for shopping at Wal-Mart."

She choked back the sourness that burned at her throat, wheeled and ran toward the bathroom at the back of the store.

The stall was empty, the room dark, but she didn't have time to fumble for lights. She retched again and again until she felt drained. Then, she sat in the dark trying not to think about the mess she was in. She had been pushing it from her mind all day, but now, it rushed in.

There must be, she told herself, things she could do. She could try to find Momma Nell, but she didn't know Fred's last name. She supposed there might be an umpires club, a place she could call, but there were probably lots of umpires named Fred.

She could call the State School for Girls to see if Rhonda Talley was still there. But stealing the ice cream truck had been Rhonda's first offense, so she was likely free.

She could call Red, but she didn't think he'd send her the money to come back to Tellico Plains. He'd already hired another waitress.

Then Novalee thought about Willy Jack. She could hitchhike, try to get to Bakersfield on her own. But she didn't know if J. Paul's last name was Pickens or Paul.

She wondered if Willy Jack had really left her. What if he had gone to get the car fixed. Or what if he was only playing a joke on her. He liked to do that. Maybe he drove off to scare her, then had a wreck before . . .

What if he had been kidnapped. Someone with a gun could have forced him to . . . She saw things like that on television.

What if . . .

Play like . . .

Just pretend . . .

But Novalee knew none of that had happened. And she knew Momma Nell wouldn't care where she was, Rhonda Talley probably wouldn't even remember her—and Willy Jack had gone on without her.

She tasted the bile rising in her throat again, felt the grip of pain in her stomach. She would have fought against it, but was too tired. She let herself slip into blackness and disappear into space.

She didn't know how long she had been in the bathroom. She had been too weak to move, too sick to care.

Her clothes were damp and sticky, her skin clammy. Her head felt disconnected from her body. When she was finally able to stand, she felt like she was seeing everything from some great height.

She got to the sink and held on while she splashed her face and rinsed her mouth. Her head throbbed and she ached all over, but she washed up as well as she could, then recovered her beach bag and eased out the door.

The building was dark and quiet. A weak light came from the front, but she knew the place was empty . . . knew she was alone.

She moved soundlessly through the store, toward the light, and found her possessions by the bench where she'd left them—the Welcome Wagon basket, her baby book, the buckeye tree. She gathered them up, as if she were preparing to leave, as if she were going home.

Then she began to wander, like people do who have come from no place and have no place to go—like Crazy Man Dan, in Tellico Plains, who walked the streets at night carrying bits and pieces of other people's lives.

She moved aimlessly from one side of the store to the other, past rows of televisions without pictures, racks of toys without children. She shuffled past stacks of sheets, boxes of candy and shelves of dishes. She walked some aisles many times, some not at all, but it didn't matter.

And then she saw a table, a round, glass-topped table beneath a red and white striped umbrella . . . a place where she could sit with the baby and drink chocolate milk and watch the sun go down. She ran her hand across the smooth glass top, swiping at dust, cleaning a place for the book and the basket. Nearby, she found some thin white trellises and moved two of them to the side of the table, then placed the tree between them.

She eased into one of the chairs, opened her beach bag and took out the pictures of Sister Husband, Moses Whitecotton and Benny Goodluck, then propped them up against the basket. She moved the book nearer the center of the table, then pushed it back to where it had been. Finally . . . finished . . . she sat still for a long time, so long that it seemed she might never move.

Much later, when she did get up, she walked to the front window and looked outside. A light rain was beginning to fall and a hard wind scattered drops against the glass. Hazy neon yellows and reds, tiny darts of color, were caught in the trickles spilling down the pane. And suddenly, a memory, long-buried, came rushing back to her.

She was very little and she couldn't remember why or how, but she was left behind at a skating rink, locked in, alone. At first, she was terrified . . . screaming, pounding on locked doors, clawing toward high windows.

Then, she stretched to a switch on the wall, flipped it up, and a huge silver ball in the middle of the rink started to turn, sending a shower of silver and blue across the floor, up the walls, around the ceiling—around and around.

Her fear broke apart then, shattered like splintered glass, and five-year-old Novalee Nation walked into that shower of light and let the bright diamonds of color dance around her body. Then, she began to turn. Under the magic silver ball, her stockinged feet gliding, sliding on the polished wood, she turned . . . faster and faster . . . arms floating free in space . . . spinning . . . whirling . . . free.

Novalee smiled at her five-year-old self, all elbows and knees, and she tried to hold her there, but the child spun away, into the shadows.

Then, Novalee Nation, seventeen, seven months pregnant, thirty-seven pounds overweight, slipped off her thongs and there, in the middle of the Wal-Mart, she began to turn . . . faster and faster . . . spinning and whirling . . . free . . . waiting for her history to begin.

Chapter Three

WILLY JACK RAN out of money in Tucumcari; the Plymouth ran out of gas eighty miles later. When the needle on the gas gauge crawled over the E, he dug in his pockets to count his change, ninety-four cents. He regretted giving Novalee the ten, which would have gotten him closer to California, but he quickly shrugged that off. Willy Jack was not one to linger on regret.

He was able to let the car coast to a grove of pines, well off the shoulder of the road. He locked his cardboard suitcase in the trunk, then pulled out the seats, front and back, searching for lost coins. He found two quarters, a dime, three pennies and his roach clip.

He hadn't walked far before he realized he had left his dark glasses on the dash. More than the heat, he was bothered by the glare of the sun, which produced a finger of pain jabbing at his eyes.

He tried to hitch a ride, but the truckers, having gotten up speed coming off the Pecos Mesa, roared past, creating small whirlwinds of dust and grit, leaving him grinding sand between his teeth.

Few other vehicles were on the road. Pickups with whole families crowded into the cabs. RVs, their windows plastered with bumper stickers that said SENIOR CITIZENS ON BOARD. Not the kind of drivers to stop for hitchhikers.

Once, a banged-up little VW full of teenagers slowed and pulled even with Willy Jack. A redhead with crooked teeth leaned out the window and smiled.

"Excuse me, sir," he said, "but would you have any Grey Poupon?"

"What? Grey what?"

But the car had already started to speed away, the sounds of laughter spilling out behind it.

"Cocksuckers," Willy Jack shouted.

The redhead leaned out the window and blew Willy Jack a kiss; Willy Jack gave him the finger.

"Cocksuckers," he yelled again, but they were far down the highway by then.

The heat was beginning to bother him; his mouth was dry, his head pounding. At the top of a rise he spotted a pond, but it was a mile or so back from the highway.

He didn't have a plan for getting gas or money, but when he saw a sign that said SANTA ROSA—THREE MILES, he figured that was a better option than walking to Bakersfield.

Just before the exit, another sign announced GAS, FOOD AND LODGING AHEAD, but Willy Jack never made it to any of the three. He never made it past a bar called Tom Pony's, a squat concrete building painted the color of weak coffee.

Willy Jack was afraid the place might be closed. An old pickup parked in front was missing the two rear tires and had been there for a while. The neon signs on the building were unlit and it looked dark behind the windows, but he could hear the sounds of music playing inside, a steel guitar sliding along the edges of a song. He tried the door, but it was locked. Then he went to the window, rubbed away a circle of grime, cupped his hands around his eyes and peered inside.

In a few seconds his vision adjusted enough for him to realize he was staring into another pair of eyes on the other side of the glass.

"Jesus," he yelled as he jumped back.

He heard someone inside laughing. A moment later a lock clicked and the door opened, but just inches. He moved to it, tentatively, then leaned in a little closer. That's when the door flew open and a hand reached out, grabbed Willy Jack and pulled him inside.

"What the hell you think you're doing peeking in my window?"

A girl who looked to be twelve or thirteen had hold of him. She had short cropped hair, a beak of a nose, a thin, sharp face dotted with pimples. Willy Jack almost laughed at how ugly she was, lean and stringy. She reminded him of pictures he had seen on television, pictures of starving people in Africa, except this girl was white. And strong.

"You can get shot doing that, you know."

"Look," he said, brushing her hand off his arm. "It's not like I was peeking in your bedroom or anything. This isn't a house."

"How do you know it's not, Mr. Smarty Pants."

"Well, is it?"

"What does it look like?"

Willy Jack scanned the room, but without interest. He had spent a thousand nights in such places, but never saw in them more than he saw in this one: jukebox, pool table, bar, girl. He never saw the cracked plastic or the splattered walls or the torn Naugahyde or the yellowed pictures of Indians, haggard and beaten. He couldn't see the gleam and shine of things still new already dulled and scarred—like the girl.

"So, is this place open or not?" he asked.

"If we were closed, you wouldn't be here, would you?"

"All I want—what I'm after is just a cold beer."

"Well, that's what we sell."

She went behind the bar, drew a beer, then slid it across the counter to him. He drank most of it in one swallow.

"So, where you from?" she asked.

"Nashville."

"Tennessee?"

"I don't know of but one Nashville. And it's in Tennessee."

"You're a smartass, ain't you?"

Willy Jack grinned.

From somewhere in the back, in a room behind the bar, Willy Jack heard a toilet flush.

"You know who you look like when you smile?" she said. "John Cougar Mellencamp. Anyone ever told you that before?"

"Sure. Lots of people. You know why? 'Cause he's my brother."

"Bullshit. He ain't your brother."

"That right? My momma thinks he is."

"You're not."

Willy Jack finished the beer and held the empty glass out to her.

"Show me your driver's license."

"Why? You a cop?"

She laughed then, and Willy Jack saw that she was missing her two front teeth. Her gums, where the teeth should have been, were deep red, like she'd put lipstick in that place. Willy Jack was surprised to feel the beginning of an erection.

She filled his glass and handed it back to him.

"Come on. Prove you're who you say."

"Wish I could."

"I knew that was bullshit."

"Some son of a bitch stole my wallet last night. Right out of my hotel room. Money, credit cards. The works."

"You mean you don't have no money? How you gonna pay me for them two beers?"

"Oh, I got a little change." Willy Jack acted like he was going for his pocket.

"That's okay. They're on the house."

"Jolene?" The voice from the back room, a woman's, was husky, flat.

The girl squinched up her eyes and made a face like she'd gotten a mouthful of raw egg.

"Yes, ma'am?"

"You filled the salt shakers?"

"Yes, I did."

The girl grabbed a sack of Morton Salt from a shelf behind her, then twisted the tops off a couple of chunky plastic shakers on the bar. She upended the salt and waved the sack back and forth above the shakers.

"Jolene," the woman called again.

The girl grinned at Willy Jack as the salt spilled over the shakers and onto the counter. She held the sack until it was empty, the shakers buried beneath a pound of salt.

"Jolene." The voice was more insistent now.

"What?"

"Put the rest of the Coors and Millers into the case," the woman yelled.

"Okay."

The girl walked into a curtained area at one end of the bar and returned with two cases of beer, one on top of the other. She handled the cases easily, without strain. Willy Jack watched as she opened the cold case behind the bar and began loading the hot beer into it. Her jeans pulled up tight into her crotch each time she bent forward, but that wasn't what excited him. It was that space in her mouth where she had lost her front teeth.

"You a musician, too?" she asked.

"Yeah. Got a gig in Las Vegas if I can get there by tomorrow night."

"Why it ain't but eight hours. And that's doing the speed limit."

"Hell, I ain't good at speed limits, but I—"

"Jolene?"

The girl held her finger to her lips, a signal to Willy Jack to be quiet, but he didn't need a signal. He could hear the impatience in the woman's voice.

"You talking to someone out there?"

"No." Jolene rolled her eyes in disgust. "I'm just singing."

"You can make it easy in eight hours," the girl whispered to Willy Jack.

"But my car's out on the highway, out of gas. And I don't have any cash . . . no credit cards."

"Why don't you call your brother?"

"That's the problem. He's in London. On tour."

"Then call your wife."

"Don't have one."

"Girlfriend?"

"Naw, that's over. I dumped her."

"You could hitchhike. Unless you think you're too good."

"I done my share of it. But I can't leave my car."

"Well, maybe I can help you out."

"How's that?"

"I got some money."

"I sure would—"

"What the hell's going on?" The voice from the back room belonged to the heavy woman standing in the door. She was wearing a man's undershirt, black lace underpants and pink Reeboks.

"You open up, Jolene?"

"No, ma'am, but he—"

"You the one decides when we open? Huh? You setting the hours now?"

The woman crossed to the bar, got right in the girl's face.

"You running the place now?"

"This guy—"

Then the woman turned to Willy Jack. "We're closed."

"That right?" he said.

She reached across the bar and grabbed the beer from in front of him.

"You pay for this?"

"I was going to, but—"

"I gave it to him," the girl said.

"Oh. You open up and you give away beer. My, oh my. I don't know how I ever run this place without you. Yes sir, the day you . . ."

The girl scooted around the woman and across to the front door.

"He's just leaving." Jolene motioned to Willy Jack. "Go on. Get out."

Willy Jack pushed back from the bar, then slid off the

stool and headed for the door, but he didn't rush . . . didn't hurry.

"You damned right he's leaving. And so are you if you don't shape up."

As he stepped through the door, the girl slammed it behind him. He could still hear the woman's voice, even when he reached the road. She was yelling about salt.

On his way into town, he passed several trailer houses set back on treeless lots, a roadside fruit stand, abandoned, and a burned barn in a field thick with sagebrush. He crossed over railroad tracks that ran beside a boarded-up filling station—the place where the girl was waiting. She was standing on the concrete island beside the pumps.

"You cleaned up that salt real quick, Jolene." He tried to say 'Jolene' the way the woman had said it.

"I didn't clean it up."

"Then I bet you're gonna get your ass whipped."

"She ain't the boss of me."

"No. I could see that for sure."

She walked to the road and fell in beside him. "Listen. I've got over two hundred dollars I can let you have if you're interested."

He stopped walking then. "I'm interested."

"But you've got to take me with you. Take me to Las Vegas."

"Like hell. They'd get me for kidnapping."

"I'm no kid. I'm nineteen."

"And I'm Elvis."

"Well, I'm older than I look."

"What do you mean, take you with me?"

"Let me come with you, help you in Las Vegas."

"Help me with what?"

"With your equipment. Instruments and stuff. I'm

strong. I can lift. Speakers . . . amplifiers. Hell, I can move a piano all by myself."

She picked at her shirt as she talked. Willy Jack had the feeling she was about to push up her sleeves and show him her muscles. He knew if she did, he'd laugh and give it all away.

"What are you smiling about?" she asked.

"About how nice it would be to have someone with me. Someone to take care of my costumes . . . sew on sequins, buttons, stuff like that."

"Yeah, and I can run errands, take your phone calls—anything."

"Okay. Let's do it."

She smiled then, a smile that crinkled up her eyes and pulled her lips back tight against her teeth—and he saw again that empty space at the front of her mouth.

"Let's go," he said.

"Well, I can't go right now."

"Why not?"

"I've got to get my money. Some clothes. Take care of a couple of things."

"Well, when can you go?"

"Tonight."

"Tonight? What the hell am I supposed to do all day? Stand out here in the sun and jerk off?"

"I don't know. Go to the park. Look around. Just go somewhere. Then I'll meet you at the high school."

"Where the hell's the high school?"

"Right in the middle of town. You'll see it. There ain't that much town."

She waited for some sign of approval from him, but Willy Jack crammed his hands in his pockets and stared past her.

"Okay?" she asked.

"I don't seem to have much choice, do I?"

"Now where's your car?"

"On the highway. 'Bout three miles east of here."

"What are you driving?"

"Seventy-two Plymouth. Why?"

"Give me the keys." She held out her hand, trying to act certain she could pull this off.

"The hell I will."

"Look. I can get a ride out there . . . take a can of gas. Then I drive it in, fill it up, oil, the works. I pick you up at eight. We're outta here."

"Naw." He shook his head. "I ain't gonna hand my keys over to—"

"You think I'm gonna steal a '72 Plymouth? Shit. Let's forget it." She turned around and started back down the road. "Just forget the whole thing."

"Okay," Willy Jack yelled. "Let's do it."

But the girl kept walking away from him. He hurried to catch up with her, then dangled the keys in front of her nose.

"I said, let's do it." His voice had a harder edge to it then.

She plucked the keys out of his hand without missing a step.

"Eight," she said—and then she was gone.

Willy Jack was at the school by seven, hoping the girl might get there early. He'd had all he wanted of Santa Rosa, New Mexico, by then. He had spent an hour at the pool hall watching two fat men play pool like they were spearing fish. When he finally got in the game, he let them win his change so he could sucker them in for a few bucks, but they quit then and left with his money.

In the drugstore, he'd jimmied a gum ball machine for enough nickels to buy a Pepsi and a Slow Poke. After that, he had gone to a cafe called Peaches where he drank water and watched cartoons on a twelve-inch black-and-white with a vertical problem.

Finally, he had walked to the high school where he waited and swatted at mosquitoes that left welts on his face and neck.

But Jolene wasn't early; she wasn't even on time. She pulled in at a quarter after nine, driving too fast and without any lights. She missed the school driveway by a foot, jumped the curb and smacked the front bumper against an iron railing that lined the sidewalk.

"Where the fuck have you been?" he yelled.

"I got tied up."

Willy Jack started for the driver's side of the car.

"Go around," she said. "I'll drive."

"Like hell." He jerked the door open and she slid over.

"Did you get the money?"

"Sure."

"How much?"

"Two hundred eighteen," she said.

Willy Jack leaned over to her then as if he were about to whisper, so she bent toward him. But his hand shot out, grabbed the back of her head, twisted a thick hank of hair between his fingers. He yanked her head to his, mashed his face against hers, his nose pressed flat into her cheek.

Then, staring into her eyes, he ground his lips against hers and forced her mouth open with his teeth, his tongue. He pushed between her lips, his tongue ripping into her mouth, pushing, probing until he found what he was after.

And when he did, his tongue began to fondle her there, in that empty space where she had no teeth, stroking the ridge of her gums, sliding across, slipping into and out of that place . . . moving in and out, back and forth, rocking her head forward and back . . . his mouth hot against hers, filling her with his heat . . . and then he made a sound, some dark sound back in his throat, and his mouth went slack as his tongue slipped out, slipped free.

Moments later, he twisted away from her, pushing her away, back against the seat.

"Give it to me," he said.

"What?"

"The money." The girl stiffened at something she heard in his voice, something jagged and sharp, like words torn by the blade of a knife.

She pulled the money out of her purse and put it in his hand. He didn't look at the bills, didn't count them, just stuffed them in his pocket, then started the car and pulled away.

He was quiet until they reached the edge of town when he saw the neon sign over the bar where he had met the girl.

"Who's Tom Pony?" Willy Jack asked.

"My daddy."

He laughed. "Don't suppose you'd like to stop in and say goodbye."

She didn't answer him, only slumped down a little as they drove past.

Out on the highway, Willy Jack opened it up and took the big Plymouth up to seventy-five, then he stretched out, putting his arm up on the seat, his hand resting just above the girl's shoulder. She pulled herself nearer the door.

"What's the matter with you?" he asked. "Think I'm gonna hurt you?"

She didn't look at him, but kept her eyes on the road.

"Tell me something. Are you a virgin?"

"Hell no," she said too quickly.

"You are!" He grinned. "Well, I'll be damned." Then he let his hand slide down the seat, across her shoulder and onto her chest where he ran his fingers across her breast and around her nipple.

"I'll just be damned. Got me a virgin! Well, we'll have to do something about that, won't we?"

And that's when he saw the lights flashing in his rear-view mirror. He slowed, hoping the vehicle would go around him, hoping it was after someone else, but he knew better. Then they heard the siren.

"Oh, shit," the girl said.

Willy Jack pulled onto the shoulder and stopped, then waited while the sheriff crawled out of his car and walked up to the Plymouth.

"Like to see your driver's license, sir."

Willy Jack reached into his back pocket and got his wallet.

"Thought you got that stole," the girl whispered.

Willy Jack scowled at her as he handed his license through the window and waited while the sheriff studied it in the beam of his flashlight.

"What did I do?" Willy Jack asked, but the sheriff had walked to the back of the car where he was copying the license tag number onto a ticket.

"You lied to me about your wallet, didn't you?" the girl asked.

"I took care of it today."

"How? How did you take care of it?"

"Look. Let's pull together on this. Okay? We both want

the same thing, don't we? To go to Las Vegas. Together." He reached across the seat for her hand. "Right?"

The lights from the patrol car cast his face in a neon hue.

"Isn't that right?" he asked as he tightened his hold on her hand.

Willy Jack turned when he heard the swish of gabardine at the window.

"You just passing through, Mr. Pickens?"

"He's with me, Frank," the girl said.

The sheriff bent down and flashed his light across the front seat.

"Hello, Jolene. I didn't know you were in there."

"We're going to Albuquerque to see a movie," she said. "This is my boyfriend."

"I see."

Then he directed the light into the back seat. Jolene had loaded it with boxes and suitcases. Clothes hung from a hook over the back door; the floor was a jumble of shoes.

"You're taking a lot of stuff just to be going to a movie."

"We're going to stop at the laundrymat. Do some washing."

"Wonder if you all would mind stepping outside the car."

Willy Jack took his time, but the girl scrambled out, too fast, too eager to cooperate. When the lights of a passing car moved over them, she ducked her head.

"How long you been in town, Mr. Pickens?"

"Not long," Willy Jack answered.

"Just a few days," Jolene said. "Three or four."

"Sir, would you open the trunk for me?"

Willy Jack leaned through the window, grabbed the keys, then went around to the back and unlocked the trunk. It was more or less the way he had left it, except his suitcase was open and there was a plastic garbage bag beside it. The sheriff pushed things around inside the suitcase, then untied the bag and rummaged through it for several seconds.

"You smoke, Mr. Pickens?"

"Yeah."

"What brand?"

Willy Jack pulled a pack of Marlboros from his shirt pocket and held them out for the sheriff to see.

"Wonder what you're doing with fourteen cartons of Winstons then."

"What?" Willy Jack's voice sounded squeezed. "They're not mine."

Then the sheriff looked at Jolene.

"I don't smoke," she said.

"Mr. Pickens, you're under arrest. You have the right to remain silent . . ."

Willy Jack had watched *Hill Street Blues* back in Tellico Plains, so he knew the words, knew them by heart. He even thought the sheriff there behind him sounded a little bit like Renko.

A deputy stood near the door. Frank, the one who had arrested Willy Jack, sat beside a desk, facing him. The girl was in a chair beside him, but he never looked at her. Not once. The money she had given him was spread out on the desk.

"Look," Willy Jack said. "I run out of money. I just come here to see what I could hustle up."

"And you hustled up two hundred eighteen dollars and fourteen cartons of Winstons—Winston Light 100s. And you run into the strangest coincidence because that's exactly what someone stole from the 7-Eleven in Puerto De Luna on Wednesday morning."

"I wasn't even here Wednesday morning. I was in Oklahoma."

"Anyone who can prove that?"

"Yeah. My girlfriend, Novalee. She was with me."

Jolene shifted in her chair; one of the wooden slats at the back made a sharp cracking sound.

"Where is she now?" the sheriff asked. "This girlfriend."

"I left her in Oklahoma. Some town starts with an S."

The sheriff pulled an atlas from a drawer in his desk, thumbed through it a few seconds, then turned it toward Willy Jack.

"There's Oklahoma. Find the town."

Willy Jack ran his finger part way across the map, then tapped it twice.

"Sequoyah, right there."

"So, you left that girlfriend in Sequoyah, Oklahoma. With a relative?"

"No."

"A friend?"

"No. I left her in a Wal-Mart store."

"She have a job there? In the Wal-Mart?"

Willy Jack shook his head as he began to pick at a tear in the knee of his jeans.

"Was she going to meet someone there?"

"No." Willy Jack pulled at the loose threads, giving the hole in his pants all his attention. "I just left her there."

"What do you mean you left her? You let her out?"

Willy Jack nodded, then hooked his finger inside his torn jeans.

"You dumped her out?"

"Yeah." He pulled at the faded denim then and ripped the jeans open from the knee to the hem. "I dumped her out."

"That's what you were going to do to me, wasn't it," the girl yelled."Dump me off like some stray dog." Her voice slid into a higher register. "You son of a bitch."

"Now Jolene, don't be harsh," the sheriff said. "Let's give Mr. Pickens the opportunity to be heard." The deputy at the door laughed. "So what time was it on Wednesday when you dumped this girl out?"

"I don't know. 'Bout ten. Maybe eleven."

"That's a lie," Jolene said. "He was here with me on Tuesday night. Asked me to go to Las Vegas with him. That was late Tuesday night. Said he'd figure out a way to get the money if I'd just go with him."

"No," Willy Jack yelled. "I said—"

"That's right, Mr. Pickens. You *said*. But can you prove it?"

The sheriff stared at Willy Jack a moment, then raised his eyes to the other man beside the door. When he looked back at Willy Jack, he was shaking his head.

"You're a piece of work."

"Let me call. See if I can find her."

"Call? Call where?"

"The Wal-Mart store."

The sheriff laughed then, like he'd heard a joke that wasn't funny. "You think she's still there? Waiting for you?"

"Well . . . no, but . . ."

"Besides, the Wal-Mart's closed now."

"But there might be someone there. Someone who's seen her or knows where she went. A night watchman, maybe. Or a janitor. Don't I have the right to make one phone call?"

"Yeah, you do. One. This one."

The sheriff got the number from the long-distance operator, then dialed. When it started to ring, he pushed the phone across the desk, smiled again, and said, "One."

Willy Jack cleared his throat, then put the receiver to his ear. On the third ring, he scooted up to the edge of his chair. By the eighth, he was biting at his lip and twisting the phone cord beneath his fist. At ten, he started whispering. "Ten Mississippi . . . eleven Mississippi . . . twelve . . ."

The receiver was slick and the sound coming through it was distorted, like an alarm echoing through a tunnel.

The sheriff held up his index finger and mouthed the word, "One."

"Twenty-one Mississippi . . . twenty-two . . ."

Suddenly, Willy Jack shot up out of his chair and hammered the receiver across the edge of the desk, sending splinters of plastic flying across the room. Then, Willy Jack bellowed, the words roaring out of his mouth like sounds riding on strong winds.

"God-dammit!" he shrieked. "Answer the phone. Answer the god-damned phone."

One of them hit him just below his ear. The other one took him to the floor, but Willy Jack managed to hang on to a piece of the receiver. He heard someone speaking, but he didn't know who. A child somewhere whimpering in the dark.

"Thirty-one Mississippi . . . thirty-two . . ."

Chapter Four

NOVALEE HARDLY MOVED when the first alarm went off, but when the second one sounded, she turned and stretched inside the sleeping bag, slow and sluggish like a caterpillar nestling in its cocoon. The third alarm, an irritating whistle, got her moving, wiggling out of the bag, then plodding down the aisle to the clock counter. She always set three alarms for fear the first employee to arrive would discover her sleeping—a Goldilocks without her bears.

She had not needed alarms in the beginning when she hardly slept more than minutes at a time. Strange noises would jerk her from dreams and leave her rigid with fear, her eyes creating monsters in the shadows of coffeepots and hunting jackets. But once she got used to the building, got to know the look of the dark and the feel of the sounds, sharp and metallic, she began to sink into sleep too thick for sounds to slip through.

She rolled up her sleeping bag, then stuffed it behind the others at the bottom of a shelf. A sharp pain poked at her lower back when she straightened, but she rubbed it away as she shuffled to the bathroom at the back of the store.

She splashed her face with cold water, then brushed her teeth. When she pulled the nightshirt off, she stood on tiptoes to see her belly in the mirror. Her skin was stretched so tight it looked like the color of thin milk. She ran her fingers across her navel and thought of the baby attached to the other side of it, imagining it could feel her touch so that it might even reach out to her.

The sound of the garbage truck behind the store jarred her from the daydream. She washed and dried herself with paper towels, then dressed quickly in the blue pantsuit she had picked from the maternity rack in ladieswear, the one she alternated with the tent dress she was wearing the day she arrived. She washed both outfits on Sunday nights when the store closed early, so they would have the extra few hours to dry.

She was combing her hair when the back door slammed. Her heart raced as she crammed her things inside the beach bag, then turned off the light.

"Stupid, stupid, stupid," she whispered to herself, angry that someone had arrived so early. She waited until footsteps echoed off the plastic tiles out front, then stepped soundlessly out of the bathroom, slipped around the corner and squeezed into her hiding place, the closet housing the hot water tank. She held her breath as she eased the door closed behind her.

These were the times she hated most . . . hiding before the store opened and after it closed. The airless little closet was too small for a chair, or even a stool, so Novalee had to stand, wedged between the door and the tank. And the bigger she got, the less room she had.

She had tried other hiding places, but they didn't feel as

safe. The first couple of weeks she was there, she had climbed a shaky ladder to a crawl hole into the attic, but the height made her dizzy. Then, she made a space for herself in the storage room by rearranging large cardboard boxes of pillows. But a few days later, a stock boy taking inventory came within inches of her before he was called to the front. That's when she found the hot water tank closet.

She usually stayed hidden about an hour in the mornings, a little less if everyone was on time. She counted them as they came in, all eighteen of the morning crew. But they fooled her occasionally, when two or three came in together. One morning she stayed hidden for over two hours, waiting for a straggler to arrive.

Novalee's stomach growled then, so loud she was afraid whoever was out front could hear it. She wished for biscuits and gravy, but would settle for the granola bar and peanut butter in her bag. She had given up Paydays and Pepsis after the first few days in Wal-Mart, but she still worried she wasn't eating right for the baby.

When she was sure the morning crew had arrived, she opened the closet door just a crack, checked the stock room, then slipped out and crossed quickly to the tool locker. She lifted the buckeye tree out, then hurried to the employee entrance and stepped outside.

The day was already hot. By the time she walked the half block to the stop light, her hair was plastered to her neck and her blouse was wet across the shoulders, but she still had a long walk ahead of her.

The library was on Main Street, less than a mile from Wal-Mart, but Novalee was going to walk an extra four blocks to avoid passing the nursery. She didn't want to take the chance that Benny Goodluck or his father might see her carrying the tree around, its roots still tied in burlap. But more than that, she didn't want them to see that she had let it get sick.

She had tried to take good care of the buckeye, had watered it every night, had taken it outside two or three times a week. Sometimes she took it to the city park and placed it between the large oaks that grew in straight rows at each side of the fountain near the entrance. Occasionally she took it to a wooded field behind the King's Daughters and Sons Nursing Home where she left it hidden in a grove of young pines.

But some days she left it in the tool locker. She knew it needed sunlight, but on days when she didn't feel so well, the tree seemed too heavy, too bulky, too much for her to manage. Besides, she knew a pregnant girl carrying a buckeye out the door of the Wal-Mart every morning was bound to attract someone's attention.

Then the buckeye got sick. Some of the leaves had turned the color of oatmeal and patches like liver spots covered their underside. The trunk, spindly and twisted, was so dry it left a film of powder on her hands when she touched it. And it hadn't grown at all since Benny Goodluck had given it to her four weeks earlier. She wanted to make herself believe nothing serious was wrong, but the truth was, Novalee was scared. If buckeyes really did bring good luck, she couldn't imagine what trouble she'd have if she let it die.

So, she had to get to the library to find a book on buckeye trees, to find out what she needed to do to save it.

She had wanted to ask someone for advice, find someone who knew about trees who would tell her what do do, but she didn't know who to ask. She couldn't ask the Goodlucks and let them know she hadn't planted the tree yet. She had checked the phone book to find other nurseries, but the Goodluck was the only one in town.

She had read a book in the Wal-Mart about plants and trees, and had learned when to plant zinnias, where to plant pansies and how to plant daisies, but she didn't learn what was wrong with her buckeye tree.

And then she thought of the library, a two-story brick building with a black wrought-iron fence, the lawn planted with joseph's coat, calendula and foxglove, names she had learned from the gardening book. She had passed the library many times on her way to the park, but she never thought of going inside.

Novalee hadn't walked far before a dull ache spread between her shoulder blades. The buckeye, light as it was, felt like it weighed a hundred pounds. She shifted it from one hand to the other and waited through several green lights at each corner so she could stop and stand the tree on the sidewalk beside her.

She stopped in a small cafe called Granny's Oven and asked for a glass of water. The waitress, who smelled of White Shoulders and fried onions, didn't seem pleased that Novalee wasn't a paying customer, but she was too busy with the breakfast trade to do more than roll her eyes.

While Novalee sipped at her water, she studied the menu to show she was at least thinking about food. Since she had been living at Wal-Mart, she had eaten so many Del Monte carrots and Green Giant peas, unseasoned and cold from the cans, that her mouth ached at the thought of a cheeseburger and fries.

Novalee jumped when the sound of a police siren rattled the front window of the cafe. She looked outside to see the sidewalk filling with people as a police car, lights flashing, crept by.

"Hey, Dooley," the waitress yelled back to the kitchen. "Parade's startin'."

She poured coffee for a woman seated at the end of the counter. "Our cook," she said, motioning toward the back. "His kid's a drummer in the band."

Novalee emptied her glass, then went outside where she pushed in behind two little girls at the curb. A flatbed truck decorated in red, white and blue crepe paper moved down the middle of the street. Banners attached to the doors had WESTERN DAYS printed on them, and on the bed an old man dressed in a white suit played the fiddle.

Then Novalee heard the music from a marching band as it turned onto Main Street. Boys and girls in blue uniforms marched in crooked rows and broken lines as they followed eight majorettes, their batons gleaming in the sunlight. Novalee watched them, their boots high-stepping, their batons sailing into the air while they posed, their bellies flat, their breasts high. They were girls with shiny hair and freckles, girls with dimpled wide smiles . . . their lips too red, their eyes too bright, their faces too young. They were girls who made brownies in home ec, who cut hearts out of red paper for Valentine's dances. Girls who had their pictures in annuals, who got crowned at homecoming. Girls who ate oatmeal for breakfast with little sisters who borrowed their lipstick and sweaters. Girls who were Novalee's age . . . girls who would never be as old as she was.

Chapter Five

THE ONLY LIBRARY Novalee had ever been inside before was the bookmobile that came to the grade school in Tellico Plains, so when she stepped into the Sequoyah County Library, she was filled with a sense of expectation. This library didn't have wheels under it.

Even before the door closed soundlessly behind her, Novalee knew she had entered a special place. She hardly breathed as her eyes played around the room, a room with dark wood carved into intricate designs, tall windows of thick, frosted glass and red velvet drapes held back with silver cord, chandeliers whose crystal drops caught fragments of light transfused into rich blues and deep greens, paintings in gold frames of nude women with heavy bellies and thick thighs. And books. Racks of books, stacks of books, walls of books. More books than Novalee had ever seen.

Then suddenly Novalee knew something was different in this place. Not the light filtering silver through the frosted panes. Not the stillness. Not the smells—varnish and oils and strong wood. But something. Something.

"What do you want?"

Novalee looked around to see who had spoken, but her eyes had trouble spotting the figure at the far side of the room. He was folded into a chair much too small for him, propped over an opened book on a long, narrow table. He had a beard the color of copper, but his hair, mostly hidden beneath a brown stocking cap, was darker than heartwood.

"I'm looking for a book," she said.

"Librarian's not here."

"Oh."

Novalee waited for him to say more, but he returned to the book he was reading without looking back at her. She didn't know if she should wait for the librarian or try to find the book for herself. In the bookmobile kids had just grabbed whatever was the brightest and biggest, but she knew that was not the way to find a book about buckeyes. She decided to wait for the librarian.

She wandered to a pair of glass cases in the middle of the room. One contained an assortment of shiny gold and silver coins from foreign places. The other held a collection of letter openers, their handles decorated with jewels or intricate carvings in ivory or jade.

She walked past the paintings on the walls, staring into eyes that seemed to stare back. Novalee stopped before a picture of a girl trying to put on her stocking. The girl was naked and very heavy. Her stomach was so round, so full that Novalee wondered if she might be pregnant. She stepped closer to the painting.

"Renoir."

It was the man's voice, the man in the brown cap, but he wasn't at the table where he had been sitting. Novalee couldn't see him anywhere.

"What did you say?" she asked, but he didn't answer. She

began to feel a little strange then and wondered if she and the man were the only two people in the building. She thought of leaving, but the buckeye, hidden just outside the front door, was going to die if she didn't do something.

She moved nearer the front, a quicker escape if she needed one, and began to walk down an aisle with books shelved on either side of her. She read titles, then pulled out *The Dream House Encyclopedia*. She flipped through the pages, but the pictures were not in color. As she started to put it back, she saw a brown cap bobbing on the other side of the shelf, so she shoved the book back, then turned to the end of the aisle and stepped around the corner. She could hear him as he rounded the other end of the aisle, moving in her direction.

"You reshelved it in the wrong place," he growled.

Novalee pressed herself tightly against the wall.

"It goes between *The Dream Garden Encyclopedia* and *The Dream Kitchen Encyclopedia*," he said. "If you're not going to take the time to put books back where they go, then . . ."

Suddenly, he was standing right in front of her.

". . . don't pull them out."

"I'm sorry," she said as she began to edge toward the front door.

"You don't have to leave." He sounded a little less angry. "Just be more careful."

"No, I think I'll just come back when the librarian's here to help me."

"Help you with what?"

"Find a book." She reached for the front door. "A book about trees."

"*I hear my echo in the echoing wood . . . A lord of nature weeping to a tree.*"

"What do you mean?" she asked. "What's that mean?"

The man studied her face briefly, then wheeled and bolted toward a cabinet of small drawers against the back wall.

"Trees!" he yelled, striding across the floor. "Trees! Forestry? Environment . . . agriculture? Botany. What do you want to know about trees?"

"I want to know about buckeye trees," she said, falling in behind him.

"Buckeye! The horse chestnut! Belonging to the genus *Aesculus* of the family *Hippocastanaceae*."

"What? I can't understand what you're saying."

While he opened one of the drawers in the cabinet and began flipping through cards, he seemed to forget that Novalee was there. His blazing black eyes narrowed in concentration and his lips moved as if he were speaking to the cards flying under his fingers.

She moved a step closer, close enough to know he smelled of mint and sweet alyssum, which she had seen in clay pots beside the front door, close enough to hear his starched denim shirt crinkle when he shifted his weight and slammed the drawer.

"*Taylor's Encyclopedia of Gardening,*" he shouted, as he raced to a shelf of books where he darted and swayed, his fingers playing across titles. Suddenly he zipped down the aisle like a child looking for a cherished toy. Novalee had to run to stay up with him.

Then he dipped and pulled a book from the shelf. "Now. What do you want to know about buckeyes?"

"Mine's sick. I think it's dying."

He dashed to the nearest table, pulled out a chair and motioned for her to sit down. Then he slammed the book down in front of her, opening it to the index.

She ran her finger down the page mouthing "buckeye."

"It's not here."

He moved in beside her, scanned the page for a moment, then pointed to a word.

"What? I can't say that."

"Yes, you can. Hip-po-cas-ta-na-cea-e."

Novalee pulled the book closer and began to read.

She had not been aware of his bringing her more books, but when she looked up, she was amazed to find the table littered with them—encyclopedias, dictionaries, almanacs, agricultural tracts, government pamphlets. And she had read from everything he had placed before her.

She leaned back. He was sitting across from her watching her face.

"Well?" he asked.

"My tree has leaf rot from overwatering."

He nodded. "More."

"It may have root damage, too."

"Go on," he said as he began to rock back and forth in his chair. "Go on!"

"It has nematode symptoms."

He rocked faster and faster.

"Traces of powdery mildew."

"Yes."

"Possible nitrogen deficiency."

"Yes!" He slapped the table. "Yes!" he shouted, then shot out of his chair, tumbling it backward and skidding it across the floor. "The words!"

"Well, I know what's wrong with it . . ."

"You've found the words!"

". . . but I don't know if it's gonna make it."

He shook his head, then leaned across the table to Novalee, his voice dipping to a whisper. "*The tree has no leaves and may never have them again. We must wait till some months hence in the spring to know. But if it is destined never again to grow, it can blame this limitless trait in the heart of men."*

Novalee watched his lips shape the words . . . the sounds, like whispered secrets, hanging in the air.

Chapter Six

NOVALEE HOPED he wasn't watching her through the library window when she lifted the buckeye from behind some evergreens, but she felt sure he was. She carried the tree to the end of the block, then stopped to dig the city map out of her beach bag. She was going to the last house on Evergreen Street, the house where Sister Husband lived.

As she walked the first few blocks, her mind was on the strange man she had met in the library. She kept going over what he had said, trying to make sense of it, but she wasn't even sure she knew what he was talking about. She hoped the book in her bag, the one he had checked out for her, would help her understand.

The trip to Sister Husband's took her to a part of the town she hadn't seen before. Usually, when she left the Wal-Mart, she stayed fairly close or walked to the north side where wide streets were lined with elms and sycamores and deep lawns were edged with geraniums, snapdragons, and moss roses. She had rested in pretty parks where children waded in blue pools while their mothers waited in the shade of broad, flowering mimosas.

But this part of town, Sister Husband's part of town, looked like the places where Novalee had lived in Tellico Plains, neighborhoods the color of cold gravy. The streets were lined by shallow ditches filled with brackish water, and the parks, where swings dangled from broken chains and merry-go-rounds leaned drunkenly on their sides, were empty except for skinny dogs and old men.

The houses, their roofs patched like scrap quilts, sat crookedly in yards littered with rusted cars on concrete blocks. And at the end of them all, at the end of the street, was Sister Husband's home: a house trailer on wheels.

A porch of raw lumber leaned against the front of the trailer and coffee cans of flowering kale and cockscomb lined the steps. The grass, recently mowed, had been trimmed around a granite birdbath and two tires that protected small bushes of hollyhock. A pecan tree bonneted by bagworms provided shade for a bald spot in the yard that served as driveway for the Toyota Welcome Wagon.

Novalee carried the buckeye to the door with her, but then changed her mind and left it at the edge of the steps. She brushed her hair back from her face and mentally rehearsed her lines, then she knocked, louder than she had intended.

From inside, she heard bare feet slapping the floor, doors slamming, water running. After a few minutes, she began to feel uncomfortable. She didn't know whether she should knock again or just leave, but before she could decide, the door suddenly opened.

Sister Husband, her hair a soft shade of blue, smiled at Novalee through the screen.

"Sister Husband, I don't know if you remember me.

Well, you probably don't, but we met one day at Wal-Mart and you gave me a Welcome Wagon basket and I took your picture which I've got right here in this bag and you called me Ruth Ann, but I'm not. My name is Novalee Nation and I—"

"Why, how awful of me to make such a mistake. Of course, now that I see you in a different light there is not the slightest similarity between you and Ruth Ann. Well, it's just wonderful to see you again, darlin'. Won't you come in?"

"Thank you."

Novalee stepped into a room of yellow—yellow lamp shades and flowers, yellow curtains and throw rugs, and the yellow shirt of a small bald man standing just inside the door.

"Darlin', I'd like you to meet my gentleman, Mr. Sprock. Jack Sprock."

"How do you do," he said as he took Novalee's hand in both of his own.

Jack Sprock smelled of baby powder and cinnamon and when he smiled, his teeth gleamed like they had been painted with white enamel.

"We were just getting ready to have some cold buttermilk and cornbread. Of course, you'll join us."

"Oh, no. I just came by to ask—"

"You just came by because I asked you to. Invited you to come to my house and be my guest. And here you are and I can't think of what would make me any happier than this. To have you and your child and my lovely Mr. Sprock here with me this beautiful afternoon."

"Beautiful afternoon," Mr. Sprock added.

Then Sister Husband smiled and led Novalee to a chair at the kitchen table. Mr. Sprock sat beside her while Sister

Husband brought tall yellow glasses to the table and filled them with buttermilk from a yellow pitcher. She put a plate of cornbread, sliced like pie on a yellow platter, in the middle of the table, then she sat down and took Mr. Sprock's hand in one of hers and Novalee's in the other. Mr. Sprock fumbled for Novalee's other hand and they were joined, the three of them, when Sister Husband bowed her head and began to pray.

"Dear Lord, we are thankful for this communion of souls here today. We pray, Lord, for the safe delivery and a healthy child for this sweet darlin' who graces our table this day. And we ask forgiveness, Lord, for the fornication that Mr. Sprock and me have committed again. Now, we pray that you will bless this food to the nourishment of our bodies. Amen."

Mr. Sprock said amen, then smiled at Novalee as he passed her the plate of cornbread.

"So, what do you think of our town, darlin'? Are you getting acquainted?"

"Yes," Novalee said as she wiped buttermilk from the corners of her mouth.

"Oh good. I think that's good."

"I met someone new just today. At the library."

"That would be Forney Hull," Sister Husband said.

"Yep, Forney Hull," Mr. Sprock seconded.

"Oh, he's a brilliant man. Just brilliant. If he'd of had a chance to finish his schooling, why there's no telling what he'd be."

"Nope. No telling what he'd be," Mr. Sprock said.

"You see, darlin', Forney's sister's the librarian, but she's never in the library. She's an alcoholic. Stays upstairs all the time. Never leaves her room. So, Forney takes her place downstairs in the library."

"Oh, he didn't say nothing about that."

"No, he wouldn't. Wouldn't want you to think bad about his sister, God love her. More cornbread?"

Novalee had two glasses of buttermilk with four slices of cornbread, Sister Husband smiling at every bite she took. Finally, Novalee decided it was time.

"Sister Husband, I have a favor to ask of you, but it's okay if you say no. I'll understand."

"Why whatever is it? You just go ahead and ask."

"Just go ahead and ask," Mr. Sprock said.

"Well, this is gonna sound pretty strange, but I have a tree I'm needing to plant."

"Then we'll help you."

"No, that's not it. See, the place where I'm living right now . . . well, they won't let me put a tree there."

"Oh, isn't that mean."

"Mean." Mr. Sprock shook his head and sighed.

"So, what I was wondering is . . . do you think I could plant it here? Just till I settle someplace permanent. Then I'll come and take it up."

"Plant it in my yard?"

"Yes, ma'am, but just temporary like."

"I can't—"

"And I'll take care of it, too. While it's here. It's not too pretty right now, but I'm gonna doctor it and maybe it'll be okay."

We must wait till some months hence in the spring to know.

"Darlin', I can't think of anything I'd like better than to have you plant your tree in front of my home."

And with that, Mr. Sprock was up from the table and out the door.

Novalee and Sister Husband hurried behind as Mr. Sprock took a shovel from Sister Husband's shed; then Novalee had to decide where to plant the buckeye. From her reading in the library, she had learned that she should plant the tree on a slight rise for drainage, so she chose the highest point in Sister Husband's yard, a spot nearly in the center.

"Right here," she said. "This is it."

Mr. Sprock nodded, then started to dig, but Novalee stopped him.

"No, thank you, Mr. Sprock. I'll do it."

"But darlin'," Sister Husband said, "that's heavy work. Do you really think it'll be good for you?"

"Yes, ma'am. It'll be good for me."

By the time Novalee had the hole deep enough, she had blisters on her hands, and a pain in her lower back that would not rub away.

She loosened the burlap, then very gently lowered the tree into the hole, being careful not to disturb the roots. She had guessed right. The hole was twice as wide as the tree's root ball and plenty deep enough.

She was so tired before she finished filling the hole that Sister Husband and Mr. Sprock used their shoes to scrape dirt over the roots when they thought Novalee wasn't looking.

When she finished, Sister Husband and Mr. Sprock took her hands once again and they circled the tree while Sister Husband sang "A Fig Tree in Galilee," a song Novalee had never heard.

Then, Sister Husband said, "Now, I quote from the Good Book, Mark 8:24. *And he took the blind man by the hand, and led him out of town; and when he had spit on his eyes, and put his hands upon him, he asked him if he saw ought. And he looked up and said, I see man as trees, walking."*

By the time Novalee crossed the parking lot, bedraggled and grimy, it was nearly dark. She had specks of dried buttermilk on her blouse and grass stains on the knees of her pants. Her fingernails were caked with dirt and she had a dark smudge across her cheek, but she was too exhausted to care.

She was too tired to enjoy the beauty of the sun setting behind the hills west of town, too tired to welcome the cool evening breeze, relief from the early spring heat. And she was far too tired to notice the man in the brown stocking cap standing across the street . . . the man watching her as she slipped inside the back door of the Wal-Mart.

Chapter Seven

FORNEY TOLD NOVALEE if she was late for her own birthday dinner, he'd feed her grasshopper stew. She made sure she wasn't late. In fact, she got to the library twenty minutes early. But Forney had made such a fuss about being on time, she figured he might be as upset about her arriving early as he would about her coming late. So instead of going inside, she waited on a bench near the iron gate while she tried to brush some of the frizz from her still-damp hair.

She had come directly from the truck stop on East Main, where she went to shower and shampoo her hair whenever she could. A few weeks earlier she had discovered the shower stalls in the back of the station had an outside entrance. All she had to do was get in and out fast before the manager or one of the truckers walked in on her. So far, she had been lucky.

After her shower she had changed into a new dress from the maternity rack at Wal-Mart. Though she hated writing another charge in her account book, this was a special occasion, something Forney had been planning for weeks.

Soon after they had met, on her third or fourth visit to the library, when Forney found out about her birthday, he started acting secretive. She had seen him scribble hurried notes, always shielding the writing from her, always with some good excuse. Once, when she saw him writing on a dollar bill, he said he was alerting the Treasury Department to a forgery. Then, with the expertise of a secret agent, he held the bill to the light, popped it to test its strength, and nodded shrewdly before he crammed it deep in his pocket.

About the same time, he started asking Novalee odd questions about food—what she thought of veal, if she could eat curry, whether she liked orange food better than red. When he asked her if she liked the smell of tarragon, she said she didn't like fish at all, a comment Forney found so delightful his eyes teared.

What she had wanted to tell him was that she was sick of beef jerky, tuna packed in spring water, and Vienna sausages—that she would never eat deviled ham or Treet again—that Stokely's peas and carrots tasted like the cans they came in—and that after living on Wal-Mart food for nearly two months, a home-cooked meal of veal, curry and even tarragon, orange or red, would suit her just fine.

Thinking of food made her stomach rumble. She checked her watch and though she was still a few minutes early, she stood up and brushed the wrinkles from her dress. The street lights had just come on, casting shadows stretching from the heavy evergreens at the edge of the sidewalk to the letters chiseled into stone pillars at the front of the library.

Forney was watching her from the window just behind the reference section. He had been watching her since she first sat down on the bench.

When she was halfway up the sidewalk, he stepped away from the window and started for the entry hall. He tried to slow his steps, to match her pace, but he had the door opened before she had even reached the top of the stairs.

He knew she had pulled her hair back and fastened it with a silver comb and he knew she was wearing a dress just a shade darker than wisteria, but he didn't know until he opened the door that her hair would smell like honeysuckle or that the deepening light would make the green flecks in her eyes look the color of willows in early spring.

"Good evening," he said in the voice he had practiced.

Novalee could hardly believe the man standing before her was Forney Hull. He was not wearing his stocking cap, the first time she had seen him without it. His hair, so brown it was almost black, fell loosely across his forehead. He had shaved, exposing skin that looked too smooth, too tender to belong to this giant of a man.

He was wearing a strange suit with a long coat and velvet collar. Novalee had seen such suits in movies and old photographs, suits worn by rich men who wore shiny top hats and drank tea from china cups.

"Hi, Forney. You sure do look nice."

"Oh. I . . . uh . . . well." This was a line he hadn't rehearsed.

"You want me to come in?"

"Please, come in," he said, a bit louder than he had intended.

"Are you catching a cold?"

Forney shook his head. "I don't think so."

"You sound stopped up."

He closed the door behind her. "So do you," he said.

"I sound stopped up?"

"No! I mean, look nice. So do you . . . look nice . . . too."

"Thank you."

"Well," Forney said, trying to get back on track. "Well." Suddenly, with both arms, he made a grand, sweeping gesture toward the reading room, a gesture he had refined in front of his mirror. "This way, please."

He walked a bit behind her as she moved down the hall, sure now that the whole thing had been a mistake, certain she would think he was crazy, afraid she would laugh when she saw it.

But when she stepped through the reading room door, when she saw what Forney had done, she sucked in her breath and clapped her hands together, struck by the wonder of it.

The entire room glittered in candlelight. Golden, shimmering light flickered in every corner, on every surface. Candles burned on tables, shelves, cabinets and carts. And wherever there were candles, there were roses, dainty tea roses in soft pinks and pale yellows—rosebuds, full blooms, bouquets of roses in vases and bowls. Candles and roses crowded onto planters and stands, clustered on desks, arranged in windowsills. Candles glowed on thick marble and polished wood, sending ripples through shadows that danced on the ceiling and floor.

And in the center of it all, Forney had prepared a table for Novalee's birthday dinner—a round table covered with ivory damask, set with crystal goblets, white china and pink tea roses in a ruby red vase.

"Oh, Forney. It's so wonderful," Novalee whispered. Then she began to circle the room, marveling over everything she touched—a fragile pink vase shaped like a Chinese fan, a pair of silver candlesticks engraved with bows of ribbon, a green ceramic bowl painted with seashells, a candleholder made of dark, carved wood.

Forney watched her moving slowly around the room, candle-glow lighting her face as she traced the design of a candlestick, then put the palm of her hand over the flame, feeling its heat. When she found a fallen yellow rosebud, she put it in her hair. Forney couldn't see it from where he stood, but he knew the tiny scar at the corner of her mouth was silver-white in the candlelight.

"I feel like we're in a movie, Forney. Like we're the stars. Velvet curtains open up and there we are, up on the screen, smoking cigarettes in silver holders and—"

"I don't have any cigarettes, but I could go get some."

"No, we don't need cigarettes. This is perfect, just the way it is."

Novalee picked up a vase painted with blue dragons. "Where did you get all this, Forney? All these vases?"

"They belonged to my mother. She kept flowers in every room."

"It's hard for me to imagine this place as a house. I mean, it's so big."

"Oh, it's changed a lot now. Walls have been knocked out. Doors sealed up. See, this room was originally three rooms—a parlor, a dining room and my father's study. The kitchen is back there and the bedrooms are upstairs."

"You were a rich kid."

"Well, my grandfather was rich. And my father inherited from him. Yeah, I guess we were rich. A long time ago."

"It must be neat to live in a library, to have all these books to read and—"

A scraping sound from upstairs caused Novalee to look up, to glance toward the ceiling, but Forney didn't move. She might have thought he hadn't heard it except for the tightening of the muscles in his jaw.

Suddenly, he crossed the room to the table and pulled out a chair. "Let's sit down."

Novalee followed him to the table, then settled into the chair he had pulled out for her. She felt awkward as he scooted it up to the table.

"Do you like wine?" he asked.

"You mean Mogen David?"

"Well, something like that."

"Sure."

Forney brought a full decanter to the table and filled their glasses, then he raised his and held it across the table toward her.

Novalee smiled and said, "Don't tell me this isn't a movie." Then she picked up her glass and touched it to Forney's.

"Happy birthday, Novalee. Happy eighteenth birthday," Forney said, exactly the way he had rehearsed it.

When Novalee took a drink of the wine, she tried not to make a face, but she shivered with the effort.

"It's too dry for you, isn't it?" Forney asked.

"What do you mean?"

"It's . . . not sweet."

"Dry wine is sour, you mean?"

"I'll get you something else to drink."

"No! It's wonderful. I love dry wine . . . always have." She pretended to take another sip from the elegant glass that felt so good in her hand.

Forney reached under the table then, came up with a package wrapped in yellow paper and handed it to Novalee.

"Oh, Forney . . ."

"Open it, Novalee."

She began to unwrap the package, being careful not to tear the paper or crush the ribbon. Inside, she found a book bound in dark leather with gold lettering across the front: *Gardener's Magic and Other Old Wives' Lore.*

"It's beautiful," she said as she brushed her fingers across the title. "And you don't know how much I need some magic."

"Maybe you'll find some way to save your buckeye."

"This is my first book, Forney. And you know what else? This is my first birthday party. Ever."

Forney cleared his throat to deliver the speech he had prepared, but two quick thumps from the floor above them caused him to forget his lines.

"Forney, is there—"

"I guess we'll eat then." He stood up and started toward the kitchen.

"Can I help you?"

"No. You're the guest of honor. You're not allowed in the kitchen," he said as he stepped through the door and closed it behind him.

Novalee could hear kitchen sounds—a spoon scraping metal, the clink of glass against glass, but she could not imagine Forney managing ovens and burners or skillets and lids. She could see him dipping and swaying between history and fiction, but not between a stove and a kitchen sink.

When he came back in, carrying a tray, he said, "Dinner is served," trying to speak with a French accent, the way he had practiced.

He set the tray on a cart beside the table, then placed a bowl in front of Novalee and one at his place. "Your soup, madam."

"I've never seen orange soup before."

"It's orange almond bisque," he said as he sat down.

Novalee took a taste, a wonderful nutty taste . . . tangy, velvety smooth—but cold.

"Forney, it's just great."

She knew when he tasted it he would be embarrassed that it had gotten cold, but she couldn't imagine it would taste any better hot.

She tried not to eat too fast, at least no faster than Forney, but he wasn't doing much eating. Mostly, he was watching her.

"You made this yourself?"

Forney nodded.

"How'd you learn to cook?"

"I just read about it."

"You learn everything from books, don't you?"

Forney ran a finger under the stiff white collar of his shirt.

"I want to get this recipe."

"You like to cook?"

"Well, where I'm living now, I'm not set up to cook, but when my baby comes . . ." She didn't finish what she started to say, didn't really know how.

Suddenly, Forney jumped up and dashed across the room. He swooped around a counter, dipped down, then bobbed back up, a book in his hand.

"*The Physiology of Taste: or Meditations on Transcendental Gastronomy,*" he said, as he sailed back across the room. He handed it to Novalee.

"Is this a cookbook?"

"Well, it has recipes, but it's history and philosophy and . . ." Forney looked at his watch. "Uh-oh, it's time." He took up the soup bowls and raced to the kitchen.

Novalee checked her watch, too. She would have to be

back before nine, otherwise she'd be spending the night in the park. She felt like Cinderella.

She was still looking at the book when Forney returned with another tray, this one loaded. It smelled so good Novalee felt dizzy.

"This is asparagus mousse," he said as he dipped a large serving spoon into a quivering mound of something that looked, to Novalee, a bit like green vanilla pudding.

"What are those?"

"Tournedos Wellington."

"They look like fancy biscuits."

"A pastry, with beef inside."

"Beef!" She had to fight herself to keep from snatching food from the tray, tearing into it with her hands. To hell with knives and forks.

"And this . . ." Forney picked up a small silver pitcher filled with dark brown liquid. "This is Madeira sauce." He put a tournedo on Novalee's plate, then poured some of the sauce over it. "And finally, green peas with cream."

"The only thing I can recognize."

After Forney filled their plates, he sat down across from Novalee again.

"Forney, I've seen pictures of food like this in magazines, but I never thought someone would fix it for me."

He couldn't imagine what to say.

"This is the most perfect night of my life."

Nothing he had practiced would sound right now. He had never anticipated that she would say, "the most perfect night."

She had just cut into the beef and seen the juice seep into the pastry when a terrific crash directly above them jolted the chandelier, sending a shower of dust adrift. Forney was frozen, his look fearful, his eyes disbelieving. Then he vaulted from his chair, colliding with the table as he rose. Glasses tumbled, wine sailed through the air and a plate crashed to the floor.

"Forney!"

"Stay here, Novalee," he yelled, then he was across the room and through the kitchen door.

Novalee raced through the long, narrow kitchen following the sounds of Forney's heavy steps somewhere beyond her. She found the stairway to the second story at the end of a poorly lit hall, then took the steps two at a time to a broad landing at the top. She rushed toward light spilling from an opened door, then stopped when she reached it.

Forney was bent over the crumpled body of a woman, a woman whose bony arms and legs reminded Novalee of the stick figures she had drawn as a child. The woman had thinning gray hair and skin like tarnished silver. Novalee thought she was dead until she saw her fingers curl like claws around Forney's wrist.

The floor was wet and sprinkled with shattered glass. When Novalee stepped into the room, the smell of whiskey was so strong it stung her eyes, but there was something else, something she—

Forney spun around so suddenly, Novalee jumped back.

"No, Novalee. Don't come in."

"Let me help, Forney," she said as she edged nearer to him. And then she knew what it was, a stench so powerful she tried to hold her breath. The woman had soiled herself.

"Novalee," Forney said, in a voice he hadn't practiced, "I'd like you to meet my sister, Mary Elizabeth Hull . . . the librarian."

Chapter Eight

IN THE WEEKS following her birthday, Novalee felt herself growing heavier and slower each day.

One morning in early May, when Forney offered to drive her home from the library, she was tempted to say okay, to let him find out that "home" was the Wal-Mart . . . but she didn't.

And then, that night, just after she had crawled into the sleeping bag, a hard cramp gripped her lower belly. At first, she thought maybe her time had come, but the pain didn't last and didn't hurt much more than a bad stomachache. But if she was going into labor, if this was the worst of the pain, she figured it wasn't going to be as awful as she had feared.

She had heard dozens of horror stories about childbirth when she worked at Red's. Seemed like every woman who got drunk had a delivery story to tell. They told her about being in labor for four days, begging to die. They talked about pain so dreadful they bit through their tongues or pulled wads of hair right out of their heads. They described the way their flesh was ripped apart when their babies came.

But maybe that was just liquor talk; maybe they told those stories to scare girls like her who had never had babies. Maybe it wasn't going to be so bad.

She had read, in one of the books Forney had told her to read, about a pregnant Chinese woman who worked in a rice paddy until her contractions began, then birthed her child alone, hardly interrupting her labor . . . bending, stooping, wading in water up to her knees. Novalee figured if a woman could manage that, having a baby must not be too terrible.

Besides, she wasn't totally unprepared. She had been reading about delivery; she knew what she would have to do. And she had gathered the supplies she would need—scissors, rubbing alcohol, cotton pads, receiving blankets. She had packed everything in an overnight bag, the way some women packed to go to the hospital when their time came. But Novalee knew she wouldn't be going to the hospital.

But the bag was in the storage room and when she thought of going back to get it, just to be on the safe side, she was too tired to get up. She yawned and rolled onto her side. She wasn't sure she should go to sleep in case she was starting into labor. She was afraid she might sleep right through it, then wake up and find her baby already born, but she was having a hard time keeping her eyes open.

Early that morning she had walked to Sister Husband's to plant some pyracantha cuttings she had taken from a planter outside City Hall. The week before, she had started a flower bed in the corner of Sister's yard with cuttings of hydrangea and mock orange; a couple of days later, she had added some morning glory seeds and a few stems of crepe myrtle.

The flower bed would have been shaded by the buckeye tree if it had had any leaves. The last one had fallen off a week after the tree was planted. But Novalee thought it might still make it. She didn't know why she thought that; it was a little less hardy than a Charlie Brown Christmas tree, but she had hope.

Sister Husband hadn't been home, but Novalee had rested on her porch for a while, then walked to the library where Forney was waiting for her. He had brought her some carrot sticks, two bran muffins and a thermos of cold milk. He had something for her every day, something healthy. Food with bean sprouts, whole wheat and soy. And milk. Lots of milk. Milk in glasses . . . and cups. Pitchers, pails . . .

She slept then, jerked nearly to consciousness from time to time by the cramps in her stomach which seemed to coalesce with her dreams, dreams of babies lost in dark places . . . babies stuck in deep wells . . . babies calling her name.

Then she was struck by a pain unlike the others. It tore into her pelvis, shot through her hips and into her spine. She held her breath until it eased, then struggled out of the sleeping bag.

Her water broke as soon as she was on her feet. She watched as the warm liquid trickled down her legs and puddled between her feet. Even though she knew what it was, she still felt a little silly, like a child who had wet herself.

She sponged herself off and changed into a fresh nightshirt, then she cleaned the floor and dried her trail to the bathroom by skating on paper towels.

The second pain, stronger than the last, caused her to suck in her breath and grit her teeth. This was no stomachache. Her baby was coming . . . but she wasn't ready.

Why, she wondered, had she waited until the last minute? Where had the time gone? Two months had passed since Willy Jack had dumped her—and she had done nothing. She hadn't looked for a place to live, hadn't figured out how to make a living. She hadn't even picked out a name for her baby.

Then she remembered a list of names she had started on the day she and Willy Jack left Tellico Plains. She pulled the spiral notebook out of her beach bag and flipped to the back. The list was still there—one page for girls, one for boys. *Felicia, Brook, Ashley*. Novalee made a face as she read them. *Rafe, Thorne, Hutch, Sloan*. Names she had taken from soap operas. *Blain, Asa, Dimitri*. Moses Whitecotton had told her to find a strong name, but the names on her list weren't strong. They just sounded silly.

The third pain, deep and hard, left her feeling queasy. She closed her eyes for a few minutes until the nausea passed, but a heavy, dull ache in her lower back would not go away. Finally, she decided to get up and move around, to see if that would bring her any relief.

It took her awhile to get to her feet, but when she did, it was worth it. Her back didn't hurt as much. And anything, she figured, was better than doing nothing . . . just waiting. As she huffed up the aisle, she searched for names she might use for the baby. *Coleman. Prescott. Dixie. Hanes*. She grinned then at the thought of naming her baby after underwear.

She was near the front of the store when the next pain knocked her to the floor. She reached out, grabbing for support, and took a rack of cassettes with her. As they clattered across the tile, Novalee said, "Shhhh," embarrassed at the racket she was causing.

She didn't know how long she was out, and she didn't know if everything she saw was real or not. She thought she saw a mouse dart across the aisle, very near her feet. And she thought she saw a brown stocking cap bobbing around outside the plate glass window at the front of the store. *Then Momma Nell and the umpire named Fred waved at her from the television, but the screen was so thick and smoky she had to squint to get a clear picture.*

She drifted in and out . . . let sleep take her between the pain that fit her like a brace . . . pain that ran from beneath her ribs, to her pelvis, around her back . . . pain that pulled her to the edge of . . . *the edge of the highway as the Plymouth raced past, Willy Jack hunched over the steering wheel . . . the picture faded . . .*

Then she saw Forney Hull's face, but it was blurry and dark. *She adjusted the contrast and focus, pulling in a better picture as he waved, both arms high over his head. She waved back though her hands were asleep, too heavy to raise more than a few inches.*

Forney's mouth was working, but she couldn't hear him. *Then she laughed, realizing the volume was turned down. She could hear someone moaning, but that was coming from another channel. Interference. When she turned the sound up, Forney's voice came out too fast and he sounded like Willy Jack.*

"I found us a place, Novalee."

Willy Jack's voice was out of sync with Forney's lips . . . the sound coming out of his mouth just a few seconds too late.

"I found us a place."

There was so much static she could barely hear him.

"Willy Jack? I thought you went to California."

". . . a house with a balcony . . ."

The picture began to roll, faster and faster, until she fiddled with the vertical button.

". . . a balcony where we can sit with the baby."

"I'm having the baby tonight, Willy Jack."

"We can sit with the baby . . ."

"I read this book, Willy Jack, this book by a woman named Pearl Buck who works in a Wal-Mart store."

". . . sit with the baby and . . ."

"And in the third chapter . . . or maybe the sixth . . . you dumped this Chinese woman out in a rice paddy just before she had her baby . . ."

". . . sit with the baby and . . ."

"Do you remember that little fuzzy dog? The one I called Frosted Mocha 'cause she was the color of my lipstick. Do you remember her?"

". . . we can sit with the baby and . . ."

"You took her to the rice paddy and you dumped her out. Frosted Mocha. You stopped the car and dumped her out on the road. You said she was not gonna have her litter in the floor of your car . . ."

"We can sit with the baby and watch the sun go down."

"Dumped me out and you said . . ."

"Novalee, I found us a place."

". . . having a baby in the floor . . ."

". . . found us a place."

Suddenly, her voice pulled itself away from her. "Having my baby on the floor of a Wal-Mart store." The sounds seemed not to come from her mouth, but from a hole in the air above her head. "Damn you." The words, a fierce wind whipping behind them, were pushed up and out, filling the space around her. "Damn you, Willy Jack! DAMN YOU TO HELL!"

And then Forney Hull, his face pressed to the "television screen," shielding his eyes from the glare, pounded on the glass.

"You break that television and I'll have to pay for it."

But Forney Hull didn't listen. He struck the glass again and again, first with his fists, then with a length of pipe, each blow heavier, harder than the last . . . faster and faster, and then it exploded, shattered and flew in all directions, sounding like notes played on a badly tuned piano. Then Forney crawled in, crawled through the broken window and into the Wal-Mart store.

"Novalee!"

"You shouldn't have done that. They'll make me pay and color TVs don't come cheap."

Forney folded himself to the floor beside her and cradled her head in his lap.

"Big-screen TVs aren't—"

Suddenly, Novalee's body curled, found the curve of Forney's arm to fit into as she stiffened . . . hardened into a knot of gristle to meet the pain. She clenched her teeth to hold in the scream that came from deep inside, from the place where she felt herself splitting open. She held against it, rigid—unyielding, and when it passed, she collapsed, like a puppet whose strings had been cut.

"Big screen." Her voice sounded thin, uneven. "That'll cost more than you think, Willy Jack."

"No. I'm not. I'm not Willy Jack."

"Good," she said. She peered into Forney's face, narrowing her eyes as if she were trying to bring him into focus. "Willy Jack's gone."

"I guess so."

"I'm having a baby, Forney."

"I know."

"Can you help me?"

"Novalee, I don't know how."

"Yes, you do. You read the books."

"Not all of them."

"Nearly."

"Then I didn't read the right ones."

"Are there wrong ones, Forney? Are there any wrong books?"

"Well, I don't know. I suppose—"

But Novalee couldn't hear him then. She braced her arms across her abdomen as if she could protect herself from what she felt coming, but it came anyway.

Her pain carried its own heat now . . . muscle, bone, flesh burned into a single thing low in her belly, against her spine. It flared deep inside, white heat . . . combustible . . . then rising, seared her lungs, scorched her throat. When it left, it left her dry, brittle as old paper.

"Get me a drink of water, Forney."

"Is it okay to do that? Are you supposed to do that?"

"Yes, I think so. Go check the manual."

"What manual?"

She let her head fall against his chest. Her hair was wet, her face bathed in sweat.

"The buckeye lost all it leaves, Forney."

"What manual?" He wiped her face with the back of his hand. "What manual should I look in?"

"The Complete Guide to Fruit Trees."

"Novalee, I'm going to call an ambulance. You need to be in the hospital."

"In a bed with white sheets."

"Yes, a hospital. You need a doctor."

"Forney!" Her voice sounded urgent. "Get a knife."

"What?"

"A knife."

"What for?"

"Don't you remember? Rose of Sharon!"

"But I don't . . ."

"They put a knife under Rose of Sharon . . . when she was in labor. A knife . . . to cut the pain."

"Novalee, I don't think that's—"

The pain tore through her so quickly she had no time to set her body against it.

"Novalee?"

She heard an animal keening—its high-pitched cry made her throat ache.

"Novalee!"

The pain twisted inside her, pulling at her center, taking her to the edge of what she could stand.

"Oh, my God!" Forney said.

And at the edge, she gave herself to it, held nothing back.

"What am I supposed to do, Novalee?"

"Forney . . ."

Pain took her then, knotted itself around her with such force, such power that it choked off her breath.

"What should I do?"

It began to move then, the pain inside her, drawing something from her as it pushed itself deeper and deeper.

"It's coming, Novalee."

Then she felt some part of herself tearing away as it pushed lower.

"I see it. I can see it now."

There was life to the pain then as it twisted and stretched, straining against her, using her resistance to find its way.

"Yes!"

And then it was free.

"I've got it," Forney said. "I've got it." And he laughed, a kid with the Cracker Jack prize. "Look, Novalee. Open your eyes."

The release was too sudden . . . the separation too final.

"Open your eyes and look at your daughter."

Novalee squinted against the light as she blinked her eyes into focus and watched as Forney lifted the baby and gently placed it on her stomach. The tiny body, shrunken and dark, pulsed with every heartbeat.

When Benny Goodluck placed the buckeye tree in her arms, she was surprised at how light it felt and she wondered if such a fragile thing could ever take hold.

And she reached out and brushed the cheek of her daughter and she smiled at the touch . . . at the way it made her feel . . . the way she had felt when Sister Husband had hugged her, when Moses Whitecotton had taken her hand, when Benny Goodluck had touched her scar . . . when Forney Hull had held her in his arms.

And then she knew . . .

a name that means something

It came so suddenly that there was no space between knowing and not knowing . . .

a sturdy name

like two edges of time had slipped together and whatever had been between them was nothing . . .

a strong name

It drifted up from somewhere deep inside her, like a piece of music broken free. It touched empty places as it rose, brushed against her heart . . .

a name that's gonna withstand a lot of bad times . . .

floated up into the light behind her eyes. Then she felt the shape of it on her tongue, the slip and slide of it through her lips . . .

a lot of hurt

and the taste of it as she whispered, "Americus."

"Forney," she said, her voice catching, "I know her name." She smiled at him then. "Americus. It's Americus."

And as she took her baby's hand in one of her own and Forney's in the other, the teenage girl on the floor of a Wal-Mart whispered in the early hours of a new day, "Americus . . . Americus."

Chapter Nine

"WHO WAS THE GUY who broke the window?"

"Have you named the baby yet?"

"How long have you been living in Wal-Mart?"

The first reporter showed up while Novalee was still in the emergency room. The second arrived as she was being moved to a ward, and, before the floor nurse could get an IV started, two more slipped in and crowded around the bed.

Their questions came so fast Novalee couldn't have answered them even if she had wanted to—but she didn't want to.

A television crew arrived just after the staff moved her to a private room and posted a NO VISITORS sign. Even then, a brisk young man dressed as an orderly slipped into her room and started filming before one of the nurses ran him out.

"You're causing quite a stir around here," the nurse said as she fastened the blood pressure cuff around Novalee's arm. "Guess we've got us a celebrity." Her lips curled around the word "celebrity" like she had just gotten a mouthful of bitternut.

"I don't know what they want," Novalee said.

"You'd think we had Madonna in here. Whole pack of 'em sniffing around. Trying to find out how much you weigh, how much blood you lost. One of them offered me twenty dollars to let him take a picture of your baby."

"My baby . . ."

"Oh, you don't have anything to worry about. That nursery's tighter than Fort Knox. If anyone—"

Novalee's door swung open and Forney rushed inside like a man being chased. The noise from the hallway spilled in behind him.

"Hey," the nurse bellowed. "You march your ass right back out that door."

"He's not one of them. He's my friend."

"Good! Seems like you could use one." She cut her eyes at Forney then. "This girl's had a baby. She needs some rest."

"I won't stay long."

"That's what I know," she said as she opened the door and plowed her way into the throng in the hallway. As the door closed, they could hear her calling for security.

"What's happening, Forney? Why are they here?"

"It's crazy, Novalee. It's just . . . crazy. Radio. TV cameras. Some woman stuck a microphone in my face."

"But it doesn't make any sense. Women have babies in taxicabs and elevators. Why, Red's cousin had hers right in his cafe back in Tellico Plains. What's so special about Wal-Mart?"

"I don't know. I can't figure it out."

"And how did they hear about it? I mean, where did they find out?"

"It was my fault," he said, dropping his eyes. "When I broke the window out, that set off an alarm at the police station. Then the ambulance came and . . ."

"You did it to help me, Forney."

Novalee smiled at him then and when she did, he noticed again the tiny scar no bigger than an eyelash just below her bottom lip.

". . . and the doctor said if you hadn't been there, I might have . . ."

When she tilted her chin, the scar caught a glint of light and for one brief moment, it shimmered like silver.

". . . having the baby in an unsterile environment, so they'll keep me on antibiotics . . ."

Then she paused and ran her tongue across her lip, its tip barely kissing the edge of the scar, and just for a heartbeat, Forney felt he might faint.

". . . in the incubator until her temperature stabilizes, but he thinks . . . Forney, are you listening to me?"

The nurse came back then, roaring with displeasure. Forney knew he had to get up, had to walk out the door, but he didn't know how he could. Later he wouldn't remember when he left or why. He would only remember Novalee's smile, her lips and that indelible scar.

"He's a strange one," the nurse said as she rolled Novalee to one side and raised her gown over her hip. "Take a deep breath. This is going to stick."

But Novalee hardly felt the needle pierce her skin. She was too tired to care, so she sank into a troubled sleep, moving along the edges of dreams she would not recall, except for a scene becoming familiar to her now . . . familiar enough that when she heard the train, saw it speeding toward her and the baby, she shook herself nearly awake, then floated away to a place too black for dreams.

Novalee awoke to the smell of bacon, and looked up into amber eyes set in a face as broad and flat as a dinner plate.

"Good morning," the girl said. When she smiled, her eyes disappeared behind a smooth mound of flesh that swelled from her cheeks to the bridge of her nose and her chin melted into a soft layer of skin stretching to the base of her throat. But she had the most perfect mouth Novalee had ever seen. Her lips, full and luscious like ripe, wild plums, were unpainted, yet they looked moist and satiny and, for just an instant, Novalee had the urge to reach up and brush the tips of her fingers across the girl's mouth.

"I hope you're not hungry," the girl whispered, "because this is Tuesday."

Novalee looked around for Forney, but he was gone.

"The best breakfast days are Friday and Sunday, but Tuesday is the worst," she said as she fussed over the breakfast tray, rearranging containers and opening cartons. She felt the coffee cup to check for heat; touched the milk carton to make sure it was cold. She sniffed the bowl of oatmeal, stirred a glass of orange juice, and poked at a fruit salad, then peeled the covers from containers of strawberry preserves and grape jam. Novalee had never seen anyone pay such attention to food before.

When the girl reached to the far side of the tray for a napkin, her breasts swung back and forth over Novalee's face like gigantic, quivering water balloons. They surged from the neck of her tunic and billowed under her arms, her uniform straining against the unbelievable expanse of her chest.

"I'm Lexie Coop," she said as she removed the warmer cover from a plate of scrambled eggs and limp toast. The eggs were the color of mustard, the texture of hominy grits.

"If you intend to eat those eggs, you might want to give

them a shot of this." She pulled a small bottle of hot sauce from her pocket and held it out to Novalee.

"No, I don't think so."

"How about this toast?"

Novalee shook her head. "I thought I smelled bacon."

"That's my perfume. Musk of bacon." Then she laughed, a laugh that began deep in her chest, then rolled across her tongue and out her perfect mouth.

"Just kidding," Lexie said, her chest heaving as she regained her breath. "I fried bacon for my kids this morning. Guess I wore the smell to work. You sure you don't want this," she asked, motioning to the food.

When Novalee made a face, Lexie sprinkled the eggs with hot sauce, then took a dainty bite.

"Hot sauce," she said. "See, I have this theory. Hot sauce burns away the calories. You can eat anything you want as long as you eat it with hot sauce."

"Does it work?" Novalee asked.

"I've lost six pounds in eighteen days, but I've got a long way to go. I gained a lot of weight with my last baby."

"How many kids you have?" Novalee asked.

"Four."

"Four? You don't look old enough."

"Well, I started when I was fifteen and then I just couldn't stop. See, after I had the first one, I started looking to find him a daddy. Thought I found one, too. But all I got out of that was another baby. So, then I wanted to find a good daddy for the two of them. I tried, but what'd I get? Twins."

"Have you found 'em a daddy yet?"

"*No*, and I'm not looking. I figure that'll get me another baby. Number five. I don't know," Lexie said, shaking her head. "I think I'm going about this the wrong way. But I just can't seem to say no."

Lexie finished the last of the eggs, then put the cover back on the empty plate. "You know, you should eat something. Help you get your strength back."

"What I'd really like to do is take a shower. Can I do that?"

"Sure you can."

"What about this?" Novalee motioned to the IV pole.

"No problem. We'll just wheel it in the bathroom with you."

Lexie moved the breakfast tray, then peeled the covers back and helped Novalee ease out of bed and to her feet.

"Just take your time. If you feel too shaky, let's put you back down for a few minutes."

"No, I'm okay. But . . ."

"Yeah, I know. Stitches pull, don't they?"

Novalee held on to Lexie's arm as they shuffled across the floor.

"Do you know about me?" Novalee asked.

"About Wal-Mart, you mean? Yeah. I guess everyone here knows about it. The hospital's full of reporters. They say you're going to be on television at noon."

"Oh, God," Novalee moaned, more from Lexie's news than from the pain of walking.

The phone calls started coming shortly after noon, the first from a man with a soft voice and a strange accent. He said he wanted to buy the rights to Novalee's story to make a movie, but he needed a picture of her nursing the baby in order to get the project off the ground.

An old woman who said she was a doll maker called later. She told Novalee to name the baby Walmartha, then she would make a doll to market by that name. She said if she could sell the idea to Wal-Mart, they would make millions. And she told Novalee if she had another baby, a boy, and named him Walmark, they would market the dolls as brother and sister.

The seventh or eighth call—by now Novalee had lost count—was from a man who thought he might be the father of the baby. He wanted to know if Novalee was the woman he had raped in an apartment on Cedar Street nine months earlier. As soon as Novalee hung up, she unplugged the phone.

Later, the floor nurse came in with a breast pump so they could feed Americus with Novalee's milk. The nurse was rough when she handled Novalee's breasts, the pump cold and hard against her tender nipples. When they didn't produce much milk, the nurse seemed irritated.

Finally, she left Novalee to manage the pump by herself, but she didn't have any luck. But when Lexie Coop came in with a pitcher of fresh ice water, she took over the pump. Her hands, still smelling of bacon, were warm against Novalee's flesh and her voice was gentle, soothing. Novalee's milk filled the jar.

Flowers began to arrive in the middle of the day, the cards addressed to the Wal-Mart baby. They came from banks, churches, politicians, schoolchildren—people Novalee had never heard of. She had flowers in baskets and ceramic vases with plastic storks and rubber clowns posed inside.

Novalee was reading a card attached to a single white rose when there was a knock at the door, and a second later, a tall, gray-haired man in a baseball cap stuck his head inside.

"Is it okay if I come in?" he asked.

"Are you a reporter?"

"No." He stepped into the room. "I'm Sam Walton."

"Who?"

"Sam Walton. I own Wal-Mart."

"Which one?"

"Well, actually . . ." He ducked his head then, like he was embarrassed. "I own all of them."

"Oh." Novalee cringed then, knowing why he had come.

"I don't know your last name."

He made "your last name" sound like a question, but Novalee didn't say anything.

"Is it all right if I call you Novalee? That's what they called you on television."

She nodded.

"You have some pretty flowers."

"I don't know any of the people who sent them though."

"Well, I guess they heard about you having your baby in the store . . ."

He didn't finish what he started to say, but just let "store" drift for a few seconds while he examined some ivy leaves in a ceramic planter shaped like a baby shoe.

"A little girl, they say. How is she?"

"She's in an incubator, but that's just a precaution."

"Americus. I heard you named her Americus."

"I did."

"That's a fine name."

"A strong name," she said.

Sam Walton nodded, then stared at Novalee like he expected her to say something, like he wanted her to explain, but she didn't know what to say. They were both quiet for a long time, so long that Novalee finally coughed, but it wasn't a real cough.

"The reason I came . . ."

"Mr. Walton, I kept track of it all. The food. The clothes. And the sleeping bag. The other stuff, too."

"But I . . ."

"I have it all written down, the cost of everything. And it's a lot of money. Over three hundred dollars."

"Well, that's one of the things I want to talk to you about."

"I'm going to pay you back. Every cent. Even for the window Forney broke."

"See, the thing is, I want to forgive that debt."

"What do you mean?"

"I want to cancel it."

"Oh, no. I can't do that. I owe you."

"No, I owe you."

"Why?"

"Because you made me a lot of money."

Novalee pulled herself up in bed, narrowing her eyes in puzzlement. "I don't understand."

"Look. The whole country's probably heard about the baby born in Wal-Mart. Now that's good advertising. People are going to read about Wal-Mart, see it on TV. That's free publicity and it's good for business."

"But . . ."

"And that's why I want you to forget about the window, forget about your bill. Forget all that. And I want to offer you a job in my store. In this store, right here in town, where you had your baby."

"Well, that's awful nice of you and I really appreciate it. I need a job, that's for sure. But . . . I don't know."

"Why? What is it that bothers you?"

"There'll be people coming in there to look at me, ask me questions and I don't . . ."

"Oh, not for long. This whole thing'll settle down in a

few days. Folks will forget all about it by the time you're ready to start to work."

"You reckon?"

"I reckon. So, is it a deal?"

"Okay. It's a deal."

Sam Walton reached over, shook Novalee's hand, then pulled an envelope from his pocket and put it on the bedside table.

"You take good care of yourself and when you're ready, just go to personnel, in the back of the store. They'll know about you." Then he turned and in three long strides he was across the room.

"Goodbye," Novalee said, but she didn't think he heard her. When he opened the door, the hallway blazed as camera strobes popped and film lights flared. A dozen voices vied for his attention.

"Mr. Walton, what did you say to her?"

"Sam, did you see the baby?"

"Mr. Walton, let me ask you . . ."

Novalee picked up the envelope which had her name printed on it and took from inside it five one-hundred-dollar bills, the most money she had ever held in her hand at one time.

Much later, when the floor nurse came in, Novalee was still holding the money. The woman cut her eyes and glared at Novalee.

"It's stupid to keep cash in your room," she said.

Novalee had seen that look before. On the faces of clerks as they watched welfare mothers count out their food stamps. In the eyes of some teachers when kids lined up for free school lunches. Behind the tight smiles of secretaries who patiently explained that the water couldn't be turned on again until the bill was paid.

The nurse pushed Novalee to her side to give her another shot. But this one was not like the last. This time she jabbed her twice, her movements hard and punishing.

Forney slipped soundlessly through the door and tiptoed to the side of the bed. Novalee had fallen asleep with one arm shielding her eyes from the glare of a fluorescent bulb; the other was tangled in the IV tubing twisted and caught beneath her shoulder.

He turned off the overhead light, then gently moved her arm from her face, and as he did, she pulled her mouth into a frown and shifted to one side.

Forney eased the tubing from under her, then smoothed it into place on the back of her hand where her skin looked tissue-paper thin. He let his fingers close softly around her wrist, dizzied by the pulse there that throbbed in time with his own.

His lungs filled with her smell . . . soap and milk and roses. He saw her bottom lip quiver with a sudden release of breath and heard the small whimpering sounds she made when she brushed her fingers across her breast. And when her eyelids fluttered, like the heartbeats of baby birds, something tightened in his chest, caught his breath just below the hollow in his throat, and a sound too soft to hear vibrated deep inside him.

Chapter Ten

NOVALEE DISCOVERED the next morning that Wednesday breakfasts weren't much tastier than Tuesday breakfasts. She was trying to deal with cold oatmeal and warm Jell-O when a white-haired woman dressed in a pink pinafore brought her a fistful of mail.

At first, she thought it was a mistake, but when she shuffled through the envelopes, she saw they were addressed to THE Wal-Mart BABY, to THE WOMAN ON THE FRONT PAGE OF THE TULSA WORLD, to BABY AMERICUS and to THE Wal-Mart MOTHER. They came from Texas and Arkansas, from Louisiana and Kansas, one from Tennessee, and the rest from Oklahoma.

Novalee opened the one from Tennessee first, afraid it was from someone in Tellico Plains who had seen her on television, someone who knew who she was. Inside was a note that said, "I gave birth to a baby in the back of a VW van where I lived for nearly a year. My baby didn't make it. I hope yours does." There was a ten-dollar-bill clipped to the note.

Then she opened an envelope from Texas. Inside was a dollar bill and a note written with crayon on yellow construction paper. It said, "Dear Americus. I read about you in the paper. I think your a very brave baby and I love your name. My name is Debbie and I am seven years old."

One letter typed on stiff white paper had a twenty-dollar-bill folded inside it. "Americus. What a wonderful name. I fought in World War II and Korea, my brother died there. We need more Americans like you who are proud of our country and not afraid to show it. Some of them won't stand up for the National Anthem. God Bless You."

One woman wrote, "I wish I could send you money, but I don't have any." Inside the envelope was a coupon for one dollar off a package of Huggies. A little boy wrote to ask if he could get a baby brother at Wal-Mart. There were offers to adopt, offers of foster care. One couple wanted to buy Americus. Someone sent an outdated credit card, another a fishing license. One envelope had a check for a thousand dollars, but it was signed, "The Tooth Fairy." One ad came from a diaper service, one from a modeling agency. One man proposed marriage; one warned of breast-feeding. Two of the letters had no notes, only money. And one said, "I wish you had bled to death on the floor of that Wal-Mart. I wish your baby had been strangled by it's imbellycal cord. Your nothing but white trash and so is your baby and that's all it will ever be."

Novalee read the hate letter again and again, trying to imagine why anyone would want to say those things to her. She wondered who would write it and even tried to get a picture in her mind of what the writer looked like, but every time she did, she saw the face of the killer in *Carnage*, a movie Willy Jack had taken her to see at a drive-in.

When one of the doctors came in, Novalee shoved the mail under her pillow. She decided when she was alone again, she would tear the letter up and flush it down the toilet.

The doctor was not the one who had stitched her up in the emergency room the day before, but Novalee had seen him there in one of the cubicles. He told Novalee if her temperature remained normal and if Americus had no problems develop, he would release them both the next morning. He said the baby was stabilized and had no sign of infection, but he wanted to keep her in the incubator for another twenty-four hours.

Novalee wanted to ask him some questions, but he seemed to be in such a hurry to leave that he walked backward to the door while he was still talking. He reached the hall just as he said, "twenty-four hours," and then he was gone.

Novalee didn't realize she was smiling until she padded to the bathroom and saw herself in the mirror. "Americus is all right," she said to her reflection. "My baby is all right."

Then came the sound of a commotion in the hall. An electricity of voices, angry and urgent, crackled like dry sparks. Moments later, Momma Nell charged through the door and into the room.

"Who the hell's the geek playing bouncer?" she snapped as she flung a red plastic shoulder bag onto a chair near the bed.

Novalee remembered her as round and soft—full, meaty hips, a pillowed belly, fleshy breasts. But that had been ten years ago. There was nothing soft about her now. She was bony, sharp, her body all angles, her features hawklike.

Her skin was threaded with spider veins and her eyes, the color of shale, were as flat and hard as a cheap motel bed.

She had bleached hair, yellowed and brittle, like late-summer jimsonweed. Her eyebrows, created with a black grease pencil, were drawn too high, too thin. She reminded Novalee of the pinched, bony victims in slasher movies.

Momma Nell stopped a couple of steps short of the bed, then flashed a smile as full of happiness as a beating. She smelled of rented rooms and cheap perfume and her voice, ravaged by too many Camels and too much Jim Beam, sounded scratched and raw.

"I hope you don't think this kid's gonna call me Grannie or nothing like that," she said as she fished in a pocket for cigarettes and a lighter.

"What are you doing here?"

"Thought you'd be surprised."

"How did you know where I was?"

"Hell, saw you on television. I was just flippin' channels and all of a sudden, there's your face. They was wheeling you down the hall. Looked like you was dead, but I seen you open your eyes. Then I hear the story about you having a kid inside a Wal-Mart, so I wrote down the name of this town, got me a map and here I am. Drove nearly ten hours."

"From where?"

"Well, I was on my way to New Orleans."

"Any woman on her way to New Orleans can't have too many Lamentations," Novalee said, though she hadn't intended to.

"What? What the hell's a lamination?"

"You live in New Orleans now?"

"No. But I been in Louisiana a couple of years."

"What about Fred?"

"Who?"

"Fred. The umpire."

Momma Nell screwed up her face in concentration while she stubbed out her cigarette in a soap dish on the bedside table. She tossed her head a couple of times as she tried to shake loose the name of "Fred."

Suddenly, she wheeled. "That shithead," she yelled. "Told me he was a major league umpire. Said he traveled from coast to coast, stayed at fancy hotels in Los Angeles, New York, Chicago. Said I'd get to meet famous ball players. That lying little son of a bitch! He umpired softball games in Little Rock for the VFW."

Momma Nell lit another cigarette. "Fred. That little bastard." She blew the smoke through her nose and left the cigarette dangling from the side of her mouth. "What in God's name made you think of him?"

"Because he was the reason you left."

"Left what?"

"Me."

"Well, that's water under the bridge now," Momma Nell said as she waved her hand through the air, erasing the past. "That's not why I come here, to talk over old times."

"Why did you come?"

"To tell you the truth, I thought you might need some help. Didn't sound like you was doing too good. Living at the Wal-Mart's not my idea of success."

Novalee ran the sheet between her fingers, smoothing it into pleats, working hard to avoid looking at her mother.

"So, how are you going to help me?"

"Oh, I don't know. You got any plans? Someone to help you out? You got a man?"

Novalee shook her head.

"Where's the prick put you in this mess?"

"Gone to California."

"That figures. You got a place to live? Or was you planning on moving back to the Wal-Mart?"

"No," Novalee said, trying not to whine, trying not to sound seven years old again.

"Well, you gotta have someplace to take that baby. You give any thought to maybe moving into Sears? How about Kmart? That might be—"

"If you just came here to make fun of me—"

"I told you I come to see if I could give you some help. Look, Novalee, I was working for some asshole at a bar in Baton Rouge, but it was a dump and I wasn't making enough money. Heard it was easy to find work in New Orleans and the money was better, too, then I seen you on television and I think, 'Okay, I'll go see Novalee and her kid.' And here I am."

"She's in the nursery."

"Yeah?"

"I named her Americus. She's so beautiful. She has brown hair, real thick and curly."

"The way yours was when you was a baby."

"I haven't got to see her but just a few minutes because they put her in an incubator as soon as we got here. I can't wait to get out and start taking care of her myself."

"When do you think that'll be?"

"Tomorrow. One of the doctors said tomorrow."

"Any idea where you're going then?"

"Not for sure."

"Well, since I'm not in any hurry to move on, maybe I could find a place. A place for you and the baby and me."

"You mean you'd stay here and—"

"Sure. Help you and the kid till you're on your feet. Rent us an apartment, maybe a duplex. I've got a little money."

"Oh, I've got money."

Novalee reached under her pillow and pulled out the envelope from Sam Walton and the letters and checks that had come in the mail. She handed them to her mother.

"I've got almost six hundred dollars," she said.

"Where did you get this?"

"People I don't even know sent me money. And the man who owns the Wal-Marts, he gave me five hundred dollars and offered me a job, too."

"Why?"

"I'm not sure. But with my money and your money, we can probably get a nice place."

"You bet we can."

"And we're gonna need some things for the baby. A bed, maybe a cradle. And some diapers and blankets."

"Sure. She'll need gowns, and booties and—"

"A rocking chair. I want a strong rocking chair. And get her a teddy bear, too. A white one."

Momma Nell was pulling the money out of the envelopes and counting it.

"You think we'll have enough for all that stuff?" Novalee asked.

"Plenty. We have plenty of money."

Momma Nell grabbed her purse and stuffed the money inside it. "Well, don't you worry about anything. I'll take care of it."

"You want to go down to the nursery and see Americus? I know they'll let you see her if you tell them . . ."

"I better get going. I've got a lot to take care of today, but I'll see her tomorrow."

"Okay. But be here early. Say by nine o'clock."

"Yeah. Nine o'clock." And as suddenly as she had swooped in, she swooped out.

And later that night, after Novalee had napped, when

the rooms were dark and the halls quiet, she tried to imagine what kind of place Momma Nell would get for them. She hoped for sunny rooms and winding staircases, for tall windows and broad yellow porches. But she had trouble picturing such places. The rooms in her head were dark, the light hazy and dim.

She tried hard to remember her magazine pictures . . . rooms papered in soft spring flowers, glass doors overlooking bright gardens, but the images looked blurred, the colors faded.

She covered her head with her pillow, hoping sleep would bring dreams of white cradles, wicker chests and glass music boxes that, spinning, catch the light.

Early the next morning, after a flurry of release forms and goodbyes, Novalee and the baby were wheeled downstairs by a teenage candy striper with bleached hair and braces. She waited with them for nearly an hour before she reclaimed the wheelchair and wandered away.

Novalee and Americus waited in the lobby until just before noon, and might have stayed there longer, but Novalee thought people were whispering about them, so she took the baby outside to wait on the sidewalk.

She knew then Momma Nell wasn't coming; knew she and the money were gone. But Novalee had no place to go . . . and so she waited.

They were still there at straight up two o'clock when Sister Husband's Toyota came ricocheting up the curbed drive and screeched to a stop. Like a shepherd coming for lost sheep, Sister rounded up Novalee and Americus, herded them into the covered wagon, then raced away, heading for safety . . . heading for home.

Chapter Eleven

SAM WALTON WAS RIGHT. By the time Americus was a month old, folks were starting to lose interest in the baby born in Wal-Mart. Just out of the hospital, Novalee continued to get mail, forwarded to Sister Husband's. A widow in Dallas sent an invitation to her daughter's wedding and a boy named Moe Dandy sent a bookmark made from a snake. A Sunday School class in Topeka sent twenty dollars and a Vietnamese family in Fayetteville sent ten. A ninety-year-old Quapaw Indian named Johnson Bearpaw mailed a sack of worn comics and a five-dollar-bill. Mostly though, Novalee got notes of encouragement and prayers for Americus, but even those tapered off quickly.

Now and then a reporter would phone from Tulsa or Oklahoma City and sometimes an out-of-state call came, someone wanting to know about the child named Americus Nation. Once, a man and his wife came to the door and told Sister Husband they had driven all the way from Midnight, Mississippi, to bring the word of God to Novalee, but Sister told them she already had it, then gave them a copy of Ecclesiastes and sent them on their way.

The locals were curious and stared as she walked down Main Street on her way to the library. Those who knew who she was pointed her out to those who didn't. When they had family from out of town, they drove them down Sister's street so they could take pictures of her trailer. The clerks in the IGA, where she bought baby talc and Vaseline, were polite and soft-spoken as they handed her change, but winked at each other over the top of her head and made Wal-Mart jokes when she walked out the door.

But she didn't see them, never noticed. She was too busy falling in love with her baby . . . memorizing the soles of her feet and the pattern of thin curls at the back of her neck . . . tracing the curve of her lips while she nursed . . . learning the heft of her hips palmed in one hand . . . listening for her breath in the dark of the night.

Sister had set out to spoil them as soon as she got them moved in. She would pick Americus up at her first whimper and dance her around the trailer to a music box that played "My Funny Valentine." She cut stars from construction paper and hung them on strings above the crib, claiming babies got their sense of direction from stars.

When Novalee tried to help with the dishes or vacuum the floor, Sister would lead her to the front porch swing and make her sit down. Whenever she went to town, she brought Novalee some special gift—a plastic barrette shaped like a butterfly, a tiny Bible no bigger than a match box, a sample lipstick from the Merle Norman store.

For the first few days at the trailer, Novalee had felt stiff, a bit shy. She was careful not to use too much hot water and kept her door closed at night. Her speech was polite; she said "thank you," "excuse me," and "please," and always cleaned her plate at the table, even when Sister served her lima beans.

But what changed all that was when Novalee ran into the gas stove. She had just put Americus to sleep after the two o'clock feeding, then slipped down the hall and into the bathroom without making a sound. She eased the door shut behind her and left the light off so it wouldn't shine into Sister's bedroom. Barefooted, feeling her way in the dark, she misjudged the distance and crashed into the heavy old gas stove, cracking her shin against one of the sharp ridges that curved over the jets. The savage thwack of bone against iron splintered the silence just before Novalee bellowed in pain and fell to the floor.

Sister flew out of bed, ran into the bathroom, turned on the light. "Oh darlin', what happened?"

Novalee, cradling her leg, rocked back and forth in the middle of the floor. The skin along the bony ridge of her shin had been split open—peeled back, scraped to the bone.

"My word. Let's get something on that. I know it must hurt like the dickens."

Between clenched teeth Novalee hissed, "dickens," while Sister rummaged in the medicine cabinet, talking to herself as she poked through jars and tubes. She found the bottle she was looking for on the top shelf. Kneeling, she took the injured leg firmly in one hand, uncorked the Merthiolate and upended it on Novalee's ravaged flesh.

"Oh, shit!" Novalee screamed as she beat her fists on the floor. "Shit!"

Suddenly, she froze, her face rigid as she realized what she had said. "Sister . . ." Her voice trailed off into silence.

Sister looked solemn as she eased Novalee's leg to the floor. "Darlin'." She spoke slowly, choosing her words carefully. "Didn't you forget to say please?"

Sister forced her face to frown, then covered her mouth, trying to hide the smile that played at her lips. She choked back the first hard release of air, swallowed the sound of a snicker, then exploded with laughter—laughter that robbed her of breath and made her eyes tear.

Novalee, her color rising, cracked an uncertain grin, holding it just for a moment, just until the first thin squeak slipped out . . . and then it was over. They laughed, they hooted, they squealed, their chests heaving as they gulped for air, until, minutes later, still gasping for breath, they struggled to their feet, then padded to the kitchen, made coffee and talked until dawn.

Novalee told Sister about Willy Jack and the Wal-Mart. She told her about Momma Nell, too, but not about the old stuff, she didn't tell about that. She only talked about her coming to the hospital, running off with the money.

"Nearly six hundred dollars," Novalee added.

"Now just imagine that," Sister said. "Strangers who cared so much about you and that precious baby that they sent their money. Don't that beat all?"

"I should've known what she'd do."

"But that don't change the goodness of all those folks giving it to you, does it?"

"Sister, I been wanting to ask you. Why did you show up at the hospital when you did? I mean, how did you know?"

"Why, darlin', the Lord has a way of telling us what we need to know."

Novalee nodded her head like she understood, but she didn't. She hadn't understood much of anything that had happened to her. Like when Sister brought her and Americus to the trailer that first day. Sister had told her if she would just trust the Lord, everything would work out. Novalee had nodded her head then, too, even though she hadn't really believed it.

But that afternoon, a Mexican family named Ortiz, from the trailer next door, brought over a handmade pine crib and some hot tamales wrapped in corn shucks. The father spoke no English, but smiled while the mother and the three daughters took turns holding Americus. Dixie Mullins, from across the street, brought diapers and gowns, things her granddaughter had outgrown. Dixie had a beauty shop in the back room of her house, but she didn't do much business. Sister said it was because she carried on conversations with her dead husband while she worked. Henry and Leona Warner, from three doors down, brought a watermelon, some receiving blankets and a sterilizer. They agreed the baby was beautiful, but they got into an argument about the color of her eyes. Henry said they were cornflower blue; Leona insisted they were azure. Sister explained, after they left, that they lived in a duplex—Henry on one side, Leona on the other.

By sundown, Novalee and Americus had everything they needed. They were fed, settled and in bed in their new home. Maybe Sister was right, Novalee thought. Maybe everything would work out, but she couldn't see how.

The little spare room at the back of the trailer barely held Novalee's bed, the crib and the tall chest for their clothes, but Sister fixed it up with a new bedspread and curtains from Goodwill and some framed pictures she bought at a flea market east of town. Novalee worried about the money Sister spent on her and Americus. She figured the Welcome Wagon job didn't pay much because most weeks when Sister went by City Hall to get the names of new people in town, there wouldn't be more than two or three. Now and then, she worked at the IGA handing out samples of sausage or cheese or some new cracker, but those were long days that kept her on her feet for hours. She never complained, but she took pills for days afterward. "To improve my disposition," she said. Novalee hoped when she went to work at Wal-Mart, she'd make enough so Sister could give up the IGA.

Forney came by each evening as soon as he closed the library. He always knocked three quick raps, then waited for Novalee to come to the door, no matter how many times she called, "Come in."

Each time he came, he brought an alarm clock and two books, one of them for Novalee. He brought her books about convents. He brought books about cowboys. Books on gambling, whales and molecular biology. She read about the planets, jazz and Mexican architecture . . . about polar expeditions, bull-fighting and the Russian Revolution. Once he brought her a collection of essays about love which he handed to her inside a brown paper sack. She read a book about shepherds along the river Tweed in Scotland and one titled *Rats, Lice and History*, a chronicle of infectious diseases and how they altered the world. Novalee started all of them, finished most, skimmed some, gave up on a few, but she couldn't keep up with Forney. The stack of books beside her bed stretched to the window.

The second book he brought was for Americus. He would prop her in her carrier on the kitchen table, then put his chair directly in front of her. After he cleaned his glasses and got a glass of water, he would set the alarm, then begin to read.

He read for thirty minutes exactly, a different author each night. He read Shakespeare, Plato, Freud, Nietzsche, Rousseau, and he read with deep concentration. From time to time he looked up at Americus to judge her reaction to something he had read.

She never dozed, never fussed, but stayed alert from the first word, her attention focused completely on Forney.

While he read, Sister and Novalee sat quietly across the room. Occasionally, Sister would nod her head at something she felt deserved a response, or now and then whisper "Amen" when she heard something she believed to be true. She became so involved when Forney read *Romeo and Juliet*, that she cried and held Novalee's hand.

When the alarm went off, Forney would close the book, then repeat, from memory, three key passages from the reading, as if to suggest to Americus there might be a test.

After the readings, Forney manufactured lots of reasons why he had to hurry away, but he never did. He liked sitting on the porch with Sister, peeling peaches or shelling peas. He liked holding Americus at bedtime, liked the feel of her soft cotton gown, the smell of Novalee's milk still on her breath. He liked watching Novalee as she smiled at something he said, lifting her hair from the back of her neck, bending to put Americus into his arms.

Mr. Sprock's visits were not nearly as predictable as Forney's. Sometimes he came in the mornings, bringing fresh tomatoes or peppers from his garden. Sometimes he came in the evenings to sit on the porch and drink tea. He always had something interesting to show them—a rock shaped like a rabbit, a potato that looked like a man's butt. He brought peacock feathers and foreign coins, arrowheads and old postcards. Once he brought a gold tooth in a bottle that he found floating at the lake.

Novalee didn't know when or where Mr. Sprock and Sister found time to be alone, but sometimes, when Sister said grace, she asked the Lord's forgiveness for fornicating again.

Mr. Sprock often brought Novalee seeds and young plants for her garden, which was beginning to burgeon with color. The morning glories, a foot tall and climbing, wound around a trellis Mr. Ortiz had made for her. All the geraniums and pansies she had received in the hospital were thriving in that corner of the yard, as well as white candytuft, scarlet rose mallow and purple coneflowers she had added since she got home.

In a lot behind the trailer, she had found some white rocks she used to circle the buckeye tree in the center of the yard. It hadn't grown any that she could tell, but the trunk had lost its powdery film, a sign, she had read, that indicated returning health. The gardening book Forney had given to her for her birthday was already looking worn.

Just behind the trailer she started a small vegetable garden with potato eyes and onion sets, then lettuce seeds Dixie gave her. She added asparagus crowns for Sister, who claimed if they took root, they would grow for a lifetime.

Sometimes Mr. Sprock would come in the evenings to bring some new seeds or help her weed the garden, then he'd stay over to hear Forney read. Mr. Ortiz came a few times, too, and when he was there, Forney would read louder—hoping, perhaps, that volume would ensure comprehension. Afterward, when there was talk about the reading, Mr. Ortiz would voice his opinion, always with enthusiasm, always in Spanish.

Sometimes Dixie came over with ice cream she had mixed up. Forney would turn the crank and freeze it, then they'd eat on the front porch until mosquitoes drove them inside. Dixie never ate ice cream herself. She said it gave her diarrhea. Novalee believed she went to all that trouble just so she could hold Americus for a couple of hours. Once Henry and Leona had a fish fry in their backyard, but they argued all night over whether the baby should sleep on her back or her belly. On the Fourth of July, the Ortiz girls set off their fireworks in the street while everyone gathered on Sister's porch for lemonade. Mrs. Ortiz had made Americus a bonnet of red, white and blue and the girls posed her with a flag so they could take her picture.

Novalee sometimes worried about all the attention the baby was getting. She wondered if too many could love her too much. But Americus flourished. She never grew fussy with a crowd around. They could pass her from hand to hand, from arm to arm and she wouldn't make a peep. She could sleep on Forney's shoulder, in Dixie's lap or across Leona's knees. She could awaken to the smiles of the Ortiz girls, a waltz with Sister or the touch of Mr. Sprock's hand.

Novalee could hardly imagine that one tiny creature could create so much love. And that was the problem: the more Novalee loved her, the more she feared she might lose her.

At times Novalee's fear would come rushing at her, so sudden it would be gone before she quite knew it was there, like a flash of disconnected memory. Or, it might settle on her slowly, press against her chest, build until her heart pounded with it. Now and then it was less insistent, only some vague uneasiness, a fragment of a bad dream nagging at her. But at its worst, it was real . . . a shadow, a shape lurking just beyond the edge of the light.

Always, it came without warning, without cause—while Americus was in her bath, her spindly arms and legs soaped, slippery as cooked spaghetti . . . as she drifted into sleep, a lazy eyelid just closing out the light . . . her mouth stretched into a lopsided O . . . her hand curled into a fist, the twitch of one tiny finger.

And with Novalee's new fear, the old superstitions held

greater peril. Dreams of locked doors could invite croup or measles. Gray horses or broken shoestrings might signal pneumonia or scarlet fever. Two crows in the same tree might foretell polio. Or worse.

But the greatest portent of disaster, her nemesis—number seven—now sent her running to Americus, running to feel for lumps or fever, to look for spots or swelling . . . to check her mouth, her heart, her lungs. A seven, any seven, was a scourge, a plague, an affliction, but weeks earlier, at the moment Americus had begun her seventh day of life, Novalee had confronted the most terrifying seven of all.

The night was filled with lurking strangers, the morning with rabid dogs. Every mosquito carried malaria, each gas jet leaked deadly fumes. Knife blades became savage weapons; a gentle breeze, a killer storm.

Novalee checked the windows, guarded the doors, walked the floor. She saw danger in every car that came down the street, whether she recognized the driver or not. The few times she dozed, she saw Willy Jack running at them, his face twisted into a vicious grin.

She held Americus in her arms from midnight till midnight. And when it was over, when the danger had passed, she wondered how they would survive the seventh week, the seventh month, the seventh year.

Chapter Twelve

WILLY JACK ARRIVED at the New Mexico State Prison on a Monday and by the following Friday, he had six stitches in his rectum, a broken nose, a nickel-sized chunk of flesh out of his left buttock and a bruise the size of a Frisbee on his chest. Prison was going to be a hard place for Willy Jack to get used to.

They'd fast-forwarded him out of Santa Rosa. He was in the county jail only nine days before his trial, which lasted just over an hour, and his sentencing took less than three minutes. He was going to do fourteen months in prison whether he behaved himself or not, but then, good behavior had never been a quality Willy Jack aspired to.

His prison troubles had started early. The broken nose came on the first day when the guards tried to lock him in his cell, an incident that got him three days in isolation. The chewed buttock and torn rectum came about on the second night when he was raped by a pair of brothers named Jabbo and Sammy who bought him from the guard in solitary. The bruise on his chest, seemingly the most minor of his injuries, was, in fact, the most serious. It transpired because he wouldn't give his devil's food cake to a desiccated little man called Sweet Tooth—an odd name for a man with no teeth.

By the end of the first week, Willy Jack had been in the infirmary four times. The doctor, Dr. Strangelove to the inmates, found Willy Jack to be wildly attractive, a situation that would not work to Willy Jack's advantage. Dr. Strangelove's response to sexual attraction was physical pain—and his craving for Willy Jack was strong. When he packed Willy Jack's broken nose, he stuffed it with so much cotton that the soft tissue of the septum was perforated. When he treated the wound on Willy Jack's buttock, he added a pinch of Drano to the salve he slathered across the teeth marks around the soft, torn flesh. And when he stitched up Willy Jack's rectum, he signed, with a flourish and fine suture, his name.

Willy Jack's cell mate was a Navajo called Turtle who didn't know how old he was. His eyes looked like the whites of runny eggs, and his skin was so thin Willy Jack could see the blood oozing through the veins that snaked across the old man's temples. And he didn't talk much. In fact, they didn't speak until the fifth night, the night Willy Jack's heart stopped.

He was asleep when it happened, when the pain inside his chest rolled him onto his back and pinned him to the mattress, but it was the silence that brought Turtle to the side of the bunk, silence that made him stare down into Willy Jack's face.

"This heart. It ain't beating," Turtle said. His voice was soft, his speech unhurried in the comfortable way men talk to themselves about malfunctioning carburetors and misfiring pistons.

Willy Jack tried to speak, shaped words with his lips to tell the old man to get help, but the pain inside his chest choked off sound.

"It ain't beating," Turtle repeated.

Willy Jack could feel the pressure building inside his belly, then ballooning beneath his ribs and chest where Sweet Tooth had hit him.

"My grandfather's heart stopped beating once," Turtle said. "For three moons."

With his chin tilted up and his lips peeled back tight against his teeth, Willy Jack gulped for air, fought for breath.

"Charlie Walking Away told us he was not dead. Told us to be patient. So we were."

Willy Jack's arms began to whip from side to side, his fingers scratching at air.

"But it is not an easy thing to wait for a heart to beat."

Turtle's words started drifting away, rising through something inky and thick floating over Willy Jack's body.

Willy Jack would not remember the singsong pattern of sounds in Navajo or the tapping of Turtle's gnarled fingers on his chest. But he would remember, though not until much later and always when he wanted not to think of it, the sound of Novalee's voice, thin and distant like an echo.

Give me your hand.

Willy Jack squinted, trying to see through something dark and murky that separated them.

Feel that?

He remembered then her telling him about the heart.

Can't you feel that tiny little bomp . . . bomp . . . bomp?

Had she been talking about his heart?

Feel right there.

Or maybe she had asked him . . . could it have been . . .

That's where the heart is.

And finally he felt a muted thump inside his chest. Then, moments later, another . . . then two . . . beats out of time, stumbling, staggering to fall into the rhythm Turtle tapped out, the rhythm for Willy Jack's heart to follow.

Claire Hudson, the prison librarian, had sad eyes, eyes that looked even sadder when she smiled. A big smile, which did not decorate Claire's face often, could fill her eyes with tears, as if smiling resulted more from pain than happiness.

She was a big woman who had to shop for queen tall pantyhose and size eleven shoes, double E. She wore dark clothes—stiff gray gabardines, navy twills and black serges . . . boxy suits with high necks, long sleeves and tight collars. Claire avoided garments with lace, bows and fancy buttons and she owned no jewelry, not even a watch. She held a strong disdain for anything showy, allowing herself only one extravagance: Band-Aids.

Claire Hudson carried Band-Aids in her purse and pockets, in her suits and in her bathrobe. She kept them on her desk, the dash of her car, her bedside table, with her gardening tools and in her sewing kit. She stuck them in teapots, vases and bowls, in her lunch sack, between pages of her Bible and under the pillow on her bed.

She wore them constantly and in abundance—from her scalp to the soles of her feet. She wore sheer, clear, medicated and white and she used specific sizes and shapes for certain areas of her body . . . circular spots for her throat and face, juniors for her fingers and toes, three-quarter by threes on her torso and one by threes on her arms and legs. Occasionally she mixed them to form overlapping protection if the need arose.

She covered warts, moles and ingrown hairs . . . pimples, cuts and fever blisters . . . burns, abrasions, hangnails and bites . . . eczema, psoriasis, scratches and rashes. Claire had spent her life, all sixty-one years of it, hiding her injuries from the world—until she opened the most painful wound of all to prisoner number 875506: Willy Jack Pickens.

She was just applying a fresh medicated junior to a paper cut on the pad of her index finger when she saw Willy Jack for the first time, when he entered the library with a crew coming in to clean.

"Finny," Claire shouted at Willy Jack. Then she collapsed.

She was carried to the infirmary where Dr. Strangelove revived her with smelling salts, but not before he peeked beneath a dozen of her Band-Aids, disappointed not to find raging infections and disfiguring wounds. By the time Claire had recovered and returned to the library, the cleaning crew was gone. But it didn't take her long to get Willy Jack back.

When he walked through the door, she once again called him Finny, this time her voice little more than a whisper.

Willy Jack edged a couple of feet into the room, then stopped and studied Claire suspiciously.

"Come on in," she said, motioning him toward her desk. "It's okay."

"They said I'm supposed to mop up a spill in here."

Without taking her eyes from Willy Jack's face, Claire shook her head, a gesture of disbelief.

"It's just incredible," she said. "Incredible."

"What?"

She picked up a framed photograph from the corner of her desk, stared at it several moments, then handed it to Willy Jack. An enlargement of a snapshot, it showed a young man standing on a stage playing a guitar.

"Can you believe it?" Claire asked.

Willy Jack wasn't sure what he was supposed to believe, but he nodded as she handed him another picture. In this one, the same boy held a trophy in one hand, a guitar in the other.

"That was taken at the State Fair. He was eighteen."

Willy Jack could tell the pictures were old, but he didn't know if that was a clue.

"Feel like you're looking at your twin, don't you?" Claire said.

Then Willy Jack knew what it was he was supposed to believe. He and the boy in the pictures looked alike.

"Yeah," he said as he handed the photos back to Claire. "Who is he?"

"My son, Finny."

"Oh." Willy Jack looked around the library. "What'd you spill?"

Claire's gaze wandered from the pictures to Willy Jack's face, then back again. "It's in the eyes." She touched a finger to the face in the picture. "The lips, too. One time a girl drew his picture on a napkin when he played at a club in Tucumcari. She gave it to him with a note that said he had beautiful lips." Claire smiled her sad smile.

Willy Jack moistened his lips with the tip of his tongue. Somebody had told him once that wet lips were sexy.

"This was his last picture," Claire said, nodding at the one with the trophy. "He was killed two months later." She looked up at Willy Jack then as if she expected him to say something, but he didn't. "He was hit by a drunk driver on his way home from a dance hall in Carlsbad."

"Well," Willy Jack said, "that's too bad."

"Twenty-two years ago. About the time you were born, I'd guess." Claire put both pictures back on her desk. "But I just can't get over it, how much you look like Finny. You've even got the same build . . . about the same size."

"How tall was he?"

"Five eight."

Willy Jack pulled himself to his full height and then some. "Yeah. That's about right."

He hated the prison shoes he was wearing. The only thing he'd found to stuff them with was toilet paper, but it kept working its way up the back of his heel.

"He had the sweetest voice. Everyone said so."

Willy Jack watched a tear wash down Claire Hudson's cheek, spill across a Band-Aid near her upper lip, then drop onto another taped to her wrist.

"This is all pretty strange," he said. "See . . . I'm a musician, too."

Claire's hand lifted to her mouth.

"Guitar." Willy Jack nodded, a big gesture designed to communicate the full irony of the situation. "And . . . singer."

"Musician," Claire said softly, reverence in her voice.

"Well, I mean I *was* a musician."

"But . . ."

"Seeing where I am right now, I don't figure I'm gonna be playing no music."

"Oh, but you can."

"No, my guitar . . ." Willy Jack let his voice trail off as if what he were about to say was too painful.

"What? What is it?"

"It's just . . . well, my guitar." His voice broke then. "I sure do miss it."

"But you can have your guitar in your cell. Didn't you know that?"

"No, ma'am. I didn't."

"You just tell me where it is and I'll have it sent here for you."

"Well, you see, there was a fire. My grandma's house burned . . ." He struggled to go on. "Lost everything—my house, my music. It's all gone." Willy Jack took a few moments to create a kicked-puppy look, then brightened—as much as possible. "But I'm glad you told me about your son. It almost makes me and your Finny sound like brothers, don't it?"

Claire Hudson smiled then, her eyes once more filling with tears.

And Willy Jack knew right then he was going to get a guitar, maybe even the Martin he had seen in the pictures, if it had survived. He knew he was going to get not only a guitar, but almost anything else he wanted while he was in prison. And he was right.

The next day, Claire Hudson showed up with Finny's guitar, the Martin, and by that night, Willy Jack had taught himself three chords. A week later he was playing a couple of John Cougar Mellencamp songs, and within three months he would write a song called "The Beat of a Heart," a song that would soar to the top of the country charts and that would, within three years, sell over a million copies.

Part Two

Chapter Thirteen

WHEN NOVALEE took the job waiting for her at Wal-Mart, the other employees ran wild with rumors. Sam Walton was the father of her child; Novalee was blackmailing him with the threat of a paternity suit; Americus was going to inherit the Walton millions. But by the time Novalee collected her first paycheck, gossip had already shifted to an affair between a forty-year-old married woman who managed sporting goods and her nineteen-year-old first cousin, a bushy-haired boy called Petey who worked in customer service.

But if they had been paying attention, they could have added a new rumor to the mill on that payday when Novalee took Sister Husband's Toyota in to have the brakes fixed.

She parked in front of the automotive center at the side of the store at nine-thirty. Just as she cut the motor, the big overhead door swung open and twenty-six-year-old Troy Moffatt, slim-hipped and golden-haired, stood squinting against the sun.

"Hey!" he yelled. "You can't park there. We ain't open yet."

"I know that, but I've got to get to work."

"Well, that ain't my problem. My problem is keepin' this door clear."

"But I'm bringing it in to have it worked on."

"Then bring it in at ten o'clock."

"I can't."

"And you can't leave it there."

"Let me leave the keys with you and—"

"Lady, you're gonna have to move your Toyota."

Novalee started the pickup, then revved the engine to show him how mad she was . . . until it died. She tried to start it again, giving it more gas as the engine kept grinding, but it wouldn't turn over.

"Okay. Okay!" Troy yelled as he stomped to the side of the truck and jerked open the driver's door. "Scoot over."

"Forget it!"

"Scoot over. I'll drive you to work, bring your truck back here."

"No, I'll . . ."

By then, he was sliding under the wheel, his body pushing hers across the seat. She hoped the truck wouldn't start, but it did. The first try.

"Okay," he said. "Let's make this quick. Where to?" He backed out smoothly, then turned up the lane that ran parallel to the store.

"Go around the corner, left . . . toward the street."

After he negotiated the turn, she said, "Stop right here."

"What for?"

"You said you were going to drive me to work."

"Yeah?"

"Well, this is where I work." She jabbed her thumb toward the door marked EMPLOYEES ONLY.

"Oh hell," he said. "Why didn't you say so?" His face reddened. "I'm sorry." He smiled at her then and for the first time, she noticed that his eyes were the color of brown sugar.

"It's the brakes," she said. "That scraping noise." She opened the door and slid out. "The name's Nation and I'll pick it up at six." She slammed the door and marched away, feeling his eyes on the curve of her hips—pleased, for some reason, that he was watching her.

As soon as Novalee got her lunch break, she headed for the snack bar to meet Lexie Coop, the only girlfriend she'd had since Rhonda Talley was sent to reform school back in the seventh grade.

Lexie brought her children to Wal-Mart two or three times a week, cheaper entertainment, she declared, than miniature golf or the video arcade. At Wal-Mart, she could load them into a shopping cart, then wander the aisles for as long as she wanted. They never demanded toy guns or Barbie dolls, never cried to get out of the cart or whined because they felt crowded. Their bodies, soft and sticky, malleable as warm cookie dough, pillowed together free of sharp elbows and bony knees.

Lexie always packed a sack of treats . . . jelly sandwiches or cinnamon rolls, banana bread, sugar cookies. The children shared their food and licked their fingers, then yawned and smiled while Lexie browsed the aisles in search of yarn or sequins or pastel cotton balls—materials for their holiday crafts. They produced Santa dolls and leprechauns, Easter baskets and Valentines, but they were little concerned with calendars or time. They might dye eggs in January and make witch costumes in July, but there was never a question of being early or late. Not one of them cared.

They were already crowded into a booth waiting for their order when Novalee arrived.

"Hi, Nobbalee," they said in unison.

Novalee kissed them all, then wiped at a sticky spot on her nose. The children were wedged together like Gummi Bears . . . bits of sugar and cinnamon stuck to their cheeks and chins, their fingers glazed with jelly and something green.

"I went ahead and ordered for you," Lexie said.

"Good. I didn't have time for breakfast and I'm about to starve."

"Oversleep?"

"No. Sister is working at the IGA today, so Mrs. Ortiz is keeping Americus. By the time I got all her things together and made three or four trips next door, it was almost nine."

"You're lucky to have good sitters."

"And they all want to keep her. Dixie Mullins, Henry and Leona. I think they're glad when Sister has to go to work."

At some unspoken signal, all of Lexie's children slid out of the booth together, as if they were permanently joined. They brought back trays of food that covered the table: hot dogs, french fries, nachos and onion rings. Then Lexie reached into her purse and pulled out a bundle of chopsticks held together by a rubber band. The children waited quietly as Lexie handed a pair to each of them.

"It may look strange, Novalee, but I have this theory. People who eat with chopsticks are thin. You know why?"

"Well . . ."

"You think it's because they eat rice and vegetables, but

that's not it. It's because you can't eat fast with these things."

Lexie's chopsticks clacked like knitting needles as she piled jalapeño peppers on a stack of nachos, then scooped up a glob of cheese.

"I've already lost eight pounds."

Her chopsticks cut a swath through the fries, then scissored a hot dog in half.

The two older children, Brownie and Praline, were as adept with the sticks as their mother. The twins, Cherry and Baby Ruth, whose motor skills were not as finely tuned, were, nevertheless, managing just fine. None of them complained or got angry, but each ate quietly and cooperatively, passing food, sharing drinks and, from time to time, sighing with contentment.

Lexie didn't speak again until she had finished eating and put her chopsticks aside.

"I met someone, Novalee."

"You mean . . ."

"Yeah. Someone!"

"Who?"

"His name's Woody. Woody Sams. And he's nice, Novalee. Real nice."

"Tell me."

"Monday night, I worked the late shift in emergency because one of the night aides is in jail. So Woody came in, dislocated shoulder and abrasions. Ran a motorcycle into the side of a pickup. Well, they patch him up and when he's leaving, he asks me to go out for coffee, but I tell him I have to get home to my kids and let the babysitter go. So he asks me if he can come over the next night, Tuesday, and I say okay and he does. He brought a video, *The Black Stallion*, and some presents for the kids—a puzzle and some checkers. He really likes kids. Said he couldn't have any because when he was a teenager, he got the mumps and they went down on him and—"

"What does that mean? They went down on him."

"Well, you know." Lexie pooched out her cheeks, made a popping sound, then pointed to her crotch. "They went down on him."

"Oh."

"Here honey," Lexie said to Baby Ruth, "you've got a piece of pickle in your hair."

"So did you and Woody—?"

"No! We didn't even kiss but once, when he left, but it was nice. Anyway, he can't have kids, so I don't have *that* to worry about. I think I like him."

"You think?"

"Well, he's not perfect or anything." Lexie lowered her voice, pulled her mouth into a frown. "He chews tobacco. And he's an atheist."

"Oh, I guess no one's perfect."

"I know." Lexie shook her head. "But girls like us, Novalee . . . we don't get the pick of the litter."

"Troy!" The middle-aged man at the service counter yelled to the back of the shop. "Woman's here for the Toyota."

Troy Moffatt slid out from under the pickup, flashing Novalee a smile as he came toward her. "It's more of a problem than I bargained for," he said, wiping grease from his hands with a towel already black.

"Is it going to cost a lot?"

"Probably won't be too bad, but I won't be finished till tomorrow." He dodged then, feinting as if she might be tempted to throw a punch.

"Well, shoot."

"You need a ride? I could run you home."

"No. That's okay."

"You sure?"

"Yeah."

As she walked out, she heard him say something just under his breath, but she didn't turn, didn't ask him what he'd said.

She had walked two blocks, was crossing the four-way stop, when a banged-up Ford pulled up behind her and honked.

"Come on," he said. He leaned across and opened the passenger door. "It's on my way home."

Novalee got in, shut the door. "You know where I live?"

"No. But wherever it is, it's on my way home." He eased the Ford across the intersection.

"Look, about this morning . . ." He cut his eyes at her and grinned. "I'm sorry."

"That's okay."

"I just hadn't seen you around. I know most everyone who works here. By sight anyway."

"Well, I haven't been here very long."

"That's what I hear."

Novalee eyed him suspiciously, certain then he had heard about her and Americus, but he kept his eyes on the road.

"I'm really going to need that truck tomorrow," she said. "The woman I live with, it's hers, but she lets me drive it whenever I need to."

"It'll be ready by noon."

He lit a cigarette then. Novalee wondered if he chewed tobacco, too.

"I fixed a couple of things inside. Your radio and that dome light."

"Look, I don't know if I can afford all that. See, I'm going to pay for it myself. It's a surprise for the woman who owns it, but—"

"I ain't gonna charge you extra. But when I drove it, to check the brakes, I tried the radio and then I noticed the dome light, so I fixed 'em."

"Well, thanks," she said, sounding more angry than grateful.

"You sell books?"

"What? Books . . . no."

"Well, you got a God's plenty of 'em in that Toyota."

"Oh, I forgot. You think they'll be okay . . . leaving them in there overnight?"

"You kidding?"

"I mean, they're library books. They don't belong to me."

"You think any of those boys workin' in automotive is gonna steal books?" He laughed then. "Now they might swipe a Willie Nelson tape or maybe a fishin' lure, but they ain't about to steal a book."

Novalee bit at her lip thinking how upset Forney would be if he knew where his books were.

"What are they? Love books?"

"No."

"I used to go with a girl that read them love books."

"Turn left here."

"She was all the time talkin' about the flames of love and . . . hearts on fire, and stuff." His voice slid into a higher range as he curled his lips around the words. "Oh, my burnin' soul of love."

When his voice broke, cracked like an adolescent boy's, Novalee laughed, and so did he.

"This is my street. I'll just get out here."

"No, I'll take you to your house. Which way?"

She motioned to the right. "It's the trailer at the end of the block."

"You want to go out sometime?" he asked.

"Go out?"

"Yeah. With me. On a date."

"Oh. Well, I don't go out. I have a baby."

"People with babies go out sometimes, you know."

"I guess."

"You mean you guess you'll go out with me or you guess people with babies go out?"

He smiled and winked one of his brown sugar eyes.

"So. You want to go?"

"Go where?"

Troy shrugged. "To a movie. Dancin'. Shoot some pool. Whatever you want to do."

As they pulled up in front of Sister's, Novalee saw Forney on the porch with Americus.

"How about Saturday?" Troy asked.

"I don't know."

"Well, I'll see you tomorrow when you pick up your truck. Maybe you'll know then."

"Thanks for the ride."

As soon as Novalee stepped out of the car, Troy backed into the driveway, then turned on his bright lights, catching her in the crossbeam. Blinded by the glare, she stopped, unsure of where she was going.

Chapter Fourteen

"MR. WHITECOTTON?"

When he turned, his eyes narrowed as he focused on hers.

"Do you remember me?" Novalee asked, suddenly afraid that he might not. "You gave me—"

"A baby book," he said, "and you took my picture." He reached out and took her hand in his. "I remember you very well," Moses Whitecotton said. "You like porch swings and Life Savers."

"I knew I was going to see you again someday," she said, surprised that her throat tightened, the way it did sometimes when she was trying not to cry.

For several moments after he released her hand, she left it hanging in midair, as if she hadn't wanted to break the connection.

"I've thought of you many times," he said.

"You have?"

"Many times."

"That day," Novalee said, "all the things you talked

about . . . I think about that. And I remember everything you said."

"Oh, maybe sometimes I talk too much." He turned his hands out, palms open, the self-conscious gesture of a man owning up to a weakness.

"No, you were right. What you said about time and names and . . ."

"Yes, we talked a lot about names. But you know what? You never told me yours."

"It's Novalee. Novalee Nation." She pulled back the edge of her sweater so he could see her name tag. "I work here now."

"Well, Novalee Nation, seems to me it's time for you to do the talking. Time for you to tell me about your baby."

"You didn't hear about me?"

"No. I didn't."

She could tell he wasn't the kind of man who would pretend. He wasn't like that at all.

"I had a girl."

"A girl." He nodded. "I wondered, you know."

"She's . . . she's just . . ." Novalee laughed then, language for a word unspoken.

"Oh, nothing sweeter than a baby girl." He shifted his weight in a way that made him seem expectant—wanting to know, but not wanting to ask.

"She has a strong name," Novalee said.

"I'm glad to hear it."

"It's a name that's gonna withstand a lot of bad times."

"And they'll come," he said, shaking his head at the inevitability of it.

"Her name is Americus."

Moses stared, unblinking. "Americus," he said. He looked away then, giving the sound some time . . . some distance. Finally he looked again at Novalee. "Americus Nation," he repeated. "It'll do. It surely will do."

They were silent for several moments, but it was a comfortable silence . . . broken, finally, when a voice on the intercom called for additional checkers at the front.

"That's me," Novalee said.

"I'll be working here tomorrow. Taking pictures."

Novalee smiled. "I know."

"You'll be here, then?"

"It's my day off, but I'll be here."

"With Americus?"

"We'll both be here."

Reggie Lewis, the young blond manager, walked up to customer service. "Hi, Mose. Good to see you."

Moses reached for his briefcase on the counter behind him. "Moses," he said, his voice steady and strong. "Moses Whitecotton."

That night, Novalee dressed Americus in every outfit she had. The yellow jumper from Dixie Mullins, the baseball uniform from Henry and Leona, the white dress Sister had made and the bonnet from Mrs. Ortiz. When she finished, the baby was worn out and Novalee was no closer to deciding than when she had started. Finally, it was Forney and Mr. Sprock who voted for the dress and bonnet.

The next morning Novalee got up early to get everything ready. She rinsed out the white dress and hung it on the line to dry. After she mended a bit of torn lace on a pair of diaper pants, she trimmed loose threads from inside the bonnet. She picked invisible lint from a pair of white booties and polished their tiny pearl buttons with the hem of her gown. Finally, she ironed the dress carefully, fussing over each ribbon and ruffle and bow.

With Americus fresh from her bath, Novalee brushed her hair into delicate waves and tight ringlets, then tied the top back with a narrow silk ribbon. She dressed her with the care and precision of a backstage mother . . . patting, polishing, smoothing, stroking . . . determined to make Americus perfect.

By the time they arrived at Wal-Mart, two dozen women and children were already in line, waiting for Moses Whitecotton to take their pictures. The aisle was littered with toys, diaper bags and abandoned strollers. Fussy babies howled in the arms of impatient mothers; angry toddlers strained to twist from the grasp of adult fingers. A half-dozen preschoolers cartwheeled and tumbled like a tangle of wild kittens.

As Moses settled a sobbing baby into the lap of its older brother, he saw Novalee and flashed her a quick smile. He said something then to a young woman working beside him and moments later she walked to the back of the line where she placed a standing sign behind Novalee, a sign that said, "The photographer will not resume shooting until . . ." and beneath that was a dial with the hands set at one o'clock.

Moses seemed unhurried, even when an inquisitive child discovered the snaps on his briefcase or a young mother insisted on a pose that would produce, Moses explained, a headless photograph of her child. His voice, when Novalee could hear it beneath the hooting, howling children and scolding, threatening parents, was even and calm.

She watched him coax laughter, persuade silence and gentle anger . . . taking time with each shot, adjusting the lighting, readjusting the pose, working for the right expression.

The line moved slowly and Americus, in spite of the care Novalee took to avoid it, was wilting. Her hair had frizzed around her face and a crease up the side of her bonnet gave her a dented look. Her dress was wrinkled and limp, the collar damp with drool. One of the pearl buttons from her booties had popped off and Novalee was still searching for it when she looked up to discover they were next.

"So this is Americus Nation," Moses said.

Americus, her eyes Raggedy Ann wide, fixed Moses with an open-mouthed stare, a silver strand of saliva spinning its way from her bottom lip to the perfectly ironed ruffle around her perfectly ironed dress. She was, for several moments, motionless—frozen in fear or fascination as she struggled to take him in, her eyes darting from his face to his hands to his hair. Suddenly, her decision made, a smile nudged itself into a corner of her mouth, pushed across her lips and up over her cheeks. She held out her arms, reaching out to Moses Whitecotton, her fingers curling into her palms in a "take me" gesture.

When he lifted her out of Novalee's arms, Americus exploded with excitement, her knees pumping against his chest, arms windmilling the air, a gargle of laughter catching at her breath.

"Nothing sweeter than a baby girl," he said.

"Well, she looked a little sweeter before she tried to eat her dress." Novalee wet her finger, then rubbed at a smudge on the baby's arm. "Looks like she's been cooking mud pies."

"But that doesn't have anything to do with what's here. Nothing to do with what we're looking for."

"What do you mean?"

"If that's all it was, making them look good, it would be easy. Just scrub 'em up good, put on new clothes, press the shutter release. Bingo. You've got a nice baby picture."

Novalee nodded her head to show that a nice baby picture was certainly the last thing she wanted.

"No, those pictures are about the trappings," Moses said. "The costumes."

Novalee was tempted to snatch the bonnet off Americus' head.

"But it's not that simple," he added. "This child is Americus Nation. Now, how do we get a picture that'll measure up to that?"

Moses lifted the baby, as if to offer proof of her presence, then turned and put her on the table. "Step over here, Novalee, while I get set up, make sure she doesn't tumble off."

Moses pulled down a new background, a soft blue. He reset the lights, gauging the effects of every change by the reflection on Americus' skin. Finally, he covered the camera he had been using, then moved it and the tripod around behind the background.

"Company camera," he explained. "It takes nice studio pictures—studio *portraits*, they like us to say—but that's not what you want."

Moses pulled a scuffed and battered leather satchel from beneath the table and unbuckled the flaps.

"This is mine," he said.

Then he took out a strange-looking camera, not at all like the Nikons and Minoltas Novalee had stocked in the electronics department. Those were glossy, streamlined cameras in hard plastic cases, cameras that fit in the palm of her hand. But this one, Moses' camera, looked heavy, clumsy, hard to manage.

"What is it?" she asked.

"A Rollei. Best ever made."

He removed the lens cover to reveal two identical lenses on the front, one above the other.

"I've never seen a camera like that."

"No, not many of them left. Not like this one."

Then Moses pressed a button and the top of the camera popped up, making Novalee think of poorly tinted photographs in dark oval frames . . . men and women posed in stiff collars, their yam-colored faces set with grim-lipped smiles.

He held the camera in front of him, at his waist, looking down into it to find his shot.

"Okay, Miss Americus," he said, watching her through the eyepiece, "let's get started." He moved in, closer to the table. "Now I'll do all the work. You just do whatever seems right."

What seemed right to Americus was to rake her arms across the side of her head, dislodge her bonnet and pull it halfway down her face. As she tried to peek from under it, Moses pressed the shutter release, then turned a crank on the side of the camera.

"That's it, baby," he said without looking up. "Don't hold anything back."

He kept shooting as she worked the bonnet off, then sailed it to the floor . . . shot again as she leaned forward to peer over the edge of the table, her face screwed up with concern.

By the time Americus lost interest in the fallen bonnet, she hardly heard the clicks of the camera as Moses continued to shoot. Her attention strayed to more important matters—a hair caught between her fingers, a drop of drool spilling across her knee, the tight drum of her belly discovered beneath the ruffles of her dress.

Moses was not taking the pictures Novalee had imagined—Americus posed with teddy bears and parasols, beaming angelic smiles and flaunting dimpled cheeks. Instead, he was snapping pictures as her fingers delighted at the pucker of her navel . . . while she puzzled over an empty sock still wearing the shape of her heel . . . as she pondered the miracle of toes and the magic of a finger that points.

Moses' motions were like a dancer's . . . sliding, circling, turning—his movement finding balance and his eye finding voice . . . a bark of delight when he saw the true shot, a rasp of laughter as he found the right angle, the click of his tongue when he snapped the perfect picture.

And the camera, which Novalee had thought old-fashioned and unwieldly, looked small and delicate in Moses' hands, hands that moved in magical ways, fingers that found their own rhythm and knew, without knowing, when it was right.

Chapter Fifteen

After her second date with Troy, Novalee started taking birth control pills. She wasn't sure she would sleep with him, but she wasn't sure she wouldn't.

The first time they went out, Troy took her to a bar called Bone's Place where they ate ribs and played shuffleboard. When he took her home, he kissed her twice, then tried to unbutton her jeans, but she slipped out of the car and hurried inside.

On their second date, they went to a dance at the VFW, then to the city park where they drank wine coolers at a picnic table. When Troy tried to talk her into going to his apartment, she said no. But she liked the way she felt when his breath passed across her ear. And that was when she decided to get on the pill.

Three days and three pills later, she stopped saying no and went to his apartment where she let him take off her clothes and lay her back on his bed, a thin mattress on the floor. When he began, she closed her eyes, held tightly to his shoulders and hoped he wouldn't see the stretch marks that cut across her belly.

He hadn't said anything about protection—hadn't offered, hadn't asked. She was glad she had made her own decision about birth control, glad she had, for once, used her head, glad she had started taking

> *pills . . . the pills . . . tiny pills . . . smaller than aspirin . . . thinner than vitamins . . . and she had taken three . . . only three . . .*

Suddenly, she knew, knew with certainty, that three pills couldn't protect her. It would take days and days of pills, weeks of pills before she could be truly safe. Why, she wondered, had she been so stupid? Why had she taken such a chance? And why was she on a mattress that smelled like cottage cheese with a man who didn't care if she got pregnant or not?

By then, all she could do was to will Troy Moffatt to hurry, to get it over with. *It* didn't take long.

When he finished, she dressed quickly, then hurried away.

Back at the trailer, she cleaned herself again and again, scrubbed at her body with hot water and soap, as if that might erase ten minutes spent on a mattress the color of putty. She remembered then the foolish precautions she had taken when she started sleeping with Willy Jack . . . drinking Coke and aspirin, taking vinegar baths—contraceptive practices whispered in seventh-grade gym classes by girls who had gotten "the curse."

When Novalee finally crawled between the covers of her bed, she had to fight off the urge to wake Sister, to ask her to say a prayer. But she supposed God had more to do than direct the traffic of Troy Moffatt's sperm.

Novalee called Lexie early the next morning to catch her before she left for work.

"Are you okay?" Lexie asked. "You sound funny."

"I'm fine. I just wondered if you were coming to the store today. I thought we'd have lunch."

"No, I switched shifts. I'm working the three to eleven."

"How come?"

"Praline and Brownie have roseola, so I can't take them to day care, but my neighbor said she'd keep them tonight."

"Oh."

"Novalee, is something wrong?"

"Well . . . not really. I just need to talk to you."

"Come on over now. What time do you have to be at work?"

The line was quiet for several seconds.

"Novalee?"

"Huh?"

"What's the matter? What's going on?"

"I think I might be pregnant."

Lexie lived in low-income housing at the edge of town, a complex that had, years before, been a motel. Four units surrounded a pool, which the tenants called the toxic tub. The grounds, patches of bare earth and a half-dozen stunted cedars, were littered with rusted tricycles, airless inner tubes, trash can lids and chunks of bricks. Two skinny hounds licking at a greasy spot in the parking lot were undisturbed when Novalee pulled in behind them.

The door to Lexie's apartment, number 128, was decorated with Santa and Rudolph and Christmas bells. Halloween was just a week away.

"Hi, Nobbalee," Brownie said. "I have roy-rolla. See?" He pulled up his Mutant Ninja pajama shirt to reveal a rash across his belly.

"Does it hurt?"

"Yes, but I'm a big boy," he said as he strutted back to the television and Wile E. Coyote.

"I'm in the bathroom, Novalee," Lexie called. "Coffee's on."

Novalee went to the kitchen, but settled for a glass of water. She didn't need coffee, but that was partly because her stomach wasn't ready for chocolate chip mocha, Lexie's coffee of choice, and partly because of the brightness. Lexie had painted everything with Glidden white glossy enamel, a garage sale bargain at fifty cents a gallon. On bright, sunny days the glare was blinding. The rooms were so shiny, so brilliant, that Praline, the blondest and fairest of the children, wore an old green velvet hat with a black veil to protect her eyes when she first woke up. That's when Lexie called her Madam Praline and served her milk in a dainty china cup.

Lexie sailed into the kitchen wearing another of her garage sale purchases, a filmy chiffon gown that she said was exactly like one Marilyn Monroe wore in *Some Like It Hot*.

"Tell me everything."

"Okay." Novalee took a sip of water, then ran her tongue across her lips. "The guy I told you about . . ."

"The one who works in the garage."

"Troy Moffatt. Well, I went to bed with him . . . and Lexie, I'm scared to death I'm pregnant."

"Didn't he use anything?"

"No."

"Did you?"

"No. Yes. I mean, I'm on birth control pills, only . . ."

"Then you don't have anything to worry about."

"But I've only been on them a little while."

"That's probably why you're late then. They can throw you off schedule the first couple of months."

"I just don't trust them."

"How late are you?"

"Well, I don't know if I am."

"What do you mean?"

"See, it's not time for my period yet. I'm not due to start for another couple of weeks."

"Then how pregnant could you be? I mean, if the pills didn't work, how far along could you be? Two weeks?"

"No."

"A week?"

Novalee shook her head.

"How long then?"

"Nine . . . ten hours."

Lexie smiled, squeezed Novalee's hand, then got up and poured herself a cup of coffee. "Honey, I think it's a little early to start worrying."

"No . . . it's not! It's exactly the *right* time to worry. Now! When maybe I can do something about it."

"You mean an abortion?"

"No, not that. Not like that."

Lexie looked puzzled. "Like what?"

"Well, I don't know. That's why I came to you."

"Me?"

"You work in a hospital, so . . ."

"Novalee, look who you're talking to. I have four kids. Four! You think if I knew what to do . . ."

"But there are ways. I've heard . . ."

"Oh yeah. I've heard that stuff, too. The first time, I took quinine pills. A girl at school told me that would take care of it. It didn't. My God-fearing folks kicked me out of the house because I'd sinned and 'brought shame on them' and a few months later, I named my first baby Brummett."

"Brummett?"

"Well, I called him Brownie because that's what I craved the whole time I was pregnant." Lexie sipped at her coffee, then she said, "The second time, I tried sneezing."

"I never heard about that."

"Well, I hadn't either, but there was a newspaper story about a woman who had a miscarriage because she couldn't stop sneezing. So, I figured if it worked for her, why not me? I sniffed black pepper, red pepper, cayenne pepper. I tickled my nose with feathers, cotton balls, weeds. I plucked out eyebrows till I almost didn't have any left. And it worked. I sneezed and sneezed and sneezed. And nine months later, I had a baby girl I called Praline."

Lexie stirred another spoon of sugar into her coffee.

"Now the third time, I jumped."

"You jumped."

"There was a Gypsy woman lived down by the Willis Bridge. I heard she had some kind of magic. She did. She said, 'Girl, if you jump backwards nine times before the sun comes up, you'll lose that baby.' So I jumped. But just to be on the safe side, for extra insurance, I jumped backwards for over a mile. All the way from Parrish Road to the quarry. I had blisters, stone bruises, shin splints, a dislocated knee-cap . . . and in May, I had twins. No, honey, I don't know of one thing you can do but wait and see."

"How about one of those kits . . . a pregnancy test?"

"I don't think that's going to tell you anything after ten hours, but . . ."

They turned toward the kitchen door as Praline, wearing a Minnie Mouse nightshirt and her green velvet hat, shuffled into the room, her eyes puffy from sleep.

"Oh, oh. Madam Praline's up."

As Praline crawled into Lexie's lap, she said, "Nobbalee, I got the rolly-rolly."

"I know it, honey."

Lexie adjusted the black veil over Praline's face. "Would you like to have a cup of juice?"

"Yes, and . . . and . . ." Then Praline sneezed—twice.

"Bless you, Madam Praline," Lexie said. "Bless you."

Novalee spent the next two weeks trying to avoid Troy Moffatt. He came to the front of the store several times a day, but she managed to stay too busy to do more than say hello. When he called her at home, she found excuses not to talk.

She had little appetite and didn't sleep more than a few hours at a time. She got out of bed three or four times a night to go to the bathroom, certain that she knew the cause of the pressure on her bladder. Sometimes when she got up, she felt sick and dizzy, the way she had when she was first pregnant with Americus.

Then one morning, sometime before dawn, when she was just at the edge of sleep, Novalee felt the familiar wetness between her legs and it was over. She was free again. She was who she had been . . . without quinine, without vinegar or aspirin and Coke . . . without sneezing or jumping. She had been lucky this time.

She remembered something then, something from a book she had read about India, about women of the Untouchable caste, women who aborted their pregnancies by burning themselves with iron rods heated in burning coals.

Suddenly, Novalee sat straight up in bed, sleep no longer a consideration.

She got up, turned on her light and started pulling books out of the stacks on the floor beside her bed. When she found the one she wanted, she flipped through it until she saw what she was looking for, then read again a poem about a black woman who aborted her child.

Novalee picked up another book, ran her hand across its cover. It was the story of an Arab woman who had, when she was young, put spiders inside her body, spiders whose bites, she had been told, would cause her to miscarry.

Novalee lifted a small book from the bottom of a stack, a book she had just finished reading, a story about a Jewish girl named Brenda who got a diaphragm because her boyfriend asked her to.

Novalee looked around her at a room filled with books. Books stacked in corners, standing on her dresser, crammed into her headboard, pushed into a bookcase. And in the library, Forney's library, there were more. More books . . . more stories . . . more poems. And suddenly, Novalee knew—knew what she hadn't known before. She wasn't who she had been. She would never again be who she was before.

She was connected to those women she had read about. Untouchables. Black women. Arab women. She was connected to them just as she had been to girls in seventh-grade gym classes and to make-believe women named Brenda and to real ones named Lexie.

She remembered then the first day she met Forney, her first day in the library, when he had swooped up and down the aisles, plucking books from shelves . . . reading from one, then another . . . holding books, talking to them as if they were live . . . talking about trees and poetry and paintings . . . and she hadn't understood then, hadn't understood any of it. But now she was beginning to, and was sorry she had to wait for morning to see Forney . . . to tell him that she was finally beginning to understand.

Chapter Sixteen

THE WHITECOTTON PLACE was a mile off a rutted dirt road, a county road, but it had been two years since the blade of a grader had touched it. The land, cleared for pasture half a century earlier, rolled toward a shallow creek dotted with scrub oak and bois d'arc.

Novalee turned the Toyota into the graveled drive shaded by sweet gum trees, their leaves already turning wine and gold. The house was a dignified two-story with a broad screened-in porch and wide steps lined with pots of geraniums.

Moses stepped out the front door as Novalee maneuvered Americus from her car seat.

"Have any trouble finding us?" Moses asked.

"No, not once I crossed Sticker Creek."

Americus squealed and held out her arms to Moses before Novalee had reached the top of the steps.

"Miss Americus!" he said as he lifted her to his chest.

The porch, dark and cool, was a jungle of moonseed vines and snakeroot, Algerian ivy and butterfly weed. A half-dozen fishing rods leaned together in one corner and work boots toed the edge of newspapers beside the door.

Two heavy easy chairs sat arm to arm in the middle of the porch, but it was several moments before Novalee noticed that one of them held a tiny gnarled man.

"Novalee, this is my father, Purim Whitecotton."

The old man smiled at her with the side of his face that still worked, but the broken side, the side with the hooded eye and sagging lip, had shut down on his last birthday, his eighty-third, when he bent to blow out candles on an angel food cake and a blood vessel exploded in his temple.

"Hello," Novalee said.

His left hand, defective . . . useless, fingers twisted and curled toward his palm, lay in his lap like some long-owned geegaw . . . worthless, but too familiar to throw away. He offered his good hand—palsied, warted and scarred, discolored like bruised fruit—but good. Veins, intricate purple skeins, webbed across the back of his hand and his skin, cool and soft, felt like fine, creased silk. And when Novalee touched it, she heard the lines of a poem she had read.

> *. . . ancient as the world and older than the flow of*
> *human blood in human veins.*

For a moment, the words seemed to echo and Novalee thought she might have said them out loud.

"Daddy, look here," Moses said. "Look at Miss Americus Nation."

Purim Whitecotton's good eye narrowed as it found and focused on Americus. Then he tried to speak, tried to make his broken lips speak, but a sound somewhere back in his mouth, a strangled sound back of his tongue, was all he could manage. But Moses had learned his father's language, knew what he wanted, so he stepped closer and when he did, the old man reached up and put one thin trembling finger to Americus' cheek. She held very still, hardly seemed to breathe until he lowered his hand—and then she smiled at him.

Novalee turned toward the swoosh of the screen door as a tall woman in blue linen stepped onto the porch.

"Well, I declare," she said, "I didn't know our company was here."

"Novalee, I'd like you to meet my wife, Certain," Moses said.

Certain Whitecotton had a halo of silver hair, and copper-colored skin, unblemished except for a dusting of freckles across the bridge of her nose. When she smiled, her eyes, just a shade lighter than sage, caught the light and shimmered like clear glass splashed by rain.

She took Novalee's hand and closed it inside her own, then held it still as if they were sealing a promise.

"Moses been saying some nice things about you, Novalee. So nice, I thought you might be a fairy tale."

"I'm pleased to meet you."

Then Certain turned to Americus, still in Moses' arms. "So! Here's the lady who stole my husband's heart."

Americus was clearly happy to be at the center of their attention.

"Can't imagine how," Certain said. "Unless it's that smile spread from here to St. Louis."

Americus ducked her head, pressed her face into Moses' shoulder . . . a brief flirtation with shyness.

"Oh, yes. That's a powerful smile," Certain said.

"What smile?" Moses asked. "I never saw no smile."

"Novalee, has Moses offered you something to drink? We have cider."

"Thank you, but I'm not thirsty."

"Well, I know you two want to get out back, so I won't try to keep you here with small talk or cider." Though Certain seemed to be talking to Novalee and Moses, she was looking at Americus as she spoke. "But when you finish, we'll have us some pie and coffee and get better acquainted."

"Don't let her kid you, Novalee. She wants us to leave so she can get her hands on Americus."

"Me? Now who is it standing here acting like an old fool over that baby?"

"I was speaking truth and you know it."

"Moses, give me that child and get on out of here."

"Now Mother . . ."

Then it was over. Certain slipped Americus from Moses' arms and into her own. But as she did, as she and Moses touched, something passed between them . . . something dark and sad that made him lower his eyes and caused her to turn her face away, as if each could not bear to see the sorrow of the other—as if the handing over of a child could break their hearts.

Moses said, "Certain, are you . . ."

"We'll be fine," she said. "We'll be just fine."

"Are you sure?" Novalee asked. "She can be a handful sometimes 'cause she's teething right now and—"

"Don't you worry," Certain said as she settled into one of the easy chairs with Americus on her lap. "You all go out there and have fun. Father Whitecotton and I can manage this child just fine."

"You won't spoil her, will you, Mother?" Moses tried to sound playful again, but his voice was a little too flat.

"Not before you make it out back," Certain said, and though she smiled at him, the smile had pain in it.

"Out back" was a rough-hewn oak cabin some two hundred feet behind the house.

"This is where I was born," Moses said. "My father built it, more than sixty years ago."

The windows were covered with gingham curtains, and a harvest wreath of gourds and dried flowers hung on the door.

"It looks like a playhouse."

"Well, that's Certain's doing."

The front room looked bigger inside than Novalee had expected even though it warehoused the castoffs of earlier generations—coal oil lamps, a wooden wheelchair, quilting frames.

"Certain comes in here from time to time . . . airs the place out. Threatens to clean, but . . ."

Moses stepped through a doorway and into the old kitchen, now his darkroom. As Novalee followed his path through a maze of boxes, she spotted a rocking horse half hidden beneath the front window.

"Moses, do you and Certain have children?"

The cabin was absolutely still for several moments, then Novalee could hear Moses moving again, moving around in the darkroom, switching on lights, opening drawers.

"Never can lay hands on those scissors when I need 'em," he said.

Novalee tried again. "I said, do you and Certain—"

"Come on in here and you can see how I get set up."

Novalee knew then she had asked the wrong question.

There wasn't much "kitchen" left in the low-ceilinged room: a wall cabinet without any doors and a galvanized sink, stained and discolored. Nothing else to suggest the place where families had been fed, wounds doctored, babies bathed.

Now it was a darkroom. Work tables had been squeezed in, shelves shoved into corners. The cabinet was crammed with bottles, cans, boxes and jars. Long shallow pans covered tabletops and counters. And everywhere . . . photographs. Photographs hung from a clothesline stretched across the room. They leaned against books, stuck out of drawers, stood in files; were packed in boxes and tacked on walls.

"Now as soon as I find that developer, we'll be set," Moses said.

"Is it okay if I look through some of your pictures?"

"Sure." Moses began pawing through bottles in a box on the floor. "Wonder what I did with that fixer?"

Novalee picked up a stack of photographs on a table by the door, pictures taken on the steps of a church, black men in dark suits and broad-brimmed hats, women in spring dresses with tatted lace collars, children squinting into the sun, their hands clutching Easter baskets and Bibles.

Novalee picked up another handful of pictures from a narrow shelf that ran across one wall. These had been shot on a street she didn't recognize, a tired, dusty street with tired, dusty people. In one, a teenage boy hunkered outside a pool hall, his face pulled into a scowl. In another an old woman gazed with disinterest into the window of a cafe. And in another a little boy sitting on a curb, his face smeared with grime, watched a bony cat carry a dead bird across an empty street.

"These are good."

"What have you got there?"

Novalee held the pictures out for him to see.

"Shot those in Tangier, out in the western part of the state. Two, maybe three years ago."

As soon as she put those back on the shelf, she scooped up more. These pictures were older, many brittle and yellowed with age. She flipped through them quickly . . . a barbershop, a parade, some fences. She looked at hawks, horses and sunsets, then came to the last of them, the one on the bottom of the stack, a photograph in grainy black and white. Purim Whitecotton, strong and whole, feet firmly planted on the back of a flatbed truck, body straining to lift a hundred pounds of baled hay. Purim Whitecotton, muscles pushing against the sleeves of a stained white shirt, tendons corded across the backs of thick, broad hands. Purim Whitecotton, fierce dark eyes, eyes that would dare and resist, eyes that would be subdued by nothing except a tiny explosion inside his head when he would bend over eighty-three candles on an angel food cake.

And that's when she knew she was hooked! Even as Moses began showing her the way . . . as he stared into the pans of amber liquid . . . whispering to the images swimming just under the surface, urging them to life, Novalee knew.

Later, while Moses was cleaning up the last of it, and after she had wandered back into the other room, she stood beside the rocking horse beneath the window. It was handmade of pine with marbles for eyes and tufts of rope for a mane. Novalee put her hand on its head and set it rocking, and when she did, the only sound in the cabin was its rhythmic creaking. Then, from the darkroom, Moses' voice . . .

"We had Glory."

"What?"

"We had Glory. But we lost her when she was three."

Novalee put her hand on the horse, stilled its rocking.

"Certain got rid of the other stuff . . ." He turned on a tap in the darkroom, ran water into a basin. "Topper. Glory called him Topper—Hopalong Cassidy's horse." A cabinet door slammed. "See that mark on the back of its head? Between its ears?"

Novalee bent to examine the wood and found a tiny chip, right between the ears.

"Glory's front tooth made that. She fell and cracked her mouth, busted her lip."

Novalee rubbed her finger across the dent, a dent just about as wide as Americus' front tooth, her first.

"Glory cried. Cried, she said, 'cause she bit Topper." Moses turned off the water, then Novalee heard the ping of metal against glass. "We lost her in the spring. That spring. Drowned in Sticker Creek."

The cabin was quiet again.

"You can't see the creek from here, but it's down the hill . . . down below that pecan tree."

Novalee stepped to the front window and parted the gingham curtains.

"I carried her up the hill," he said. A gust of wind pushed against the branches of the tree and a single pecan fell near the trunk. "Certain saw me coming . . . ran out across the yard. Met me right there . . . to the side of the well-house."

Novalee knew Moses was looking out the darkroom window, looking at the spot by the well-house, seeing again what had happened there in another lifetime.

And then Novalee saw it, too . . . saw Certain slip her daughter out of Moses' arms and into her own . . . saw him lower his eyes and her turn her face away as if each could not bear to see the sorrow of the other . . . because the handing over of a child had caused their hearts to break.

Chapter Seventeen

NOVALEE FOUND THE ROLLEI at a flea market in McAlester, crammed in a box with cookbooks, bowling trophies and remnants of cotton ticking. Moses had told her it could take months to find one, but she'd gotten lucky.

She tried not to act excited when she saw it, remembering what Sister Husband had said.

"Never act like you want it, darlin'. Act like you wouldn't own it if they paid you. Tell them it's dirty, broken . . . a useless thing. Then make an offer."

The case looked like it had survived a battle, but just barely. The strap was broken and the top stitching had pulled loose, causing the leather to curl at the corners.

The camera didn't look quite as worn as the case, but it was dinged and scratched . . . streaked with something black and sticky. She removed the lens cover and blew at layers of dust, but it was too big a job for breath to handle.

The vendor pretended not to see Novalee while he faked interest in a plastic cuckoo clock that didn't work.

"This camera's filthy," she said, intent on following Sister's advice.

"Yep."

"Looks like it's broken, too."

"Nope."

"Don't know what in the world I'd do with it."

"Be me," he said, "I'd take some pictures."

"What do you want for it?"

"Askin' price is thirty, but I might go—"

Too fast, she blurted, "I'll give you thirty!"

Moses kept the camera for a week, repairing the shutter. He told Novalee he would need some time, but she drove out every day, hoping it would be ready.

When he did finally hand the Rollei over to her, it looked new—spit-polished, gleaming. And he'd also had the case repaired: the strap reattached and the seams stitched up. He'd used saddle soap to clean the leather, then rubbed it with wax until it was soft as kid.

The next morning, Novalee strapped Americus to her back and was on the street before eight. She took pictures of everything—the Rhode Island Reds in Dixie Mullins' backyard, Halloween jack-o-lanterns lined up on the Ortiz porch, Leona's scarlet mums that grew in clumps along her fence. Novalee shot Henry's calico cat asleep in the mailbox and got one of a mockingbird dive-bombing a squirrel.

She took pictures of children hurrying to school, juggling lunch boxes and books as they waded through mud over the tops of their shoes. She got shots of a bald-headed man waiting outside a barbershop beneath a sign that said, HAIRCUTS WHILE YOU WAIT. And she took several more of a large woman squeezed into a child's Star Wars bathrobe as she crawled out of her stalled car in a busy intersection.

That evening, as soon as she got off work, Novalee

skipped dinner and went at it again. At the cemetery she shot old headstones; at the park she photographed splintered merry-go-round horses and broken swings. She took pictures of trees, dead and bare, their branches and trunks blackened by a recent fire. She went downtown, took pictures of graffiti, a bumper sticker that said NO MORE BUMPER STICKERS . . . a cowboy boot, scuffed and dusty, standing alone in the middle of a street . . . and a Bible in a Dumpster, an indication, according to Sister Husband, that someone had gotten too confused.

Novalee took pictures of anything and anyone—all were fair game. Americus was her most accessible victim and certainly the least able to defend herself. Sister Husband didn't object to being a subject—as long as she had enough warning to suck in her stomach and take off her glasses. But Forney would have none of it and took to wearing his stocking cap again, so if Novalee caught him out in the open, with no place to hide, he could at least pull the cap down and cover his face, a practice that resulted in two dozen photos of a giant man with a brown knit head.

Novalee worked in Moses' darkroom every night, some nights until after the Whitecottons were all in bed. She worked until her eyes stung . . . until her fingers were stained, her skin chapped and raw . . . until her clothes, her hair, her skin smelled like fixer. And later, in her bed, she dreamed of taking pictures, the same pictures all over again.

The neighbors came often, each time she had new pictures to show. They praised her talent; they were proud of her work. And they brought her rolls of film—gifts, they said, for their friend, the artist.

They asked her to make pictures for them and they wanted to pay, begged her to name a price, but she wouldn't charge them. She took their pictures and loved doing it, pictures of their cocker spaniel puppies, their prize-winning hot rolls, the fresh dents in their fenders. She took pictures of their birthday parties, their anniversary celebrations, their piano recitals. She filmed the oldest Ortiz girl in her white communion dress, she took a picture of Leona's antique Victrola for her niece in New Jersey, she filmed an egg with three yolks, a grandbaby's footprint and a can of green beans with a worm inside for which Mr. Sprock was threatening to sue the Green Giant Corporation.

And the more pictures Novalee took and the more she developed, the more she wanted to learn about what she was doing. She studied photography magazines—*Camera & Darkroom* and the *Photo Review*. She made calls to photo labs in Sacramento, California, and wrote letters to Kodak in Rochester, New York. She asked Moses a thousand questions and remembered everything he said.

Forney brought her stacks of books and she read about Gordon Parks and William Henry Jackson. She studied the work of Dorothea Lange and Alfred Stieglitz, Ansel Adams and Margaret Bourke-White.

Once, on a rare weekend off, she drove the Toyota to Tulsa and went to a photo exhibit, her first. She wandered the rooms and halls of the gallery and wrote pages of notes, then talked to herself all the way home about what she had learned.

Then, after all the hours she spent learning . . . after hundreds of pictures, days and nights in a darkroom, questions about shutter speeds and sepia tones and light vibrations . . . after all that, Novalee discovered what was important to her about pictures of cats and children and merry-go-round horses . . . about girls in white dresses and old women tasting tea . . . about birthday dinners and anniversary kisses. What was important to her was knowing that at the moment she took a picture, she was seeing something in a way nobody else ever had.

On a crisp morning in late November, Novalee got up well before dawn, pulled on jeans and sweatshirt, grabbed a coat and her camera, then slipped out of the trailer as soundlessly as she could.

She was going to Rattlesnake Ridge ten miles east of town to film the sunrise. The ridge ran between two hills that Sister Husband called mountains, the Cottonmouth and the Diamondback, and she told stories of how they had gotten their names.

"Why, darlin', a boy I knew died the most horrible death up there on the Diamondback. They could hear him screaming all the way into town. When they brought him down, wasn't a spot on his body didn't have fang marks. Even got struck in the eyes. Counted near five hundred bites, so I was told."

Such stories gave Novalee goosebumps and bad dreams. She wouldn't think of going to Rattlesnake in warm weather, but they were far enough into the cold season that she wasn't worried about snakes.

After she parked the Toyota on the shoulder of Saw Mill Road, she took a flashlight from the car pocket, then climbed through a barbed wire fence enclosing a broad meadow smothered by an early morning fog.

A quarter-mile or so to the north, the flat land gave way, dropped ten or twelve feet to a low-water creek at the back of the meadow.

Novalee used a willow branch to measure the depth of the stream as she picked her way across the water on flat rocks and fallen trees. At its deepest, it was little more than two feet. She was almost across when something slapped at the water just inches from her feet, sending drops splattering against her pant legs. She aimed the beam of light toward the sound, but whatever it was left behind only ripples.

Just across the creek, the land rose sharply. The fog thinned as she began to climb. Pine needles crunched under her feet, making snapping sounds that caused her to stop once and look back, half expecting to see something behind her.

When she heard a rooster crow in the distance, she looked up to see the sky reddening in the east, so she picked up her pace, determined to be on the top before sunrise.

She liked the feel of her Rollei, still in the case, brushing against her hip as it swung from the strap over her shoulder. For a few moments, she enjoyed the fantasy of being a war correspondent climbing a mountain to get shots of a battle in the valley on the other side, a scene she remembered from an old war movie.

Though the morning was cool, by the time she was halfway up the mountain, she shed her jacket and tied it around her waist. Not only was she hot, she was also winded, an indication, she was sure, that even at eighteen, she was already growing old.

She stopped to catch her breath, but when she realized she no longer needed the flashlight, that there was enough morning light to see by, she began to climb again, her own private race with the sun.

She knew she didn't have much farther to go . . . could tell by looking down to the meadow below. Whenever Sister Husband talked about these hills and called them mountains, Novalee would tease and call them molehills.

She had, after all, lived with the Appalachians in her backyard. She knew what real mountains were—the only thing about Tennessee she missed.

She could hear the sounds of mysteries darting out of her way beneath the needles and dry leaves . . . insects, field mice, tree frogs . . . but they moved too fast for her to see. Louder sounds from farther away—sounds of animals working through the trees and underbrush—were most likely squirrels and raccoons, but she liked to imagine they were deer.

When she broke through the last tree line before the top, she had a clear view of the ridge that stretched for more than a mile between the two hills. As she studied the last of the climb before her, trying to decide the best way to go, movement caught her eye, something running along the ridge, no more than a blur. Whatever she saw had appeared and disappeared so fast, she wasn't sure she had seen anything at all, but her heart raced as she fumbled at the buckles on her camera case.

She had just removed the lens cover when she saw it again, racing across the clearing between an outcropping of rock and a stand of young pines. She looked down to adjust the focus on the camera, looked down for only a split second, but by the time she found the ridge again in the viewfinder, whatever it was had disappeared.

A deer, she thought, though the shape was not quite right. A coyote, maybe . . . or even a bobcat, but from her distance and in the half-light, she couldn't be sure.

She had a decision to make. She could stay where she was, gamble that she might get some shots, deer or not, or she could give up and push hard for the top of the ridge so she could shoot the sunrise she came for. The decision was easy.

She scanned the ridge through the viewfinder, set the focus, found the angle she wanted and waited. Watched and waited until she saw it again . . . still running. She snapped, turned the crank, snapped again . . . watched it cross treeless ground, then saw what seemed impossible to see. So sure it wasn't what she thought, she looked up, needed to see it with her eyes, as if the camera had distorted the sight. So she looked up, had to look at it directly because it wasn't a deer—not coyote, not bobcat—but a boy. A naked boy running across Rattlesnake Ridge.

And at that moment the first rays of the sun just cleared the ridge to form a golden luminous arc and, in the middle of it, was a naked boy running . . . a lean brown boy named Benny Goodluck who was running like the wind.

Chapter Eighteen

THE FIRST CHRISTMAS Novalee could remember, she was five. She and Momma Nell were living in a trailer not far from the Clinch River with a red-headed man called Pike. The trailer set down in a bog that sucked at tricycle wheels and dog paws even without rain. But after three days and nights of it, mailboxes and fences had nearly disappeared.

On Christmas Eve, sometime after midnight, the rain washed out an earthen dam at Sharp's Chapel, a half-mile away. Momma Nell and Pike were gone, had been gone for two days and nights, and Novalee was asleep when the water started rising. The next morning when she crawled out of bed, their scrawny aluminum Christmas tree and two lengths of red plastic garland floated down the hallway toward her like spiny sea creatures adrift in strange seas.

Novalee couldn't remember much about other Christmas mornings. The first few years after Momma Nell left with Fred, the years of foster homes and state homes and Baptist homes, she had asked department store Santas to bring her Mickey Mouse watches and puppies, drum sets and

Momma Nell, but it didn't take long to discover that Santas didn't come to Tennessee on Christmas mornings and mommas didn't either.

But this Christmas, the first one for Americus, was going to be different. This one was going to be perfect, just like the pictures in magazines . . . gifts tied in silver ribbon, a turkey and pumpkin pies, candy canes, mistletoe . . . and the most perfect Christmas tree in Oklahoma.

The second Saturday in December, Novalee loaded Americus and Forney into the pickup and headed to the lake. They walked "eight thousand meters over savage terrain and uninhabitable topography," according to Forney, and looked at "three hundred dog-eared, bald-topped, antigogglin, butt-heavy trees," according to Novalee. So, with Americus beginning to sniffle and Forney complaining about a bruised metatarsus, Novalee called off the search and they went home empty-handed.

The next Saturday, Americus got a reprieve because of a cold, but Forney was dragged out at just after six and they went at it again.

"Perhaps we should take a different approach today," Forney said.

"I think we'll start north of Shiner Creek."

"No, that's not what I mean."

"We can work our way around to the bridge."

"I mean let's start with a list." Forney pulled a small notebook and a pencil from his pocket. "A list of specifications."

"We could go out to Catfish Bay."

"A statement of particulars."

"Or Cemetery Road, toward the interstate."

"For instance," Forney said, opening the notebook. "What about height? Over four feet? Under six?"

"Sister said she saw a stand of pines at Garners Point."

"Genus." Forney licked the pencil lead. "*Homolepis? Veitchi? Cephalonica?*"

Novalee slowed, then steered the Toyota onto the shoulder of the road. "If you'll get the shovel, I'll—"

"A statement of particulars, Novalee," Forney cried out in desperation.

"Oh, Forney," she said, her tone patient, her explanation logical, "I'll know it when I see it."

Forney groaned, Novalee grinned—and they crawled out of the pickup.

"Come on, Forney."

"Novalee, it's a parasite."

"But it's a tradition."

"It's a parasite! And you expect people to stand under it and kiss?"

"Yes! That's what people do with mistletoe."

"Why not hang up some kudzu . . . or maybe some bagworms."

"Please?"

"Novalee, that tree's forty feet tall."

"It is not! Thirty, maybe."

"I didn't even climb trees when I was a kid."

"What's wrong, Forney? You too old?"

She had him then. Grumbling, he jumped, grabbed a branch above his head, then pulled himself up with a strength that surprised her.

She had never asked him his age. Hadn't even guessed. But sometimes when she was reading, she'd look up, unexpectedly, and find him watching her. And in that second just before he would look away to pretend he hadn't seen her, he would look boyish . . . embarrassed and shy. At other times, in the shadows of the library, when sharp sounds from upstairs caused him to look up, lines cutting across his forehead, something dark behind his eyes, he would look suddenly weary and old . . . older than Novalee wanted him to be.

A branch cracked and pieces of bark showered down on Novalee.

"Forney, be careful!"

"I used to have nightmares about this kind of thing. I'd be stuck at the top of a skyscraper or a mountain—or in a fifty-foot oak tree."

"That tree's growing, isn't it?"

Forney was halfway up, moving cautiously, staying close to the trunk.

"Hey," Novalee called, "there's a dead branch right over your left shoulder. Looks like crown gall got it. Why don't you pull that down."

"Novalee, tree surgeon was not one of my career choices."

"What was?"

"Ventriloquist. Shepherd."

"Librarian."

"I never wanted to be a librarian."

"Really?"

"I wanted to be a teacher." Forney snapped the dead branch off, then looked down to make sure it would fall clear of Novalee. "History teacher. But I never finished college."

"Why not?"

"Well, when my father died, I came back home. By then, my sister was . . . too sick, so I stayed."

"Forney, what happened to your sister?"

"Oh, I'm not sure. She was twenty when I was born, so I was just a kid when she . . . when she started drinking. I was ten, I guess, when my father sent her away the first time. To a sanatorium somewhere in the East . . ."

Forney was close enough to the mistletoe that, by stretching, he could almost reach it.

"Then, just after I went off to school, he sent her away again, a place in Illinois. By then, I knew she was an alcoholic, but we never used that term in our house. My sister had 'an indelicate condition.'"

Forney tore loose a handful of mistletoe and let it fall.

"Anyway, when my father died, my sister asked me never to send her away again."

"Forney, will she ever . . . do you think . . ."

"Here comes the last of it," he said as he yanked the rest of the mistletoe from the top of the tree and flung it to the ground.

They stopped for lunch when they reached the bridge. Novalee had fixed bologna sandwiches and a jar of Kool-Aid, but she'd forgotten the paper cups, so they shared the jar.

"Hope you like mustard. We were out of mayonnaise."

"Anything to keep up my strength." Forney rubbed at a sore knee. "This quest of yours for the perfect tree might kill me."

"We'll find it. Just be patient."

"Patient?" Forney looked at his watch. "You know how long we've been at this?"

"We just haven't seen it yet."

"I thought that spruce looked nice. The one with—"

"The one with a bare spot halfway up the trunk?"

"Well, the cedar . . ."

"Too short."

"Novalee, what is it about this tree? Tell me."

"I never had a real tree before."

"What do you mean 'a real tree'?"

"Real. Living. Not dead, not plastic, not cardboard."

Forney smiled then at an old memory. "When I was in grade school, third, maybe fourth grade, we made Christmas trees out of egg cartons. Ugliest things. I cried because my father wouldn't let me put one on our mantel."

"One year when I was in the McMinn County Home, we made a tree out of coat hangers and aluminum foil."

"It's a wonder you weren't struck by lightning."

Novalee said, "I'll tell you about the funniest tree I ever had." She took a drink from the Kool-Aid jar, then handed it to Forney. "I was eight, living with Grandma Burgess, and—"

"You've never mentioned your grandmother before."

"Oh, she wasn't my real grandma. I don't know if I ever had a real grandma. Anyway, the way I came to live with her was that right after Momma Nell went away, I stayed with a family there in the trailer park—three girls about my age, and Virgie, their mother. She'd been real nice to me, let me stay for supper a few times and took me with them to a movie once. So when Momma Nell left, I lived with them for the rest of the school year.

"But then, Virgie got transferred to Memphis, so she moved me in with her grandmother, Grandma Burgess. She had a little silver trailer out on the edge of town. Kept chickens and a cow, had a garden. Sort of like a farm."

Novalee reached into the picnic sack and pulled out another sandwich. "I brought you two."

"Thanks." Forney took the sandwich, then handed Novalee the Kool-Aid jar. "So how long were you with her?"

"Couple of years. It wasn't a bad place to live, and

Grandma Burgess was a sweet old woman, but she had spells, so—"

"Spells? What do you mean?"

"Well, she just didn't always know what was going on. Like, she'd take off all her clothes, then go out to milk the cow. Sometimes, she'd eat chicken feed, stuff like that."

Forney shook his head.

"She got a check of some kind every month, but once in a while, she'd have one of her spells—cash her check, then give the money away . . . or she'd buy something crazy. Once she bought a trampoline . . . just all kinds of weird things. A trumpet. A wedding dress. She'd hate it later, when she came to her senses, but . . .

"Anyway, when Christmas came, that first year we were together, we made all kinds of plans. She was going to buy me a bicycle and I was going to get her a heating pad. But right after she got her December check, she had one of her spells and ended up spending all the money on a forklift. An old Clark Clipper."

Forney, mesmerized by Novalee's story, put his sandwich on the ground.

"By the time Christmas came, we were living on milk and eggs and we'd killed two of her chickens. And there wasn't a bicycle or a heating pad or a tree. Grandma Burgess felt awful about spending all the money. So, you know what she did?"

Forney shook his head.

"She got some green paint she had out in a shed and she painted a Christmas tree on the living room wall. A big tree!" Novalee stood up and stretched her hand over her head. "From the floor to the ceiling. We made some decorations and taped them on." She shrugged. "That was our tree."

"My God. And you were eight? An eight-year-old kid expecting a bicycle and—"

"Well, I got something better than a bicycle." She smiled. "She gave me the forklift."

Novalee rummaged in the sack. "You want some peanut butter cookies?"

They had, by Forney's account, walked eight miles along the mill road . . . over fences, across cattle guards, up the landfill, along the creek, and it was late afternoon when Novalee suddenly stopped.

"That's it, Forney," she said. She pointed to a stand of half-dead pecan trees—but at their edge was a blue spruce, a spruce with a straight trunk, full boughs, and "a tip made for an angel."

"It's perfect," Novalee said.

And Forney knew she was right.

By the time he dug up the spruce, carried it back and loaded it into the pickup, the light was fading. When they got back to town and Novalee turned down Evergreen, it was dark, but the street was bright with color.

Henry and Leona had strung lights around the eaves of their duplex—green ones on his side, red on hers. Dixie Mullins' yard, bathed in an iridescent glow from sack candles that lined her sidewalk, looked shimmery, like silver. The nativity scene on the front porch of the Ortiz trailer was lit by a spotlight Mr. Ortiz had rigged up in an oak tree at the edge of the street.

There were more lights at the end of the block, bright swirling lights flashing red and blue like neon in the street in front of Sister Husband's trailer.

Novalee's mouth went dry and her legs began to tremble. She mashed on the gas and the Toyota shot across the rock garden at the edge of Dixie's drive, then bounced across the gully that ran beside the Ortiz sidewalk.

"Novalee," Forney called, but she had already thrown the door open and tumbled out, then was up, running . . . jumping across the rose garden and stumbling into the branches of the buckeye . . . racing past the police cars parked in the driveway, their red and blue lights making clicking sounds as they turned, splashing Novalee's face with color.

She was flying up the steps when Sister rushed out the door, her face pulled into hard lines of hurt.

"Darlin', I don't know how—"

"Sister, what's—"

"No more than turned around—"

"But how could—"

"Gone, Novalee."

"Oh, God—"

"Gone."

"No!"

"Americus is gone."

Chapter Nineteen

THE POLICEMAN who asked the questions had seen Novalee before. He had been on duty the night Americus was born, had been the first one to arrive at Wal-Mart after the alarm was called in.

"And the front door was unlocked?" he asked.

"Yes, but I just went out to the shed," Sister explained. "Wasn't gone more'n a few minutes. Went to get a box of Christmas decorations, seeing as how Novalee and Forney were bringing a tree."

"So whoever took the baby came in the front and went out the front."

"Had to. I would've seen 'em if they'd come in the back. Shed's not twenty feet away from the back door."

"But when you came back in . . ."

"She was gone." Sister's voice broke then and she grabbed Novalee's hand. "Oh, darlin'."

"Was anything else missing? Jewelry? Money?"

"No, I don't have nothing except for my wheat pennies,

right there on the sideboard." Sister pointed to a jar filled with coins.

"Did you notice anything unusual today? Anyone strange in the neighborhood? A car you didn't recognize? Anything like that?"

"No. Not that I can remember."

The policeman turned to Novalee, giving her a stiff smile. "Miss Nation, will you describe your little girl for me?"

"I have lots of pictures."

"Good. But I'm going to need a written description, too."

"Well, she weighs nineteen pounds. She has green eyes and light brown hair that grows . . . like this." Novalee blinked back tears as she touched her own hairline to illustrate. "In a widow's peak."

"How old is she?"

"Seven months," she said. "Seven." And her mouth burned with a bitter taste, the taste of something scorched and dry. She had been hovering over Americus for days trying to get past that seven, then had risked it all for a Christmas tree.

The policeman wrote down everything Novalee said in a small notebook.

"Is there anyone you can think of who might have taken your daughter?"

Novalee squinted as if she were trying to "see" the question, to bring it into focus.

"Anyone who might be mad at you," he said, "or jealous. Someone who might have a score to settle?"

"No." Novalee bit at her lip. "No, I can't think of anyone."

"Miss Nation, you think there could be any connection between this and your baby being born at Wal-Mart?"

"What do you mean?"

"Well, it was all over the news . . . on the TV, in the papers. Lots of people knew about it. And I suppose some of them wrote to you? Called you on the phone?"

"Yes. They did."

"Did you hear anything strange? A threat of any kind? I mean, there are some real crazies out there."

"I got a few letters like that. People who said they wished I'd died. Me . . . and Americus, too."

Novalee was gripped by a sudden chill that left her weak and trembling. Forney picked up an afghan from the couch and put it around her shoulders.

"Did you keep any of those letters?" the policeman asked.

"No, not the mean ones. I didn't keep those."

"Do you remember any of the names? The signatures on those letters?"

"They weren't signed."

"So you can't think of anyone who might want to hurt you or maybe just scare you by taking your daughter."

Novalee shook her head.

"How about the baby's father?"

"Who?"

"Your baby's father."

The words came spinning at her. "Baby's father." Novalee was stunned to realize that she had never, not once since Americus was born, let herself think of Willy Jack as "the baby's father."

"Have you seen him?" the policeman asked.

"No."

"Any idea where he is?"

"I don't know. California, I guess."

"You know where we can reach his family?"

"He has a cousin in Bakersfield. And his mother lives in Tellico Plains, in Tennessee. But that's all I know."

"And what's his name . . . the father?"

"Willy Jack Pickens," she said. Then she began to tremble again.

While the police poked around outside, their flashlight beams crisscrossing the yard, neighbors slipped into the trailer, bringing sandwiches and pitchers of spiced tea. They spoke quietly and dabbed at red eyes as they squeezed Novalee's shoulder and patted Sister Husband's hand.

The oldest Ortiz girl brought Novalee dried rose petals from her communion corsage while her two younger sisters cried almost soundlessly as they sat on Forney's lap. Mr. Ortiz prayed in Spanish while his wife worried at a rosary, shaking her head in sad disbelief. Henry questioned everybody about a blue Ford he'd seen earlier in the day; Leona read a poem on faith that she had cut from an Ann Landers column. Dixie Mullins said she had had a premonition because of a conversation with her dead husband earlier in the week.

They tried to tempt Novalee to eat and encouraged her to rest. They offered help with money and the promise of more food, but they knew that what Novalee needed was something they couldn't give, so, one by one, they slipped outside to stand in the yard and wait.

Sister put on another pot of coffee, the third of the night. Novalee handed a pad and pen to Forney.

"Will you make the list? I'm too shaky to write."

"Sure."

"Okay," Novalee said as she pulled the afghan tight

around her shoulders. "There's a woman at work doesn't like me much. She wanted the job I've got. But I really don't think she'd take Americus. She's close to retirement. Besides, she teaches Sunday School."

"Darlin', old women who teach Sunday School got just as much meanness in 'em as the rest of us, I'm afraid," Sister Husband offered.

"The policeman said to write down anybody who might be trying to get even with you," Forney said.

"All right. Her name's Snooks Lancaster."

Forney wrote the name on the pad Novalee had given him.

"Now. Let's see. There was a guy named Buster Harding stole a waffle iron from a cafe where I worked once. Said he was going to get me because I told the boss and got him fired. But that was almost four years ago. I can't imagine Buster would know where I am now."

"You never know," Sister said. "All that publicity, he could've seen you on the TV."

"Can you think of anyone else here in town, anyone you've met since you've been here?" Forney lowered his eyes, pretending to study the two names on the list. "Like that guy you go out with."

"Troy Moffatt? I don't go out with him anymore."

"He still calls here sometimes," Sister said. "Won't leave his name, but I know his voice."

"Would he have something against you, Novalee?"

"Well, he might, but . . ."

"Then maybe I'd better add his name to the list."

"Okay, but I don't know any reason he'd take Americus. Truth is, I don't know why anyone would."

* * *

When the Gremlin parked in Sister's driveway, the policemen clustered near the street eyed Lexie suspiciously until one of them recognized her as she climbed out of the car.

She charged across the yard and onto the porch, then stopped just short of the door. Taking a deep breath, she tried to strip the concern from her face, but as she walked in and wrapped Novalee in her arms, she couldn't hide the fear in her voice.

"Have you heard anything yet?"

Novalee shook her head. "Not a word.

"How long has she been gone?"

"Long enough to be scared. Long enough to be sick. Or hurt."

"Do you know—"

"I don't know anything, Lexie. I don't know where she is or who she's with. I don't know if she's cold, if she's hungry."

"I'll bet she's fine, honey." Lexie twisted her lips into a smile that felt wired to her mouth, but it was the best she could manage. "I'll bet whoever has her is taking good care of her."

"You do?"

"Yeah, 'cause the woman who took her—"

"A woman? You think a woman took Americus?"

"Well, the police think so, I guess. They got everyone at the hospital going through admission records."

"What for?"

"They're looking at OB-GYN admissions. Every woman who's miscarried or still-birthed a baby."

"But lots of women miscarry without going to a hospital. And even if she did, there must be—"

"They're gonna find her, Novalee. I know they're gonna find her."

* * *

Sister had called Mr. Sprock shortly after the police left, but he was at the pool hall playing moon until ten-thirty. When she did reach him, he came right on over.

He kissed them all when he arrived, even Forney, and his eyes reddened every time someone spoke Americus' name. He carried a handkerchief, kept it near his mouth and talked only in whispers.

He took over jobs wherever he found them—emptied the trash, kept the coffee brewing, wiped up crumbs and swiped at coffee rings. When Forney said they needed a calendar, Mr. Sprock took one from the wall and spread it out before them at the kitchen table.

"Let's see," Sister said. "I delivered one Welcome Wagon basket on Monday morning, before Novalee went to work. Then I worked at the IGA passing out cheese puffs on Wednesday."

"So you were home the rest of the week?" Forney asked.

"Oh, I went to my AA meeting on Thursday night."

"Anyone there who might have some grudge against you?"

"At AA?"

"Someone who would want to hurt you for some reason?"

"No, Forney. We're alcoholics. We're generally satisfied just to hurt ourselves."

Forney considered that for a moment, then he nodded. "Let's go through the week and try to figure out who came here, to the trailer."

"Okay. On Monday afternoon that Douglas boy with the gas company came to check the furnace."

"Would he be a suspect?"

"Oh, no. I've known him all his life. Went to school with his granddaddy. They're good people."

"Good people," Mr. Sprock whispered.

"I was here on Tuesday with the kids," Lexie said.

"That's right, and Dixie Mullins came right after you left. Brought over some sourdough bread."

"Sister, how about door-to-door salesmen, that sort of thing."

"No. I get some of the school kids selling Girl Scout cookies, or candy for the band, but not here lately. Jehovah's Witnesses came by—no, that was last week, or the week before. I can't remember."

"Anyone else?"

"Well, Mr. Sprock came to me on Tuesday evening, while Novalee and the baby were at Lexie's for supper."

Mr. Sprock smiled a sad smile and stroked Sister's hand. "Tuesday evening," he whispered.

"I'm afraid that's it, Forney. No one very dangerous, I guess."

"You're right." Forney leaned back and ran his hands through his hair. "I just hoped you might recall someone . . . a stranger . . . a phone call . . ."

"Forney!" Sister yelled, then slapped her hand on the table. "That woman!"

When Forney jumped up, his chair turned over backward and tumbled to the floor. "What woman?"

"I knew it," Lexie hollered. "I knew it was a woman."

Novalee came running from the bathroom, wide-eyed and pale.

"What happened?" she screamed.

"A woman came in to use the phone."

"When?"

"Yesterday. No, the day before. Said her car broke down and she needed to call her husband."

"Can you describe her?"

"She was about as tall as me, a little heavy. But I can't really say what she looked like. She wore a scarf and dark glasses. Said she'd just had cataract surgery."

"Does she live around here?"

"Have you ever seen her before?"

"I . . . I don't know. Something about her seemed familiar, but I can't say. She just used the phone, then she left."

"Did you see her car? Did you see where she was parked?"

"No. Just as she walked out, Americus woke up from her nap and I went back to get her out of bed."

Mr. Sprock dabbed at his eyes when Sister said, "Americus."

"Oh, Forney. I did a bad thing letting her in here, didn't I?"

"No, Sister. You couldn't know."

"You couldn't know," Mr. Sprock whispered.

"Besides," Forney said, "we don't know if she had anything to do with this."

"She did," Sister said. "I just know she did."

After the police had come and gone a second time, Novalee was in the bathroom, sick again. The policeman had explained that without a description of the car or more details about the woman, they weren't much further along then they were before.

When Novalee came dragging back to the kitchen, Sister made her drink a cup of comfrey tea, then insisted she rest for a while. But she felt worse on her bed when she was still. Her heart raced and her legs twitched and her head felt like it was caught in a vise.

As she crawled out of bed, she could hear Forney and Sister and Lexie trying to be quiet in the other room.

Novalee opened the top drawer of a chest where she kept Americus' clothes—stacks of gowns and undershirts, socks rolled into pairs. She lifted out a white gown printed with clowns and held it to her face.

She couldn't stop thinking about the description she had given the policeman. Americus—her weight, the color of her hair, her eyes. But he didn't know about the smacking sounds she made when she was hungry. Or the way she closed her eyes when she laughed. He didn't know about the mole in the bend of her knee and the tiny cut on the pad of her thumb put there by Henry's cat, Patches.

Novalee refolded the gown and put it back in the drawer, then picked up a basket of diapers fresh from the line and stacked them on top of the chest. She wondered if Americus had been changed, wondered if she'd had her evening bottle, wondered . . .

Novalee pulled down the window shade just above the baby bed, then smoothed the blue blanket and fluffed the pillow—and then she saw the Bible. A small Bible with a silver gray cover just under the satin edge of the blanket.

She exploded into the living room. "Sister! This isn't your Bible. It can't be yours, but I—"

"No, it's not!"

"I found it in the baby bed."

"I don't own a Bible with a cover like that."

"Then who put it there? How did . . ."

"It's hers! Novalee, it's hers!"

"Whose?"

"The woman who came in to use the phone! I know who she is!"

"Sister . . ."

"She came here. She and a man, right after you got out of the hospital. Said they came from Mississippi to bring you the word of God. They wanted to see Americus, too, but I sent them away. And they had Bibles with silver covers. Just like that!"

Chapter Twenty

JUST AFTER THREE in the morning, Novalee went to the kitchen, put her coffee cup in the sink, then grabbed the keys to the Toyota from the hook beside the door.

She had just called the police station again, her third call in an hour. On her first, she learned they were still waiting for some response to the inquiries to Midnight, Mississippi. During the second call, she found out that a man and woman driving a Ford with Mississippi plates had stayed for two days at the Wayside Inn, a motel west of town. And on the third call, her last, a policeman told her the Mississippi couple had checked out earlier in the day.

Forney slumped in a straight-backed chair, roused from half-sleep when Novalee walked into the living room. "Novalee, what . . ."

"I can't sit here, Forney. I can't just sit here and wait."

"What do you want to do?"

"I don't know! Drive around. Ask some questions. Do something!"

"All right. Let's go."

Mr. Sprock, folded into the recliner and covered with a quilt, mumbled softly in his sleep, a word that sounded like "sundown." Sister, huddled into a corner of the couch, flinched when Novalee touched her shoulder, then waved her hand through the air as if to push away sleep.

"Yes, darlin'. I'm awake."

"Sister, me and Forney are going to go out and look around. Maybe stop by the police station."

"Where's Lexie?"

"I made her go home. No sense in her paying a sitter all night." Novalee smoothed Sister's skirt. "Will you be okay while we're gone?"

"I'll be just fine," Sister said as she patted Novalee's hand. "Mr. Sprock will be here with me. We'll be here by the phone. You call if you need us, you hear?"

Novalee nodded, kissed Sister on the cheek, then slipped out the door.

The night air was cold and Novalee, still wrapped in the afghan, pulled it up around her neck as she slid inside the truck.

"Where do you want to start?" Forney said as he backed the Toyota out of the drive.

"Let's go out to that motel."

"The Wayside?"

"I know the police have been there, but I want to see for myself."

The Toyota was the only vehicle on the street until Forney turned onto Commerce where they saw one more, the town's lone taxi. The car was an old Dodge Charger and the driver, a Comanche woman name Martha Watchtaker, had been driving it since 1974. Forney waved when they passed, but Novalee turned to stare, wondering if there could be a seven-month-old baby hidden inside.

A few blocks later, when Forney saw a police car in front of the twenty-four-hour Get N Go, he pulled in and parked beside it. They could see the policeman inside the store at the counter, smoking a cigarette and drinking coffee.

"You want to wait out here?" Forney asked. "I'm going to talk to him."

"I'm coming, too."

The policeman, a heavyset man near fifty, smiled when they walked in. "Forney, what're you doing out this time of the morning?"

Forney turned and ushered Novalee to his side. "Gene, this is Novalee Nation, mother of the baby that's . . . uh, missing."

"Ma'am." Gene ducked his head. "Sure sorry about your trouble."

Novalee nodded.

"Can you tell us anything, Gene?" Forney asked. "Anything at all?"

"I can't, Forney. Just came from the station. They're keeping the lines to Mississippi hot, but nothing yet."

"Well, just thought I'd check."

The clerk, a baby-faced boy wearing a heavy turquoise earring, leaned across the counter and smiled. "Y'all want a cup of coffee? Fresh pot. And it's on the house."

Novalee shook her head, but Forney said he'd have a cup.

While the boy poured the coffee, Novalee stepped up to the counter. "I was wondering," she said, "if anyone had come in to buy things for a baby. Things like diapers, bottles . . . maybe a pacifier or a teething ring. Stuff like that."

"No one I didn't recognize," the boy said. "I know all the girls here in the neighborhood who's got babies and they're the only ones in tonight for things like that."

"Ma'am," the policeman said. "We been checking since

the call came in this evening. Every store in town. Even the clerks who'd already finished their shifts and gone on home. We checked out all the drugstores, too. And the Wal-Mart. But I don't blame you for thinking about it. I'd do the same thing."

Novalee nodded, then headed for the door.

"Forney, how's Mary Elizabeth gettin' along?" the policeman asked.

"She's just about the same, Gene."

"Well, give her my best."

"I will."

"And ma'am? We'll let you know the minute we hear a word."

"Thank you."

When Novalee climbed back in the pickup, she was shivering.

"You want to wait inside while the heater warms up?"

"No. I'm okay."

Forney headed west, and a mile later, when they passed Wal-Mart, Novalee craned her neck staring at it.

"What do you see?"

"A car over there."

Forney pulled in and drove across the lot toward the car parked in a dark corner. He slowed as they neared it, a blue Ford, backed up to a retaining wall.

The lights of the Toyota swept across the Ford's windshield as Forney pulled up in front of it and parked.

"Novalee, you stay here. Okay?"

"Okay." Her voice sounded pinched and thin.

Forney got out, approached the car, then began to circle it. He walked to the back, ducked down and disappeared. Novalee opened her door and started to step out. Suddenly,

Forney popped back up, went to the far side of the Ford, pressed his face to the window and peered inside.

Moments later, he stepped away, then hurried back to the Toyota and climbed back in.

"Oklahoma tag," he said. "And it's empty. Nothing inside but a couple of boxes."

Novalee made a sound as if all the air had just been sucked out of her.

"It's got a flat, right rear. That's probably why it's out here, someone without a spare."

As Forney pulled away and headed the Toyota back toward the street, Novalee slumped like she'd been hit and let her head fall back against the seat.

Closer to town, they passed the Risen Life Church where a life-sized nativity scene was lit by spotlights. Just beyond the church the Kiwanis Club had set up a Christmas tree lot. Novalee couldn't believe that only hours earlier she and Forney had been out looking for a tree. It seemed to her that days, weeks . . . a lifetime had passed since then.

Minutes later, Forney turned onto Main Street, absolutely deserted, but bright with Christmas lights. Lamp posts had been transformed into candy canes, and plastic trains trimmed in red garland stretched across the intersections.

"I brought Americus here the other night to see the trains, Forney."

"I'll bet she liked that."

"You won't believe this, but when I said, 'choo choo,' and pointed up there to the engine, she made the sound of a train whistle."

Forney cut his eyes at Novalee and clicked his tongue, a teasing accusation.

"No lie!" she said. "I swear."

"Novalee . . ."

"She did. Like this." Novalee took a deep breath and filled her cheeks with air. But instead of the sound of a whistle, a long mournful wail spilled from her lips.

Forney slammed on the brakes, stopped the Toyota in the middle of the street, then reached for her.

"I'm so afraid," she said, but her voice was torn, ripped by powerful sobs that shook her body.

She slipped her arms around his shoulders, pressed her face into his neck. He cupped her head in one hand, circled her back with the other . . . and they held together and cried.

The vacancy sign was lit at the Wayside Inn, a squat two-story building. They circled the parking lot three times, but the closest they could find to a Ford from Mississippi was a Mazda with Georgia plates.

When they finally parked and went inside, the night clerk, an elderly man asleep on a couch in the lobby, couldn't help them at all. He hadn't come on until ten, hours after the Mississippi couple had checked out.

"Can't you tell us what they looked like?" Novalee asked.

"I never seen 'em. I been off for over a week, down with the flu. Tonight's my first night back."

"How about their car? Someone saw it, someone said it was here."

"Well, that was probably Norvell. He's been workin' my shift while I been gone."

"Where is he?"

"Lives over to Sallisaw, I think, but—"

"Is Norvell his last name?"

"Can't rightly say. He hadn't been here but a few weeks."

"But there has to be some way we can—"

"Girl, I sure do wish I could help you, but I just don't know how I can. That's what I told them police. Now they went and found Norvell, so I was told. Maybe he had somethin' to say."

Forney took Novalee's arm and led her outside. "Why don't we go down to the police station? See what this Norvell had to say."

"Sure, that's a good idea," she said, but without enthusiasm.

As Forney pulled back onto Main, they heard a siren in the distance, growing louder as the flashing lights came up fast behind them. Forney slowed and stayed well into the right lane until the police passed. Then, at the intersection of Main and Roosevelt, a second police car raced by.

"Wonder what's going on?" Forney asked. "Might have had a wreck out on the interstate."

When a third police car sped around the Toyota, Forney hit the gas and took off behind it.

"Forney?"

"I don't know, Novalee. I don't know. But we're going to find out."

When they topped the hill just west of the Wal-Mart, they could see flashing lights from all three police cars parked on the lawn and in the driveway of the Risen Life Church.

Forney wheeled in and slammed the Toyota to a sudden stop.

"Novalee, I don't know if this has anything to do with Americus, but—"

"Look! Look, Forney!"

But by then, she was out of the truck and running toward the church, running to the nativity scene where the three policemen were converging as they raced past plastic camels and goats, darted between donkeys and sheep, pushed back angels and shoved aside the wooden Joseph and Mary . . . jostled their way into the heart of the stable to bend over the crib, to kneel by the manger, where, from a bed of straw, one tiny fist was flailing at the air.

Halfway across the lawn, Novalee fell, went down on one knee, pulled herself up, then gasping, ran on . . . pushed her way through the policemen . . . and stared down into the face of her baby, crying in the manger.

"Highway Patrol saw the Mississippi plate. Stopped them over in Adair County, on the Arkansas line.

Americus, her body shuddering with cold and terror, had cried herself tearless. And though her breath convulsed for air, she sobbed almost without sound.

"Admitted they took her. Said they left her here, right here in this manger.

Novalee scooped Americus into her arms and pressed her to her chest, one heart pounding against another.

"Said God told 'em to do it. Told 'em to take her to a church . . .

Americus, warming, curling into familiar flesh, finding comfort in some old knowing of smell and voice, hiccoughed air and snuffled breath . . . testing safety.

"Said God told 'em to take her to a church and baptize her. And that's what they did. They baptized this baby!"

Forney stepped over Mary and around a fallen angel, then made his way into the stable and to Novalee's side. He tried to speak, but could find no sound, so, instead, he bent and kissed Americus, tasting straw and tears and lips . . . as she tested happiness again.

Chapter Twenty-One

WHEN THE GREYHOUND pulled into the station, Willy Jack was the first one out. He grabbed Finny's suitcase and the Martin, then flagged a taxi. His pocket was full of Claire's money and he'd had enough of buses to last a while.

Willy Jack didn't realize it then, but Claire Hudson had finally sent her Finny to Nashville, the place she knew he belonged.

The taxi driver delivered Willy Jack to the Plantation Hotel where he picked up a hooker in blue spandex and steered her to his room.

He spent the next three days and nights forgetting about prison, but it took some Wild Turkey and woolly women to get it done.

On the fourth morning, when Willy Jack slipped out the service entrance of the Plantation, he left behind a sleeping whore and a hotel bill of over three hundred dollars, but he took with him a headache, a pain in his gut and a dose of clap he wouldn't know about for another week.

When he checked into a Budget Inn a few hours later, he

decided it was time to get his career off the ground. He uncorked a new fifth of Turkey, tuned up the Martin, then ran through several songs he would play at auditions, concentrating on "The Beat of a Heart," the song he had written in prison.

He had studied the videotapes Claire had supplied, concert performances by Waylon Jennings and Willie Nelson, Grand Ole Opry films with Chet Atkins and Roy Clark, and TV clips of Johnny Cash and George Strait. And after Claire bought the Walkman, Willy Jack kept tapes playing even while he went to sleep.

He had spent hours posing in front of a full-length mirror in Claire's office where he practiced his stance, his moves and his bow. He taught himself how to caress a guitar and fondle a mike and he learned when to tilt his head so that his thick dark curls fell forward and covered his eyes.

At the end of a year in prison, he had the stage presence of a pro. He had won two talent contests and played at the dedication of the new maximum security annex. Several times he got out to perform because Claire pulled some strings. He sang the national anthem at the state football playoffs in Roswell and at the Socorro rodeo. He sang "Amazing Grace" at the warden's father's funeral in Moriarty and played for the Punta de Ague prom. Once he even played in Santa Fe for a prison reform conference chaired by the governor.

By the time he landed in Nashville, he was ready for bigger things.

He hit the top agencies first—Monterey Artists, William Morris, Buddy Lee Attractions—the swanky places on Sixteenth and Seventeenth Avenues where they had lobbies with gold records and Grammys, framed pictures of Hank

Williams and Bob Wills and Patsy Cline . . . offices with genuine leather couches and ankle-deep carpets, places where real live stars hung out. At Monterey, Willy Jack was sure that when he walked in, Brenda Lee walked out.

But walking in, it seemed, was the easy part. Willy Jack never got beyond the receptionists at the front desks, the thirty-something women in dark tailored suits who invited him to leave his card, his picture, his tape . . . women who smiled and said they were sorry, but their bosses were in meetings, out of town, at auditions, in taping sessions, on vacations—unavailable.

Willy Jack ran every bluff he could think of—the boss was his cousin, his uncle, his brother-in-law. He was there to deliver a personal message, to pick up a contract, to work on the telephones. But nothing he said got him more than a smile and an invitation to have a nice day. Once, when he decided to push it, he got an escort to the sidewalk by security, brothers who sang backup on a Roy Acuff record twenty-five years ago.

Two days and two bottles of grain alcohol later, Willy Jack tried the recording companies, but with a different approach. He went to RCA with a recommendation from Dolly Parton, and was sent to Warner Brothers by Roy Orbison. MCA's head recording engineer was waiting for him to deliver a tape and Arista's director of production wanted one of his songs for Kenny Rogers' new album. But Willy Jack's stories never clicked. He couldn't get in to see the janitor.

He spent his nights hanging out in the Hall of Fame Bar and Douglas Corner down in Music Square. One night he signed up to sing at the Bluebird Cafe, but by the time his turn came, he was too drunk to tune the Martin.

After ten days in Nashville, he had ducked out of two

hotels and two motels and was holed up in a flophouse on Lafayette. He had given up Wild Turkey for Mad Dog Twenty-Twenty—and T-bones for corndogs and fries. He could no longer afford the cheap prostitutes, so he had to settle for tired women who would give it away for a beer and a smoke or a free bed. He had called Claire Hudson twice for money, but hadn't caught her at a phone.

By the time he walked into the old Boston Building on Jefferson, he had one cigarette in his shirt and two dollars and change in his pants. And he was hungry, dirty and tired.

The building, a six-story brick with a frayed awning over the front door, smelled like stale coffee and old books. An out-of-order sign on the elevator had yellowed with age.

The two-line ad in the paper hadn't promised much—auditions for bookings in local clubs—but it was the best offer Willy Jack had seen. He climbed the stairs to the fourth floor and found the Ruth Meyers Agency at the end of the hall, next to the men's room.

When he stepped into a dusty gray office not much bigger than a Dumpster, no one seemed to notice. A middle-aged man sat in a corner, hunkered into his harmonica, his eyes closed in concentration. A teenage redhead in a Western-fringed miniskirt, a fiddle case clamped between her thighs, teased her frizzy hair into a four-inch pomp.

The white-haired receptionist looked surprised when she hung up the phone and saw Willy Jack at her desk.

"Hi. Are you here to see Ruth Meyers or Nellie?"

"I saw an ad in the paper and—"

"Then you want to see Ruth Meyers. Just go on in," she said as she pointed to a door marked PRIVATE.

Willy Jack didn't knock, just barged in, squinting as his eyes adjusted to the gloom in the large, high-ceilinged room. The only light came through the grimy panes of two windows.

The room was a jumble of amplifiers, filing cabinets, pianos, stereos, speakers, microphones, drums and a massive conference table a foot deep in dead plants, take-out cartons, straw hats, sheet music, violin cases and an empty birdcage.

"Jesus Christ. Another guitar player."

She stood up then and walked around the table, came to stand against him, her hard round belly pressed to his chest.

"What's your name?"

"Willy Jack Pickens."

"And you didn't even have to make that up, did you?"

"What?"

She was tall, over six feet, and she smelled of Vicks. She wore a black velvet skirt with half the hem pulled loose and a satin blouse stapled together where buttons should have been. Her stockings were rolled down to her ankles and the toes of her felt houseshoes were cut out.

"Well, do you just carry that guitar around for balance?"

"You want me to play?"

"What the fuck you think I want you to do? Call bingo?"

Willy Jack opened the case, took out the Martin, then slid onto the conference table, sending a doughnut box sailing to the floor. While he tuned up, the woman pulled a jar of Vicks from her pocket and rubbed some just under her nose.

"One tune," she said without interest. "Your best shot."

Willy Jack cleared his throat, then began playing "The Beat of a Heart," while the woman searched through the pile of debris on the table.

Just as he started to sing, she found what she was looking for—a can of Diet Pepsi.

"No matter how lonely you are
There's someone in this world who loves you

She lifted sheet music from the top of a dead begonia, then poured a dollop of Pepsi over it.

"No matter what troubles you have
There's someone in the world who cares

She walked the length of the table pouring Pepsi onto blackened ferns and leafless ivies.

"And if God really loves you
He's not the only one

Her gardening done, she uncapped a package of Alka-Seltzer, popped two of them in her mouth, then downed them with the last of the Pepsi.

When the white-haired receptionist opened the door and stuck her head inside, Ruth Meyers held up her hand, a signal to be quiet.

"Just feel it in the beat of a heart"

After the sound of the last note died away, the room was still for several moments, then: "It's gonna cost me a thousand dollars to get you cleaned up," she growled. "Pictures will be another two hundred." Then, to the receptionist, "Jenny," she boomed, "type up a note for twelve hundred bucks, then call Doc Frazier. He can work us in. Cancel the trio from Fort Smith and set up the bluegrass singer for Friday afternoon."

"Wait just a damned minute," Willy Jack said as he slid off the table.

"My name's Ruth Meyers. Call me Ruth Meyers."

"Then let me ask you something, Ruth, what's this about—"

"Goddammit! Can't you hear? I said to call me Ruth Meyers. Not Ruth. Not Meyers. You call me Ruth Meyers!"

"Okay, *Ruth Meyers!* What the hell is this twelve-hundred-dollar note? And who's this doctor?"

"Dentist. Doc's a dentist. You've got a cavity the size of a raisin between your two front teeth. And you're gonna get 'em cleaned. They're green," she said as she made a face.

"I'll be the one who decides—"

"Jenny, call Preston's. Tell them we'll be in this afternoon for a fitting. And I want Jake Gooden or we'll go to Newman's. Jacket, trousers, shirts . . . the works. We'll go to Tooby's for boots." Then to Willy Jack, "What's your shoe size?"

"Nine, but—"

"Tell Tooby we want two-inch heels. Then get in touch with Nina at the Cut-n-Curl. He'll need a style and color." Ruth Meyers checked her watch. "We can be there by four. He needs a manicure, too."

Willy Jack said, "Now, by God . . ." but he never got to finish.

"Now here's the deal." Ruth Meyers slashed another shot of Vicks beneath her nose. "You'll sign the note and a contract. I take fifteen percent of everything you make. You'll start tomorrow night at Buffy's out on Hermitage. It pays a hundred a night. You'll work clubs until we're ready for a record deal."

"Well, that don't sound bad, but—"

"If you came to Nashville to be a star, if that's what you want, then I'll see you get it."

"That's damned sure what I want."

"And that name? One Willie in the business is enough. You're Billy Shadow now."

"Billy Shadow," Willy Jack said, trying it out. "Billy Shadow." Then he nodded his head and grinned. "Yeah. That'll do."

Ruth Meyers leaned across the table, right in Willy Jack's face. "There's one other thing."

"What's that?"

"Never . . . *ever* . . . lie to me."

"Sure, Ruth . . . Ruth Meyers. You got a deal."

Part Three

Chapter Twenty-Two

THREE YEARS LATER than when she had started, Novalee was going west. Not to Bakersfield, but to Santa Fe. Not with Willy Jack, not in a Plymouth with a hole in the floor and not to live in a house with a balcony, but Novalee was finally going to go west.

When the letter had come, back in August, she had prepared herself for disappointment. But when she opened it and read, "such stunning work," her breath came fast. As her eyes raced ahead to "pleased to announce," her fingers trembled. And by the time she saw "first place winner," she was jumping up and down, sending a tremor through the trailer that caused Sister Husband to rush out of the bathroom in a panic.

"What is it? What happened?"

"The Kodak contest! The Greater Southwest! I won! My picture won!"

"The boy on Rattlesnake Ridge?"

"Yes!" Novalee screamed, then grabbed Sister and danced her around the room. They took wide, prancing steps, tossing their heads like flamenco dancers. Then they collapsed on the couch, giggling and breathless as girls.

"Darlin'," Sister asked as she struggled for air, "what did you win?" a question that set them laughing again.

"A weekend in Santa Fe."

"Oh, my word. Just listen to that."

"And they're going to put my picture in an exhibit."

"Why Novalee, you're going to be famous," Sister said, suddenly struck by the gravity of the news.

In the days that followed, Sister's prediction came true, at least in Sequoyah County. Novalee's picture was in the paper with a caption that read, LOCAL PHOTOGRAPHER ACCLAIMED.

She was named Employee of the Week at Wal-Mart, the First National Bank sent a card of congratulations, and the art teacher at the high school asked her to come to his classes to speak.

Dixie Mullins, confusing New Mexico with the Old, offered her a Spanish phrase book. Henry and Leona gave her luggage, but couldn't agree on color or brand, so she got a red suitbag by American Tourister and a blue duffel made in Taiwan.

Lexie Coop and the children took Novalee and Americus to dinner at the Pizza Hut, where all the Coops ate standing up, Lexie's latest method of combating obesity.

Moses and Certain made a star with Novalee's name on it and put it on the door of the darkroom and Moses gave her a fountain pen that had belonged to his father, Purim, who had died the previous winter.

Americus had a thousand questions about "Messico," and Mr. Sprock asked Novalee to call an old friend in Santa Fe, a World War II buddy he hadn't heard from in over forty years.

But Forney was the most excited of all because Novalee had asked him to go with her.

At first, he had said no . . . *had* to say no. He did, he explained, have his sister to care for and, he insisted, the library could not just shut down. But when Retha Holloway, president of the Literary Guild, jumped at the chance to take over the library for a few days and when Sister Husband insisted on taking Mary Elizabeth's meals by, Forney's decision was made.

As they drove away from the trailer, Novalee continued to wave even when she could no longer see Americus, Sister Husband or Mr. Sprock.

"I hope Americus isn't crying."

"She wasn't upset when we said goodbye," Forney said.

"Well, she didn't show it, but . . ."

"What's wrong? Are you a little disappointed that she let you go so easily?"

"No." Novalee's eyes brimmed with tears. "But it's the first time I've left her since . . ."

"You leave her with Sister when you're at work. Sometimes with Mrs. Ortiz or . . ."

"You know what I mean."

"She'll be fine," Forney said in the same reassuring tone he had been using since Novalee found out she had won the trip. "You know Sister won't take any chances."

And though Novalee couldn't erase the worry from her face, she knew Forney was right. Ever since the kidnapping, nearly two years earlier, Sister had become more watchful than the FBI. She got up two or three times a night to check the yard and the street, on the lookout for "vigilante baptizers."

The Mississippi couple who had taken Americus were still in prison, but that did not completely ease Novalee's fears. She was still suspicious of blue Fords and had once followed a dark blue Fairmont from the Wal-Mart parking lot all the way to Tahlequah, some fifty miles away. The man and woman in the front seat had a child between them, a child whose head was framed by dark ringlets. But the "vigilante baptizers" turned out to be an old Indian man and woman and their "baby," a mixed-breed terrier.

Forney, always the voice of reason, had a difficult time convincing Novalee and Sister not to call the police every time a stranger walked down the street. But he had an even tougher job trying to persuade them that Americus had not been scarred by the ordeal. He didn't, for example, believe there was a connection between Americus' disdain for water and her forced baptism. Novalee and Sister were certain the immersion was the reason Americus refused to ride the kiddy boats at the fair, hated to take baths and despised the taste of water. And nothing Forney could say would make them change their minds.

For the next forty-eight hours, Novalee tried to cross every street in Santa Fe. Forney just tried to keep up.

After they had checked into their rooms at the Rancho Encantado, Novalee changed into jeans and tennis shoes, slung her cameras around her neck, then dragged Forney out of his room and into the streets. Eleven rolls of film later, Forney fell into bed and a deep sleep that lasted exactly four hours before Novalee was at the door threatening his life if he made her miss the sunrise. He didn't.

She shot eighteen rolls of film that day, one for every

mile they walked, according to Forney. He was still complaining of sore feet and an aching back as they raced back to their hotel to get ready for the awards banquet.

Forney was just pulling on his jacket when Novalee tapped on the door between their rooms.

"Are you ready?" she asked as she stepped inside.

"Just barely, but . . ."

She was wearing a dress he'd never seen before, dark green of some soft material that whispered against her breasts and hugged her close at the waist. She wore a silver chain around her throat, a chain almost as thin, almost as delicate as the tiny scar just below her lip.

"We'd better go," she said. "The man at the desk downstairs said it's a fifteen-minute drive."

"You look lovely," Forney said, his voice raspy, thick.

"Thanks." And then Novalee smiled at him and he thought that his heart would stop.

"Now come on," she said. "If I'm late, they might give it to someone else."

The main gallery of the Fairmont Museum had been transformed into a dining room. Tables were covered with linen, set with sparkling crystal and china. Waiters in white jackets rushed about with bottles of red wine and baskets of bread.

Novalee and Forney sat at the head table next to a podium where a silver-haired man in a tuxedo tapped his finger on a microphone, then waited for the room to grow quiet.

"Good evening," he said.

Novalee had grown increasingly nervous throughout the meal, so nervous she had not been able to eat more than a few bites. And now that it was time for the presentation, her mouth felt as if it had been dusted with powder. She sipped at her wine, "dry wine," she had whispered to Forney, but she managed not to make a face.

". . . my pleasure to unveil the winning photograph entitled *Oklahoma Benediction.*"

Then the silver-haired man turned to a covered tripod and removed a black silk cloth from an enlargement of Novalee's picture, the silhouette of Benny Goodluck running, the sun rising behind him. The crowd broke into applause.

Moments later, the man at the mike said, "And now, I'd like to introduce you to the winning photographer, Ms. Novalee Nation."

When Novalee stood and stepped to the podium, she was so shaky she wondered if her legs would hold her up. As the heavy applause died down, she said, "Thank you," surprised by the sound of her voice amplified in the spacious room.

"Mr. Mitford asked me to tell you a little bit about the photograph, uh . . . so, I will. But I didn't know I would be making a speech and . . . well, I'm kind of nervous." Polite laughter ran through the crowd, but it was friendly, encouraging.

"I shot this picture with a Rollei Twin Lens Reflex at F28, using ASA four hundred. I took it at sunup, in winter, when first light in Oklahoma has a blue-silver look to it. I don't know how to describe it exactly, but it's like you're looking through the cleanest, clearest pool of water in the world. It's not the same as first light here in Santa Fe, but . . ."

Someone seated near the back said, "We wouldn't know. No one here's ever been up that early," and the whole crowd laughed.

Novalee's face reddened, but she smiled and felt more relaxed. "Anyway, back home, the light's wonderful in the mornings . . . like when it catches a hawk in a glide or when it touches the spikes of Indian paintbrush."

The room was suddenly still, so still that Novalee suffered a new wave of stage fright and had to take a sip of water.

"Well," she said, "maybe you'd like to know about the boy in the picture. He's a Sac and Fox Indian and he was running that morning, his last run for a long time. You see, his grandpa had just died, so the boy was giving up something he loves as a tribute to his grandpa. It's a custom in the boy's tribe.

"But I didn't know that then, when I took the picture. I just happened to be there, trying to get to the top of a mountain before sunrise.

"Later, when I got to know the boy better, I told him I had seen him there that morning. I told him I had taken his picture and he asked to see it. When I gave it to him, he smiled. He said he could see his grandpa's spirit there in the light of the sunrise.

"Sometimes," she said, "I think I can see it, too."

When Novalee and Forney got back to the hotel, she called room service and ordered dinner. She still wasn't hungry, but she thought eating in a hotel room was glamorous. After all, she explained, she had watched Jane Fonda do it, and Elizabeth Taylor, too. But the real reason was because she had promised Lexie Coop she would.

Forney had offered to take her out to dinner, but Novalee had her heart set on room service and there was no way he could talk her out of it. But he didn't try very hard.

Dinner was exactly the way Novalee had pictured it. The young man from room service rolled in a serving cart, the dishes covered with silver warmers. He brought a rose in a slender vase, and two candles in crystal holders. And he dimmed the lights before he left.

"Forney," Novalee said, "do you ever feel like you're playing grown-up?"

"What do you mean?"

"Like you're a kid who's just acting like an adult."

"I am an adult."

"So am I. But when I get this feeling, I don't feel like one. I feel like a kid."

"You mean like when you lock your keys in the car or . . ."

"No." Novalee kicked off her shoes, shifted her weight and tucked her feet beneath her. "Look. Say you're doing something . . ."

"Like what?"

"Like . . . packing a suitcase 'cause you're going to New Mexico. You're packing, see?" Novalee pretended to be folding clothes. "You put your shirt here . . ." She pantomimed arranging a shirt on the table. ". . . and you put your underwear here. Then all of a sudden, it dawns on you. Packing a suitcase is something adults do."

Forney nodded in agreement.

"But right then, at that very moment, you don't feel like an adult. You feel like a kid *playing* adult. You know you're just *playing* grown-up."

"And is that the way you feel now?"

"Forney, that's the way I've felt for the past three days. Winning an award. Making a speech. Having dinner in a hotel room. All of it! I've just been playing grown-up."

Forney shook his head.

"You've never felt that way?"

"No," he said. "Never."

"Well, maybe I'm just . . ."

"Unless you mean the way I felt when I was about to help deliver a baby."

"Then you do know what I mean."

"Now *that's* playing grown-up!"

"We'll never forget that night."

"Oh, God, no!"

"I remember when you handed her to me and . . ." Novalee slid away from the table. "I'm going to call home." She hopped onto the bed, studied the dialing instructions on the phone on the night table, then punched in Sister's number.

"Sister, it's me."

"Oh, darlin'. Did you get your award?"

"Yes. And I made a speech and got a plaque and they're going to put my picture in the paper."

"Why, Novalee, you are above approach, just above approach."

"How's Americus?"

"She's wonderful. She's been in bed an hour and I haven't heard a peep out of her, not a peep."

"I knew she'd already be asleep, but I wanted to call."

"Well, she's fine, darlin'. Don't you worry."

"No, I'm not."

"You tell Forney I read her another chapter of that book they started last week."

"Which one?"

"Oh, I can't remember the name of it, but it's by that Charlie Dickens."

"*David Copperfield*?"

"That's the one. And Americus laughs every time I say 'Micawber.' She tells me that's not the way Forney says it and . . . oh, oh! Little pitchers have big ears."

"Is she up?"

"Just came shuffling in like a little sleepwalker, dragging her blanket and poor old Night-Night. Come here, sweet thing."

Novalee could hear the rustle of Americus settling herself into Sister's lap.

"You want to talk to Mommy?" Sister coached.

"Hi, sweetheart," Novalee said.

"Mommy in Messico?" Americus asked.

"Yes, I am, but I'm coming home tomorrow."

"Forney too?"

"Forney is coming home, too. Americus, what are you doing out of bed?"

"My jamamas are wet."

"What happened? Did you have an accident?"

"No. Night-Night did."

"I didn't know teddy bears wet the bed."

"Uh-huh. They do."

"Well, Sister will change your pajamas."

Sister said, "Tell Mommy you learned a new song today."

"New song today."

"You did? Can you sing it for me?"

"Tinkle, tinkle little star . . ."

Novalee motioned for Forney and whispered, "Hurry, she's singing."

Forney crossed the room in three steps, then scooted in beside Novalee on the bed. When she turned the phone receiver so he could hear, he curled his hand around hers, and with their fingers intertwined, the receiver resting between their faces, they listened to Americus sing.

When she finished, Forney praised her and Novalee asked her to sing again, but she was clearly at the end of her performance and not inclined to render an encore.

"Kiss Night-Night," she said. "Kiss Americus." As she

began smacking, her goodbye ritual of sending kisses through the phone, Novalee turned her face toward the receiver and kissed the air, her lips only a whisper away from Forney's, her breath so close he could breathe it. And for an instant, for just one motionless instant, Forney thought he could tell her, thought he might be able to say the words . . . but then it was gone, floating somewhere beyond that time and that place.

Chapter Twenty-Three

Novalee had been working in the stockroom since lunch, so she hadn't seen the sky begin to darken in the south or the sharp zigzag lines of lightning spiking far off in the west. But later in the afternoon, when she came to the front to work at one of the registers, the storm had moved close enough that she could hear the low rumble of thunder in the distance.

Her last customer was a lanky middle-aged man with two flats of Big Boy tomato plants.

"You going to try to plant those before the rain moves in?" Novalee asked.

"Gonna get more'n rain, I judge."

"That right?"

He pulled up his shirt sleeve to show her old wounds that had left his skin crimped and pitted with scar tissue.

"Shrapnel from Vietnam." He studied his arm for several seconds as if the sight of it still puzzled him, then he pushed his sleeve back down. "When a storm's coming, I know it first. Sooner than a weather bulletin. And right now, this arm's telling me a big one's on the way."

When Novalee closed her register at three o'clock, the store seemed almost empty. Most of the customers had hurried away, leaving half-full baskets parked in the aisles, while others had rushed through the checkouts, their eyes on the darkening sky.

Some of the clerks wished they could leave, too. They wanted to get home to frightened children—babies who couldn't sleep when the wind came up and toddlers who became hysterical at the sound of thunder. One woman said her six-year-old had nightmares about flash floods and another talked about her daughter who memorized weather bulletins.

Novalee had never gotten used to the Oklahoma storms herself, storms that often sent them running to Dixie Mullins' cellar, even in the middle of the night. But Sister had turned those hours underground into adventures, so Americus wouldn't be afraid. Sister performed finger puppet shows and did magic tricks. She sang songs and made up stories for Americus to act out, spotlighting her with the beam of a flashlight.

But Sister wasn't quite as clever at covering her own fear, fear of "crawly things" that sometimes shared the cellar with them. She always sent Novalee on ahead to relocate anything that crawled, jumped or slithered. But about all she ever found were daddy longlegs, which had better odds of surviving inside the cellar with Sister than outside with the wind that could blow them all the way to Auntie Em's farm in Kansas, according to Americus.

By the time Novalee clocked out, the sky was closing in, dropping down over the Snake Mountains. She decided to go straight home even though she needed to stop at the

IGA. She could skip the grocery store, could always come back later, but passing up the Texaco station would be a little more risky because the Chevy was empty, the needle resting squarely over the E.

The old Toyota seemed to have gone for weeks on one tank of gas. Sister said it ran on magic. But the new car guzzled unleaded and used more oil in a month than the Toyota had in a year. Even so, Novalee was proud of it, the newest car she had ever driven and now, nearly paid off.

As she pulled in and parked beside the trailer, a bolt of lightning cracked near enough that the hair on her arms stood up.

Americus and Sister were in the kitchen fixing the "cellar bag," as much a staple of Oklahoma storms as wind.

The bag always held a transistor radio, a flashlight and some candles, then Sister would add whatever she could put her hands on that wasn't mushy, smelly or sticky. She always took enough to share with the neighbors who showed up in Dixie's cellar—hard candy, a chunk of cheese, gingersnaps, whatever came fast and easy from the refrigerator or cabinets.

"Mommy, storm's coming," Americus said as she wrapped a skittish kitten in a bath towel, preparing for the trek to the cellar.

"TV just put out a tornado warning," Sister said. "They spotted a funnel cloud over in Vian."

"I've gotta get Doughboy," Americus yelled as she headed out the back door.

"Don't worry about Doughboy. He'll go under the house."

"No, he wants to go with us."

"You stay close," Novalee called. "We're about to leave."

"Darlin', get those new batteries from under the sink, will you?"

"How's Dixie feeling today?"

"No good. Her sister said she didn't sleep at all last night."

"Suppose she's going to the cellar?"

"Oh no. Cellar's too damp, worst thing for pleurisy. Besides, Dixie's not really afraid of storms. She just goes to the cellar to visit."

Novalee put the batteries in the sack. "Are you ready?"

"You go on with Americus. I made Dixie some potato soup. I'll take it by on my way."

"And if I get there first, I can clear out all the boa constrictors and tarantulas and . . ."

The lights dimmed for an instant, followed by a sharp crack of thunder, causing Novalee to flinch.

"That was close," Novalee said.

"No, that was God tellin' you to take that baby and get on to the cellar."

"Okay, but you hurry."

"Darlin', if you don't go on, I'll be there before you are."

Novalee grabbed the sack and scooted out the back door. Americus was at the foot of the steps pulling at the collar of a fuzzy mongrel.

"Come on, Doughboy!"

The kitten, agitated by the whining dog, had worked its way out of the towel and was climbing up Americus' shoulder.

"Help me, Mommy."

Novalee picked up the little dog, knowing Americus was not going to be happy until she had her entire menagerie with her.

"Let's go."

The air was so still that nothing moved, so heavy that even pollen was held to ground. No stir of leaves, no whisper of wind. The sky, dark and growing darker, was green—an eerie shade of green, like light trapped in a bottle.

The neighborhood looked abandoned—no life in the streets or the yards. Dixie's Rhode Island Reds had retreated to the hen house and Henry's cat, always on the prowl, had vanished. Even Leona's bird feeders were deserted.

Nothing barked or chirped or crowed . . . nothing called, nothing answered. Doughboy lay limp against Novalee's hip and the kitten peeked wide-eyed and silent from the folds of the towel where it was once again settled. And as Americus stepped over the garden hose in Dixie's backyard, she swiped at a bluebottle fly glued to the soft flesh just below her eye.

The cellar door had been thrown open, so Novalee knew they were not the first to arrive. Mrs. Ortiz and the girls were bailing water from the floor into a tin bucket.

"Where is Sister Husband?"

"She's on her way."

"My husband is painting a house. Somewhere on Commerce. I tried to call, but . . ." Mrs. Ortiz eased onto the wooden bench against the wall and pulled her rosary from her pocket.

"Maybe this will blow over," Novalee said, trying to sound reassuring. She lit the candles, then turned on the transistor, but the local station had been knocked off the air. From Tulsa she got static and two country and western stations, both playing the same song, "The Beat of a Heart."

As soon as the bucket was full, Novalee carried it up the

steps and emptied it beside the cellar door. The wind had started to pick up, quick gusts lifting the lower branches of the sycamores in Dixie's yard and sending dust devils skipping down the alley.

Novalee supposed Sister had already left the trailer, but she wondered why she hadn't seen her crossing the street on her way to Dixie's.

By the time Novalee went outside with the second bucket of water, there was little hope the weather was going to blow over. The wind had grown so strong she had to lean into it to keep her balance. A powerful gust picked up the cellar door, a solid piece of oak crisscrossed by heavy strips of metal, then slammed it back to the concrete platform on which it rested.

Just as Novalee scurried back into the cellar, hail began to fall, sending the Ortiz girls to huddle on the bench beside their mother. A storm the previous summer had left them horrified when Cantinflas, their Chihuahua puppy, had been pounded to death by hailstones the size of walnuts.

"Mommy, where's Grandma Sister?" Americus asked.

"She's coming, honey."

Novalee stood inside the cellar and watched the hail bouncing in the yard—pellets springing up, colliding, spinning across the grass, an odd dance of ice. Stones pelted the daffodils in Dixie's flower bed, stripping off the petals, slicing into the stalks.

The tin roof of the chicken house clattered, the sounds staccato and disconnected. When they heard glass shatter, Mrs. Ortiz and Novalee locked eyes.

As hailstones began bouncing down the cellar steps and rolling across the floor, the smallest Ortiz girl started to cry.

"Do you think we should shut the door?" Mrs. Ortiz said.

"Uh, let's wait for Sister. Just a few more minutes."

Suddenly, the hail stopped and it was quiet once again.

"Thank God," Mrs. Ortiz whispered.

Novalee nodded, then hurried up the steps. Dark clouds blistered the sky—bubbling, exploding into strange, fierce shapes . . . clouds moving fast and low, so low Novalee believed she could touch them. And from somewhere above her, she thought she could hear the sound of breath, the sound of old and powerful breathing.

Then a siren began to wail. Novalee wanted it to be a police car or a fire truck, but she knew what it was—a tornado warning coming from the grade school two blocks away. Goose bumps rose along her forearms and she said, "Damn," but her voice was lost in a violent gust of wind.

Mrs. Ortiz climbed the lower steps of the cellar so she could see outside. Debris was beginning to sail around Dixie's yard. Trash cans were flying, tree limbs waving wildly.

"Novalee, maybe you should come in."

"I think I'll run in the house, check on Sister and—"

Then Novalee saw it. Coiling, spiraling . . . dipping down like a giant gnarled finger reaching for the earth. The air filled with a roaring noise and the sky turned hot and began to swirl, stinging her skin, biting into her flesh.

Just as she started for the house, something struck her in the arm, something small and hard that skipped across the yard and into the street. She saw Dixie's beauty shop sign sail into one of the sycamores, and watched Henry's johnboat hurtle down the alley and smash into the hen house.

Novalee knew she couldn't make it to the house, so she struggled back to the cellar, got one foot on the top step, then grabbed the door. She was able to lift it a few inches before the wind slammed it back against the concrete slab. She tried again, but the wind was too strong, and when she leaned farther out, farther away from the cellar steps, she felt a powerful current of air lift her, felt her body grow lighter as if she might be swallowed up by the sky.

Then hands grasped her ankles, pulled at her legs. She bent her knees, ducked down and reached behind her, found Mrs. Ortiz' hands and gripped them as hard as she could, held on as Mrs. Ortiz ripped her away from the wind, pulled her down the steps and onto the cellar floor.

Americus cried out as she flew into Novalee's arms, but the sound was lost in the roaring that filled the cellar. They closed their eyes against the grit swirling around them, so they didn't see Mrs. Ortiz scrambling into a corner with her daughters. They didn't see Doughboy howling behind the overturned bench. And they didn't see the kitten, lost and bewildered, creeping across the floor.

Suddenly the air, punishing and hot, began to rush out of the cellar, sucking the flames from the candles, extracting leaves and gingersnaps, a mildewed sock, a paper cup . . . snatching daddy longlegs from the walls and flinging them outside . . . hurling the kitten against the steps, lifting and tossing it, sucking it out into the spiraling wind.

Then a tremendous crash from outside shook the walls and sent a tremor across the floor as a savage gust of wind picked up the door and slammed it shut, leaving the cellar as dark and silent as a tomb.

Chapter Twenty-Four

HENRY AND LEONA were buried three days after the tornado. They had died wrapped in each other's arms in the closet on Leona's side of the duplex. Some thought their decision to get in the closet together was probably the only thing they had agreed on in forty years. But it wasn't. They were buried in adjoining plots that they had bought on their twenty-fifth wedding anniversary.

Their funeral was the first; others followed in quick succession. A family from Muldrow—mother, father and two children—had been killed in their pickup on the interstate when they had tried to outrun the tornado. Three teenagers had died in the rec room of the First Methodist Church where they were playing Ping-Pong. Sister Husband was the last to be buried on a rainy Tuesday morning in the Paradise Cemetery north of town.

Forney was the one who found her, pulled her from the tangle of the trailer, which had been pleated like an accordion and hurled into the street. She was alive then, but not by much. Her heart stopped once on the way to the hospital and again in the emergency room. Following surgery, she was on life-support for five days.

Novalee didn't leave the hospital until it was over. She could only go into ICU for ten minutes every two hours, but now and then she got to stay a little longer. Lexie Coop called in a favor with one of the nurses in intensive care, and when she was on duty, Novalee got some extra time with Sister.

For the first couple of days, Novalee and Mr. Sprock went into ICU together. The head nurse talked with them, explained that comatose patients probably responded on some level to what went on around them.

"That's why it's important for you to touch her. Hold her hand. Stroke her hair."

Mr. Sprock nodded and said, "Stroke her hair."

"And talk to her. Talk about good times you've had together. Tell her funny stories. Laugh if you can."

"Laugh," Mr. Sprock repeated.

"Yes. You think you can do that?"

"I don't know," Novalee said. "We'll try."

And Mr. Sprock *did* try. He would go in prepared to tell a joke, something he had rehearsed with Novalee. Or he would try to do his Barney Fife impression, or start to read *Shoe*, Sister's favorite comic strip.

But when he stood over her, when he saw her broken body and the snarl of tubes, when he heard her machined breathing and the rattle of breath in her chest, he would begin to sob and have to be led away. Finally, he stopped going in. He just sat in the waiting room and waited.

Novalee learned early how to shut off the part of herself that wanted to cry, to scream . . . the part that wanted to rip out the tubes, pick Sister up in her arms and carry her home.

"Americus said one of the new kittens in Moses' barn

opened her eyes today, the yellow one she named Butter Bean. Anyway, she told me to tell you that you were right. When the kitten opens her eyes, the first thing she sees is her mother."

And when Novalee learned how to shut out the sounds and smells of the living and dying, she could almost pretend she and Sister were shopping in the IGA or planting moss roses in the garden or sitting in the kitchen waiting for coffee to brew.

"I just talked to Certain on the phone. She told me our Americus has become a doctor. Seems Forney went out, took her a present. A doctor's kit. So Certain makes her a little white jacket and embroiders 'Doctor Nation' on it. And Moses fixes her a shingle and hangs it on the door of her room . . . and she's in business.

"Certain said she's doctoring everything that moves—Moses, chickens, dogs. And today . . . cows."

Novalee smiled as she adjusted the sheet across Sister's chest.

"Anyway, Moses took her with him this morning, out to the barn, and while he was milking, Americus was doctoring. He said she hunkered down beside their old Holstein, the one Americus named Polly."

Novalee took a tissue from the table beside the bed and dabbed at spittle in the corner of Sister's mouth.

"He said Americus was fussing at Polly while she examined her, told her to hold still, to take a deep breath. Then, after Americus listened through her stethoscope to Polly's udders, she shook her head and said, 'Well, Polly, you have to go on a diet 'cause your titties are too big.'"

Novalee laughed and pretended Sister was laughing, too. Sometimes Novalee was so good at make-believe that she really thought she could see Sister smile,

> *home gives you something no other place can . . . your history . . . home is where your history begins*

or hear her sing,

> *cheer up, my brother, come live in the sunshine*
> *we'll understand it all by and by*

or feel the curl of her fingers as they held hands while Sister prayed,

> *and we ask forgiveness, Lord, for the fornication that Mr. Sprock and me have committed again*

But those were the bad times, the times when Novalee had to work harder to shut herself down, so when it was over, when they unplugged Sister and let her go, Novalee could gather up Sister's yellow rayon dress and her Timex watch, put them into a paper sack . . . and walk away.

After the funeral, Novalee went to Moses and Certain's, to a pine room with a feather bed and soft yellow sheets where she slept for eighteen hours. She might have slept longer, but Americus came tiptoeing in at two the next afternoon, carrying a small black bag.

"Hi, sweetheart," Novalee said.

"Memaw Certain said Mommy sleeping."

"I was just waiting for you to come in here and give me a kiss."

Americus held her arms up and Novalee lifted her onto the bed. They kissed, then Americus fumbled with the catch on the bag.

"What have you got there?"

"Doctor bag." Americus took out her medical instruments—a plastic stethoscope and a wooden tongue depressor. "Mommy sick." After a bit of struggle, she fastened the ear pieces to her cheeks, then listened to Novalee's chest.

"What's wrong with me, Doc?"

"Pepaw Moses said Mommy's heart was breaked."

Novalee managed a smile she couldn't feel as Americus concentrated on her examination. After she poked Novalee's mouth with the wooden stick, she nodded wisely, put the instruments back in the bag and took out a package of M&Ms. She fished out two. "Take this and you be all well."

"What is it, Dr. Nation?"

"Biotics." She put one of the M&Ms into Novalee's mouth and one into her own. Then she said, "I have a breaked heart, too."

For the next week, Novalee dragged through the days and nights, the consequence, she reasoned, of a breaked heart.

When she slept, her dreams were ravaged by voices calling to her from flattened duplexes and twisted trailers, live wires hissing in broken trees, flashlights slicing through darkness to reveal cats impaled on splintered fence posts and beheaded chickens flopping down cellar steps.

Awake, she struggled to fill the hours until she could sleep again. But nothing she did made her feel whole. If she ate, she didn't taste the food. If she read, she couldn't remember the words. If she rested, she still felt tired.

Everyone around her wanted to help. Forney came out each evening, bringing some new book he thought she'd like. Lexie called twice asking her to come to dinner. Moses put his Rollei out on the kitchen table where she'd be sure to see it and Americus continued to give her medical care. Only Certain offered no enticements, for she knew nothing could ease the pain. Not books or photography or food. Not even love.

The Whitecotton phone never seemed to quit ringing. Mr. Sprock called two or three times a day, but he broke down each time he tried to say Sister's name. Mrs. Ortiz phoned to let Novalee know they had been able to salvage a few things from the trailer before it had been cleared away.

Dixie Mullins called twice to report conversations with her dead husband, conversations with rather vague references to Sister Husband.

In the beginning, Novalee tried to speak to everyone who called. She accepted their condolences, listened to their advice, laughed with them and cried with them, shared their memories and their pain. But she had enough pain of her own and, little by little, she began to find ways to avoid the phone. When she'd hear it ring, she would duck outside or slip into the bathroom, discover dishes to be washed, laundry to be done, a child to be scrubbed.

It seemed everyone in town knew where Novalee was, so Certain became practiced at telling "sugar lies," and taking down messages. She wrote the calls on slips of pink paper that soon filled an unused ashtray beside the phone. The director of the funeral home called with some unfinished business and so did a woman with Paradise Cemetery. Two florists phoned to get directions to the Whitecotton place and the electric company got in touch to see about reestablishing service. Someone with the Social Security Office called wanting Novalee to return Sister's last check and a hospital records clerk needed to see where to send the final bill.

Some of the callers were people Novalee had never heard of—a woman named Grace, a boy called Ted, an attorney named Ray who phoned twice. But Novalee guessed they were members of AA because Certain said they all started their conversations the same way. "Hi, my name's Grace . . . Hi, my name is Ted . . . Hi, my name's Ray."

Several Wal-Mart employees called, each of them worried about their jobs. The store had been practically destroyed in the tornado. Most of the roof was gone, walls flattened, the stockroom gutted, merchandise scattered all over the county.

No one knew for sure what was going on, but everyone had heard a rumor. Snooks Lancaster said she heard that Sam Walton was coming to town to inspect the damage himself. Betty Tenkiller said the employees were going to get disaster bonuses. And Ralph Scoggins said the city manager told him Wal-Mart was going to buy the old National Guard Armory, refurbish it and reopen the store within the month.

But not one of them could have anticipated what was really going to happen. Not one of them had the least idea.

"I've got some good news and some bad news," Reggie Lewis said. "What do you want to hear first?"

What Novalee wanted to do was hang up the phone, but she said, "I guess I'll hear the bad stuff first."

"Okay. Here it is. Wal-Mart's not going to rebuild here. They're pulling out."

"What?"

"I just got the word from the head office. Woman on the big man's staff in Bentonville called me not more than an hour ago."

"No. That can't be."

"Our store would have to be completely rebuilt. From the ground up. They had a couple of engineers in here for three days going over what's left out there and they said, 'No way!' There's just too much structural damage, Novalee. Wal-Mart's out of here."

"If you've got some good news, then . . ."

"I do. They've decided to build a Super Center over in Poteau."

"Poteau!"

"One of those gigantic buildings. I don't know . . . a hundred thousand square feet. Groceries, pharmacy, optical, bakery. Whole damned shooting match. Over fifty checkouts."

"I thought you said this was good news."

"It is! Now listen. We're all guaranteed jobs there."

"Reggie, Poteau's fifty miles from here."

"Fifty-four. But they're going to pay moving expenses and half-pay until the store's up and open."

"We have to move to Poteau?"

"Well, it'd be a long way to commute, wouldn't it?"

"But this is home. I can't just move."

"If you want to keep your job with Wal-Mart, you will."

The news of Wal-Mart's closing was followed by a new round of calls to the Whitecottons' and within an hour, Forney was ricocheting around their living room, as agitated as the first day Novalee saw him in the library. He darted from the fireplace to the picture window, raced toward it as if he might crash right through it, then, at the last second, he spun and lunged toward Certain's china cabinet where her collection of tiny porcelain cats trembled with each thunderous step he took.

"What else can I do, Forney?"

"Do? Find another job. There's work here, Novalee."

"Right." Novalee picked up the paper, already opened and folded to the help wanted section. "Drivers to pull mobile homes," she read. "Live-in needed for disabled man. Address envelopes at home. Make money selling nationally advertised product."

"But people do find decent jobs here."

"Where?" She held the paper out to him. "Show me."

"Novalee . . ."

"You think I want to leave? Do you? This is my home, Forney. The people I care about are here."

"Yes!"

"But I have a job at Wal-Mart. The pay's decent. I have sick leave, health insurance for Americus."

"You can live with me!" Forney's face reddened. "And my sister," he added quickly. "Live with us in the library."

"Forney." Novalee shook her head.

"I know that's not the best solution, not the best place for Americus, but we could work it out. Maybe . . ."

"Forney, having a place to stay isn't the problem. Moses and Certain asked me to live with them . . ."

"Then . . ."

"But I can't do that."

"Why? Why not?"

"I've had people taking me in since I was seven years old, Forney. I can't do that again."

"Novalee, I wish you, uh . . . I want you, you and Americus . . ." Forney threw his hand in the air, a magician's gesture, but there was no dove, no bouquet, no white rabbit.

Mr. Ortiz drove out that evening with the few odds and ends he had retrieved from the trailer—some wheat pennies, a few pictures, a ceramic vase . . . and Sister's Bible.

That night, after Novalee gave up on sleep, she turned on her light and took the Bible from the bedside table. She turned the first few pages until she came to the family record where names and dates had been recorded, written by different hands. Some in old-fashioned script with intricate curls and flourishes, some in print, plain block letters, studied and carefully drawn.

Novalee read the entries, dates of births and deaths—Sister's mother and father, a brother who died in infancy, a brother dead at fourteen, two aunts, an uncle, some cousins—and Sister's last brother, Brother Husband, who died in 1978.

The most recent entry was the one Sister had written four years earlier.

> *Americus Nation, born on May 14, 1987*

Then Novalee got a pen from her purse,

> *You're gonna die. But your name's not. No. It's gonna be written in somebody's Bible . . .*

placed the Bible in her lap

> *See, that name has a history. And that history is gonna be there even when you're not.*

and made one more entry.

> *Thelma Idean Husband, born October 9, 1922*
> *died May 6, 1991*

When Novalee finished, she closed the Bible. And that's when she knew it was time . . . it was finally time to cry.

Chapter Twenty-Five

"Hurry, Mommy."

Americus squirmed as Novalee brushed a tangle from her hair. They were going to meet Lexie and the children for lunch at McDonald's, and Americus, eager to be turned loose in Playland with the other kids, had been antsy all morning.

"Okay, let's go."

Certain was in the kitchen folding a basket of fresh laundry. "Oh, don't you look nice," she said, bending to give Americus a hug.

"Mommy brushed my hair."

"And it's beautiful."

"We should be back by two-thirty or three," Novalee said. "Need anything from town?"

"Well, why don't you pick up three or four lemons. And a can of black pepper. Get the big can. Let's see, I'm out of vanilla extract, too."

"Is that all?"

"I think so. You want me to write those down?"

"We can remember."

"That's what Moses always says, then he ends up calling me from the store."

"Where is he?"

"Outside messing with that tractor. Doing whatever he can to keep his mind off you two moving away. Breaking his heart to think of that."

Certain shook her head at the sorrow of it. "Be more'n one breaking heart, that's for sure. I saw the look on Forney's face when he left here yesterday."

"You know I don't want to leave, but . . ."

"Come on, Mommy," Americus said as she tugged at Novalee's skirt.

"Okay."

"Oh, I almost forgot," Certain said. "That man named Ray called again."

"Did he say what he wanted?"

"No, but he left his number this time."

"I'll give him a call." Then, with Americus pushing her through the door, she added, "When we get back from town."

Moses was half buried under the hood of an old John Deere tractor, but he looked up when he heard Americus calling.

"Pepaw Moses!"

"I hear you're going to town, Miss Americus."

"Going to Playland. With Praline and Brownie and Baby Ruth . . . uh-oh." Americus slapped her forehead, a gesture she'd copied from TV. "Forgot my doctor bag," she said as she wheeled and ran for the house.

"Now why in the world you need to take your doctor bag to McDonald's?" Moses called after her, but she had already darted through the back door.

Moses grinned, then dug in a toolbox and pulled out a wrench.

"You okay, honey?" he asked.

"Yeah."

"Heard you up in the night."

"I was looking for a pen."

"You wanted to write? At three o'clock in the morning?"

"Well, it was something I had to finish up."

Americus struck a trail from the front door of McDonald's straight through to Playland where Praline, Brownie and the twins were taking turns at the slide. Lexie was wedged into a booth sipping a cup of coffee. She was forty pounds and six months into a pregnancy that had thinned her hair and sapped her energy.

"You been here long?"

"Oh, that depends on how you look at it," Lexie said. "We came this morning at nine, for breakfast. Then we went to the clinic for my ten-thirty appointment and here we are, back in time for lunch."

"You all are good customers."

"Customers? Novalee, we're family. We spend so much time here that Baby Ruth calls Ronald McDonald 'brother.' "

Novalee laughed—a real laugh, her first in a long time. "You're good for me, Lexie."

"Well, somebody needs to be." Lexie reached across the table and pushed Novalee's hair back from her face. "You look like hell."

"I didn't get much sleep last night."

"It shows. How'd it go with Forney?"

"About like I figured."

"That bad, huh?"

"Yeah. But he's just so crazy about Americus. If we move away . . ."

"And he's not crazy about you?"

"Sure. We're best friends."

"Oh, Novalee, open your eyes! You are *not* his friend. I've told you before. Forney Hull is in love with you."

"Lexie, do you know the difference between love and friendship?"

"Is this a test?"

"Forney's a wonderful, decent friend who's stuck with me through some of the worst times of my life. Lexie, the man delivered my baby! That kind of friendship . . . well, it's maybe even stronger than love."

"Oh, give me a break. He wants you so bad. I bet he dreams about sweeping you up in his arms and—"

"You read too many Harlequins."

"Novalee, listen to me. The man is wild about you. He comes alive when he's with you."

"You're talking crazy."

"No! I see it . . . I watch him when you're around. He thinks everything you say is wonderful. He loves the way you walk, the way you smell. He loves your hair, your skin, your little boobs . . ."

"Lexie, Forney's not like us."

"What does that mean?"

"Well, he's different. His people were educated. They had money. Lexie, Forney lived in a house with a parlor. I've never even known anyone who *said* 'parlor.' "

"I've said 'parlor.' "

"He's been to Europe. He's studied music. He speaks three languages!"

"So what do you mean he's not like us?"

"Lexie, I'm here, in this town, because a guy threw me away like a piece of trash. I'm poor and I'm ignorant and—"

"You're not ignorant. You know things. You read more'n anyone I know."

"I could read three books a day and I'd never know what Forney knows. I'd never be able to talk to him about great ideas or—"

"Novalee, will you listen to what you're saying. A man can't love you because you haven't read as many books as he has? He can't love you because you don't speak French or because you don't go to operas? You're telling me we have to fall in love with people who are just like us?"

"No, not exactly."

"If you're right, then I deserved Woody Sams and I deserved what he did to me. He said he was gonna be a daddy to my kids because he couldn't have kids of his own. 'The mumps,' he said. Well," Lexie rubbed her swollen belly, "I've got his mumps right here."

"Lexie, I didn't mean—"

"So he hangs around longer than most of the others, long enough to get me knocked up, then he walks out on me . . . no, let me correct that. He *rides* out on his Harley, with *my* dutch oven and *my* king-sized pillows. Rides out of town in the middle of the night, leaves me pregnant with number five, and you're telling me we can only get what we deserve? That's the best we can hope for?"

"Well, Lexie, you said it yourself. Girls like us don't get the pick of the litter."

"Vanilla," Certain said.

"Right." Novalee turned away from the pay phone in the IGA and whispered "vanilla" to Americus, who thumped her head again, a gesture she was about to perfect.

"Novalee. That Ray called here again. Said he needs to talk to you today."

"Did he tell you why?"

"No. Just that it's important."

"All right. What's that number?"

"765-4490."

"I'll call him."

As soon as Novalee hung up, she put another quarter in the phone and punched in the number Certain had given her. A man answered on the first ring.

Ten minutes later, Novalee pulled into Sister's driveway and parked behind a dark brown Buick as a small, thin man slid out of the driver's seat and walked back to meet her.

"Hi. My name's Ray," he said.

Novalee shook the hand he offered, but she wasn't aware of the pressure of his fingers or the smoke from his cigarette or the clean, pine smell of his aftershave. She didn't see the fleck of tobacco stuck to his lower lip or the deep-set gray eyes that looked wounded and tired.

She was looking past him, just over his shoulder . . . looking past his Buick, past the driveway.

The trailer was gone. And the place where it had been showed no evidence it was ever there at all.

Nothing was left. Not the braces that had been wedged against the wheels, not the concrete blocks that had supported the tongue, not the aluminum that had wrapped around the underpinning. There wasn't a shard of glass or a strip of tin . . . not a block of wood or even a brick.

It was all gone—the porch and the storage shed, the trellis and the birdbath. Swept smooth and clean. Swept away.

"Is this the first time you've been here? The first time since it happened?"

Novalee nodded as Americus slipped in beside her, reached up and took her hand.

"I'm very sorry," he said. "I know you were close. She talked about you a lot."

"You and Sister were . . ."

"Both alcoholics. That's where I met her, at AA. Four years ago, about the time she found you. She was my sponsor."

"Oh, you're the one. The one who called . . ."

"In the middle of the night? Yes. I'm the one. The one she picked up at the Hi-Ho Club or the Red Dog Saloon . . . Bone's Place." Ray tossed his cigarette away and lit another one. "Wherever I ended up, she came after me."

"Mommy?" Americus pulled at Novalee's hand.

"She never gave up on me," Ray said. "After I lost my practice, about to be disbarred . . . well, she's the one who helped me turn it around."

Novalee looked across the yard. "I just can't believe it's all gone."

Americus unwrapped her hand from her mother's, then scooted away.

"Yeah," Ray said. "This must be quite a shock, but it might have been worse if you'd seen it before I had everything hauled off."

"You did that?"

"I'm executor of the estate, so . . ."

"Estate?"

"Sister had a will." He reached into his pocket and pulled out a thick envelope. "It's all in here."

"What?"

"Her will, the deed, some checks . . . receipts. You'll need to sign some papers, then—"

"Why?"

"Because she left it all to you, Miss Nation. The land. And the trailer. Insured, but just for the minimum. Eight thousand. And eight thousand on the contents. State Farm. The check's in here." Ray handed the envelope to Novalee. "And a check from National Republic, a life insurance policy for ten thousand, and you're the beneficiary."

"Mommy," Americus called from across the yard.

"Anyway," Ray said, "it's all yours."

Novalee took the envelope, her movements stiff and mechanical.

"Have you made any plans?"

bedrooms with old quilts and four-poster beds

"Will you be staying in this part of the country?"

kitchens with copper pots and blue china

"Mommy!"

walls covered with family pictures in gold frames

"Mommy, look!"

Novalee turned and saw Americus skipping around the buckeye tree—still tall, still straight, still alive.

it's lucky . . . helps you find your way home if you get lost

"Or are you going back to Tennessee?"

home is where your history begins

"What?"

"I was just wondering if you'd be going back to Tennessee?"

"No. I'll be staying here. Staying home."

Chapter Twenty-Six

THE REDHEAD at the bar lit another cigarette and re-crossed her legs, letting the fringed miniskirt slide farther up her thighs to reveal the crotch of her lace panties. She wanted to make sure the singer who called himself Billy Shadow kept her in his sights. She had nothing to worry about.

Willy Jack had her spotted, her and all the rest of them—the little brunette in tight jeans and halter top that just covered her nipples . . . the leggy Hispanic in red boots and denim shorts that didn't quite cover the cheeks of her ass . . . a doe-eyed girl who sucked her thumb every time he looked at her. Willy Jack hadn't missed a one.

But tonight, he wasn't looking for women. He was watching for Johnny Desoto, one of the biggest agents in the business, who was coming to hear him sing.

"So what can I do for you, Billy?"

"Well, Shorty Wayne said I ought to get in touch with you, Johnny. Said you like my song."

"The Heartbeat, right?"

"The Beat of a Heart."

"Nice tune."

"Shorty said if I was in Dallas, I should give you a call."

"You do that."

"Well, that's why I'm callin'."

"You're here in Dallas? Now?"

"Yeah. I opened at Cowpokes last week."

"How long you gonna be around?"

"I'll be here till the tenth."

"I see."

"So I thought . . ."

"Billy?"

"Yeah?"

"You still with Ruth Meyers?"

"Yeah, but I'm thinkin' about makin' some changes, Johnny. If you know what I mean."

As Willy Jack pumped his fist in the air to let the drummer know he was half a beat behind, he let his voice slide into the chorus of "Mama, Don't Let Your Babies Grow Up to Be Cowboys," the first song of the set by Billy Shadow and Night River.

Cowpokes had gone over the occupancy limit of four hundred, even before Night River took the stage. An hour later, customers were still spilling through the door, eager to shell out the ten-dollar cover so they could pay five bucks a bottle for Lone Star longnecks. On the trendy end of Greenville Avenue in Dallas, Cowpokes catered to the young, monied crowd—fresh-faced professionals in Stetsons shading their eyes from disco strobes, fraternity boys from SMU wearing six-hundred-dollar Lucchesi boots that would never cover rougher terrain than inlaid parquet, and thin golden women, their looks hard won by exercise coaches and tanning beds.

But Cowpokes was a long way from the places Willy Jack had started in, the cut-and-shoot clubs where Ruth Meyers had booked him in the beginning, mean places in tough towns—the Back Stabber Bar in Trinidad, Colorado . . . the Forked Tongue in Winslow, Arizona . . . Coonasses and Crackers in Biloxi, Mississippi.

Ruth Meyers had wanted to see if Willy Jack had staying power, see if he could survive the glamorous world of entertainment. He could—but sometimes not by much.

In Chillicothe, Missouri, a place called the Hole in the Wall, a man in a wheelchair tried to kill him with a claw hatchet because the band couldn't play "The Sound of Music." In Decatur, Alabama, in Baby's Bar and Grill, a woman held an ice pick to her husband's ear and demanded that Willy Jack sing "Your Cheatin' Heart."

In Hot Springs, Arkansas, three brothers holding a wake for their father brought his body to the Rubber Rooster where they made Night River play "Blue Eyes Crying in the Rain" from midnight till four the next morning.

And in Valdosta, Georgia, Willy Jack played in a bar called the Fang where he shared the stage with half a dozen cages of snakes. At feeding time, the bartender sold live mice for three bucks each and whenever a customer dropped a mouse into one of the cages, the band provided a drum roll and a chorus of "There Goes My Everything."

Willy Jack scanned the Cowpokes crowd again, wondering why Johnny Desoto hadn't shown up. Even with the place packed, he'd be easy to spot because he wore an eye patch, which, according to rumor, covered the ruins of an eye gouged out by a bull when Desoto had been on the rodeo circuit thirty years earlier.

"Can we have another round over here?" Willy Jack called to the bartender.

"No," Johnny Desoto said. "It's a little early in the day for me. Besides, I have a lunch meeting in an hour."

"Then I'll get right to the point." Willy Jack leaned closer to the table, his tone confidential. "I think Ruth Meyers has went about as far with me as she can."

"Is that right?"

"Man, she ain't got the clout."

"Oh, I wouldn't underestimate Ruth Meyers. The woman's got a track record."

"Sure, she's put a lot of musicians on stage, but—"

"She got your song recorded, Billy."

"Shit!" Willy Jack shook his head in disgust. "A damned single by Shorty Wayne."

"Now Shorty's had some hits. He's been up there. And he made a lot of people a lot of money, including Ruth Meyers."

"Well, he ain't made me rich."

"He's getting some air time."

"That ain't doing my career a hell of a lot of good." Willy Jack held his empty glass up for the bartender to see.

"So what do you have in mind, Billy?"

"An album. My album . . . and a video. Some TV time. That's what I need, someone to promote me."

"And you don't think Ruth Meyers is?"

"Hell, Johnny, Ruth Meyers ain't got the clout."

Willy Jack caught the attention of a barmaid and signaled for another shot of Wild Turkey as the piano player, a scrawny little guy called Davey D., kicked off "Misery and Gin."

Davey D. was the only musician left of the four Ruth

Meyers had put together to form Night River while she was creating Billy Shadow.

She had hired the best she knew, the best of a hundred bands she had formed and re-formed, mixed and blended—good musicians who knew the ropes and the road. She tracked them down, rounded them up and put them with Billy Shadow.

Then, remembering her days as a girl back in Missouri, memories unaccountably jarred loose by the shape of Willy Jack's lips, and thinking of that Missouri girl and those first delicious nights along the Current River with that first delicious boy, Ruth Meyers called her new singer and her old musicians Night River, feeling somehow that shadow and night might coalesce.

But that hadn't happened. Not because the drummer couldn't keep the rhythm. Not because the bass player couldn't take a solo. Not because the guitarist didn't have perfect pitch. It hadn't happened because they were too tall. Only Davey D. was shorter than Willy Jack—and only Davey D. was still around.

And though the replacements were not as good, not as polished as the originals, Billy Shadow's star seemed to be rising nevertheless. Ruth Meyers had done her work well. But it had been a job of work and it had taken a small army to get it done. Willy Jack had needed a lot of cleaning up.

On that day back in Nashville, Doc Frazier, the dentist, had nearly cried when he looked into Willy Jack's mouth where he found decay, gingivitis and more than twenty years of gunk to scrape through. But a month later, when Doc was finished, Billy Shadow had climbed out of the chair, his teeth capped and bridged and crowned—as clean and white as hospital sheets.

Nina, the beautician who took Willy Jack on, had to first

cure him of dandruff, which infected his scalp, his eyebrows and the corners of his nose, a condition she treated for a week with a tar and hot castor oil paste. Next, she cut and reshaped his hair, creating a soft, casual look with curls that tumbled across his forehead. Then she gave him a dark chestnut rinse, a color that made the most of his violet eyes. She toned his skin with mudpacks and treated the puffiness under his eyes with a cucumber and mayonnaise gel. Finally, after she gave him a manicure and pedicure, she took a picture of Billy Shadow, proof that her beauty school training had paid off.

Jack Gooden, the tailor at Preston's Western Wear, had ushered Willy Jack into the fitting room with instructions to peel off his clothes, the polyester pants and plaid shirt Claire Hudson had given him back in prison. An hour later, Willy Jack was adrape in yards of fine worsted wools and gabardines in rich amber and deep russet, while Gooden pinned and measured and chalked. Two weeks later, Billy Shadow slipped into his new suit that hugged his slender hips and padded his narrow shoulders and swished against his thighs as he walked.

Tooby the bootmaker had looked away that first day, pretended he hadn't seen the newspaper stuck to the heel of Willy Jack's sock. He knew without looking inside the cheap Acme boots that they were crammed full of paper. Willy Jack wasn't the first short customer he'd ever had. Tooby also knew, several weeks later, when the boy slid his feet into the hand-stitched alligator boots with two-inch heels, that Billy Shadow had never stood straighter and never looked taller than he did that day.

So when Ruth Meyers and her army had finished, Willy Jack Pickens stepped in front of a mirror, smiled at what he saw and watched Billy Shadow smile back.

And Ruth Meyers knew even then how much grief he would cause her. She knew someone's wife would get caught with him in the back seat of a Lincoln or Cadillac. She knew someone's daughter would get pregnant and swear he was the father. She knew someone's kid would get busted supplying him with weed and cocaine. Ruth Meyers knew what was coming.

She knew he'd bend the rules and break the law, sell her short, cut her throat and try to walk away. Ruth Meyers knew who she was dealing with, so she should have known better.

But when Billy Shadow stepped back from that mirror, grabbed Ruth Meyers and kissed her as he danced her around the room, he caused her heart to race and her blood pressure to spike and her throat to tighten at fresh memories of that delicious boy on the Current River.

"Glad you could make it, Johnny."

"I'm running a little late, but I got tied up. Couldn't find a graceful way to get up and leave."

"Well, we get the next set cranked up and—"

"I'm not going to be able to catch the next set, Billy."

"Hell, you didn't hear but those last two numbers. I figured you'd—"

"I liked what I heard."

"Yeah?" Willy Jack took a long pull at his drink. "You like it enough to represent me, Johnny?"

"Whoa! We might be moving a little fast here."

"I'm ready to move fast. I been on this slow track long enough."

"You need to understand something, Billy. As long as you're still tied up with Ruth Meyers . . ."

"Look. I don't owe Ruth Meyers a damned thing. Not a damned thing."

"She may think different."

"I can end that this quick." Willy Jack snapped his fingers, accidentally spilling the last of his drink. "She don't have nothin' to say about it, neither."

"Billy, Ruth Meyers can be a powerful ally, but she makes a hell of an enemy. You sure you're ready for that?"

"Now what you figure she can do to me?"

"I'm just telling you. Ruth Meyers has got a mighty long reach."

"Shit. Ruth Meyers ain't got that kind of clout."

Willy Jack punched in Ruth Meyers' calling card number, then took another hit of the joint before he pinched it out. She answered on the first ring.

"Well, we're here," he said. "But it was a bitch. Rained all the way. And I gotta tell you, Abilene, Texas, looks like the asshole of the world."

"You're in the Ramada?"

Willy Jack could hear something in her voice, something to be careful of.

"Yeah. Let me give you this number." He had to hold the phone close to his eyes because the numbers were swimming. He knew he was fucked up, but he didn't want Ruth Meyers to know it. "764-4288."

"I tried to call you before you left Dallas."

"Is that right?" He knew then, with the silence hanging between them, that something was wrong. But it couldn't be about Johnny Desoto. She couldn't know about that. "You call the hotel or the club?"

"Both."

"Well, we got away a little earlier than we expected. What's up?"

"I got a call from an attorney in Albuquerque."

"Oh, hell. If this is about that girl back in—"

"It's about a woman named Claire Hudson."

"Who?"

"You know Claire Hudson?"

"No. Never heard of her."

"She says you didn't write 'The Beat of a Heart.'"

"Bullshit!"

"She says her son wrote it."

"That's bullshit! Her son's dead." Willy Jack knew Ruth Meyers was still on the line. He could hear her breathing. "Okay . . . I knew her, but . . ."

"You lying little son of a bitch."

"No. Listen, Ruth, listen! I wrote 'The Beat of a Heart.' It's my song and—"

"No, Willy Jack. You're wrong. It's Claire Hudson's song."

"What are you talkin' about?"

"Claire Hudson holds the copyright—in her dead son's name."

"God-damn, Ruth. I swear to you. Listen, god-dammit. I wouldn't lie to you. I would never lie to you, Ruth."

"Really? You really wouldn't tell me a lie, Willy Jack?"

"No! I need you. I need your help with this."

"Well, you need some help all right—but not mine. Maybe Johnny Desoto can give you a hand with this."

"Ruth? Now let's talk about this. Ruth? Let me tell you about that, Ruth? Ruth Meyers?"

Chapter Twenty-Seven

NOVALEE KNEW Forney would be worried. He'd probably called the highway patrol already to check on the roads. And she knew if she didn't get home before nine, he would more than likely start calling hospitals.

Snow had started falling in the late afternoon, but changed to sleet about dark. By the time Novalee got off work at seven, the windshield of her car was covered with half an inch of ice. She pulled a cardboard box from the trunk, a box Forney had filled with window scrapers, cans of deicer, flares, candles—dozens and dozens of candles. He had read that the heat from one candle kept a stranded motorist alive for two days in a North Dakota blizzard, so he had started buying candles and couldn't seem to stop.

The Wal-Mart parking lot, a mile of concrete with spaces for five hundred cars, looked almost deserted as Novalee eased the Chevy toward the exit. They had closed down nearly all the registers inside the Super Center as soon as the first snowflake had drifted to ground. And now they didn't need any registers at all.

She hoped the sand trucks had beaten her to the highway, but no one was expecting an ice storm in April, so she wasn't surprised to find the interstate glazed and slick. It was going to be a long drive home.

The commute hadn't been so rough the first few months she drove it. But the bad weather, which had started early in November, hadn't let up yet. She had driven through sleet, hail, freezing rain and snow—nearly twenty inches fell in December alone.

Moses and Forney had weighed the little Chevy down with concrete blocks and Novalee bought a new set of snow tires. Even so, she had slid and skidded all through the winter and had enough close calls on slick roads that she thought several times of giving it up and taking a job close to home.

She wasn't sure what it was that kept her chewing up five hundred miles of highway each week. She didn't know why she stayed with it, leaving for work at sunrise and driving home after dark. She sometimes wished she could do what others did and call in sick now and then, just roll up in her quilt on one of those dark icy mornings, say to hell with it and stay in bed.

Lexie tried to talk her into applying for a job at the hospital, a ten-minute drive across town. Dixie Mullins wanted her to go to beauty school so she could work with her in the shop. Mrs. Ortiz urged her to try for a federal job, something with the post office.

But for some reason, Novalee had stayed on with Wal-Mart, one of the few who made the transition to Poteau and the Super Center, and the *only* one who made the drive back and forth each day. She wasn't sure why, but she felt a tie to Wal-Mart. Probably because she had lived in one when she was pregnant . . . or because her daughter had been born there.

When the sleet changed to snow, Novalee thought of stopping to call Forney, to tell him she'd be late, but the exit ramps looked slicker than the highway, so she didn't chance it. Besides, Forney and Americus were in the middle of *Puck of Pook's Hill* and that would keep his mind off the weather for a while.

Mrs. Ortiz kept Americus during the day and would have kept her in the evenings, but Forney wouldn't hear of it. As soon as he closed the library and got dinner for his sister, he came to the house and stayed until Novalee got home. He had to be there, he explained, to try to catch up. He had read Americus so little nineteenth-century history and he had so little time. She would, after all, start kindergarten in the fall.

But Novalee was glad he was there. She liked seeing him when she walked into her house. No matter what kind of day she'd had, regardless of how tired she was or what mood she was in, she always felt better when she saw Forney smiling his crooked smile as she came through the door.

She always knew, when he looked shy and uncertain, that he'd brought her a surprise, a special treat. Like the morel mushrooms, "genus *Morchella*," he tracked down each spring to cook in his secret batter, or the first strawberries of the season, sugared and arranged on a thin blue china plate. Sometimes he'd bring her something he'd found tucked in a library book—a lock of auburn hair tied in a green silk ribbon . . . a love letter from a man named Alexander.

Forney brought her things for the house, too. A set of glass knobs he'd found at a garage sale, and delicate gold frames for the Polaroids Novalee had taken that first day in the Wal-Mart, the day Willy Jack had left her behind.

All three photographs bore traces of damage from the tornado, but Novalee didn't see the spots and scratches and dents. She saw only Sister Husband's miracle smile, Moses Whitecotton's gentle dark eyes and Benny Goodluck's thin brown body, stiff and awkward in his camera pose.

Novalee had hung the pictures on the living room wall before the paint was dry, before the windows were covered, before the furniture was even moved in.

Though she'd been in the house for over six months, it still had unfinished spots—kitchen drawers without handles, a strip of molding missing, some trim work yet unpainted. But it was home, a home without wheels, a home fixed to the ground.

She had designed the house herself. Four rooms and a bath, and a deck that circled the buckeye tree. Some thought she'd never be able to build it for twenty-six thousand dollars, the money Sister had left her. She did, though. But she had a lot of help.

Moses did the foundation work, Mr. Ortiz the framing. Benny Goodluck and his father laid brick; Forney and Mr. Sprock did the roofing. Mrs. Ortiz hung the paper and Certain made the curtains.

Novalee did a little bit of everything. She drilled, nailed, caulked, measured and sawed, lifted, climbed, carried and carted. She sweated, cussed, laughed, ached and cried, putting in weeks of eighteen-hour days and six-hour dead-to-the-world nights.

Then one steamy August afternoon it was finished. The house Novalee had only dreamed of was hers.

a home with old quilts and blue china and family pictures in gold frames

Forney was at the window when she pulled into the drive at half past nine. He had already scraped the steps and scattered rock salt on the porch.

"I've been so worried about you," he said as he whisked her inside and took off her coat.

"I would have called, but I couldn't find a good place to get off the highway."

"Did you have any trouble?"

"Well, traffic was moving, but just barely. I saw some cars banged up south of the Bokoshe turnoff. Overpasses were like glass."

"Mr. Sprock said they'd closed down 31."

"Was he here?"

"No, but he called twice. Worried about you getting home in one piece."

"I'll call him in a minute."

"You look bushed."

"Yeah. I am."

"How about a cup of coffee."

"That sounds great."

Novalee backed up to the fire, finally letting herself feel the strain of maneuvering the Chevy over miles of ice and snow.

The fireplace was something she hadn't counted on when she built the house, something she knew she couldn't afford. But Moses insisted she could, because he could build it. And he had. A real rock fireplace. He and Forney and Mr. Ortiz had hauled chunks of granite from the bed of Sticker Creek for two days.

Forney came back into the room and handed Novalee a steaming cup.

"Thanks. When did Americus go down?"

"About an hour ago, but it was a struggle."

"Too excited about the snow?"

"Too worried about the animals. She was scared they'd freeze. Wanted me to fix them some soup. 'Give them a hot meal,' she said."

"And you did it, didn't you?"

"Make soup? For a bunch of cats and dogs?" Forney threw his hands in the air to let Novalee see how ridiculous her question was.

"What did you make them?"

Forney ducked his head, dropped his voice. "A pan of gravy."

"Forney, you're a pushover."

"It's freezing out there, Novalee."

"No doubt about that."

"And if Americus is determined to take in the strays of the world, I figure she's going to need some help from time to time."

"Don't suppose you kept any of that gravy for me?"

"Americus wouldn't let me. She said there wasn't enough. But I made you some creamed chicken."

"Good. I'm starved." She picked up a brochure from the coffee table. "What's this?"

"Benny Goodluck left it for you. It's that information you wanted on winter honeysuckle."

"Did he say his dad ordered it?"

"No."

"Did he mention the Indian hawthorn I asked about? Or how much it would cost for—"

"Novalee, that would be an awful lot of talking for Benny. He's not real crazy about words."

"Oh, he talks, Forney."

"To you, yes. To me? No." When the phone rang, Forney pointed to it. "That'll be Mr. Sprock again. Ready to round up a Saint Bernard and go rescue you."

Novalee picked up the receiver, then stretched the cord across a chair so she could stay close to the fire.

"Hello?"

"Novalee?" Lexie's voice sounded hushed. "You got the TV on?"

"No. I just got home."

"You haven't heard the news?"

"What news?"

"About Sam Walton?"

"Mr. Sam?"

"He's dead, Novalee. Sam Walton just died."

Novalee was working returns when the announcement came on the intercom.

"Attention Wal-Mart customers and employees . . .

The woman leaning over the service counter smelled of horseradish and wore a fake fur coat that was buttoned crooked. She pulled a cotton sweater from a paper sack and shoved it across the counter to Novalee.

"I ain't never had it on 'cause it's too small."

The sweater might have once been white, but it had grayed with age. Stains circled the underarms and the neck was stretched and misshapen.

". . . because Sam Walton gained the respect of . . .

"It might fit a small-chested woman, but that ain't me."

Novalee turned the sweater inside out looking for a code tag, but it had been cut away.

"I'll just take the refund 'cause I got too many sweaters now. My boyfriend says I take up the whole damned closet 'cause I got so many clothes."

". . . for a moment of silence in memory of Mr. Sam."

"I paid nineteen ninety-five, plus tax."

Novalee bowed her head and closed her eyes.

"Listen, I got my kids in the car. I gotta take them by my sister's place and get to work by two."

". . . the valley of the shadow of death . . ." Novalee mouthed the words.

"Hey. Did you hear me? I'm in a hurry."

". . . goodness and mercy shall follow me all the days of my life: and I will dwell in the house of the Lord forever."

Chapter Twenty-Eight

ON HER FIRST photography job Novalee got paid seventy dollars. Out of that, she spent twenty for film, five for gasoline, and she gave Benny Goodluck ten. If she'd added another three-fifty for their lunch at McDonald's, she'd have cleared just over thirty dollars. But that didn't matter. That didn't matter to her at all.

She got the job because of Benny, whose math teacher was looking for someone to take pictures at her wedding. Carolyn Biddle didn't have much money to spend and Novalee wasn't looking to make much, so they struck a fast bargain.

"I got it, Benny. I got the job," Novalee said as soon as he answered the phone.

"That's great!"

"The wedding's on the twenty-fourth, which is perfect because I have that weekend off and the Whitecottons will keep Americus so she won't have to make the trip with me."

"What trip?"

"To Tahlequah. Miss Biddle's going to get married at her mother's house in Tahlequah."

"Are you going by yourself?"

"Sure."

"What if you have a flat or something?"

"Benny, I know how to change a flat."

"Yeah, but I was just thinking that maybe . . ."

"If the weather's nice, they're going to get married outside. She's got everything planned. She even asked me to wear pink."

"Why?"

"Because everything's going to be pink. The flowers, the cake, the dresses."

"What if someone shows up in purple. Or yellow? What'll she do?"

"Benny, she's a teacher. If she says, 'wear pink,' you wear pink."

"Yeah, that's right."

"You know, I think I'll shoot with Vericolor. Pink can be tricky if you shoot in the sun."

"Maybe I could help you?"

"What?"

"Maybe I could go with you. Load your camera. Stuff like that."

"Well . . ." Novalee tried not to sound surprised, but she was. "Well, sure. Sure you can."

"Really?"

"I'm not kidding. I'm going to need some help because . . . now don't mention this to Miss Biddle, but I've never been to a wedding."

"Me neither."

Novalee laughed, then she said, "Well, I've seen some on *As the World Turns.*"

"I guess they're all the same, aren't they?"

"These were. It was the same woman who got married every time."

"I don't think Miss Biddle's been married before."

"Don't worry, Benny. We'll figure out what to do."

"Novalee, what should I wear?"

"You don't have a pink suit, do you?"

For the next three weeks, Novalee spent her breaks at Wal-Mart looking through bridal magazines for interesting pictures, but she didn't see much beyond the traditional shots. Getting those wouldn't be a problem unless the camera fouled up or the film was bad, possibilities that were beginning to make her a little nervous. From what she could tell, women got real crazy over their wedding pictures.

Then, just a few days before Carolyn Biddle's wedding, Moses told Novalee a story about his aunt.

"Effie, my mother's sister," Moses said, "married in 1932, right smack dab in the middle of the Depression, so I don't suppose it was a fancy wedding. She and her man both came from poor people.

"But it was a church wedding and beautiful, so I was told. Aunt Effie wore a satin dress made by my mother, and everyone had flower gardens back then, so the church was filled with color.

"Well, Aunt Effie's man was killed ten years later in the Battle of Midway. Aunt Effie never married again. Worked as a housekeeper till she was seventy or so.

"Then, when she was up in her eighties . . . eighty-four, eighty-five, her house caught fire. Aunt Effie was at a neighbor's house when they saw the flames, so she wasn't in any danger. None at all. But you know what she did? Ran home! Ran into that house on fire to save the pictures of her wedding. Pictures of a bridegroom dead over fifty years."

"She died for some pictures," Novalee said.

"No, Aunt Effie died for love. And I guess there's a lot worse to die for. A lot worse."

That night Novalee had bad dreams—dreams about blackened pictures and smoking cameras and wedding dresses burned to ash. The next morning she was still groggy from a restless night when Lexie called with exciting news.

"His name's Roger. Roger Briscoe. And Novalee, he's a professional man. A CPA. Has his own business in Fort Worth."

"Fort Worth? Where'd you meet him?"

"At the Texaco Station. We pumped gas together. Now listen to this! He drives a new Buick. Brand-new! Still has the dealer's tag on it."

"So what's he like?"

"Smart. Real smart! And you should see him. He dresses better'n a banker. But I looked a mess. No makeup, my hair was frizzy. We'd just come from the laundrymat and the kids were just filthy. But Roger said they were beautiful and he couldn't believe they were all mine.

"He took them inside and bought them Cokes and then he asked if he could take us to dinner and I said, 'All of us? Right now?' And he said yes, so we went over to the Golden Corral. It cost him over fifty dollars and I didn't even eat."

"Why not?"

"I'm on that new grapefruit diet. Anyway, guess what. He's going to come after us next weekend and take us all to Six Flags. You have any idea what that's gonna cost?"

"A bunch."

"But he doesn't act like the money even matters. He's just . . . just a generous, kind man. I could tell that right off. He liked us, too. He really liked us."

"Well, why wouldn't he, Lexie?"

"Oh, you know how some guys are. They act like they're interested till they find out you have kids. But he's not like that at all. He told Brownie he had lovely long fingers like a piano player and he said Praline was pretty enough to be in the movies. He just makes people feel good.

"You know, you never can tell, Novalee. Maybe someday you'll be taking my wedding pictures."

Novalee was up at six on the morning of the wedding, an hour before her alarm was set to go off. The day before, she had made a checklist of everything she needed to take, but she'd spent the night thinking of things she'd failed to put on the list.

While she was packing, trying to fit in lenses, Forney called to wish her luck. He was ordinarily a late sleeper, but he said he'd been up since three though he wouldn't say why. But Novalee could guess.

In the past month, Mary Elizabeth had started a grease fire in the kitchen and she'd fallen twice, bad falls that sent Forney rushing her to the emergency room. And one early morning the week before, she had been naked on the front library steps before Forney found her, wrapped her in a blanket and led her back inside.

Forney didn't talk much about his sister, but other people did.

Novalee had just hung up the phone when Certain came to pick Americus up. They rushed through a quick breakfast and tried to hurry Americus through her ritual of saying goodbye to her flock of strays, whose number was growing fast. She had recently taken in a pregnant cat she named Mother and a three-legged beagle she called Sir.

By the time Certain and Americus drove away, Novalee was running late. She threw the rest of her equipment together, jumped into her pink dress and raced across town to pick up Benny Goodluck.

Novalee and Benny arrived at the Biddle home with time to spare, but the wedding was less than an hour away when Novalee discovered she had left the film at home on her bed. She tried not to panic after Benny searched the car once more and came up empty-handed again. She wanted not to think about what Miss Biddle would do when she found out her photographer had no film for the camera.

But Novalee supposed the wedding would go on, with or without pictures. After all, the preacher had arrived and so had the groom. The patio was arranged with baskets of flowers; chairs had been set up in the yard for the guests. The wedding cake was ready to cut and the punch was chilled. This wedding was going to take place, ready or not. So how important, Novalee wondered, could film really be. And then she remembered Aunt Effie who had died for her wedding pictures taken sixty years ago.

Novalee floorboarded the Chevy, followed the directions she'd been given and found the tiny camera shop—closed and locked up tight. From a 7-Eleven on the corner, she got the shop owner's number and ten minutes later, a gnarled little man with eyebrows like steel wool unlocked the door of the Shutterbug and let her inside.

"I was taking a nap," he growled.

"I'm sorry, but your wife said—"

"My wife said you were shooting a wedding, but you didn't bring any film."

"And the ceremony starts in about half an hour, so—"

"Why didn't you bring film?"

"Well, I meant to, but I forgot it. Look, I'm really in a hurry and—"

"You're a photographer? A professional photographer? And you forgot the film?"

"It's my first job."

"Might be your last. Now. What do you want?"

"Vericolor. A pro pack."

"What are you using for light?"

"I'm shooting outside."

"Aren't you going to use fill flash?"

"Well, I . . ."

"You have any idea what I'm talking about?"

"Sure!" Novalee tried for bold, but couldn't quite pull it off. "Sort of."

"Hell." He jerked a flier off the wall, then slapped it down on the counter. "Dr. Putnam! She teaches photography here at the college."

"Oh."

"That's eighteen dollars and sixty-six cents, but I'll settle for twenty seeing I don't have any change in the register. But then I didn't plan on opening up on Sunday."

"I appreciate it." Novalee pushed two tens across the counter, then took a step toward the door.

"Here!" He flipped the flier in her direction. "I didn't take this down for the exercise."

"Okay." Novalee grabbed the paper and backed across the room. "Thanks," she said, then she pulled the door closed behind her and ran to the car.

On the way back to Carolyn Biddle's wedding, Novalee thought of a dozen comebacks to the old man in the camera shop, a dozen ways to cut him down . . . and they were all clever.

Hell no, I didn't forget the film! Someone stole it.

Who do you think you're talking to? You ever heard of the Greater Southwest Award?

You damned right I'm a photographer! Now give me that film before I cut your throat.

Benny Goodluck broke into a run when the Chevy rounded the corner and he had the door open before the car had rolled to a stop.

"Hurry!" he said. "They just started the music."

Novalee loaded the camera as she ran for the backyard and she took her first shot as Carolyn Biddle, her pink dress floating around her, stepped out of her mother's door and into the sunlight of her wedding day.

"Yeah," Benny said, "but I never knew she was so pretty."

"They say a woman's her most beautiful when she's in love."

Benny took the last bite of his Chicken McNugget, then licked away a smear of ketchup in the corner of his mouth.

"Well, she never looks that good at school."

"Here." Novalee shoved her french fries across the table. "You eat these. I had too much wedding cake."

Benny took a fry, then paused, waving it in the air. "It just seemed so weird watching my teacher get married, watching her kiss." Benny's face reddened.

"I thought it was romantic."

"Novalee, you think you'll ever get married?"

"I might. If someone asks me."

"Not me!"

"Oh, you'll fall in love someday, Benny, and when you do . . ."

"I don't know nothing about love."

"I'll bet you do."

"No. I've thought about it, but I just can't figure it out."

"What do you mean?"

"Well, sometimes love seems easy. Like . . . it's easy to love rain . . . and hawks. And it's easy to love wild plums . . . and the moon. But with people, seems like love's a hard thing to know. It gets all mixed up. I mean, you can love one person in one way and another person in another way. But how do you know you love the right one in every way?"

"I'm not sure, but I think you'll know. I think if it's the right person, it'll be better than rain and hawks and wild plums. Even better than the moon. I think it'll be better than all that put together."

"Novalee, do you . . . I mean, are you . . ."

"What?"

"Are you in love with someone?"

Novalee was so still that for a moment Benny thought she hadn't heard him. But then she moved . . . tilted her face to catch a slender shaft of sunlight . . . shifted her gaze to something the boy couldn't yet see.

"I think I am, Benny," she said. "I think I am."

Chapter Twenty-Nine

Novalee was in the kitchen sorting negatives when the phone rang, but before she lifted the receiver, the caller hung up. She was almost disappointed. Talking on the phone would have been a lot more fun than trying to deal with the mess in her kitchen.

In the two months following Carolyn Biddle's wedding, Novalee had shot a family reunion, two birthday parties and a dance recital. Now she was struggling to conquer the mountains of negatives and prints on the verge of avalanching all around her.

If she got to shoot the Chamber of Commerce banquet and the Miss Sequoyah Pageant, then she'd probably have to build on another room. And if she didn't reorganize the clutter in Moses' darkroom, she wouldn't blame him if he canceled her membership.

She was just beginning to make some headway when she uncovered a picture of Forney, a shot she had taken one evening in her backyard. She had caught him with his dark eyes turned to her and a familiar softness around his mouth, the way he looked just before he smiled.

She ran her finger over the photograph, touching his throat, the ridge of his jaw, his lips. Then, as she lifted the image of Forney's face closer to her own, the phone rang again and she jumped like she'd been caught doing something she shouldn't.

"Hello?"

No one answered, but the caller was still on the line. Novalee could hear the quick catch of breath.

"Who is this?" she asked.

"Brummett."

"Who?"

"Can you come over here?"

"Brownie?" Novalee was trying to connect the sound of the boy's voice with the child who had called her "Nobbalee" since he was four, but this voice didn't belong to a child.

"Can you help us?" he asked.

"What's wrong? What happened?"

"We need you."

"Are you at home?"

"Yes."

"Where's Lexie?"

Novalee knew the boy moved the phone away from his mouth. She could hear him talking, but she couldn't make out the words. Then, from somewhere more distant, she heard a girl crying.

"Is Lexie there?"

When he didn't answer, Novalee pressed the phone tighter against her ear, straining to hear every sound. She thought she heard him say, "hold still," but she knew he wasn't talking to her.

"Brownie?"

She heard a door close, then far from the phone he said, "Pauline," but it sounded like a question.

"Brownie!" She cupped her hand around her lips, trying to amplify her voice. "Brownie!"

A moment later she heard shuffling sounds, then his breath, thin and uneven, against the mouthpiece.

"Let me talk to your mother." Novalee tried to sound calm.

"She can't."

"Why? Why not?"

"Because . . . because . . ." Something gave way then—a splinter of sound, sharp and pointed, ripped through his voice.

Novalee said, "Okay. I'm coming." She heard the phone slide across fabric, a stiff crackling like static.

"Did you hear me?" she yelled.

She knew the receiver had hit the floor; she heard it bounce against the tile.

"Brummett?" The connection hadn't been broken, but there was no sound coming from the other end of the line.

"Brummett, can you hear me? I'm coming."

Novalee drove the ten minutes to Lexie's in five, slammed the Chevy into a juniper bush when she parked and jumped out of the car so suddenly she forgot to cut the engine.

The door to Lexie's apartment was draped in red tinsel and covered with a crayon drawing of the Christ Child even though the Fourth of July was only days away.

When Novalee stepped inside, she squinted against the whiteness of Lexie's enameled walls. The living room was undisturbed—magazines lined up on the coffee table, the spread on the couch smoothed free of wrinkles, toys picked up. The room looked just as it should. But something was wrong.

"Lexie?"

The apartment was absolutely silent. No clinking glasses, no flushing toilet, no laughing children. The only sound came from a distance, the whine of an eighteen-wheeler on the interstate half a mile away.

As Novalee started down the hall leading to the bedrooms at the back of the apartment, she nearly stepped on Madam Praline's green velvet hat. The crown was crushed and the veil torn almost in two.

Suddenly, a figure flashed across the doorway of the front bedroom, a naked child, bare feet slapping the floor as it darted like a dragonfly, then disappeared.

When Novalee reached the doorway and looked inside, she didn't see them. The bed was unmade and, at first, she couldn't see them huddled together in the jumble of pillows and quilts. But they were there, the twins, locked in each other's arms, identical faces pressed cheek-to-cheek.

"Are you all okay?"

They stared, wide-eyed and unblinking.

"What's happened here?"

Baby Ruth put her finger to her lips, then whispered, "Roger," and at the sound, they both came crawling across the bed and grabbed at Novalee, wrapping themselves around her legs, pressing their faces into her skirt.

"Where's Peanut?" Novalee asked, her voice hushed.

Cherry pointed to a lump in the bed. "There," she said, then she pulled her hand back quickly and twisted it around Novalee's arm.

With the twins clinging to her, Novalee shuffled to the bed and lifted the covers. The baby, sound asleep, had wiggled out of his diaper and lay in a widening ring of fresh urine.

"Let's go find your momma," Novalee said, but as she began to guide them toward the door, they broke away and scrambled back to the bed, back together in the safety of pillows and quilts.

When Novalee stepped back into the hall, she was tiptoeing.

Lexie's door was closed and if there was sound on the other side, Novalee couldn't hear it for the pulse pounding against her eardrums. She started to knock, but didn't—started to call Lexie's name, but couldn't.

When she turned the knob, the door swung open on its own.

"Oh, my God."

Praline was hunkered in a corner, naked except for a pair of limp gray socks. Her hair was wet, plastered against her face, her eyes vacant and tearless. She rocked back and forth, keening softly like a frightened animal. A string of saliva dripped from her bottom lip onto an old scab on her knee.

Brummett was sitting on the side of the bed trying to work the childproof cap off a bottle of Tylenol.

"This damned thing," he said.

"Brummett, can you tell me . . ." but Novalee never finished what she started to say because that's when she saw Lexie.

Someone had pulled the covers up to her neck and someone had put a wet washrag across her forehead, but no one had hidden her face.

One eye was so swollen the lid had turned inside out. The other eyelid was torn open and the eye, bulging from between the ripped tissue, followed Novalee's movements as she neared the bed.

A clump of hair was matted in the dark mucus seeping from Lexie's nostrils and a chunk of flesh had been bitten from her cheek. Part of her upper lip was severed . . . a piece of it hung against her teeth.

She made a sound then and her lower lip tried to shape a word, but her chin tilted at a crazy angle as if her face had been broken in two.

"Lexie, don't. I'm going to call . . ."

Brummett's head jerked up as if he had just heard Novalee come in.

"You found her hat," he said.

Novalee was surprised to see the velvet hat balled up in her fist.

"Oh. Praline's hat. I, uh . . ."

He crossed the room quickly. "Don't call her Praline," he said as he yanked the hat out of Novalee's grip.

He was wearing a pair of white jockey shorts and when he turned away from her, Novalee saw that the seat was smeared with something dark. Blood crusted in the soft blond down on the backs of his legs.

"Here," he said to his sister. "Let's put your hat on."

When he touched her shoulder, the girl yelped and twisted away, but he made a shushing sound and smoothed her hair until she began rocking again. He gently worked the hat down on the top of her head, then pulled the torn veil across her face.

"Her name's Pauline," he said. "And she's not a baby anymore."

Chapter Thirty

WHEN HER SICK LEAVE ran out, Lexie had to go on medical leave without pay, so Novalee emptied the white enameled apartment, moved her things to Moses' barn and moved the kids in with her and Americus. By the time Lexie got out of the hospital, they were already settled in.

Lexie's broken jaw would be wired shut for six more weeks and her eyelid and lip would need some plastic surgery later on, if she could ever afford it. She also had a couple of cracked ribs and a sprained wrist, but damaged more than anything was her spirit.

Pain pills kept her asleep most of the first week while Novalee tried to ease them all into a routine without too much friction. As soon as she arranged for ten days of vacation, she got Brummett and Pauline set up for therapy through Human Services.

She worked out a way to get the twins into nursery school for three hours a day and she let the Ortiz girls take the baby to the park every afternoon. Then Novalee tackled the house.

After she rigged up more clothesline in the backyard, she found a rhythm to doing five loads of laundry every day. But cooking for eight instead of two took some practice.

Her garden still had onions, okra, tomatoes, and peas, enough to last for a while. And Mr. Sprock, who always complained of his harvest going to waste, delighted in bringing baskets of corn, squash and potatoes.

Mrs. Ortiz taught her how to make *calabazas mexicana*, a kind of squash soup everyone liked except Brummett. Forney threw a little of everything in a pot to make gallons of a mystery he called slumgullion and Certain brought boxes of sweet potatoes that Novalee baked in breads and pies.

Lexie lived on whatever could be sucked through a straw, but she drew the line at sweet potato milk shakes. When she began to lose weight, she wrote Novalee a note saying she'd finally found a diet that worked.

Lexie could talk even with the wires in her jaw, but had to contort her mouth into grotesque shapes that scared Pauline and made her cry, so Lexie wrote notes if she had something to say. In a way this was a blessing, for she seemed to find less pain in silence.

Americus fussed around like a five-year-old nanny. She helped the twins get dressed, gave the baby his bottle, and brushed Pauline's hair without pulling at tangles. She left small treats for Brummett, on his plate or under his pillow, but he usually swatted them away or tossed them on the floor. She gave Lexie a bell to ring when she needed fresh water or wanted to close her door.

When Lexie was able to get up and around, she helped out wherever she could, but she had little energy and tired quickly. Novalee could see the pain in her eyes, but she didn't think it came from stitches and wires. She waited for Lexie to talk about what had happened, what Roger Briscoe had done to them, but she didn't push.

Two policemen came by once with a picture for Lexie to see, but it wasn't Roger Briscoe. When they left, she went to bed and stayed all day. Pauline, who couldn't bear to be separated from her, went to bed, too.

Brummett stayed away from his mother as much as he could, avoided rooms where she was, spoke to her almost not at all. But he watched her when he was sure she wasn't looking.

On their first visit to the psychologist at County Mental Health, Novalee drove them over and waited while they were inside. When they came out an hour later, Pauline was crying, clinging to Lexie. But Brummett stomped out alone, then rode home in sullen silence, his body pressed against the door. When Novalee parked in the driveway, he bolted from the car, running toward the woods a block away. He didn't come back until after supper.

That night, Novalee dreamed of Forney, something she had done often in the past few months. He was outside her house trying to find his way in, trying to find his way to her. But there were too many doors, hundreds of doors, all of them locked except for one.

Novalee wanted to call out, tell him which door would open, but she couldn't. She could only wait.

And then she heard the whine of the screen, and knew Forney had found the unlocked door. But when she heard a familiar metallic click, she sat up in bed, no longer dreaming. Someone had just opened her front door and she knew it wasn't Forney Hull.

Slipping out of bed without waking Americus, she tiptoed down the hall to the living room. The twins were asleep on the couch, but Brummett and his cot were gone.

"He moved his bed outside. To the deck." Lexie was sitting at the kitchen table in the dark.

"Lexie, are you okay?"

"I got up to go to the bathroom."

"You want some water? Something to drink?"

"I was standing beside the cot, watching him sleep. But then he woke up and stared up at me . . . and I saw something in his eyes."

Novalee sat down, folded her legs under her and tucked her gown around her feet. "Did he say anything?"

"Not a word. Just jumped up, grabbed his cot and went out the front door."

"Well, he's moved that cot before. Never know where he'll be come morning."

"He hates me, Novalee."

"No, he doesn't. He's just confused."

Lexie pulled in a deep breath, then said, "I was supposed to work until four o'clock that day, but I skipped my lunch hour and got off at three because Roger was coming in from Fort Worth."

"Are you sure you're ready to do this, Lexie?" Novalee reached for Lexie's hand.

"I stopped by the day care for the twins and the baby, then hurried home. I wanted to take a shower and shampoo my hair before Roger got there. Get the smell of hospital off of me.

"Anyway, his car was parked out front when I pulled in. I was surprised because he said he wouldn't be in until after four. But Praline and Brownie were home, so I knew he hadn't had to wait outside in the heat."

Lexie tightened her grip on Novalee's hand, her thumb beginning to move in hard circles.

"When I opened the door, I heard a sound coming from

the back of the apartment. It sounded like Brownie, like he was choking. All I could think was that he was strangled on something.

"I shoved the baby at Cherry and I ran to the back, ran toward the sound. My bedroom."

Lexie's fingernails were cutting into Novalee's palm, her hand locked like a clamp around her fingers.

"Something was against the door. I had to push to get it open. It was Pauline, crumpled in the floor, her hands over her eyes.

"Roger had Brummett on the bed, bent over the end of the bed, and he . . . Roger had . . ." Lexie's breathing quickened. "He had his . . . he was inside Brummett, Novalee. Inside my baby."

Lexie shook her head as if she might dislodge the image.

"I flew at him. I was going to kill him. I wanted to, more than anything in the world. I think I hit him twice before . . ." Lexie shivered. "That's all I remember." She dropped Novalee's hand and let her head fall forward.

"You couldn't save them that, Lexie. But you may have saved them from something worse. After he beat you, he ran. And as horrible as it was for Brummett . . . and for Pauline . . ."

"You know he didn't rape her, don't you?"

"Yes, they told me at the hospital."

"When he tried . . . tried to put it in her mouth, she threw up on him. And that's when Brownie walked in. That's when he took Brownie instead."

"Lexie, Brummett knows it wasn't your fault. But he's just a little boy. He's going to need some time."

"How much time, I wonder. A lifetime?"

"Maybe when the police find Roger Briscoe, when they get him in jail, maybe then you and the kids can . . ."

"We'll never be the same, Novalee. Never."

Lexie pulled herself up from the table and padded across the kitchen. For a second, Novalee thought she was going back to her room, but then she stopped, turned.

"How did a man like Roger Briscoe find me? How did he find me and know he could do such a thing to me? To my kids?"

"What do you mean?"

"He had to be looking for women like me, women with children, women alone. Women who were stupid."

"Oh, Lexie . . ."

"But the others, those other women, they saw through him, didn't they? They could tell he was evil. But I didn't see it. I didn't know. And now, I've got to live with that, but I don't know how. I don't know if I can."

"You can! You can, Lexie! This isn't the first time you've been hurt. It's not the only time you—"

"But this time it's not just me. It's my kids, goddammit. It's my kids."

"That's right! And they're in pain. Maybe the worst pain they'll ever feel in their lives because they've lost something they can't get back, something they'll never have again. That's gone, Lexie. Roger Briscoe took that!"

"That bastard!"

"Yes, he is. But you've survived others. Every time one of them left you pregnant, walked away from you and your baby, he hurt you both. And I know that kind of pain. But look what they left behind."

"Yeah. Dirty underwear, hot checks, shitty toilets."

"They left us with these little people who celebrate the wrong holidays all year long . . . who get roseola and ringworm . . . bleed on our blouses and pee on our skirts, lose our keys, drag home dogs with mange and cats with worms . . ."

"Spill nail polish on our best pair of shoes," Lexie said, "and drop our favorite earrings down the garbage disposal."

"Flush our only good bra, wear a velvet hat with a veil . . ."

"But Novalee, what am I going to say to Brummett and Pauline when they ask me why this happened to them? What will I say?"

"Tell them that our lives can change with every breath we take. Lord, we both know that. Tell them to let go of what's gone because men like Roger Briscoe never win. And tell them to hold on like hell to what they've got—each other, and a mother who would die for them, and almost did."

Novalee went to the kitchen window and pushed the curtain aside.

"Then tell them we've all got meanness in us . . ."

She could see Brummett asleep on his cot, one arm dangling over the side, his face dappled by moonlight shining through the buckeye tree.

"But tell them that we have some good in us, too. And the only thing worth living for is the good. That's why we've got to make sure we pass it on."

Chapter Thirty-One

NOVALEE HAD NEVER BEEN on a college campus before and she was sure everyone who saw her knew it. She tried to look like she belonged there, but she didn't figure she was fooling anyone. Most of the people she passed had backpacks or armloads of thick textbooks. She had a camera and a thin spiral notebook with a picture of Garfield on the cover, a gift from Americus and Forney.

She wasn't even sure where she was going. She stopped outside a red-brick building and dug in her purse for the brochure the college had sent her a few days earlier.

When the hateful little man at the camera shop had shoved the flier in her face, she never dreamed it would lead to this. She hadn't even intended to keep the flier, but she had carried it in her purse for three months until she finally made the call. Two weeks later, Novalee had become a college student.

She was there for a photography seminar—four Saturdays at Northeastern State University in Tahlequah, to study printing techniques—for seventy-five dollars. And she would earn one hour of college credit.

She had been sure she wouldn't be accepted, certain she couldn't be enrolled as a student because she hadn't even finished the tenth grade. But her enrollment papers had been processed and she had a copy in her purse in case anyone wanted to see it.

According to a campus map in the brochure, she was in the right place. Regents Hall, a majestic three-story building draped with ivy, just the way she had imagined it. She found the seminar room on the second floor.

She was the first to arrive so she slipped inside, afraid someone might hear her, call out and ask to see identification. Demand proof that she had a reason to be in such a place.

She had expected desks and blackboards, but the room looked more like an auditorium than a classroom. Tiers of theater seats were arranged in a semicircle with a stage in the center.

She took a seat in the first row, but she felt like a kid at the movies, so she got up and moved to the back.

A steady stream of people entered, nearly two dozen, and they all sat near the front. Just as Novalee made up her mind to switch seats again, a thin, deeply tanned woman took the stage.

"Good morning," she said, then pulled a pair of glasses from one pocket and a folded piece of paper from the other.

Novalee would never have imagined her to be the teacher. She carried no books or briefcase, and she looked more like a construction worker than a college professor. She wore a baseball cap, work boots, slacks and a canvas jacket.

"I'm Jean Putnam," she said. "You don't need to bother with the 'Doctor.' Just call me Jean."

She counted heads then and when she came to Novalee, she smiled and said, "Why don't you come down front with the rest of us."

Everyone turned to stare as Novalee made her way down the aisle. She turned her notebook so they couldn't see Garfield and wished like hell she had worn her jeans.

She knew she was dressed all wrong, had known it as she watched the others file in. She was wearing a skirt and blouse, hose and a brand-new pair of navy pumps. She had dressed the way she supposed college students dressed. But the ones in this class were wearing pants, sweatshirts and tennis shoes.

Novalee slid into a seat in the second row and tried her best to disappear.

Dr. Putnam spent the first hour giving an introduction to the course, talking about "slow-sync modes" and "built-in slaves," "hard shadows" and the "afterglow of filaments." Sometimes Novalee knew what she was talking about, but sometimes she didn't.

"Now," Dr. Putnam said, checking her watch. "Our bus should be out front. Let's get going."

Novalee had no idea where they were going, but she fell in behind the others as the teacher led them outside and onto a university bus. From the conversation around her, Novalee learned they were going to an outdoor lab, whatever that might be.

The man who sat beside Novalee was friendly and they made small talk a couple of times, but mostly Novalee's mind was on a conversation she and Moses had had a few nights earlier.

"You go on and take that class," he said, "and don't you be scared."

"But I might be getting in over my head."

"You'll be fine, honey. Just fine."

"Moses, I'm not sure about that."

"Listen. They're going to teach you some things I can't. There's lots of technical stuff I don't know. But you remember this. You know something that no one can teach."

"What's that?"

"You know about taking pictures with your heart."

The bus trip, which took nearly twenty minutes, ended on a gravel road a hundred yards from the Illinois River. From there, they walked to a wooded area where Dr. Putnam stopped, the students fanning out around her.

"We're going to make our way upriver for a mile or so. You'll find plenty to shoot out there, but remember, the best part of a good picture takes place in the darkroom. That's where we'll be heading when we're finished. Any questions?"

Two hours later, when they crawled back on the bus to return to the campus, Novalee had a blister on her heel, cockleburs in her hose and tree bark in her hair, but she was no longer worried about how she looked.

She had taken three rolls of film along the river and somewhere in those seventy-two shots of dragonflies and honeybees and horny toads, she might have one that would tell her a secret. And her adrenaline was pumping with the odd excitement she always felt in knowing she was about to find out.

"Remember this," Jean Putnam said, "bleaching is a process that can't be learned from books. No one can tell you how to do it or show you how to do it. Oh, they can demonstrate. They can suggest and they can advise, but bleaching is learned by doing. Learned by touch."

The campus darkroom was large enough that every student in the class had a separate work station at a counter with a sink. Jean Putnam strolled around those counters as she talked.

"Now you can use a Q-tip selectively to lighten portions of the print, spots with too much shade or small dark areas threatening black."

Novalee had slipped off her stiff new shoes and her shredded stockings and was working barefooted, the tiles of the darkroom floor cool against her feet.

"Or you can use a sponge if you're working with a large area," Dr. Putnam said. She stopped then beside the man who shared Novalee's seat on the bus and bent close to the print he was working on. "You've probably gotten that a little too light, but it's hard to tell."

When she resumed her pace, she said, "Remember, the bleaching process doesn't stop when the application does. Potassium ferrocyanide is like that rabbit on television. It just keeps on going."

Novalee was working on one of the lizard prints, the first one she had shot.

She had been stumbling down a dry rocky gully in pursuit of a monarch butterfly when she saw the horny toad and when it saw her. The lizard lifted hooded eyes in startled response, but it did not race away. As Novalee bent and swung the camera around, the creature backed up, but still it did not run, instead held its ground just at the edge of an outcropping of rock.

When Novalee pressed closer, the horny toad puffed itself up in a show of boldness, the spiked horns at its neck menacing and dangerous. Novalee cut her eyes to the viewfinder just as the horny toad hissed, a fierce little dragon in an ageless ritual of courage and dread.

Now Novalee was remembering what Dr. Putnam had said earlier in the day. "The best part of a good picture takes place in the darkroom."

Novalee dipped a Q-tip into the mixture of potassium ferrocyanide, then began to move it in small, tight circles on a darkened area of the print, a shaded area in front of the horny toad's eyes.

Suddenly, without Novalee realizing she was there, Dr. Putnam was at her shoulder. "You'll know when it's right," she said softly. "Your fingers will tell you."

"But how . . . "

"Some kind of magic that tells you it's enough, just exactly enough to find what you're looking for."

"I don't really know what I'm looking for."

When Novalee wiped the Q-tip once more over the print, her fingers began to tingle and she pulled the swab away.

"You felt it, didn't you?"

"Yes. Yes, I did."

As they watched, the shaded area continued to lighten and Novalee saw what she was looking for, a tiny arc of blood spurting from the eyes of the mighty horned lizard, *Phrynosoma platyrhinos*, and Novalee knew she had begun learning the secret of seeing into shadows.

Chapter Thirty-Two

WILLY JACK dropped another quarter in the jukebox, punched B7, then slid back onto the stool at the end of the bar. He settled an invisible guitar on his lap, then strummed a few warm-up chords while he waited for his song to begin. When it did, he closed his eyes, played along with the melody and sang harmony with Wayne Deane to "The Beat of a Heart," which had climbed to number three on the charts.

"When you are without a friend
And got no company

The bartender, beefy and black, cut his eyes at Willy Jack. "Jesus Christ, man, don't you know another song?"

"World has kicked you over and over
You're crying 'Woe is me'

"You got something against Whitney Houston or Tina Turner?"

"Well, you're not the Lone Ranger
This I know for sure

"I'm about sick of listening to that cowboy shit."

"I wrote this god-damned song." Willy Jack swung around to point at the jukebox, then had to fight to regain his balance.

"Yeah, I know! You told me already," the bartender said, clearly as sick of the story as he was of the song. "You wrote it and someone named Freeny stole it and—"

"Finny! I told you it was Finny! But he didn't steal it. Hell, he was dead. It was his mama. It was Claire Hudson."

"Right. The mama did it."

"You damned right, she did. And now, I ain't got shit!"

The bartender nodded his head. "That's about the way I see it."

"Now Claire Hudson's rich. Shorty Wayne's rich. Wayne Deane's rich. And Billy Shadow ain't got shit."

A woman with a nervous face leaned over to Willy Jack and said, "Honey, let's get outta here." But when she tried to take his hand, the one holding the neck of his make-believe guitar, he shook her off.

"If you're one who has lost everybody
You may find just one more

Her name was Delphia, but Willy Jack couldn't remember it. Sometimes he called her Della; sometimes it was Delilah. But mostly, he didn't call her anything.

"No matter how lonely you are
There's someone in this world who loves you

When Willy Jack made it to the chorus, he let his head fall forward the way he had on stage so that his hair swung across his eyes.

"No matter how lonely you are
There's someone in this world who loves you

But he hadn't spent much time on stage in the past two years. Not since Ruth Meyers had cut his throat.

After she'd called her Night River musicians back to Nashville, she'd canceled Willy Jack's credit cards, she'd canceled his bookings—and she'd canceled his career. He couldn't get a gig in a choir.

He'd made the round of lawyers, glad-handed men in dark suits who couldn't wait to see justice prevail. They'd verified that "The Beat of a Heart" was a posthumous copyright filed by Claire Hudson while Willy Jack was in prison—the same prison where she worked as a librarian. And the lawyers verified that an Indian named John Turtle had been Willy Jack's cellmate and a witness to the creation of the song. But the Indian had died, the librarian had disappeared and Willy Jack had run out of money.

So much for justice.

"When you're tired of fighting
Feel like saying 'I give'

Willy Jack had made his way back to Dallas, but Johnny Desoto wouldn't touch him by then. Ruth Meyers had already poisoned that well.

So Willy Jack picked up a half-assed drummer in Oklahoma City and a fair piano player in Abilene, musicians as down and desperate as he was, and they'd headed west.

Billy Shadow and Sunset. A scruffy trio of dopers and drunks living out of a rusty VW van, picking up work in pistol-whipping bars that even Ruth Meyers wouldn't bother to mess with. They never got paid much more than their bar tabs, just enough to score some meth or a gram of coke whenever they could.

"And if God really loves you
He's not the only one

They were together for nearly a year before the drummer got busted up in a fight in Greasewood, Arizona, and lost the use of his left arm. Then in Prescott, the piano player took off with a redhead named Rita, so by the time Willy Jack drifted into California, Billy Shadow was a solo act.

Two days after he crossed the state line, he went to jail in Barstow on a charge of public intoxication. He was there for nearly a week before he reached J. Paul, his cousin in Bakersfield, who wasn't thrilled to hear from him, but sent the two hundred dollars for bail.

"You'll discover a family you never had
Before your life is done

Billy Shadow had spent the next year picking up gigs in the border towns . . . dives in Potrero and Plaster City where the owners charged him double for whore's whiskey . . . bars in Jacumba and Campo where pushers sold him bad dope.

But he could still find a stage now and then. He could still draw an audience. He could still please a crowd. And if Billy Shadow knew anything about show business, it was that an artist had to have fans to make it to the top.

But that was going to be hard to do now because yesterday Willy Jack had made a big mistake. Yesterday, he had pawned Finny's guitar, the Martin.

"When you think you can't remember
what it felt like
when you had a friend
You'll have one again"

"Come on, Willy Jack. Let's go," Delphia said. "He's not gonna show."

"He's gonna show! And the son of a bitch better have my money or I'll stomp his ass."

Willy Jack narrowed his eyes and tried for his Clint Eastwood glare. But he didn't feel nearly as tough as he looked. He was beginning to get worried.

He'd hocked the Martin because a street hustler named Pink had offered him a deal he couldn't pass up, a deal that would net Willy Jack nine hundred bucks.

what it felt like
when you had a friend

Pink had a friend who had to turn two pounds of smoke fast, but he couldn't get out on the street to do business because someone was after him. If he showed his face, he was liable to get it blown away, so he had to get out of town quick and he needed money.

Pink said his friend would sell the reefer to him for two hundred dollars if he could get the money now. And Pink had already lined up a buyer—a guy who'd pay two thousand dollars when he had the stuff in his hands.

But Pink was a hundred shy of what he needed and that's

where Willy Jack came in. For a hundred bucks, Willy Jack would get a return of a thousand, half the purchase price.

Of course, Willy Jack didn't have a hundred and the only thing he had to raise the money on was the Martin.

"Well, how long are we gonna wait?" Delphia asked. "I'm getting hungry."

When the song ended, Willy Jack motioned the bartender for another drink, picked up a quarter from a stack of change in front of him and turned toward the jukebox.

"Dammit!" Willy Jack kicked the dash of Delphia's Pinto. "God-dammit!" He threw his head back against the seat and rubbed his eyes.

He had driven all night to get to Bakersfield, five hours on the highway and another two to find J. Paul's house, and he'd been popping bennies for two days.

"Want me to talk to him?" Delphia asked.

"Now that'd be real smart, wouldn't it. If he won't give me the money, why the hell would he give it to you?"

"I just thought that . . . "

"I'm the fucker's cousin. I'm family, for God's sake."

"Well, maybe he told you the truth. Maybe he don't have a hundred bucks."

"Oh, he has it all right. Damned railroad paid him a fortune 'cause he got his thumb cut off. Just look at that place he's living in."

Delphia glanced at the townhouse, a two-story no-frills brick in a neighborhood going to seed. A miniature golf course across the street was boarded up and covered with graffiti.

"I guess family just don't count for much no more," Willy Jack said.

"But you said he helped you out once. Sent you money for bail."

"Yeah, and he ain't forgot it, neither. Threw that in my face, too. I had to stand there and listen to a damned sermon."

"Well." Delphia yawned. "What do you think we oughtta do?"

Willy Jack fished another benny from his pocket and pulled the tab on a warm can of Coors.

"Wanna go back to San Bernardino?" she asked.

"What the fuck am I gonna do in San Bernardino? Sit around with my thumb up my butt waiting for that bastard Pink to show up? Wait for him to hand me my goddamned money so I can get my guitar out of hock?"

"Maybe you could get another guitar. Maybe you could find something cheaper for now and—"

"How many times do I have to tell you this," Willy Jack said, his patience running thin. "There ain't *another* guitar. The Martin is the *only* guitar. Now do you understand that?"

"Okay. Okay!" Delphia started up the Pinto. "So what do you want to do?"

"Drive, Della. Just drive and let me think."

He reached into the back, dug through the debris of fifty thousand miles and came up with what he was looking for, a half-full fifth of Beam's 8 Star. He took a long hard pull at the bottle, then eased back in his seat and fixed his eyes on the road.

He needed to figure out what to do about the Martin, figure out some way to get it back. Because without it, he was nothing. He'd known that the first time he held it in his hands. Maybe, he thought, he'd just break into the pawn shop and take it. Or maybe he'd track down Pink.

Beat him, kill him if he had to. But he knew that was crazy. He knew that didn't make any sense.

But making sense was not going to be easy. For the last forty-eight hours, Willy Jack had been gobbling bennies and eight balls, he'd dropped some acid and smoked some grass and he hadn't slept a wink.

Give me your hand

He wasn't surprised when he heard her voice. When he was fucked up, he could almost count on it.

It had started while he was still in prison, sometime after the Indian had restarted his heart. In the beginning, it wasn't so bad. Just her voice . . . always her voice.

Feel that?

But later, when he was with Night River, she started talking to him while he was asleep. He'd wake up with a pain in his heart that twisted and burned . . . but the voice wouldn't go away.

Can't you feel that . . . ?

He turned the bottle up, swallowed again and again until he felt the warmth of the whiskey spread through his chest and into his belly. The yellow line in the middle of the highway was beginning to blur, so he closed his eyes and tried once again to think about the Martin.

Can't you feel that tiny little bomp . . . bomp . . . bomp?

"I don't feel nothin'," he said.

"What?" Delphia stared at him. "What are you talking about?"

"I didn't say anything."

They were quiet for the next few miles until Delphia pulled off the highway and the Pinto rattled to a stop outside a hardship cafe on the edge of town.

Willy Jack said, "What are you doing?"

"I'm beat. Let's have some coffee, get something to eat."

"Hell, we don't have time."

"Why not? What's the big hurry?"

"I gotta get some money."

"Where? Where you gonna come up with money?"

"Gotta go . . . gotta get my guitar." His words were so slurred that Delphia had to guess at what he said.

"You need to get something in you besides that whiskey."

"Now don't you start . . ." Willy Jack tried to shake his fist in her face, but it floated up and hit the rearview mirror.

"Suit yourself." Delphia slipped the keys out of the ignition, crawled out of the car and slammed the door.

Willy Jack fell over a curb and tore the knee out of his jeans. When he pulled himself up, he dug a piece of gravel out of the heel of his hand, then veered away from a complex of empty loading docks.

He'd walked more than a mile from the cafe where Delphia had parked the Pinto, wandering through a maze of deserted streets with boarded-up warehouses and weed-choked parking lots.

The sun was almost directly overhead when he crossed a viaduct and slid down a grassy hill into the train yard. The heat had softened the tar under his feet so that he felt like he was wading in molasses.

He saw a train backing down the rails across the yard, an engineer at the controls. He caught a glimpse of a brakeman perched on the back of an engine as it pulled slowly out of the yard. And he saw a teenage boy asleep inside a box car. But no one saw Willy Jack. No one saw him stumbling down the tracks, lurching from side to side.

When he fell against the tank car, he knocked some skin off his forehead, but he was able to stay on his feet.

"Shit," he said as he swiped at a trickle of blood in his eyebrow.

He pushed away from the car and staggered back and that's when he saw the letters swimming only inches away from his eyes. He had to squint to bring the words into focus.

"Union Pacific," he said as clearly and distinctly as a sober man. "Union Pacific." And with the sounds of the words came pieces and parts of an old memory.

Willy Jack's breath quickened as he reached up and traced the letters with his fingertips. Then he rested his head against the warm metal of the tank car and hoped, more than anything, that he wouldn't cry.

He wouldn't know for five days that he still had his fingers, wouldn't know until then that he still had his thumbs.

But he would remember the smell of something dark and fresh . . . and a pain that had teeth and claws.

And he would remember someone picking up one of his legs and bringing it back to him . . . someone who, like him, was trying not to cry.

Give me your hand.

And he would remember the sound of her voice calling from somewhere above him.

Feel right there . . . That's where the heart is.

Part Four

Chapter Thirty-Three

"LEXIE, what do you think of this?" Novalee pulled a denim shirtwaist from a jumble of clothes piled on a patio table.

"It looks okay."

"Here." Novalee held the dress up to Lexie, then made a face. "No. This would swallow you," she said as she tossed it back on the pile.

They had been making the round of garage sales since seven-thirty to find Lexie some "skinny" clothes. She had lost sixty pounds and four dress sizes while her jaw was wired shut and even now, months later, she was still in her old size 22Ws. But Novalee was determined to change that.

"How about this?" She held up a black and white striped pantsuit.

"Isn't that a referee's uniform?"

"No. You'd look good in this. Why don't you . . ."

But Lexie was as little interested in clothes as she was in food. The only thing she'd bought all morning was a game of Operation, which was keeping the kids entertained in the car—all the kids except Brummett.

He had just left for Outreach, a summer camp for boys in crisis. And ever since Roger Briscoe, Brummett had been in crisis. He became more angry and sullen every day and had been caught twice stealing baseball cards from the IGA.

Pauline wasn't stealing, but she still had nightmares and she was still fearful of men. The psychologist at County Mental Health said she needed a strong male role model in her life, which had sent Lexie into a spell of depression that lasted for weeks.

"Lexie," Novalee said, "here's a pair of elephant earrings. Look at their trunks." Novalee handed the earrings to Lexie, who believed elephants with raised trunks brought good luck. When she worked the posts through her ears and posed for Novalee's approval, it was clear Lexie could use a change of luck.

Her ruined eyelid drooped and blinked out of sync with the other. And her lips, her once-perfect lips, were crimped and pinched with zigzag ridges of scar tissue, even when they smiled.

When they got back to the car, they found Peanut asleep, the twins in a fight, and Americus and Pauline sitting on the hood singing "Old McDonald."

"Novalee, I guess we'd better get back to the house. By the time we get the kids some lunch, it'll be noon and I'm supposed to look at that apartment today."

"Lexie, I wish you wouldn't be in such a hurry to move."

"Hurry? We've been there long enough now that by squatter's rights, we own your house."

Lexie hustled Americus and Pauline into the car, then crawled in behind them.

Novalee said, "You want to stop by and see the apartment now, on our way home?"

"No, I need my car." Lexie leaned close and lowered her voice. "Remember, I have to stop by the police station." As she settled Peanut on her lap, she added, "For all the good it'll do."

The police had turned up four Roger Briscoes, but only one was from Fort Worth, and he was fifteen years old. Of the others, one was black, one was blind and one had been in prison for twenty years.

By now, the case was growing old, but a policeman would call from time to time and ask Lexie to come in.

Novalee started the car, then pulled into the street when the first fire truck raced by.

"Hope I turned off the coffeepot," Lexie said.

Seconds later, they heard another siren.

"Can you smell smoke, or is that my imagination?" Novalee asked.

"I smell it, too," Americus said.

At the next light, a police car blocked the right lane and a policeman was directing traffic, moving cars one at a time into the left lane.

"Everyone wants to go see the fire," Lexie said.

"Can we, Momma?" the twins screamed. "Can we?"

"No."

When Novalee reached the corner, she rolled down her window. As she eased the Chevy around the policeman, she said, "Can I get through on Taylor?"

"I doubt it," the policeman said. "They're backed up six blocks in both directions from Locust and First."

Novalee's grip on the steering wheel tightened. "Locust and First?"

"Yeah," he said. "The library."

"No!"

"Yes, ma'am. The library's on fire."

On the day of his sister's funeral, Forney moved into the Majestic Hotel, a decrepit 1920s brick with sagging floors and stained ceilings. Whatever majesty it had enjoyed sixty years earlier was buried now beneath layers of chipped paint and the smell of cooked onions.

The pensioners who lived there, old men with milky eyes and clotted voices, looked up when Novalee opened the front door. They smiled at the sunlight shining through her white cotton dress as they recalled other summer days, other dresses. They sighed at the sound of her voice when she asked for the room of the librarian, and they remembered the smell of gardenias as she passed through the high-ceilinged lobby and hurried up the stairs.

She knocked three times before she opened the door. At first, she didn't see him. The room was dark and he was wearing a slate-colored suit.

"Forney?"

He was sitting up straight on the side of the bed, his hands folded in his lap.

"I was worried about you," Novalee said.

"I'm sorry."

"No, don't be sorry. I don't want you to feel sorry. I just wanted to see you."

"Oh."

"Forney, can I come in?"

"You want to come in?"

"If that's okay."

"Yes."

When Novalee closed the door, the room was so dark she could barely make out Forney's shape.

"You want to turn on the light?" he asked. "We can turn on the light."

"No. This is fine."

"I used to be afraid of the dark," he said. "But sometimes, it's the best place to be. Sometimes you can see things in the dark that you can't see in the light."

"What do you see here in the dark, Forney?"

From somewhere down the hall, Novalee heard canned laughter, then the voice of Fred Flintstone.

"When I was six," Forney said, "in the first grade, my father always picked me up at school."

As Novalee's eyes adjusted to the dark, she could see a wedge of reflected light shimmering on the ceiling.

"But one day, he didn't come. It was raining, so lots of parents came for their children, but my father didn't come."

Forney shifted his weight and the bedframe creaked beneath him.

"I watched everyone else leave, even the janitor . . . and then I was the only one left. I started crying because I thought I'd have to stay in the school all night by myself.

"Anyway, it was getting dark when I heard footsteps in the hall. It was Mary Elizabeth. She smoothed my hair and wiped my face, but I couldn't quit crying.

"She took my hand and we started to leave, but when we passed the auditorium, she stopped. I knew she wanted me to stop crying, but she didn't say anything, just looked at me for a moment, then led me inside."

Someone shuffling past Forney's door coughed, the thick, phlegmy cough of an old man.

"Mary Elizabeth took me to a seat on the front row, then walked up the steps to the stage. She looked out at me and began to hum a song, some tune I didn't know. And then she started to dance.

"She lifted her arms, turned her body slowly and began to glide. Moving to the sound of her song, she danced. She danced just for me.

"I sat very still and watched her. Never took my eyes away from her. She was so beautiful. And when she finished, she smiled at me."

The TV was shut off down the hall and a door closed somewhere nearby.

"You know what, Novalee? I don't think I ever saw her smile again."

The room was so still that Novalee felt suddenly afraid.

"Forney . . ."

"I want to tell you about this morning, Novalee, and why I couldn't go."

"You don't have to."

"I tried. Walked right up to the church, right to the door, but I couldn't walk in."

"Forney . . ."

"I had four white roses . . . for her. But when I got to the church, they'd turned brown." Forney wiped his face with the back of his hand, then he looked up at Novalee. "I couldn't take her brown roses."

Novalee would barely remember crossing the room and wrapping him in her arms . . . but she would never forget his breath against her throat as he murmured her name again and again. And when his lips found the silver scar at the corner of her mouth, she didn't know that the voice whispering "yes" was her own.

Chapter Thirty-Four

FOR THE NEXT FEW DAYS, Novalee's life seemed routine. She started on the inventory at Wal-Mart and finished up a photography job for the Chamber of Commerce. She made Americus a costume for Western Days, had dinner with Moses and Certain and completed her enrollment for another class at Northeastern—a course in American literature. She was everywhere she was supposed to be and she did everything she was supposed to do, but she was only going through the motions. Her mind was with Forney Hull.

She thought about him all day and dreamed of him at night, troubling dreams in which Forney was always saying goodbye. Each time the phone rang she hoped she would hear his voice. Even at work, when she was paged, she imagined it would be Forney on the phone.

She wrote him twice, but each time she tore up the letter because she sounded like a schoolgirl declaring her love. Novalee loves Forney. NN + FH.

She found herself doing silly things . . . singing love

songs in the dark, reading poems that made her cry. She cut her hair too short, bought herself a keychain shaped like a heart and watched *Casablanca* at two o'clock in the morning.

She was in love for the first time in her life, had been for months, and just couldn't keep it to herself any longer.

"Oh honey, I'm so happy for you," Lexie said as she took Novalee in her arms. "Forney's been crazy about you from the beginning. I told you so myself."

"Lexie, I've never felt like this before. I thought at first I was coming down with the flu."

"You're in love, Novalee. Trust me. I've *had* the flu. Now, tell me, what did Forney do when you told him?"

"Well, I haven't told him yet."

"Wait a minute! You made love in his hotel room. He said he loved you and you didn't tell him?"

"No. But . . . it was strange."

"Sure. It always is."

"No, you don't understand. When we . . . well, when we finished, Forney acted . . . strange."

"Novalee, Forney *always* acts strange."

"This was different."

"So, you're telling me you just left?"

"Oh, we talked—a little. Just 'How long will you be gone,' and 'I'll call you.' Stuff like that."

Lexie smiled and shook her head.

"Lexie, did I make a mistake?"

"Novalee, I know a little something about algebra and I can make a cherry cheesecake. I'm a pretty fair bowler and I used to be able to twirl a baton. But love? I just don't understand it."

And Novalee didn't think she understood it either. She

couldn't understand why she had hurried away from Forney's room when all she wanted to do was to stay.

She kept replaying what had happened at the Majestic Hotel. She saw herself in Forney's arms and heard him whisper her name—like lovers in a movie. She only wished she could rewrite the end of the scene so she could hear herself say, "I love you, Forney Hull. I love you."

Novalee was on her way to the Chamber of Commerce to drop off some photographs when she ran into Retha Holloway, the president of the Literary Guild.

"I've been meaning to call you, Novalee. I need to get Forney's mailing address."

"His mailing address?"

"Yes. I thought you might have heard from him."

"No, but he'll be back in a few days."

"He's coming back here? To Sequoyah?"

"Sure."

"Well, I'm surprised. I figured he'd just stay there until it's time for the new term to begin."

Novalee looked puzzled. "Miss Holloway, Forney went to Maine. He went—"

"To bury Mary Elizabeth. My, my. What a tragedy."

"He should be back today or tomorrow."

"You know the Hull family came from Maine." Retha Holloway's voice took on the singsong rhythm she had used in teaching English for over forty years. "Why, the first Hulls were Brahmin. Boston Brahmin. An aristocratic family," she said making sure to enunciate all five syllables.

"I knew Forney's mother quite well. His father only slightly. A difficult man to get to know. But very cultured, very well-bred.

"I don't think they were ever happy in this part of the

world. I know Mary Elizabeth wasn't. And I suspect Forney would have chosen a different life if he could have. But all that is getting ready to change, don't you think?"

"What do you mean?"

"Well, with Mary Elizabeth gone and the Hull mansion destroyed, Forney can get on with his life. After all, he's still a young man. Thirty-six was thought to be old when I was a girl, but not anymore. Why, Forney can go back to school now, finish his education."

Novalee nodded as if she understood.

"You know, Forney was attending Bowdoin College in Brunswick when his education was cut short by Mary Elizabeth's condition." Retha Holloway shook her head to emphasize the tragedy. Then, as if she were giving a test, she said, "Did you know, Novalee, that all the Hull men graduated from Bowdoin? As a matter of fact, Mr. Hull's great-grandfather lived in the same dormitory with Nathaniel Hawthorne. Just imagine!"

Retha Holloway's voice slipped into a higher register as she began to recite.

> *"Half of my life is gone, and I have let the years slip from me and have not fulfilled the aspiration of my youth . . ."*

"Beautiful, isn't it, Novalee. And so apt." Miss Holloway dabbed at the corner of her eyes. "Longfellow went to Bowdoin, too. Henry Wadsworth Longfellow. And now . . . it's Forney's turn."

"Yes, I guess it is."

"Anyway, I have some papers for Forney to sign. Just some legal work for the city. So we can close things out."

"But what about the library?"

"We already have an architect to draw up plans for the

new building. And Mayor Albright's daughter will take over, run things for us. A lovely girl. She has a degree in library science and she's a librarian now in Dallas, but she wants to come back here. Her mother's our incoming Literary Guild president. A fine family."

When a car pulled up at the curb, Retha Holloway motioned to the driver, an elderly man. "Well, Novalee, here's my ride. Nice to talk to you."

"Yes, ma'am."

"And when you hear from Forney, please tell him to get in touch with me."

Novalee stood on the sidewalk until the car was out of sight, but the sound of Retha Holloway's voice had been left behind.

. . . now he can get on with his life . . .

Novalee had been in bed an hour when the phone call came, but she wasn't asleep. She dressed quickly, woke Lexie to tell her she was leaving, then slipped out of the house as quietly as she could.

The night was muggy and still. When she drove past the bank, she noticed the temperature was eighty-four.

She parked across the street from the Majestic Hotel, then sat in her car for a few minutes watching the windows of Forney's room, watching his shadow cross the shades.

The lobby was empty except for one old man, shrunken like a museum mummy and slumped into a corner of a stained couch.

Forney's smile was in place when he opened the door as if he had been rehearsing while she knocked.

"Hi."

His hair was still wet from the shower and he had a fresh razor cut on his chin.

"Hello."

She started to hug him, but it caught him off guard and by the time he realized what was happening, she had backed off a step and stood awkwardly in the doorway, her hands hanging at her sides.

"Come in," he said.

As she stepped through the door and slipped past him, she smelled the soap he had bathed in. Something lemony and sweet.

"I'm sorry I called so late."

"I'm glad you did."

"Did I wake everyone up?"

"No."

The lights were on now, an overhead bulb and a lamp by the bed, so for the first time she really saw the room. The walls were papered with faded forest scenes; the furniture looked like painted army surplus. The only decoration was a framed print of a sad clown.

"How was your trip?"

"Long."

"Did everything go all right?"

"All right?"

"I mean with the ceremony. Your sister . . ."

"Mary Elizabeth." Forney nodded, then said her name again as if he needed to hear the sound. "Yes. Well, there was no service, nothing like that. There was no one there. Just me. And Mary Elizabeth. But no one else."

"Forney, are you okay?"

"Oh yes," he said, but he turned away, looked at the clown on the wall. "Well, I guess I am."

Novalee shifted her weight from one foot to the other

and Forney shoved his hands into his pockets. A toilet flushed in a room above them. To cover the sound, they both spoke at once.

"While you—"

"I wanted—"

"Novalee, would you like to sit down?" Forney made a hospitable gesture, but there weren't many choices. A metal office chair with a cracked vinyl seat, and the bed. Novalee took the chair.

"You must be tired," she said.

"A little."

"I was beginning to worry. When you weren't back by Wednesday . . ."

"I stayed longer than I intended. Rented a car. Acted like a tourist. I had forgotten how lovely it is there. Very different from here."

"I'll bet."

"You know, my mother and father were born there. Mary Elizabeth, too. I never really lived there, except when I was in college, but it felt almost . . . familiar."

"Skowhegan, you mean?"

"Well, that whole part of Maine. Skowhegan, Waterville, Augusta, Brunswick."

"Brunswick. That's where you went to college?"

"Yeah. I drove over there to poke around for a couple of hours and wound up staying two days. Spent some time on campus. Bowdoin has a great library. Saw a couple of professors I studied with. One of them has a new book coming out."

"Sounds exciting."

Another silence settled on them, but this time they waited it out.

"I thought about you, Novalee."

"Forney . . ."

"I wanted to talk to you, but I thought what I had to say . . . well, it wouldn't seem right over the phone."

"What did you want to say?"

"It was about the last time we were together. I was afraid . . . I mean, I wondered if I might have, uh, hurt you or something."

"Hurt me?"

"I suppose I wasn't very . . . well, I was worried that I might have been clumsy . . . not exactly . . . gentle."

"No, Forney. You didn't hurt me."

"I wouldn't want to, Novalee."

A noisy compressor in the window air conditioner kicked on and the lights dimmed for just a second.

"So, what's happening here?"

"Not much. Lexie found a place. A duplex. They'll be moving out on the first."

"You'll miss her."

"She won't be far away. Right across from the school."

"How's Americus?"

"Fine. She's going to be Annie Oakley in the Western Days Parade on Saturday."

"I brought her a book." Forney dug in an opened suitcase on the bed behind him and came up with a package wrapped in red paper. "*The Maine Woods*. Thoreau. We had two copies in the library here, but . . ."

"Retha Holloway wants to see you."

"Any plans yet for the new library?"

"Yeah, but I don't think you want to hear it."

"What?"

"Well, Retha said the mayor's daughter is going to be the new librarian."

"Oh, I'm not surprised. Albright's wanted to move her in

for a long time. But that's okay. It's time for something new." Forney wiped his hand over his face, then rubbed the back of his neck. "I hear they're hiring at the plastics plant."

Novalee had seen the workers from Thermoforms come into Wal-Mart to get their checks cashed—tired men and women, their ID badges still clipped to their pockets.

"Novalee?"

Unsmiling men and women waiting for the thin stack of bills they got paid for pushing the same plastic forms down the assembly line day after day, week after week.

"Novalee, are you okay?"

"Sure."

"You were a thousand miles away."

"Forney, what about teaching. You said once you wanted to be a teacher."

"Well, that was a long time ago."

"But if it's something you want, then time doesn't matter. Time doesn't matter at all."

"What I want, Novalee . . . what I want, is to be with you. To be with you and Americus."

"Forney."

"I love you. I love you more than anything in the world and when we were here together . . . when I had you in my arms . . ."

"Forney, maybe we made a mistake. I don't know how it happened or why it happened when it did. But maybe it wasn't the right time for us. Maybe we . . ."

"Novalee, did you . . . did you make love to me because you felt sorry for me. Was that it?"

"Oh, no. Don't think that."

"Because if that was the reason . . ."

"No, Forney. It wasn't."

"Then what? Just a bad decision? Just a spur-of-the-moment thing? Or one of those times when you were feeling low, needed a boost?"

"What do you mean?"

"I mean . . . do you care for me at all?"

"Care? Of course I care. You're the best friend I've ever had, Forney."

"But do you care?"

"You delivered Americus."

"Do you care!"

"You taught me to learn, Forney. You showed me a new world. You—"

"But do you love me, Novalee? Do you love me?"

"Forney, if I . . ."

She tried not to remember the way he held her after they made love . . . the way his lips felt on hers, the way his hands . . .

"You know, Forney, that I . . ."

She knew if she let herself remember, she couldn't tell him the lie he had to hear.

"Forney . . ."

She wouldn't be able to break his heart . . .

"No, Forney. I don't love you. Not in the way you need to be loved. Not in that way."

. . . and she wouldn't be able to break her own.

Chapter Thirty-Five

FOR THE FIRST FEW WEEKS after Forney left, Novalee thought she might be going insane.

She cried for no reason and in the strangest places. Once while she was pumping gas at the Texaco, she wept openly, didn't even try to hide her face. When she went to Parents Day and the second-grade teacher told her Americus was reading at eighth-grade level, Novalee sobbed uncontrollably and had to be led to her car. And one day when she was working in electronics, she saw—on three TV screens at once, Julia Child preparing orange almond bisque, and she cried so hard she couldn't finish her shift.

But crying wasn't what upset her most. It was the fear of losing her memory that would cause her throat to tighten and her skin to go clammy. Her first indication that she had a problem came when she read a novel called *An Episode of Sparrows,* read it all the way through, before she realized she'd read it before. A few days later she signed a check and misspelled her name. Then at work she clocked in on somebody else's time card and twice gave customers too much change.

By then she'd already bought a book called *Memory Magic* and she'd started taking large doses of Vitamin E, which she had read was "the brain vitamin." But she couldn't tell much of a difference. It seemed the harder she tried to concentrate, the more she forgot.

She'd find herself lost only blocks from the house. Dial the phone, but forget who she was calling. She'd go shopping, but buy things she didn't need. One day Lexie counted eighty-four carrots stuck in the crisper drawers of Novalee's refrigerator.

Her friends wanted to help, but they didn't know how. They couldn't ease the ache in her chest, the place that felt tender and bruised. They didn't know how to bring back the light to her eyes. They couldn't rewrite her dreams or fix her hurt or help her repair her heart.

Americus, as devastated by Forney's absence as Novalee, turned quiet and strangely detached. She took in another stray, a lame rabbit she named Docker, and she alphabetized all her books. She learned to make root beer floats and she got Dixie Mullins to teach her how to sew on buttons. She memorized the names of the Supreme Court Justices from John Jay to Mahlon Pitney before she began writing poems that she hid in a box under her bed. And in her prayers every night at bedtime, she asked God to bring Forney Hull back home.

If Novalee had only herself to worry about, she might have just gone to bed . . . crawled between the sheets, pulled a pillow over her head, and prayed for a deep, dreamless sleep. But she couldn't do that because her daughter needed her. So she forced herself up, faked an energy she didn't have, feigned a cheerfulness she couldn't feel and pretended Americus believed her performance.

She found places for them to go and things for them to do, but everywhere they went, there was Forney. He was the tall man under the umbrella running across the park . . . the thin guy who sat behind them at the movie. He was the figure in the stocking cap at the top of the ferris wheel . . . the lone skater at the rink . . . the face they saw through the window of the doll museum.

Then one evening at the mall in Fort Smith they heard Forney Hull paged over the intercom. They ran from one end of the mall to the other and arrived breathless at the security office where they met a boy too young to shave, a boy named Farley Hall.

Minutes later they crossed the parking lot trying to hide their tears, but when they crawled into the car, they gave up on being stoic. They cried and held each other, then went home and ate ice cream. Then they cried some more.

Forney's first letter came the very next day.

Dear Americus,

Enclosed please find a study schedule I have made out for you. This schedule will take you through the rest of The Latin Primer *by the middle of August. It is imperative for you to finish it before you start third grade. And don't forget, conjugation of verbs is only memory work. I love you. I stopped at the library in Washington, D.C., and stayed four days. Did the chocolate stain come out of your yellow dress? I reread* I Hear America Talking *and now realize that you must read it, too. The book is, unfortunately, out of print, but I have a used bookstore mailing you a copy, which you should have by the end of the week. You cannot know how much I miss you. Americus, you must keep pushing to get Latin added to the curriculum in your school. Remember this: change is brought about by good purpose. I dreamed about you three times and you were always smiling, but you had cat whiskers. Be sure to add* Word Origins and Their Romantic Stories *to your reading list. You will find it fascinating.*

Sincerely,

Forney Hull

Please tell your mother I extend my best wishes.

The letters to Americus kept coming, but with little regularity. She might get three on the same day, then wait a month for the next one. Sometimes they would be wrinkled and stained, dated weeks ahead of when they were mailed—or weeks after. They arrived smelling of shoe polish or mustard or glue. One had a bit of brown lettuce inside. Another came with a cracked green button.

They were written on recycled paper, hotel stationery and the backs of letters addressed to "Occupant." One came on the back of a menu, another on a flier announcing a poetry reading.

They were postmarked from St. Louis, Washington, Indianapolis, Pittsburgh, Kansas City, Baltimore, Akron and Louisville—and in that order. Americus traced his route on the map he had tacked up in her room. But if he was working his way toward some destination, she couldn't tell it.

Mostly he wrote about books and study. He continued to add to Americus' reading list, which had grown to over six hundred titles. He said little about himself and nothing about Novalee, but the last line of every letter was always the same: "Please tell your mother I extend my best wishes."

It wasn't much, but it was something and Novalee and Americus would take whatever they could get. When Forney had left, they had lost a piece of their lives, something that couldn't be filled by photography or Latin, by movies or ferris wheels . . . not by root beer floats, not by lame rabbits and not by all their tears.

Novalee thought of trying to find him, driving to all the cities where he'd been. She even thought of putting a "Come Back" message in the papers and hiring a private detective to track him down.

"And what would you do if you found him, Novalee?" Lexie asked.

"Well . . ."

"Would you tell him you love him?"

"Oh . . ."

"Would you ask him to come back?"

"Lexie . . ."

"You couldn't, could you?"

Novalee took a deep breath, then shook her head. "No," she said. "No, Lexie, I couldn't do that. Have him come back here and work in a factory? Flip burgers at Lita's Drive In?"

"Maybe he could get on at Wal-Mart?"

"No," Novalee answered too quickly.

"Oh. It's okay for you, but he's too good for it. Is that it?"

"That's not true."

"Here's the truth, Novalee. You never thought you deserved Forney. Never thought you were good enough."

"Listen to me, Lexie."

"No, you listen to me. I know your mother threw you to

the wolves. And I know what that asshole Willy Jack did to you, but . . ."

Novalee started to push away from the table, but Lexie reached over and took her hand.

"But look at what you've done, Novalee. Look what you've done for yourself. You have a wonderful child and a home. A family of friends who love you. You have a good job. You're a great photographer—an artist. You've read a whole library of books. You even go to college. You've got it all, honey. You've got it all."

"No, Lexie. I haven't got Forney. I haven't got him."

Four letters came for Americus on the same day, all postmarked Chicago. Novalee didn't think much about it at the time. She figured from the dates that Forney might have written the letters in four different cities, carried them with him for days and days, then mailed all four at the same time from Chicago. But two weeks later, another letter arrived with a Chicago postmark and that was a definite break in the pattern. Six days later, there was another and the next week, one more.

Novalee tried to talk herself out of what she was thinking, tried not to do what she did. She knew it was silly and wouldn't change the way she was feeling, but even as she dialed the phone, even as she started, she knew she wouldn't stop.

First, she called the Chicago Library, but they had no record of a Forney Hull. But she knew about Forney and books, knew he had to be around them if he was to breathe, so she called the Tulsa Library, then waited a week for the copies of pages from the Chicago phone book. Nine photocopied pages—from the Abraham Lincoln Book Shop to Waterstone's Book Sellers, Inc. She hoped she wouldn't have to go all the way to the end, and as it turned out, she didn't.

Forney answered on the first ring. "Chaucer's Book Store," he said.

For an instant, she thought she could tell him, thought she might be able to say the words, but then it was gone, floating somewhere beyond that time and that place.

"Chaucer's," he said once more.

Moments later, the phone clicked . . . and Novalee knew they were disconnected.

Chapter Thirty-Six

THE TINY HOSPITAL CHAPEL had not been designed for weddings. The five short pews crowded together might be enough for grieving families and the room would probably hold anguished classmates or mournful friends. Novalee could imagine such quiet huddlings in the early hours of painful mornings, but the chapel might be too small to contain the joy of this wedding.

Seven giggling, squirming children were jammed into the front pew; smiling adults were wedged butt-to-butt in the others. Several nurses, doctors and aides, in uniform and on duty, squeezed in late and stood at the back, ready to run if they were paged.

The hospital chaplain, a pleasant-looking man with dyed titian hair, waited at the end of the aisle, his back to a stained-glass window. At his elbow was the groom, a grinning and red-faced Leon Yoder.

When the door opened, everyone stood and turned to stare as Lexie stepped in and started down the aisle. She wore a slim suit the color of goldenrod and carried a corsage of seven white roses, one for each of her five children and Leon's two, all of them standing now at the front of the chapel—Brummett holding on to a renegade four-year-old, the twins with a waving toddler between them and Pauline, smoothing the hair of her youngest brother.

Novalee made a final adjustment to her camera and began shooting as Lexie, halfway down the aisle, flashed a radiant smile to Leon, the man about to become her husband.

They had met when Lexie had been able to go back to work at the hospital. Good nurse's aides were hard to come by, so she hadn't had any trouble getting her old job back.

Leon had been an aide, too, for nearly six years. But then he'd gone to nursing school and come back to County General, a registered nurse specializing in pediatrics.

He asked Lexie to go out one day while they were sharing a table in the hospital cafeteria. Even though she'd said no, he didn't give up.

"Sure, he *seems* nice," she had told Novalee. "But so did Roger Briscoe."

Weeks later, when Lexie finally agreed to go out with him, Leon took her fishing. Lexie, her kids and his kids, too.

"Nine of us," Lexie said. "It was a real circus, Novalee. We had kids with worms in their hair. Fish hooks flying. Ants in our sandwiches. And Leon's little girl, Carol Ann, she poured all the minnows in the lake."

"Did you have fun?"

"We had a great time. And Brummett caught a fish. A bass. Leon said it'd weigh three pounds. Thrilled Brummett to death. Of course, he couldn't show it. He'd grumbled all day about having to go and he acted mad the whole time. Until he caught that fish."

"Well, do you like him?"

"Leon? Sure."

"Sounds like you two hit it off. Sounds like maybe you all—"

"No! He's not my type, Novalee. I mean, he's a nice guy and all, but there's no electricity there. None at all."

"Dearly Beloved, we are gathered here today to join this man and this woman in Holy Matrimony

"I've tried to call you a dozen times, Lexie, but you're never home."

"Yeah, I know. Leon took us bowling last Saturday and on Tuesday we went to play miniature golf. If I don't stay home and get some laundry done, my kids are going to have to give up wearing underwear."

"Where were you last night? I drove by your place about eight. Thought we might take the kids out for ice cream."

"We went to the mall with Leon and his kids. He had to buy his little boy some pajamas, so we went to Sears. And I bought Pauline a blouse. Then the strangest thing happened, Novalee. While we were there, I put on this funny hat. Black with red flowers all over it. And you know what? While I was acting silly, posing in that hat, Leon told me I was pretty. He touched my lip and my eye and he said I was pretty. Can you imagine that?"

"Because marriage is ordained by God and is built on a firm foundation of trust and respect

"So yesterday when I told Leon that Brummett was in another fight at school, he said he'd go with me to see the counselor."

"Why do you have to do that?"

"It's something called a disciplinary conference. Remember when Brummett wrote 'Larry Dills french kissed a goat' on the bathroom wall?"

"Yeah."

"Well, I had to go to a disciplinary conference then. Mostly they talked about Brummett's 'behavior pattern' and his 'inability to control his emotions.' "

"He's doing a lot better though."

"Yeah. He's easier to live with. Leon's going to take him to meet one of his friends, a guy who runs a karate studio. Leon said martial arts teaches more than self-defense. He said it teaches self-control."

"Sounds like something I ought to take."

"Me too. I got so mad at work today I could have punched out a nurse on the cardiac unit. She spilled a cup of coffee on her desk and she made me clean it up. Acted like I was her janitor. I might just take Leon's advice some day and go to nursing school."

"Oh, Lexie. You should. You'd be wonderful."

"Well, if I ever get the chance, I just might. Anyway, I called for two reasons. Brummett and Leon caught a tub of crappie Wednesday night and they're going to treat us to a fish fry this evening. We want you and Americus to come."

"Can I bring anything?"

"No. Just come on over whenever you get in from work. Now, the second thing is this. Can I borrow your straw hat?"

"Sure."

"I'm going to be out in the sun all day Saturday and you know how I burn. Leon's taking us to Arlington to see the Rangers play a doubleheader. Can you imagine what that's going to be? Seven kids in a ball park all day with nachos and hot dogs and . . ."

> *"Do you Lexie take this man to be your lawfully wedded husband? To have and to hold . . .*

"I'm in love, I'm in love, I'm in love," Lexie yelled as she came bursting into the kitchen and whirled Novalee around.

"Whoa," Novalee said as she fell into a chair. "Lexie, do you know what time it is? I haven't even had my coffee yet."

"Did you hear what I said? I'm in love, Novalee!"

"Why is it so early and who are you in love with?"

"Leon! I'm in love with Leon Yoder! And I haven't even slept with him."

"But you said he didn't appeal to you."

"Forget what I said. King's X on what I said."

"Lexie, what's going on?"

"You're not going to believe this story, Novalee. You will *not* believe it."

"Try me."

"Okay. Listen to this. Leon's daughter, Carol Ann? She is *not* his daughter."

"That doesn't make any sense."

"Cody is his son, but Carol Ann isn't his daughter."

"And that's why you're in love."

"Now! Let me tell you how he got her."

"Lexie, let's have some coffee. I think you need it more than I do."

"Listen. Three years ago, Leon met a woman named Maxine. Max, he calls her. She had a little girl, Carol Ann. Well,

Max moved in with Leon. Max and Carol Ann. You with me so far?"

Novalee nodded and rubbed her eyes with the heels of her hands.

"Okay. Max gets pregnant with Leon's baby and Cody is born. So they have these two babies. Her Carol Ann and their Cody. Right?"

"Right."

"Well, when Cody was just a few months old, Max up and says she's leaving. Going to Mexico. Just like that. She's through with Leon and she didn't want their baby, Cody. She didn't want her Carol Ann, either, until she found out Leon did. He said he was scared of what would happen to her if Max took her to Mexico because by then, he could see that Max was a shitty mother.

"So, when Max found out Leon wanted the girl, she knew she had something to bargain with. Now, here's the clincher!

"Leon had a bright red '67 Camaro. And Max wanted it. So she traded her daughter for it."

"What?"

"Yes! She traded her daughter for a car."

"Lexie!"

"Leon never saw Max or the Camaro again."

"That's amazing."

"Novalee, when he told me that, I knew Leon Yoder was the pick of the litter." Lexie's eyes filled with tears, but she smiled. "And that's when I knew I was in love."

"I now pronounce you Husband and Wife."

Chapter Thirty-Seven

AT FIRST NOVALEE thought the music was in her dream. Slow romantic song. Lots of violins. She rolled over and pressed her face into her pillow, then realized she wasn't dreaming. The music was coming from outside her window.

She checked the time as she crawled out of bed. Eighteen minutes before midnight. She tiptoed down the hall to the living room and peeked out the front window.

Benny Goodluck was sitting on her deck.

She eased the front door open, then stepped outside. The music was coming from his pickup parked in the drive; the volume was up, the windows rolled down.

"Benny, what are you doing?"

"Did I wake you up?"

He was wearing a tuxedo and cummerbund. His snap-on tie had come undone, the bow now dangling down the front of his stiff white shirt.

"What's wrong, Benny?"

"Nothing."

"Then what are you doing here?"

"Are you mad, Novalee?"

"No, I'm not mad. But you're supposed to be at the prom."

He was folded into a lawn chair, his long legs stretched out in front of him. Pretending a sudden interest in the toe of one shoe, he bent to inspect it. "I was," he said, "but I left early."

"Where's your date? Where's Melissa?"

"I took her home."

"You sure ended the evening early."

"Well, Melissa didn't care," he said, but his words slid together and "Melissa" sounded like "Melissha."

"Benny, have you been drinking?"

"No. Well, not really. I had two beers."

"Is that why Melissa wanted to go home? Because you were drinking?"

"Yes. I mean no. I didn't drink until after I took her home, but . . ." Benny twisted in his chair. "I didn't have a date for the prom, Novalee. I told you a lie."

Novalee pulled up another lawn chair and sat down, pulling her legs up under her long cotton gown.

"I asked Melissa, but she already had a date and Janetta Whitekiller did, too, so I went by myself. But I wasn't the only one. Some other guys went without dates. Some of the other dweebs like me."

"Benny, don't say that. I'll bet both of those girls would've had a better time with you than whoever they went with. I'll bet they—"

"I didn't ask them, Novalee."

"What?"

"I didn't ask Melissa or Janetta. I lied about that, too."

"You'd better be careful, Benny. All this practice at telling lies, you'll get good at it."

"I'm sorry, but . . ." Benny shrugged his shoulders, then slid down in his chair and put his head back.

"But what?"

"You want the truth?"

"Sure."

"Okay. I've never had a date, Novalee. I've never even been with a girl."

"Well, you've got some time. I mean, you're . . ."

"Seventeen! Almost every guy I know has already . . . they've already had two or three girls by the time they're seventeen."

Novalee sighed and shook her head.

"What's that mean?"

"Oh, a lot happened to me when I was seventeen."

"Well, nothing's happened to me! Nothing good. Nothing bad. Nothing period!"

"Benny, what are you talking about. You're a track star, won all those awards. You think that's nothing?"

"Look, Novalee. I know what happened to you when you came here, when you were seventeen. I know some guy ran off and left you. And I know you had Americus in Wal-Mart."

"Yeah?"

"Well, that was awful for you then, but those were *real* experiences. You know what I mean?"

"No, I don't."

"I mean, you weren't stuck in Mr. Pryor's algebra class at eight-thirty every morning. You didn't have to suit up for basketball on Friday nights so you could sit on the bench. You haven't spent your whole life in Sequoyah pruning pear trees and mulching pines at the Goodluck Nursery. See, everything about my life is the same. Always the same."

"Benny . . ."

"I read those books you gave me, Novalee. All those stories about people going off to places like Singapore and Tibet and Madagascar. People who race cars and hop freight trains. Go up in balloons, climb mountains. Explore places where no one else's ever been. Stories about people who write plays and make movies. People who fall in love."

"You're going to do some of those things, Benny."

"Going to? When? I'll be eighteen tomorrow—and I haven't done anything yet."

"Good! Then everything's out there in front of you, isn't it?"

"I guess so."

"Think about this, Benny. What if you'd already done it all?"

"What do you mean?"

"What would be left? What would the next thrill be? What would be the fun of waking up every morning if you'd already done it all? Huh? What would you do?"

"I guess I'd do some of it again."

"But it wouldn't be as wonderful the second time around. Benny, we can't all go to Singapore, and some of us are never going to climb mountains or make a movie. But you run races and I take pictures and everyone looks for someone to love. And sometimes, we make it. Sometimes, we win."

"Yeah."

"Things will look different in the fall, when you go off to school."

"Oh, Novalee. I'm afraid I'll just be doing more of the same old stuff."

"No! You'll be learning new things, meeting new people. Exciting people. Lots of girls."

"That'd be nice."

"And I'll bet you'll meet some special girl. Some girl you'll want to be with all the time. Why you won't be able to sleep or eat because she'll be on your mind all the time, and—"

"Novalee, I've never kissed a girl."

"You will, Benny. You'll kiss a whole lot of girls."

"But I don't know how. I won't know what to do."

"Oh, it comes pretty naturally, I think."

"Can I kiss you?"

"Benny . . ."

"Just once. And I'll never ask again."

"I don't think that's a good idea. I'm not a girl."

"Twenty-five's not old."

"It's a lot older than seventeen."

Benny lifted his wrist and looked at his watch. "I'll be eighteen in three more minutes."

Novalee studied his face for a moment—the face of the ten-year-old boy who had leaned out of a truck and touched her . . . the face of the boy at twelve, running on a mountain ridge . . . the face of the teenager who loved rain and hawks and wild plums. Then she leaned across the arm of her chair, leaned toward Benny Goodluck and took his face in her hands and brought it to her own. As their lips met, he closed his eyes, and in the light of the moon and under the branches of the buckeye tree, they kissed. And it was the greatest adventure of his seventeenth year.

Chapter Thirty-Eight

NOVALEE WAS CONVINCED that luck could be passed on from parent to child just like the shape of a nose or bowlegs or a craving for chocolate. Americus did, after all, have Novalee's widow's peak, her green eyes, the same smile. So it seemed almost natural for her to inherit her mother's bad luck with sevens.

So far they had survived it, but sometimes just barely. They had lived through the seventh month of the pregnancy together. They had endured the seventh day of Americus' life and managed to make it through the seventh month. But now, they faced the greatest challenge of all—the seventh year. Americus had just had a birthday.

Novalee had kept the celebration small and quiet, as if too much attention might invite disaster. But the party had been without incident. There was no earthquake, no flood. Not a scraped knee or a bee sting, not even a sunburn. The weather was beautiful, the ice cream didn't melt and no one spilled the Kool-Aid. An almost perfect day.

Even so, in the weeks that followed, Novalee couldn't ignore the dread she felt, dread that chilled her skin and tingled her scalp. She knew something was coming. She just didn't know what or when. Sometimes she almost wished whatever was going to happen would come on, so she could get it over with.

She didn't have long to wait.

The newspapers had stacked up for three days while she finished developing pictures of a wedding she had shot in Keota the weekend before. She didn't get around to Monday's paper until Thursday night, just after Americus had gone to bed. She was working through them quickly because she still had to wash her hair and dry a load of clothes.

She was scanning pictures and headlines when she saw it, a short column tucked between ads on page seven.

VICTIM'S WHEELCHAIR STOLEN

A legless man identified as W.J. Pickens was discovered Sunday afternoon in the men's room at a rest stop near Alva. Pickens, who lost his legs in a train accident, had been trapped since sometime late Friday night when he was robbed of his wheelchair.

According to Pickens, an unidentified male picked him up outside of Liberal, Kansas, where he was hitchhiking. As they neared Alva, Pickens became ill and the driver pulled in and parked at the rest stop. Pickens said he wheeled himself into the men's room, but the driver followed him inside and fled with the wheelchair.

> On Sunday afternoon a survey crew heard Pickens' calls for help and notified the Sheriff's Office in Alva.
>
> Pickens, who left California two weeks ago, said he was hitchhiking to Oklahoma to search for his child and the child's mother, whom he had not seen since 1987.
>
> Pickens was admitted to Woods County General where he remains in guarded condition.

Novalee didn't do her laundry or her hair. She made two quick calls, then got Americus up and took her to Moses and Certain's. After she filled her car at the Texaco, she headed for the highway.

Willy Jack's eyes were closed when she stepped inside the room and for a moment she thought he was dead, but then she could see the rise and fall of his chest beneath the thin hospital gown. His skin, a sickly yellow, seemed too big for his body, like he'd shrunk inside it.

She watched him sleep and wondered what pictures he saw behind his twitching eyelids. Suddenly, his body jerked, a powerful jerk that shook the bed. He twisted toward the door.

"What did you say?" He fixed her with his eyes. They were the color of bile, the skin beneath them puffy and gray. "What did you say?" he asked again, insistence at the edge of his voice.

She let him struggle to pull her image into focus. She hadn't come to help him with anything.

"Novalee?"

When he lifted his head off the pillow, she could see his scalp through the thinning hair at his temples.

"I can't believe it," he said. "I can't believe you're here."

He pulled himself up on his elbows and stared across the room at her. "Novalee." Then he smiled. "I was coming back to find you."

"Why?"

The question hung between them like something solid and thick.

"What were you going to do, Willy Jack?" Her voice was even, without heat. "Were you going to come back to the Wal-Mart where you dumped me out?"

"Novalee . . ."

"Did you think I'd still be there waiting for you?"

"I just wanted to see if you were all right."

"Really?"

"Look . . ."

"You're a little late though. About seven years."

Willy Jack let his head sink back into the pillow, then rubbed at his forehead. An IV needle in the back of his hand had made the skin look waxy and bloodless.

"I come back because I needed to tell you something about Americus."

Novalee stiffened. Her muscles tensed, her weight shifted. Then her eyes went flat and hard as she measured the threat of him.

"How do you know about her?"

Willy Jack heard something in her voice, something strong and dangerous, something he didn't know.

"How did you find out?"

"My cousin, J. Paul."

"You're telling me a lie!"

"He said the police called him a few years back. The baby was missing and they wanted to know where I was."

"Willy Jack . . ."

"Hell, I was in prison. I never heard nothin' about it till a year ago when I saw J. Paul. But that's how I knew about her. That's how I knew where she was."

"But you didn't know if I got her back. You didn't know if she was dead or alive."

"You're wrong, Novalee. I knew. I knew she was okay and I knew she was with you. In Sequoyah."

"How? How did you know that?"

"I called your house."

"You what?" She was fighting for control, but the words crackled with anger.

"Oh, I never said nothin' to her. Anyway, you usually answered the phone. But a few times, she did." He seemed to drift away, then he smiled. "I heard her voice . . . and that was enough. Got me through some bad times."

"You were coming for her, weren't you?"

"Coming for her? What do you mean?"

"You were going to try to take her." Novalee could feel the muscles of her face tighten. "You were going to take her away from me."

"How could I do that?"

"What? Willy Jack Pickens do something so low as to steal a child?"

"Steal her? That's what you think?" Willy Jack grabbed the rails of the bed and pulled himself up. "What the hell you think I'm gonna do, Novalee. Run away with her?"

He yanked at the sheet that was covering him and threw it on the floor. "I'm not doing a hell of a lot of running these days."

His legs ended just below the knees. Novalee wanted to

look away, but she didn't. She knew that's what he was after. He wanted to shock her, but she wouldn't let him get by with it. She wouldn't let him get the best of her. Not ever again.

She walked to the end of the bed and looked, without flinching, at the puckered flesh. The thick, ugly scars.

"How did you know I was here, Novalee?"

"I read about you in the newspaper."

"What did it say? Poor pitiful cripple can't get off the floor of the john?"

"Something like that."

"Well, if the cripple can't even manage to get out of the toilet, how the hell's he gonna get in your house and steal your girl? 'Course, if he finds a phone booth and changes into Superman, then—"

"Don't try to get funny. Don't try to change this."

"And how would the cripple take care of her once he got her? Now if he could grow legs and if he could get a new liver, then maybe . . ."

"If you think I'm going to feel sorry for you, you're wrong."

"Then *maybe* he could run Disney World."

"Why did you come back here?" Novalee's voice was growing louder.

"Or *maybe* he'd go into banking."

"If it wasn't for Americus, then why?" She knew she was losing it, but she couldn't stop.

"I suppose he *could* become a judge."

"Why?" she screamed. "Why are you here?"

The only sound came from the hall, cushioned footsteps and the swish of nylon as a scowling nurse marched in.

"You have a problem in here?" She looked from Willy

Jack to Novalee. "I could hear you all the way down the hall."

"Sorry," Willy Jack said.

Then she saw the sheet on the floor. "What in the world is going on?"

"It just slipped off."

"Oh." She gathered up the sheet and dropped it beside the door, then pulled a fresh one from the top of a closet. "I thought maybe you were jumping on the bed." She flipped the sheet open and let it settle over Willy Jack, then she checked his IV. "I've got a shot for you if you need it."

"I'm doing all right. Let's wait."

"You let me know," she said. "And no more rough stuff down here." Then she wheeled and walked out, closing the door behind her.

Novalee went to the window and stared out. The sky, almost cloudless, appeared to be a strange shade of green through the tinted glass.

"Novalee." Willy Jack's voice dropped nearly to a whisper. "I done a bad thing to you. The worst I ever done to anyone, I guess. But then, most of what I've done's been bad."

Novalee was listening, but she didn't trust what she was hearing. She knew better.

"Now I know there's not much to redeem me. Not much at all 'cause I only done two good things in my whole damned life. And I don't suppose it took much to do either one . . . but they was both my doin'."

Novalee listened for the snarl, then turned to look for the smirk he could never hide, but she couldn't see it.

"I fathered a child, a sweet child, I imagine, if she's anything like her mother. And I wrote a song. A damned good song. But, of course, I screwed around. Messed myself up. I ran away from one of them . . . and I got the other stole from me. Hell, I probably deserved it. But that don't change the goodness of either one of 'em. And I hope that counts for something."

"Willy Jack . . ."

He held up one hand, a gesture for a little more time. "Now that don't make me good. That won't change anything, won't right all the wrongs I done or help the people I hurt. It's only two things, Novalee, but it means I wasn't all bad. It means it wasn't all a waste."

Novalee didn't want to feel what she was feeling, didn't want to believe what she'd heard. She had been hanging on to the Willy Jack she knew for such a long time, the one who didn't care, the Willy Jack she had taught herself to hate. She knew she could handle him, but this Willy Jack was throwing her off balance. And she knew the worst thing she could do was to lose her balance.

"Willy Jack, you said you came back here to tell me something about Americus."

"Yeah." He scooted around in the bed and grimaced with the effort. "You remember the last day? The last day we was together?"

Novalee nodded.

"You asked me if I wanted to feel the baby and you put my hand on your belly, but I said I didn't feel nothing. You said that if I tried, I could feel the heart."

Can't you feel that tiny little bomp . . . bomp . . . bomp?

"I said I couldn't and tried to pull my hand back, but you wouldn't let me."

Feel right there.

"Your voice was so soft, just a whisper, but I heard what you said."

That's where the heart is.

Willy Jack's face was streaked with tears, but he didn't wipe them away. "I lied, Novalee. I lied to you." His voice sounded heavy and tired. "I said I couldn't feel it, but I did. I felt that baby's heartbeat. I felt it as sure as I could feel my own. But I lied."

"Why?"

"Lord, I don't know. Why does anyone lie? 'Cause we're scared or crazy, maybe just 'cause we're mean. I guess there's a million reasons to lie, and I might've told that many . . . but none like that. I guess there's always that one lie we never get over."

"What?"

"Oh, maybe you don't know about it yet. Maybe you never told a lie so big it can eat away a part of you.

"But if you ever do . . . and if you get lucky . . . you might get a chance to set it right. Just one chance to change it.

"Then it's gone. And it never comes again."

"Deposit two dollars and seventy-five cents."

Novalee fumbled eleven quarters into the slot, then pressed the receiver to her ear as the phone began to ring.

"Oh, please be there," she whispered after she had counted three rings.

one lie we never get over

On the fourth ring, she closed her eyes and ran her hand through her hair.

just one chance to change it

She twisted the phone cord so tightly around her hand that by the fifth ring, her fingers had turned white.

then it's gone . . .

After the sixth ring, she felt weak and leaned against the phone booth door.

and it never comes again

Then she got lucky. He answered on the seventh ring.

"Chaucer's."

When she heard his voice, her throat tightened, choking off breath, choking off sound.

"Chaucer's Book Store."

She tried to say his name, but something hard knotted and swelled in the hollow below her throat.

Then he said, "Hello?"

She remembered dreams, bad dreams in which she would try to call for help, but the words would be tangled and trapped inside her.

"Well . . ." he said and she knew he was going to hang up.

She squeezed out a sound, more like a whimper than a word, but he heard it.

"I'm sorry. Can you speak up?"

Then something broke loose and his name tumbled out as she swallowed air and began to cry without sound.

"Novalee?"

"I . . . I called be . . . cause . . ." Her voice, broken with sobs, cracked the words in two.

"What's wrong, Novalee? What is it?"

"Forney . . ."

"Is it Americus? Is she all right?"

Snuffling breath, Novalee managed to say, "She's fine," though the words sounded pinched and bent.

"Then what's the matter?"

Novalee could feel her heart quicken. Then, squeezed between convulsions of air, the words exploded from her lips.

"I lied, Forney."

Seconds turned into lifetimes while Novalee strained to hear some sound . . . a whisper of voice, an embrace of breath.

"Oh, don't let it be too late, Forney. Please don't let it be too late." She prayed he was still on the line, prayed they were still connected.

"I lied to you . . . and I'm sorry."

Then she heard him draw a deep ragged breath.

"I thought you wanted something else—a different life. I thought you wanted to go back to Maine . . . go back to school . . . become a teacher. And I was afraid if I tried to keep you here with me . . ."

"Novalee . . ."

"So when you asked me if I loved you, I said . . ."

"You said, 'No. Not in the way you need to be loved. Not in that way.' "

"But it wasn't true, Forney. I do love you."

"Then . . ."

"I lied because I thought you deserved something better."

"Something better than you?" His voice was husky and thick. "Novalee, there isn't anything better than you."

"It's not too late, is it, Forney? We still have time. We still have . . ."

Novalee's voice was smothered beneath the siren of an ambulance pulling into the emergency entrance beside the phone booth.

"Can you hear me?" she yelled into the phone.

"Novalee, where are you?"

"Outside a hospital in Alva."

"Alva? What are you doing there?"

"I'm getting ready to leave. I'm going to Tellico Plains."

"No." Forney sounded stunned. "You can't go back."

"Oh, not to stay, Forney. Not to stay." Novalee turned so she could see her car parked at the curb. Willy Jack was in the back, his head cradled on the pillows she had stacked in the seat.

"I'm just taking someone to Tellico Plains," she said. "Someone who's trying to get back home."

"Novalee, I don't know what's going on. I don't know how you found me here. I don't know why you're there. I don't know if I understand any of this. But if it's a dream, if I've just been dreaming . . ."

"You're not dreaming, Forney. This is you and this is me—and it's real."

A light rain had started falling while Novalee was still inside the phone booth. By the time she ran back to the car and slid under the wheel, the wind was slapping drops the size of quarters against the windows.

Willy Jack was in a deep sleep, the result, she supposed, of the pain shot he'd been given just before they'd loaded him into the car.

While Novalee was fishing her keys out of her purse, the wind picked up enough to set the Chevy rocking and to make her decide to wait it out and stay put until the storm passed.

As she watched the drops spilling down the window, she saw another night, another rainstorm and a girl . . . a girl seventeen, pregnant, alone . . . a girl turning, spinning, waiting—waiting for the ones who would step from the darkness, their voices calling to her from the shadows . . .

a little woman with blue hair and a wide smile, holding open the door of a trailer house, a woman who would teach her the meaning of home

home is the place that'll catch you when you fall
and we all fall

a man with black skin who would put a camera in her hands and teach her a new way to look at the world

you don't need to be scared . . . remember, you know about taking pictures from the heart

a brown-skinned boy with a soft voice and a tree full of magic

it's lucky, lets you find things you need . . .
helps you find your way home if you get lost

a woman too full of life to say no who would teach her about friendship

look at all you've done, Novalee . . .
look at all you've done for yourself

a man in a stocking cap who would teach her about love

> *what I want, Novalee, is to be with you . . .*
> *to be with you and Americus*

and a child named Americus who would teach her to trust happiness

> *when the kitten opens her eyes, the first thing she sees is her mother*

The girl knew there would be others with new voices calling to her from places she couldn't see, so—still whirling—she waited.

Novalee smiled then at her seventeen-year-old self turning on the other side of the rain-streaked glass and she tried to hold her there. But the girl spun away into the light, the place where her history began.

Reading Group Guide

A Q&A with Billie Letts

Q. You use some strange names, including Native American names. How did you come up with them?

A. We have some wonderful names in Oklahoma, names that carry their own images, their own rhythms—Whitecotton, Nation, Goodluck, Husband. I didn't have to work hard to find them. Even the name Americus is connected to Oklahoma. It was once a small community here but it's gone now, disappeared.

Q. Why did you settle on Wal-Mart as such an important part of your book?

A. Many small towns in our part of the country have central meeting places, the social centers of the towns—churches, high school gyms, football fields, and, increasingly so, the Wal-Mart store, which has changed not only business on Main Street, but the very rhythms and movements of these communities. So, for my story, the Wal-Mart in Sequoyah, Oklahoma, was the most likely place for Novalee to encounter Sister Husband, a white woman, Moses Whitecotton, a black man, and Benny Goodluck, a Native American boy.

Q. Your book includes characters from a variety of cultures. How did that come about?

A. We hear so much about America's urban areas and the various ethnic communities in them—the great melting pot. I suspect that the common perception on the coasts is still that the great middle is populated by Anglo ranchers and wheat farmers. And they do live here. But our ethnic diversity would surprise most people.

Do you know that Oklahoma almost came into the union as a black state? That at one time Oklahoma had a multitude of black towns? And of course the various Native American tribes were in place on their lands even before statehood. But the limits and boundaries of the black towns and Indian communities have largely dissolved to contribute to a cultural diversity in the state.

Q. Why is Novalee, an uneducated, pregnant, seventeen-year-old, your main character?

A. Oklahoma has a high rate of teenage pregnancy. As a result, we have many single mothers, either recently divorced or never married. I've known many of these young women—students in my college classes. They often hold marginal jobs as waitresses, motel maids, nursing home workers. They are poor and uneducated, often victims of alcoholic, redneck, small town he-men. But these are Ma Joad's children—they keep coming, keep trying. And Novalee Nation is among the best of them.

Q. How did you settle on Sister Husband and Moses Whitecotton and Forney Hull as Novalee's mentors? How is *Where the Heart Is* an "Oklahoma story"?

A. Some people have described Sister Husband as "wacky." Let's see. She's loving, giving, accepting, and nurturing. Maybe in late-twentieth-century America that's wacky. If it is, I've had a grandmother, aunts, cousins, and friends who are, according to that definition, wacky. Come to my house and I'll invite a houseful of Sister Husbands of a variety of ages, sizes, and inclinations. Sister is as much a part of me as Saturday night family musicals and Sunday morning church.

Moses Whitecotton is based on a real man—Claude Adams—a friend who died several years ago. He moved from a difficult time and place in this society to help hundreds of people better their lives. You've never heard of him, but anyone who ever knew him will never forget what he gave to each of us.

And Forney Hull? America has a tradition of anti-intellectualism and so does Oklahoma. Intellectuals, or simply anyone who listens to a variety of music or who goes to a play or who reads too many books, are suspect. *But they are here*. And, as in any society, they are our soul.

How did I come up with these characters? Hell, they're people I know.

Q. Several of your characters' names are changed or miscalled during the course of the book. When Sister Husband first meets Novalee, she calls her "Ruth Ann." Moses Whitecotton is called "Mose" by the manager at the Wal-Mart even though he's dealt with Moses several times. Lexie Coop's children are never called by their real names until late in the story. And Willy Jack's name is changed to "Billy Shadow." I'm curious about your reasons for doing that.

A. If these characters were lawyers, bankers, corporate executives, or celebrities, there's little chance people would take the liberty of changing their names. But the characters you've mentioned are poor, uneducated—without power. When I was teaching , I often used Maya Angelou's work in my classes, in particular, *I Know Why the Caged Bird Sings*. Ms. Angelou relates an incident in which a white woman she works for decides to change her name, Marguerite, to "Mary." Can you imagine how that must feel? That someone with the power of social status and wealth could, on a whim, decide to change your name?

Q. Many of your characters are disfigured in some way. Novalee has a scar that runs from her wrist to her elbow; Jolene, the teenaged girl Willy Jack meets in Santa Rosa, is missing her two front teeth, and Willy Jack himself has teeth marred by cavities "the size of raisins." Claire Hudson has so many cuts and scrapes that it seems her entire body is covered by Band-Aids, and Lexie Coop's eyelid is ruined. You obviously wanted readers to "see" these disfigurements, didn't you?

A. Yes, I did. Think about how these people live and what happens to them as a result. Novalee's scar came from a woman in a bar where Novalee worked, a woman crazy *and* drunk. Jolene and Willy Jack are trying to survive in whatever way they can. People like that can't be overly concerned with oral hygiene. Claire Hudson covers herself with Band-Aids less because of visible wounds than because she is trying to hide, to protect herself from pain. Lexie is the victim of a man who preys on vulnerable women and children. Now I'm not suggesting that people with money and power can avoid crazy people with knives or dangerous degenerates or even bad teeth, but I believe people like the characters in my book have far fewer resources with which to deal with their disfigurements, both figuratively and literally.

Q. Did you sit down and plot out the book character by character, interaction by interaction, or did it come to life as you were writing it? Is *Where the Heart Is* the novel you set out to write?

A. I had parts of the story in my head when I started. I knew who the major characters were and I knew how the story was going to end, but I didn't know many of the twists and turns that would take me there.

The first time I actually roughed out an outline, when I was seventy or eighty pages into the first draft, I came up with seventeen chapters. As you know, the book ended up being thirty-eight chapters long, so I guess outlining isn't my strong point.

Is it the novel I set out to write? Yes, I'd have to say it is even though I got there almost by accident, just sort of stumbling from one chapter to another, from one event to another.

Q. In what ways did the novel change as you wrote it? Did you find some characters developing in unexpected ways?

A. Forney Hull was a *big* surprise for me. I knew he was going to be instrumental in changing Novalee's life by introducing her to the world of books and learning. But I had no notion that he would fall in love with her. When he did, I was really amazed. And when she discovered she loved him, I was absolutely astonished. Astonished, but pleased.

Q. Can you talk a bit about Novalee? How did she come about? Was she the impetus for writing the novel or did the story come first?

A. I was in Wal-Mart one day and the thought came to me that someone could probably live there for weeks, months . . . years, maybe, without ever having to go outside. And just like that I came up with the idea of a girl hiding out in that store, living there, because she had nowhere else to go.

Then, as the story began to take shape, the girl became a pregnant teenager faced with some very adult, very difficult decisions. And in Novalee's case, a teenager who had a history full of grief.

Q. This novel has won awards in the young adult category. What is it about the book that speaks to teenagers?

A. I've heard from young people all over the country—many have written to me; some I've met in person—but most have made similar comments: they identify with Novalee because they, too, have felt lost, abandoned, alone; they want to believe there are places in America like Sequoyah, where racism, sexism, and classism do not override hopes and possibility. And because so many of them come from splintered families, they trust that they, like Novalee, might be lucky enough to find caring people out there who will help them build "families" of their own.

Q. *Where the Heart Is* is set in America's "heartland" and deals with quintessentially American characters, yet it has been translated into twelve languages. How would you account for its cross-cultural appeal?

A. I don't know, but I'm glad. I'm glad that Scandinavians and Europeans and Asians and Latin Americans will read about Moses, Sister Husband, Forney, Novalee, and the other fine folks of Sequoyah, Oklahoma, and realize that people of good heart don't exist just in the pages of books, but live next door, in the neighboring town, in bordering nations, and countries halfway around the world.

Discussion Questions

1. The theme of "home" runs throughout this novel. Would you characterize home as a place, a family, a state of mind, or, as Sister Husband says, a place "where your history begins"? As a homeless person longing for a home, Novalee's image of home is heavily influenced by the images she sees in magazines. How influenced are we all by portrayals of home and home life in the media, movies, and on television?

2. In the beginning of the novel, Novalee is a poor, uneducated teenage mother whose own mother abandoned her at a young age. Novalee, however, seems to be remarkably maternal and responsible in her parental role. Do you think this is a believable portrayal of teenage motherhood? Is it possible that lacking a loving mother herself she would be such a good mother? Both Novalee and Lexie defy our stereotypes of poor, single mothers. Do you think this is a strength or a weakness of the novel?

3. Novalee's superstition about the number seven intensifies after the birth of her daughter. What do you make of Novalee's seemingly irrational fears? What role do superstitions play in the lives of even the most rational of us? Are there any other patterns or cycles you recognize in the novel?

4. Despite his cruelty, women are attracted to Willy Jack and are willing to take care of him. What is the attraction of cruel men to needy women? Lexie says, "Girls like us don't get the pick of the litter." What do you think of this statement? And why do you think that Novalee decides to help Willy Jack when she learns of his plight?

5. Willy Jack's story is interspersed throughout the novel. Do you think his story is necessary to the plot? Why or why not? If this novel had been told through the eyes of Willy Jack Pickens, in what ways might we see Novalee differently?

6. Novalee takes pictures to "see something in a way nobody else ever had" and Forney reads to explore the world outside the confines of his own life. Do you think books and photography help them deal with their lives or keep them from dealing with life head on? In what other ways do we use inanimate objects to either cope with life or hide from it?

7. Children play an important role in this novel. How are their stories important? What do each of the children—Americus, Benny, Praline, Brownie—teach us about love and loss of innocence?

8. Despite their struggles, Lexie's family is incredibly loving, fun-filled, and close. This is what makes the attack on Lexie

and Brownie so heart wrenching and shocking. Do you think Brownie's trust in adults can ever be fully restored? Why do you think the author decided to include such a brutal scene in a book filled with so much kindness?

9. How did you feel when Novalee spurned Forney? Did you believe they would ultimately end up together? Do you think they are well matched? Do you believe that differences in education and social class matter in a relationship, and what do you think makes it possible to bridge such differences? Or do you believe that people with similar backgrounds tend to be better matched?

10. There are no traditional families in this novel. Why do you think the author chose to write a book about home and family yet disregarded established notions of what constitutes each? Though many of us accept and embrace different forms of family life, why do you think the traditional family is still frequently portrayed as mother/father/children? Do you think this remains the "ideal"?

Billie Letts On Billie Letts

I was an only child . . . and an ugly one. I had pumpkin-red hair as untamable as tangled bailing wire, buck teeth that overlapped my bottom lip, and so many freckles that my Uncle Ed called me "Speck" and teased that I was the only girl in Oklahoma who had a dog prettier than she was.

My Aunt Zora, in a sincere act of kindness, tried to console me by telling me that I was going to be pretty when I got older and "grew into my teeth," a comment that left me mystified, yet hopeful.

But my physical imperfections, unfortunately, did not end at my neck.

My body looked like a stick figure drawn by a four-year-old with a sharp pencil and a dull sense of proportion. There wasn't enough meat on my bones to tempt a hungry chicken hawk. Even worse, I was clumsy . . . never quite in control of my feet and elbows and knees, which resulted in a pandemonium of scars, scabs, scrapes, and bruises, cross-hatched with Band-Aids.

I was a *mess*. But the Oklahoma sun was warm, and I was a kid with good friends and neighbors and relatives, and somehow I could always make them laugh. A tap step here, a piano run there, and always the jokes, the laughter.

The child of parents who were children themselves, I lived much of the time with my grandma, whose house was close enough that I could see my own from her kitchen window, where I sometimes watched my mom and dad do battle. My grandma's house was always a safe haven for me, and starting school was a reprieve.

The first in my class to learn to read, I zipped through *Dick and Jane*, then, encouraged by the school librarian, packed home each week as many books as I could carry. By the time I entered fourth grade, I was beginning to yearn for something with more substance than our library could offer.

My parents, both products of the Depression, were uneducated, hardworking, and thrifty—not the kind of people to spend money on books. In our house there were only two: the Bible and a novel my mother must have thought was of a religious nature because of the title, though I'm quite sure she never read it.

I gave the Bible a try, but, finding it very confusing, turned to the novel. *God's Little Acre*. Now there was a book! I read it several times and used it as the subject for my fourth grade book report, which caused such a stir that I knew I was on to something. If I had the power to agitate a language-arts teacher in Tulsa, Oklahoma, by simply writing about someone else's writing, how much power might I have in telling my own stories? I suspect it was then, at age nine, that the idea of becoming a writer took hold.

Fast-forward twenty years.

By age thirty, I was married, the mother of two sons, and

about to graduate from college to start my career as an English teacher, a sharp departure from my previous "professions."

I had, in the intervening years, been a roller-skating car-hop, waitress, window washer, dishwasher, dance instructor, and part-time secretary to a private detective who showed me clandestine photographs of my grandma's long-time evangelist having sex with a teenager on the hood of a car.

For the first few years of our marriage, Dennis, my husband, taught at a junior college in eastern Oklahoma, pulling down just over three hundred dollars a month. Every summer, we loaded up what furniture we owned and moved to Wagoner, my husband's hometown, which was near Tulsa, and found temporary jobs. The pay was poor, but so were we, and it was the only way we could afford to get through the next nine months on Dennis's teaching salary.

Friends and family often lent a helping hand. My husband's mother, who watched our son Shawn while I worked, always had a pot of beans on the stove, fresh vegetables from her garden, and cornbread or biscuits in the oven every evening when I came for him. And though I insisted, on a regular basis, that I had a chicken thawing to cook when I got home, she'd "persuade" me to stay for supper, knowing, too, that if there *had* been one thawing through the weeks and months I'd claimed, we would have died from food poisoning if we'd eaten it.

Not long after the birth of our second son, my husband was offered the opportunity to go to Denmark as a Fulbright lecturer. From Wilburton, Oklahoma, to Copenhagen, Denmark. A bit of culture shock? You can only imagine. Suddenly we found ourselves with friends from all over the United States and Europe. We watched each other's children, fed each other, drank beer, and talked about Vietnam and books and politics and, yes, even the human condition. My education accelerated and most of the time I felt amazingly ignorant.

When we returned to the States, I finished an English degree at Southeast Missouri State and began teaching—English in Cairo and Paxton, Illinois, journalism at Southeastern Oklahoma State, elementary school in Durant and Fillmore, Oklahoma.

In 1975, one hundred twenty-five Vietnamese refugees were brought to Southeastern and I began teaching English as a second language. Along with many of the other teachers, I had actively opposed the war in Vietnam. But whatever my feelings had been about the war, I was now faced with classrooms filled with confused, frightened, lonely students. So I learned their names and faces and stories. They met my family and many of them became our friends.

Another leap in time—another twenty years.

As I neared the time to start thinking about retirement, my days of teaching drawing to an end, I had a box of rejection slips, a thick notebook filled with terrible poetry, one play I cowrote with Dennis, six screenplays (four pretty good ones and two miserable failures), a stack of short stories, and dozens of files filled with ideas for more stories.

By then, our younger son, Tracy, was living in Chicago, acting in some good theater and turning out some powerful writing for the stage. Shawn was living in Singapore, doing the work he loves—playing, composing, and arranging music. And Dennis, who had already retired from teaching, had started acting in films. (As of now he's been in nearly forty feature films and television movies.)

I was still dreaming of becoming a "real" writer, a writer

with my name in the credits of a movie or on the cover of a book.

Then, at age fifty-five, I went to a writers conference in New Orleans where, because I had registered early, I had the opportunity to meet with a literary agent for fifteen minutes. The agent was Elaine Markson, a *real New York agent,* who listened as I tried nervously to sell myself. (I didn't get my full fifteen minutes because an old friend of Elaine's dropped by to say hello and my meeting was cut short . . . by two minutes.)

A week later, Elaine called me in Oklahoma to say she had read the screenplay I'd given her and wanted to see the short fiction I'd mentioned, the stories my husband called "Tales from Wal-Mart." I sent her two, and at the back of the one I'd titled "Where the Heart Is" I'd slipped in a note saying that the story wouldn't let me go. I was even dreaming about it. I'd left Novalee Nation, a pregnant, broke, and abandoned seventeen-year-old girl, locked in a Wal-Mart late at night and I couldn't stop thinking about how she was going to survive.

Elaine called as soon as she'd read it, suggesting that it might be the beginning of a novel. It was.

Two years later, Jamie Raab at Warner Books read the completed manuscript and bought it. It was published in 1995.

The first time I walked into a bookstore and saw *my book* with *my name* on the cover, I was finally ready to deliver the line I'd been saying in my head since I was a kid: "Now, at last, I'm a *real* writer."

But I didn't say it because I suddenly knew that I'd been a real writer for almost fifty years.

I thought back to all of the people in my life . . . Teenaged parents. Loving grandmothers. Cousins, one like a sister to me, who plugged the cavities in her teeth with gum because there was no money to pay a dentist. A mother-in-law who prepared meals for my family when an imaginary chicken was thawing in my kitchen. An amazing group of friends over the years who sustained us, helped us to raise our children, and loved us.

Then there were the writers. I didn't copy them as much as consider in amazement how they could strengthen the human heart. William Faulkner and Flannery O'Connor. Eudora Welty and Toni Morrison. John Steinbeck and Sandra Cisneros. Randall Jarrell and Lucille Clifton. Maya Angelou.

Now, when people ask me how to write a book, the answer is easy. I don't know. I only know how *I* have written two books. I had stories to tell and I began typing.